BRADFORD, BRU AND BRENDAN TOO

COLIN DEREHAM

Published by Wild One Press
Cover design by Dianna Roman

ISBN: 978-1-959553-21-2 (Trade Paperback)
ISBN: 978-1-959553-22-9 (Special Cover Paperback)
ISBN: 978-1-959553-20-5 (eBook)

CONTENT ADVISORY

While “Bradford, Bru and Brendan Too” has a definite HEA, it does contain adult content that some people may find triggering. This includes themes of domestic abuse, assault involving people and animals, frank and detailed sexual scenes and very coarse language.

I was having a wonderful
dream,

then I woke up
and it was all true.

NRL TELSTRA
PREMIERSHIP

ACKNOWLEDGEMENTS

I want to extend a huge and heartfelt thanks to the wonderful people who helped bring this book to fruition:

Dianna - your talent and patience is priceless. How you manage to take my big block o' text and package it up to look this pretty is beyond me. I'm gobsmacked and grateful as all get-out.

Deb - you are my emotional cheerleader. Every time I make it through a challenging part of my manuscript, every time I write something that wrenches at my heart, every time I create something that makes me smile, I stop and ponder *What would Deb think of this?*

Tal - your finicky comments and Taurean stubbornness are like a mirror to me. It's an immense relief to know someone as doggedly fussy as you has raked their way through my final draft.

Valentina - what a blessing it was being able to come running to you whenever I needed advice from a bonafide Italian! The Borellis and I are so grateful.

KC - your alpha input and innate skill for reigning me in was the discipline this unruly bugger sorely needed. No wonder you're the queen of whips and chains.

Doctor NC - your priceless expertise will ensure I don't make a fool of myself when it comes to all things medical in the novel. A thousand thank-yous for patiently enduring my rambling interviews and DM barrages.

Sue - a big barrel of thanks for letting me pepper you with questions about guide dogs. Brendan wouldn't be half of what he is without you.

Marianne - your super street-team coordination couldn't have come at a better time. Never doubt how much I appreciate you going the extra mile!

Darrin - my bear buddy. Your perspective always reassures me I'm on the right track. If I can do it right for you, I know I'm doing the bears proud!

Luigi - sometimes ships pass in the night and they leave an impression that will last forever. You were my inspiration for Bru (though you'd need to scoff down a lot more cheeseburgers) and your fierce belief in my abilities is something I'll always cherish.

Mark, Luke, Marjay, Carole and Finch - they say never judge a book by its cover, but we all know that's bullshit. You folks made sure that everything I wanted to convey shone through in all those promo photos, including the best special edition ever!

I started off on this writing malarkey all alone with nothing but a vague mission to cobble together a book or two that might catch the eye of publishers. What I never thought I'd find along the way was the amazing support and friendship of this community. You people - all of you - prop me up with your generosity of spirit. I can only hope to be as noble as you and pay it forward, pay it back, or spread it around wherever it's needed.

Much love!

Colin

CHAPTER 1

"Hey, Braddy?" Summer's voice cuts through the busy Friday night restaurant crowd.

I look up from my soup to see my sister staring at me. "Yeah?"

"What about Brendan? Isn't he going to have dinner too?"

"He ate early. Anyway, he's working." I eye the plate in front of Summer. "Plus, if you're gonna try and sneak him some food, I can assure you he won't eat tofu salad."

"Awww, you're such a bloody spoilsport. Look at him there. He's so good and you're making him starve." She raises a conspiratorial eyebrow and reaches across to Nathan's plate. Unlike Summer and I, her partner is a card-carrying meat eater. Summer snatches the big strip of fat Nathan's cut off his steak, then leans over the table to hand it to Brendan, who accepts it graciously. My yellow labrador looks pleased as punch, devouring the large tidbit in one bite.

"No more than that, or you'll give the poor bugger pancreatitis." I admonish Summer with a mock glare and she shoots me a sarcastic pout in return.

I'm sure I seem to be seeing quite a lot for a man who goes everywhere with a guide dog. But, you know, blindness isn't a light switch. It's more of a dimmer. Tunnel vision gives me a small window of sight in each eye, though it's not the best in terms of clarity. If I turn my head in the right direction, I can make out a reasonable amount of what I need to. Still, without Brendan, I'd definitely trip and fall flat on my face, or bump into everything outside of my tiny field of vision.

No sign of Jarrod. The bastard has let me down again. It's embarrassing, really. I told him about dinner with Summer and Nathan several times. He said he'd be here. I sneak a look at the big digital clock on my phone. *Yeah, he's not gonna show up.*

"Don't worry about it, Braddy. I'm sure it just slipped his mind." Summer is smiling at me, but we both know the score. She may have lived across the other side of the country for the last decade, but she can still read me like a book.

"Yeah, we can just catch him next time, bud." Nathan grins at me, trying to lighten the mood. I like him. He's good-natured, gregarious and a lot of fun. And he treats my free-spirited hippie sister like a precious gift.

Nathan glances over at Summer, then back to me. "Uh, speaking of next time, mate, we wanted to talk to you about something." He clears his throat and wipes his mouth with a huge paper napkin. "We didn't come to Sydney just to catch the PJ Harvey gig."

I was so happy to hear Summer and Nathan were flying over from South Australia. Summer is a mad PJ Harvey fan and she was pretty disappointed the singer wasn't including Adelaide on her Australian tour. So, they booked a hotel in Darling Harbour close to where PJ is playing, left their daughters with a friend, and made it into a whirlwind weekend holiday.

"Nathan actually had a job interview today. And they told him it's as good as in the bag." Summer grabs Nathan's hand and they beam at each other.

"You mean here in Sydney?" I can't hide my surprise. Summer's never said a word about wanting to leave Adelaide the whole time she's been over there.

"Yeah, it's time for a change," says Nathan. "Mum's been pushing up daisies for two years now. I haven't got any family left in South Australia."

"And I want Aura and Poetry to get to know their grandad better," interjects Summer.

Whenever I hear my nieces' spaced-out names, I can't help but smile. But this smile becomes a little strained at the mention of Summer's dad, Roy. He was only married to my mum for a handful of years. When I turned sixteen, he moved out, leaving my three-year-old sister behind. Good riddance, in my opinion. The whole time he was around, he definitely made me feel like I was some kind of unwanted inconvenience. To Roy's credit, though, he still played a regular role in Summer's upbringing—which is more than my own dad ever did for me.

"And we want them to spend time with Ryan and Dominic too." Nathan drains his wine glass and shoots me a grin. "Hey, you should give Ryan a call. He's living over near you in Bondi now."

I feel a little uncomfortable about this. I'm aware Nathan's gay brother and his fiancé live in Sydney. But I don't know Ryan from a bar of soap. I'm not even sure he and Nathan are all that close. Despite Nathan's honourable intentions, it kind of reeks of that thing hetero relatives sometimes do: *you're gay, he's gay, therefore you should become friends.*

I'm also more than a little aware of Nathan and Summer's concern about me. They think I'm isolated. They see this blind brother struggling to get by over the other side of the country, his life revolving around a relationship that's been crumbling for a long time. And sadly, I think they're right. I have friends, but nobody close—all the good ones have either moved away or simply faded into the background. It's funny how much our social supports shrink when we find ourselves mired in couplehood.

Nathan's still looking at me with expectantly raised eyebrows. *Oh, that's right. The Ryan thing.* I shift in my seat. "I dunno. It just seems weird: 'Hey Ryan, I'm your sister-in-law's poofter brother. Let's be mates.'" I laugh, hoping to pass it off as a joke, though I'm not entirely sure it works. Scrambling for a save, I try to find a positive angle. "I suppose with you guys moving here, I'll meet him anyway. Then I can avoid the awkward introductions."

"Sure. Have it your way, then." Nathan smirks at my crafty dodge. "The job actually won't start for a few months. We're gonna need that time to sort everything out, anyway."

"Ooooh, this is gonna be so fun!" Summer's jiggling her knees under the table; I can feel the vibrations on the wooden floor beneath us. It's impossible for me not to smile at her childlike exuberance. Given our thirteen-year age gap, there's always been this playful dynamic between us. Forever my little baby sister.

"Of course it is. It'll be awesome to have you guys living close by." I shift my gaze from Summer to Nathan and back again. "And I do mean *close by*. I'm gonna get pushy about where you're allowed to look for apartments. Brendan and I want to come and visit all the time." At the sound of his name, Brendan sits to attention.

"Eastern suburbs," says Summer resolutely. "Near you, near Nath's brother and best of all—" she bats her eyelids at Nathan, "—near the beach."

"Well, with Nathan being such a high-flying accountant, you should be able to afford a reasonable rental there. I wouldn't go getting any ideas about being a stay-at-home earth mother, though."

Summer scoffs playfully and swishes her hand at me. "Sweetie, I'd be bored in no time. Anyway, since the NDIS started, occupational therapists are in high demand—there aren't enough of us to go around. I'll get work easily." The chime of her phone slices through our conversation. "Oh, it's Michelle, about the girls. I'd better go and call her." She's standing as she speaks. "Nath, how long before we have to leave?"

Nathan steals a glance at his watch. "Gig's in forty-five minutes. We should head off as soon as you're finished. I'll get the bill." He turns to me, spotting me pulling out my wallet. "Nah, mate. No fuckin' way. Our invite, our treat." Flashing another grin, he struts off in search of a waiter.

I turn to Brendan, who's still sitting there patiently, staring up at me with his big brown eyes. "Wanna kick on to the bar with me, buddy?"

***

"I'll give you a call tomorrow after I've finished showing Nathan the sights, see where you're at. Maybe we can come out and visit you at Bondi?" Summer says, as she and Nathan get into their waiting taxi.

"Sure. I'll be home." Of course I will. I hardly get out much. Or at least, I don't leave the local area. Why would I? Everything I need is at Bondi—the shops, the cafes, the beach. "Anyway, you guys have an awesome time tonight." I lean in the door and kiss the cheek Summer's thrust in my direction.

I'm glad Summer insisted I make the trek out to Newtown. I love the long, vibrant strip of shops, restaurants and bars, and I don't come over to these parts nearly often enough. Plus, now that I'm in the area, I can go to Bears' Night at the Townie. I always feel validated when I step into the upstairs bar full of burly, furry blokes. The men are welcoming and friendly. Plus, they check me out. Lingering looks, big smiles, the odd wink or warm greeting, a meaty hand on my shoulder. My vanity sorely needs that. I have to be reminded that I'm worth something.

In any case, I could do with the distraction. Jarrod's unsurprising no-show bothers me more than I'd care to admit. He's probably blown us off because he scored a root on one of the many dating apps he lurks around on. I don't know why I'm surprised. I predicted this to the point that I prepared myself—I'm scrubbed and spotless from top to toe. Tonight I'm going to pick up any bear that takes my fancy. I'm so adamant about this, I've even swallowed half a Cialis in case nerves or alcohol get the better of me. It's been so long since I got a little action, and open relationships need to go both ways, dammit.

***

It wasn't always like this with Jarrod. We were happy once. Despite everything that's gone down between us, I still harbour fond memories of the day we met four and a half years ago.

I didn't have Brendan back then. After losing the vast majority of my sight in my early forties, I used a cane for a long while. It took some time before I managed to get a grasp on things—rehearsing journeys with a mobility therapist, learning all the tricks of the trade. Using my hearing to analyse the sounds of traffic so I could work out how and where to cross roads safely. Wielding the cane to detect tripping hazards, counting steps and calculating distances, memorising terrain and landmarks and stairs and entrances. It was such a huge learning curve that it made my head hurt, but eventually it became second nature.

Waving a white stick around also meant people got out of my way—*most* of the time. There was the constant hazard of people walking in crowded areas while texting on their phones. There were people from various cultural backgrounds who weren't used to the concept of Western manners. And there were people who were just plain arrogant. Don't get me wrong—most folks were really nice. They'd frequently offer to help. I know I was supposed to feel all offended and patronised and fiercely assert my independence, but I also know not to take kindness for granted. You can never have too much. You can never show too much.

Still, it only took one bad apple to put a dampener on your day. On the morning in question, I'd just got off at the Bondi Junction bus terminal to go to yet another root canal visit at my dentist—*thanks, mum and dad for the bad genes*. I wasn't running late. I can't afford to run late. When you're all but blind, you don't have the option of making last-minute dashes. I was walking through the crowded outdoor shopping mall, swishing my cane, my tiny window of vision showing only what was directly in front of me.

I could see her coming my way. Some skinny middle-aged woman all decked out in expensive clothes with a scowl on her face. She looked right at me. She had no idea I wasn't totally blind. Instead of moving to the side and pausing, I saw her make the snap decision to just barge forward and squeeze around me so she didn't have to break her stride. Maybe if I'd yanked hard and fast enough I could have got my cane out of the way in time. But a little voice inside me said, *Why should I? Why should I risk tripping or bumping into someone on the other side of me just to compensate for this woman's rudeness?* So I didn't. In a split second, I heard the loud clomp of her shoes as she bustled past me, stumbling over my cane and falling to the ground with a splat.

Of course, this made me lose my balance too. And once again, maybe I could have saved face. I could have wobbled and stomped and hopefully remained on my own two feet. But there was that voice in my head again. *Screw her. Why should I risk twisting my ankle, scraping my knees and elbows if I can't manage to right myself properly?* What I needed was a well-executed stage fall. Something nice and theatrical. So, with a grace and skill that surprised me, I toppled sideways, landing with a loud thud against a shop window, which I then used to brace myself as I descended spectacularly onto my arse. I was quite proud of the magnitude of my performance.

While my head was still swimming from the sudden drama, I heard a harridan's screech behind me. "Jesus Christ! Why the BLOODY hell don't you look where you're going?"

Instantly, my hackles were raised. I turned my head towards the vocal cacophony and spotted Harridan struggling to her feet. My blood boiled as I pushed on the window ledge, raising myself up to stand again. I was about to let fly. This is an extremely rare occurrence. Bugger me, I'm a *nice* man. I'm polite to everybody. I'm so damn courteous that I even thank *Siri*. But this was all too much and I'd well and truly had enough.

I almost jumped as I felt a strong, warm hand landing on my shoulder. "Are you OK, sir?" spoke a gruff male voice.

Sir? This was the first thing going through my mind. *He called me 'sir'?* I felt the strong hand guide me around and suddenly I was face-to-face with him. A shaggy-haired, bearded thirty-something with a cigarette between his lips. I moved my head up and down to take him in. Probably over six feet tall. T-shirt and jeans. Slender dad bod with a sexy little beer belly. A scruffy hipster. And *kind*. That got me more than anything.

Harridan was still screeching away, but I wasn't listening. I was busy checking out Hipster Boy. "Why don't you *fuck* off, you miserable bitch!" he barked.

OK. So Hipster Boy's also a bit of a pitbull.

Hurling out an indecipherable coda, Harridan was gone, galumphing away down the mall. Hipster Boy turned to me. "You never answered my question," he said. I gave him a blank look as he plucked the cigarette from his lips and smiled. Pitbull was gone and Kind Man was back. "Are you OK, sir?" he prompted, with a raise of his eyebrows.

"Uh... yeah, mate." I chuckled at his overtly quizzical expression. "It wasn't as bad as it looked. Oh, and I'm Bradford, not 'sir'."

Hipster Boy laughed, squeezing my shoulder with his hand. In amongst all the chaos, I hadn't even remembered it was there. It had just felt so… natural. "I'm Jarrod," he said. His green eyes twinkled. I think I smiled a little too obviously.

"Where is it?" a familiar voice snapped. Our heads flicked sideways. Harridan was back.

"Where's *what*?" Jarrod snarled at her.

Harridan was hunting around on the ground, shooting venomous glances up at us. "My heel!" she spat, brandishing a black sandal in our faces.

"Do we *look* like we have any idea?" Jarrod swished his hand around in defiance. "Anyway, didn't I just tell you to FUCK OFF?"

"These cost TWO THOUSAND DOLLARS!" Harridan shrieked, but she was already starting to hobble away again.

Jarrod turned back to me. "Bullshit," he muttered. An evil grin formed on his face. "Maybe *one* thousand."

I wanted to stay. I wanted to thank him for his kindness. Hell, I wanted to hug him—for about ten minutes straight. Plus, his warm hand was *still* on my shoulder. However, my dentist and a 275 dollar non-attendance fee were weighing on my mind. "Thanks, that was really nice of you, Jarrod. Unfortunately, I'm gonna have to run or I'll be late for my appointment."

Jarrod's hand stayed on my shoulder, swivelling as I turned and manoeuvred my cane into position. "I'll walk with you," he said. It was a firm statement, no room for negotiation. And I kind of liked it.

I don't remember what we talked about. I just remember the warmth of his hand on my shoulder making the hair on the back of my neck stand up with delight. Oh, and his scent. One part tobacco and ten parts *man.* Not stinky. A fresh masculinity. I'd like to romanticise all this and bang on about how our other senses become more acute when we lose our sight, but I'd be lying. The truth is, I'm a bit of a kinky bugger as far as these kinds of things go. I've always noticed the smell of a nice man.

After walking through an adjoining arcade, down the street behind the mall, then across the road, we'd come to the building where my dentist was. "This is my stop," I said. I couldn't hide the reluctance in my voice. I didn't want this to be goodbye, but I knew it had to be.

However, Jarrod stepped in, cutting off my thoughts. "See that cafe there?" he said, pointing back over the street we'd just crossed. An uncomfortable look came over him as he glanced down at my cane, then back up at me. "Sorry, I forgot. It's just that your eyes don't *look* blind."

I laughed at his sudden swing from confidence into awkwardness. "Tunnel vision, Jarrod. I can see it OK."

Visible relief washed across his face. "Well, I'm gonna sit over there, have a coffee and read my book." *Oh? He reads too?* "And when I see you come out of this building, if you feel like you wanna keep chatting, maybe you'll walk over and join me?" The flicker of hope in his eyes betrayed his assertive demeanour. And right then, I knew I'd fallen hard.

Jarrod fished around in his pocket, pulling out a small black object and holding it up close so I could see it. "Guess we have no need for this, eh?" he said with a sinister raised eyebrow.

I took the pointy little item and studied it. On the underside, it was cream leather. And in tiny gold lettering was the word 'Prada.' With a chuckle, Jarrod grabbed the heel from my hand, then turned and walked off, tossing it into a nearby rubbish bin.

***

I'm starting to get agitated now. I can feel the tension taking hold. *You don't need to make a big song and dance out of this*, I tell myself. *You should just let it go*. But I can't. Things between Jarrod and I have been hurtling south for ages. I can't remember the last time we had a tender moment. I can't remember the last time we kissed, or—God forbid—had sex. He's always out partying, and when he's home, he's surly and distant at best. At worst? It's all snide comments and put-downs. Even mild hostility. I've been doing my best to try and keep things on an even keel, but how long can my mindfulness hold out? How many times can I keep telling myself that kindness always wins in the end?

I want a cigarette. I quit ages ago, but right now I have this irresistible urge. I need that comfort, that relaxation I used to get whenever I lit one up after a few hours. I know it's silly. I'll probably puke; I'm not gonna be used to it after all this time. But, bugger that, I have to have some kind of crutch tonight.

If you're lucky and you know where to go in Sydney, you'll find the odd shop that sells imported smokes—the illegal ones. There's one of those shops just up ahead of me—a friend told me she buys them there all the time. And who the hell can afford legit cigarettes in this damn country at more than forty bucks per packet?

Prompting Brendan to enter the store, I sidle up to the counter, pull out my wallet and make sure my blindness pension card is visible. If the guy behind the cash register knows I'm poor, he's hardly gonna think I'm a narc.

"Uh… can I get some Manchester reds?" I ask the bored attendant. "Oh, and a lighter too, please."

He glances down at Brendan, who's waiting patiently in his guide dog harness. It does the trick—Blind Guy is clearly on the level. The man rummages underneath the counter, then resurfaces, shoving my sinful items in a small black plastic bag and charging me twenty bucks.

"Thanks for that. Have a great weekend, mate." I shoot him a genuine smile and he looks almost surprised. Maybe he doesn't get many of those in his job. Well, they cost nothing and I think they should be given a lot more often.

I don't light up straight away. As I start back down King Street, I hear the ping of a text message in my bag. Pulling up to the edge of the footpath, I take out my great big Samsung phone. People who are more blind than I am will use an iPhone, because the voice over function is definitely superior. But I'm at the stage where I can still use my eyes if things are big enough. The blindness software on my phone makes things comically large, but it's only available for Androids. This is a pain, because of course, it doesn't converse with my iPad like an iPhone would. Reckon all this is too much detail? Believe me, it's more important than you'd realise. It allows me to function like a regular person. Most of us wouldn't even stop to think about our independence till it's been stripped away from us.

Hitting the envelope icon, I see the message is from my errant boyfriend. About bloody time.

JARROD: U gonna be at the Townie? Prob see u there

That's all. No explanation. Certainly no apology. It's worth a one word reply, nothing more.

BRADFORD: Sure

I feel bad that the only semblance of a walk Brendan's getting tonight is to ferry me between venues. "I'll make it up to you tomorrow, buddy. Bondi to Bronte?" The forty-five minute coastal walk between the two beaches is one of his favourites. Of course, I avoid saying the word 'walk' to Brendan. Even though we're technically *on* one, that term has different connotations for him. It conjures up thoughts of long clifftop journeys, urban hikes up and down the hills of Bondi, bounding across beaches, paddling in the shallows.

Yeah, of course—dogs aren't allowed on Sydney beaches. But state legislation overrides this rule for guide dogs. I guess technically he's supposed to be on his harness the whole time, not romping through the surf. But who am I to deny him a little bit of happiness? At the end of the day, Brendan's my best friend and wherever I go, he goes. Anyone who doesn't like that can go to blazes.

CHAPTER 2

I've never got over that initial discomfort when I'm entering buildings with Brendan. People immediately stare at him. I'm sure some of them want to tell me to get out, before it registers that he's a guide dog and they can't stop me bringing him in. Believe me, you should try flagging down a damn taxi with a service animal in tow.

The bouncer at the Town Hall Hotel tonight, however, is an exception. He beams down at Brendan and I see his hand move out automatically, then snap back to his side. Some folks are aware guide dogs shouldn't be disturbed when they're working. I hate confronting people over that when they want to pat him. Everyone seems to adore Brendan and he adores them right back, though he steadfastly remains focused. I know he has a job to do, but in my heart it saddens me that such a loving creature can't always be showered with the affection he deserves.

Bouncer Man smiles at me as he steps to my right and waves me through to the stairwell just inside. I notice he doesn't usher me towards the main bar on the ground floor, where the straight people are. He's just assumed I'm here for the gay fellas upstairs. Geez, I must have 'poofter' written all over me. Or maybe it's just the stocky bear build and full beard. *Well... obviously.*

I climb the stairs carefully, with one hand on the rail and the other monitoring Brendan's movements. Back when I had my cane, I'd use it to flick against each step ahead, giving me a physical warning when I came to a landing. These days, though, Brendan is my cue.

Uncomfortable situation number two happens when I reach the top of the stairs, which lead straight out onto the first floor bar area. A sea of heads turn towards this burly short man bringing his dog in with him. Their initial thought is to rapidly clear a path, as if this clumsy blind fool is gonna plough through and stumble over everything. On the surface, it's a bit amusing, but it's not the kind of notice I'd like to attract. Once they've realised I'm quite capable, they seem to relax and return the smile I'm flashing at them. Heads nod, mouths morph into welcoming grins and a few hellos are sent in my direction. Instantly, I feel better.

Another path is graciously cleared for me as I make my way straight to the bar, but after giving a few thanks, I quietly wait my turn. These other guys were here before me, and blindness does not preclude me from showing manners.

It's a challenge juggling my bag, my drink and my dog through the tight crowd as I make my way to the outdoor area, but it's one that I manage without too much hassle. The skinny courtyard is long and cramped, and there are a few tall rectangular bar tables with guys milling around them. I squeeze my way past the men, apologising as they politely scramble to step aside, till I come to the fourth table, which is empty. Settling on the stool closest to the rear courtyard wall, I smile down at Brendan as he lies on the wooden deck beside me. "Good job, buddy," I croon, stretching across and ruffling his hair. He knows I have Schmackos in my bag. He's well aware he's earned a treat and he accepts my offering with studied poise. *Beautiful boy.*

The wall against my back is warm from the residual January heat. It soothes me as I take a huge swig from my rum and coke. I've already had a couple of these at the restaurant and they've started to kick in nicely, so this third one is just what I need to speed up the magic. Fishing around in my bag for the Manchesters, I unwrap the plastic and pluck out the first cigarette. I'm not sure how this is going to go. After lighting it, I take a tentative drag. It's weird. It used to be familiar and calming, but it's lost its charm. I forge ahead nonetheless, seeking that elusive thrill. Is it there? I guess my head is spinning a little. Maybe another gulp of rum will help.

My glass is barely back on the table when I detect movement in front of me. "*There* you are," says Jarrod. His impatient tone makes me bristle. Apparently *I'm* the one who's been messing *him* around.

"Just got here," I say evenly. "From dinner. Where were you?"

Jarrod screws up his face in irritation. "She's *your* bloody sister, for God's sake. Neither of them give a damn whether I'm there or not."

I stub out the remainder of my cigarette, doing my best to try and keep things calm. It isn't my style to cause a scene, and I've learnt not to inflame these situations with Jarrod. "You could have called, you know."

"Too busy living my life," Jarrod says sarcastically. "Anyway, I can't stay. Just lined myself up a hot shag with a sexy cub." He reaches across to my cigarettes and flips open the box. But he doesn't just take one and light it, he pulls out a great big handful of them.

"Jesus, Jarrod! You know how expensive they are!"

"*You're* meant to have given up, remember?" he snaps. His lofty reprimand has me teetering on the edge of anger. I expand my lungs slowly, willing the volcano inside me to simmer down, but Jarrod grabs my drink and skols the damn lot.

"What are you doing?!" I'm finally raising my voice. No doubt others nearby are pricking up their ears, but I can't hide my exasperation any longer.

Jarrod slaps down the tumbler and grimaces. "Ugh. You and your bloody rum. What are you? A fuckin' teenager?" He turns on his heel and stalks off just as an imposing figure comes into my meagre field of vision.

"That guy bothering you, is he?"

There's a big man standing in front of me by the end of the table. A hefty bear in a tight t-shirt. Large, strong arms. Rounded belly. Padded and cuddly. I have to move my face up slightly to catch a glimpse of what's above his broad shoulders. Full, well-tended beard. Bald head. God, I love a hot bald guy. Having him nuzzle my chest while I run my moustache over his chrome dome and kiss the smooth skin there.

I shake myself out of my thoughts, trying to focus, but then I see white teeth through a slight smile. A concerned furrow in his brow. And twinkling dark eyes. Large and appealing and gentle. I've been looking at him for an eternity, I'm sure. I must seem completely unhinged. Trying to pull myself together, I do my best to smile back at him. "Thanks. I'm OK. That's actually the boyfriend." I couldn't be more embarrassed by the sad little domestic this bloke must have witnessed from wherever he was.

"Oh, right," he says, with a polite nod. I can sense him mentally retreating. "I should leave you to it, I s'pose."

"Nah, he's on a bender." I shake my head with a wry grin. "Scored himself a root with some young guy. I won't see him for a day or so now."

Big Bald Bear looks upset on my behalf. It takes a moment to twig onto what he's obviously thinking.

"Oh, no," I add hastily. "We've been open for ages. I'm actually glad for the reprieve. I mean, you saw how it was." My hands are now gesturing lamely around me at nothing, as if that clears it all up. I cringe inwardly. This conversation is all kinds of wrong. He doesn't need to know any of this stuff. I have no idea how to dig myself out of the awkward hole I've created.

I look up at this dark-featured grizzly of a man. I don't want him to go anywhere. I'm desperate to think of a segue, something to make him stay a little longer. "Sorry you had to witness that." *Jesus, Bradford. The sympathy vote. You really are bloody pathetic.* Steeling myself, I give him my most charming smile. I know how to do this well. In any case, it's not like I have to fake it; he's so damn appealing.

To my great relief, Big Bear's face seems to light up immediately, mirroring my expression. "Well, it gave me the perfect excuse to come over and talk to you, didn't it?" He shoots me a cheeky little wink and I just about fall off my chair. "I'm sorry he stole your smokes and your drink. I can't do anything about those," he points at the packet of Manchesters, "but I can definitely get you another rum and coke."

He knows what I was drinking? I cringe again as I realise exactly how much of my altercation this man must have heard. "That's really nice of you, but please let me shout—" My spluttered reply falls on deaf ears; he's gone before I can finish my sentence. I feel bad. After all, *he's* the one who came to *my* aid.

I'm a little dazed by all of this, it's happened so quickly. I'm in such a state, I didn't even remember to check out his arse as he walked away. That's gotta be a first for me. I'm just sitting here, fiddling with the cigarette packet, tapping it against the table. Sure, I'm used to guys flirting with me, but on the rare occasions I'm out at a place like this, it happens over the course of an evening. I've only just got here and this big smiley bloke has fallen into my lap. Well, I definitely *hope* he has.

While I'm still lost in my thoughts, he reappears, handing me a tall tumbler. He takes a seat on the opposite side of the table and lifts his beer to me. "Bottoms up," he says. I'm pretty sure we're both silently snickering at the innuendo as we take our first gulps. I notice the potency of my drink; it must be a double. *Mate, are you trying to get me drunk? You do realise I'm champing at the bit, don't you? No need to butter me up—I'm yours.*

Wiping the foam from his moustache, he looks over at my left hand. "Oh, don't let me stop you," he says. "I'm not a smoker, but it's not like it bothers me."

I glance down and notice I'm still fidgeting with the cigarette packet. All of a sudden, I'm deeply ashamed. "Actually, neither am I. I gave up eighteen months ago, and even then I'd only been doing it for about a year." As the sentence tumbles out of my mouth, it dawns on me how ridiculous this sounds. Who the hell takes up smoking in their forties? "Well, other than when I was really young, at least. It was hard to resist slipping back into ancient habits when I started living with someone who smokes like a chimney." I dump the packet in the ashtray and push it aside. "It wasn't a nice thing to revisit, anyway."

Right at that moment, there's a huge flapping sound, amidst the jingling of a collar. This noise triggers a look of surprise on Big Bear's face. "Oh!" he says. "I'm sorry, I didn't realise you…" Craning his neck, he peers down at where Brendan is lying next to my stool. "I didn't notice him there." He glances back up at me. "Can you… uh…?"

"Yeah, I can see you," I say through my best grin. "I have blurry tunnel vision, but one eye's a bit better than the other." I move my head up and down, eyebrows slightly raised, making it clear he knows I'm well aware of the stout, sexy stud in front of me.

"Well, I'm pleased to hear you've got that much, at least." He smiles and gets up, walking around to my side of the bar table and squatting down in front of Brendan. Ever mindful that he's working, Brendan remains still, but his tail gives him away as it begins to thump against the decking. My hunky guest leans over and reaches out, before pulling back slightly. "Is it OK to pat him?"

There's no way I'm gonna rain on this man's parade. "Sure, mate. He'll love it." I train my eyes on Big Bear's left hand and notice the gold band around his fourth finger. My heart sinks instantly. Maybe I've misread this friendly interaction. Oh, well. I'm going to enjoy a bit of conversation at least. But I'll definitely probe further. "Am I disturbing you? Is your husband here?"

Big Bear leans back up from Brendan. Momentary confusion clouds his face, before he glances down at his wedding ring. "Oh, no," he chuckles. "I'm not married. I have a partner, but it's the same situation as yours." His eyes flash as he seems to take in what he's just said. "I mean, we're *open*. I love him, he's my best mate, but it's not a…" his eyes flit around as he searches for the right word, "a *sexual* arrangement anymore. Not for a long, long time." This predicament is so common it could easily be trotted out as an excuse. But I've been there myself. In a lot of ways, I'm there right now. And regardless of whether it's my hormones or my heart ruling me at the moment, I choose to believe this man.

It's jarring as I take a mental step back and consider how candid we're being with each other. At first glance, the details we're sharing are far too intimate for two people who have only just met. But I've learnt there is a very small window of opportunity in situations like this. Swift sexual negotiation is required, and after downing two thirds of my drink my inhibitions have left the building. Suddenly, I'm blurting out the clincher. "Well, handsome bear, maybe it might turn out to be my night, eh?"

He looks up at me with a loaded grin. "Maybe it might turn out to be *mine*," he says. "And I'm flattered that such a gorgeous cub thinks I'm a 'handsome bear.'" He parks his burly frame on the bar stool next to me and extends his right hand. "But it's easier if you call me Bruno." Bruno's grip is strong and warm as we shake. I instantly imagine these big bear paws of his roaming my body, holding me tight, keeping me safe.

"Phwoaaar! Get in there, Bru! Arf! Arf! Arf!" Howls, woofs and jeers sail our way from a couple of tables down. I squint over to see a bunch of what I assume are Bruno's friends pumping their fists in the air footy-style as they watch us shaking hands.

Bruno laughs, but doesn't acknowledge them, staying focused on me. "Well, my yobbo mates call me Bru. You know how it is—they find names with more than one syllable impossible to cope with."

Throughout all this, Bruno has failed to let go of my hand. Our contact has gone well beyond the expected level of politeness, but I don't want it to stop. Keeping my charming smile in place, I put a renewed vigour into our handshake. "Well, I'm Bradford. You'd be amazed at the difficulty people have with *that*." It's working. Bruno's grip is still firm and his thumb is now stroking over my knuckles. Maybe I should keep talking. Maybe he'll be so busy listening he won't remember to pull away. "It's daggy as hell, but it's my dad's name and my grandad's name. Jesus, I'm waffling. Sorry."

Bruno laughs, breaking our handshake at last. I might have been upset at this loss, but he gently rubs his palm up and down my upper arm. Gee, it feels nice to be touched like this after so long. "Um, and by the way," I add, "I'm the one who should be flattered here, because I'm far too old to be called a cub."

He studies my face for a moment. "Well, you can't be more than forty."

"Eight. Turned forty-eight just after Christmas." I give him a little smirk. "A combination of my mum's good skin and the dim lighting out here."

A familiar sound chirps out of the phone Bruno's placed on the table. He glances down at it, then up to meet my eyes again. I swear I can see a little blush forming on his cheeks. We both know what it is: Growlr. "Sorry," he says. "I gotta turn that off."

"Hey, we do what we can to find a bit of companionship. I used to be on that app as well. Years ago, before I became legally blind. It was all too much hassle after that."

"You mean, because you couldn't see a phone anymore?"

"Hmmm. Back then I guess that was part of the problem. These days I have a huge phone and iPad with every vision enhancement possible. But really, I just didn't like the idea of showing up to random guys' houses with a cane or a guide dog." I glance around the courtyard, noticing it's getting a little more packed with people. "At least in places like this, a sexy bear like you could see what he'd be getting in advance." *Oh, man, I'm putting it all out there now.*

Bruno's ears prick up at my overture. "So… do you still have your login?"

I need to think about this. It's been ages, since before I met Jarrod. *Oh yeah.* "Pretty sure I do."

"What's your profile name?" There's a wolfish smile on Bruno's face.

"'bradthethird.' Spelt out, all lower case."

Bruno taps at his phone for a while, then gazes back up at me. "You look way better in the flesh," he says, before shuffling off his stool. "I'm getting us another round."

"It's my shout," I protest.

"Nah, mate. You're gonna sit here and download the app so you can get my message." As he turns towards the door leading back round to the bar, I remember my previous lost opportunity. My eyes do not leave the beautiful chunky bear arse smiling at me from inside snug-fitting jeans as he walks away. *Thank you, whatever god there is up there.*

It takes less than two minutes for me to have Growlr installed on my iPad. It takes another couple of minutes for me to log in and navigate my way around an app that now looks totally different to how I remember. And it takes me three seconds to open Bruno's message and see he's unlocked his private photo album. There it is: a series of glorious headless nudes. A super-furry bear belly. Below that, a dense, dark bush. And below that, a large, thick uncut penis. Flaccid or not, it's formidably fat. And there's a generous selection of pics in various states of arousal. I've always said I'm not a size queen. I've been rogered by five and a half inch dicks that made me come so hard I saw stars. It's true: technique and chemistry always do it for me. But, *damn.* I'm fascinated by the juggernaut between the legs of the bear in these photos.

"You got it?" Two more glasses arrive at the table, followed by a grinning Mediterranean hulk.

"Oh, *man.*" I can't even hide the way I'm beaming. I also can't deny the erection in my slutty little running shorts, the one that is now throbbing painfully. "So, now I know three more things about you, Mister *CalabreseVers47.*"

"Yeah?"

"One. You're Italian. But your first name pretty much gave that away."

"Guilty."

"And unless you were a January baby, you're, what—forty-eight this year?"

Bruno's face flushes. "Um… that profile name is a few years old. I'll be fifty in April, unfortunately."

I'm loving this bashful side he's showing me. I bask in the cuteness of it for a moment as I gear up for the third and final part of my grilling. "And how about the 'vers' part, Bruno?"

He chuckles, diverting his eyes and fiddling with his beer glass. "Well, in practice I'm more of a top. But sometimes I go home with guys hoping I'll have my arse pounded with the same enthusiasm I show to theirs. I don't even get a look-in, though, because the second we're naked, their legs are straight up in the air."

"Ha! It's always the way—big guys with big dicks attract selfish bottoms." My God, these huge gulps of rum I've been taking have really loosened my lips. "You know, mate, I have less than ten percent vision. I can't check out men with any sense of subtlety. But my eyes were glued to that beautiful arse of yours the whole time you were walking away from me."

Bruno's now turning several shades of scarlet. I'm enjoying this. "Ah, mate, you flatter me. I have a big fat arse," he says.

"It's burly and hot and fills out those jeans perfectly." I'm on a roll now. Leaning forward, I fix him with my filthiest stare. "And I'm shocked to think any bear or chaser in his right mind would not want to lavish it with as much attention as possible." I sit back, fairly leering at him. "Of course, I'm obsessed with what you have down the front of your jocks. Who wouldn't want a joyride on top of that monster? But, you know, a pancake is never done till you flip it over."

I'm sure I can hear a low growl coming from Bruno. He's smiling at me, but he's not saying anything. Trying to fill the gap in the conversation, I take another large swig of my drink, and Bruno follows suit. After he's swallowed, he seems to have found his voice. "You just keep getting better and better, Bradford."

I'm thrilled to hear this. Maybe I've been a little forthright, but he *has* just shown me his dick. Suddenly I'm reminded of my failure to reciprocate. I pick up my iPad and squint to locate my ancient private album on the Growlr app. "These pics are easily six years old, and the most explicit one is just me in a Speedo. I was never game enough to have naked shots."

Bruno's eyes flick straight to his phone when he hears my message alert. Tapping on the screen, he smiles at the photos I've just unlocked for him. "You're one hot, hairy bear," he growls, before looking over at me, sizing me up against the outdated pics. "Gee, you were built like a brick shithouse back then, but you're even more solid these days." Another glance down, another look over to me. "And I love the full beard you have now." I can tell he's being diplomatic here. He doesn't want to sound critical of the close-cropped scruff I sported back then. It's very sweet of him, but he needn't worry.

"Thanks. I decided to embrace my inner bear. I was never muscly or athletic enough to be acceptable. So, I grew my beard and became even burlier. All of a sudden, I had an identity." I slap my hands around my middle. "I've got the bear belly now, but my legs and arse are nice and brawny thanks to all the hilly walks Brendan takes me on."

Brendan sits up tall. He's well-trained and he's always ready when he hears his name. I give his neck a ruffle, then look back to Bruno, who has an amused expression on his face. "Yeah, I know," I say. "Strange name for a dog, but he was already called that when I got him. It's even funny when you say it next to mine. 'Brendan and Bradford.' Sounds like creepy little twin boys who speak in a unison monotone."

Bruno laughs politely at my silly quip. "Brendan is actually my partner's name."

"Oh, wow. Really?" I look back down at my lab, who's staring up at me, waiting for his instructions. "You hear that, buddy? He's got a Brendan too." I don't need to mention *my* boyfriend's name. I'd rather not think about him right now.

A couple of guys pass by the table, their eyes following me. As they smile, I get the kind of teenage thrill I so rarely feel these days. "Hey, handsome," one of them calls out.

Bruno turns to see the men walking through the nearby glass door, and the guy that hadn't spoken shoots me a grin and a wink. I can't be rude, so I settle for a sunny smile and a wave. Something that I hope says, *"You made me feel better about myself, but I'm otherwise engaged here."*

Bruno turns back to me with a raised eyebrow. "I'll bet there are a ton of men here desperate for a piece of you."

"You can talk. You'd be beating them off with a stick."

He doesn't answer that one, just chuckles shyly as he gazes back down at his phone. He knows it's true. "Jesus," he croons. "You in that Speedo…"

I slide off my bar stool, getting to my feet and straightening my running shorts. "Well, if you wanna see what's underneath it, I have to visit the little boy's room." I shoot him a smug smile. "I'm sure you must need to go as well." *God, my inner slut has well and truly come out to play now.*

My assumption is right. Bruno follows close behind me and Brendan as we make our way through the courtyard. "This arse of yours is fuckin' gorgeous," he growls in my ear. "Tell me, is it furry like your chest?"

"Well, I'm wearing a jockstrap under these. Why don't you find out for yourself?"

Bruno gives a lusty laugh and I feel fingers slide underneath the leg opening of my shorts. They make their way over my hairy buns and straight to the forest in my crack. "Even hotter than I'd hoped for," he rasps.

A large breath escapes me as the foraging fingers move deep between my cheeks, stroking my hole. "Bruno, you do realise I'm not gonna be able to piss now, don't you?"

Three men exit the gents' toilets as we approach. It looks busy, so I'm surprised to see it's empty when we enter. Brendan dutifully sits near the basins.

I take my position at the trough next to Bruno. Reaching across with my right hand, I pull up the left leg of my short-shorts and underwear, letting my dick and balls tumble out in full view of him. Squinting over in Bruno's direction, I spot the great big penis he's holding, already pissing merrily away. It's just like it was in his semi-erect photos—thick and engorged, but not fully hard. I thrust my hips forward a bit to make a quick comparison with my own semi-erect dick. I definitely don't have his girth, but I have every bit of his length.

I'm still ogling the spectacle between his legs when I hear him speak up. "What a nice surprise, Bradford."

I can't stop my lips curling into a smirk as I raise my eyes. He's definitely staring at my crotch. "Yeah? Short guy must have little dick, you thought?"

Bruno's laugh is so lusty it's pure filth. "You caught me out there. That beautiful long cock of yours is a major bonus." I can see him shuffling his foreskin back and forth a bit, distorting the raging stream he's directing at the metal trough. Just the sight of it has my dick growing harder. "And here's a coincidence for you," he continues. "I have a massive kink for circumcised dicks with Prince Alberts."

"You do?"

"Yeah, I shit you not. I'll trawl porn for them when I want a good wank. I'm a sucker for a cut cock, and they show off the PA rings beautifully."

All this dirty talk he's dishing out has me so wildly turned on that I'm now fully and achingly erect. Given the fact there's also a ring threaded into the end of my dick, it's becoming impossible to finish what I supposedly came in here to do.

"Hey, Bradford?" Bruno says.

"Yeah?"

"You're getting piss everywhere."

"Oh, Jesus. Sorry!" Looking down, I realise my cock is now pointing upwards and spraying in multiple directions. I quickly try to reposition my turgid shaft so my stream hits the trough at the correct angle.

"Nah, mate. Don't apologise. It's fucking *hot*. Look what you've done to me." At his invitation, I turn my head and see that he's now finished and standing there with a proud erection. He drags his gaze up my body till our eyes lock. "And while we're at it, I love the fact you're a short-arse."

I guffaw so hard my piss stream goes AWOL again. "Short-arse? I'm nearly five-seven. It just looks worse because I'm standing next to someone who's..." I survey the top of Bruno's head. Similar height to Jarrod. "Six-one?"

"Spot on," he grins. "Now, let me get another perv on your dick before you finish."

"I might be a while yet."

I don't think I've ever done this before. I mean, sure, I've checked out countless guys' penises at urinals. What man doesn't do that? Straight or gay, they're lying if they say they haven't indulged their curiosity. But it's never been this brazen for me. This *sustained*.

Unfortunately, all good things must come to an end. I feel a twinge of disappointment as Bruno finally tucks that magnificent schlong back into his jeans. When we're at the basins washing our hands, I watch his face in the mirror. My heart is thundering with lust. I can hardly wait till we seal the deal. This *has* to happen.

The contract is signed as we share the single hand dryer. I look into his big dark eyes and something snaps. Neither of us has to work out who's going to make the first move, because our mouths are suddenly together. His lips are soft and his tongue is broad and confident, sweeping straight inside me and roaming all around in bold strokes. It's not one of those delicate kisses that gradually picks up momentum. We're grunting, warm air rushing from our nostrils and filtering through our moustaches as our sense of urgency intensifies.

I'm on fire. This hasn't happened in *so long* and I'm floored at how much I've missed it. The relief, the pent-up desire, the raging passionate need in me is coursing through every cell of my body. Bruno turns his head slightly, delving into me even deeper with his tongue. I want to kiss like this all the time. I never want it to stop. His hand moves behind my head and holds it close. My arms are wrapped around his great big burly body, pulling it towards me, revelling in the manly bulk of it. He's so substantial. So masculine. So damn perfect.

His other hand moves from its position on my shoulder, sliding down my front and stroking my nipple. Instantly, a loud and involuntary moan escapes me, the soundwaves travelling straight into Bruno's throat. He pauses, tickling his thumb over my nipple again, and I moan even louder. I can feel the shape of his face change as it's pressed against mine. The muscles tighten and his cheeks perk up as he breaks into a huge smile. Barely moving his lips away, he mumbles, "So you like it too, eh?"

"Exactly like that, yes," I pant.

He gives the tiniest of chuckles. "You mean… like this?" His thumb tickles my nipple again and the groan that escapes my mouth this time is completely unbridled. "If you keep doing that, I'm gonna have to pull out my dick and come right here on the floor." I'm not lying. My left hand has been negligent in its duty of late and I'm feeling particularly trigger-happy.

"Well, that would be a shame, Bradford. I'm hoping for a whole lot more than a wank in the dunnies."

"You and me both." I move out a little, sliding my hand around to fondle his right nipple. "You're telling me that yours work too, yeah?" I'm always fascinated when I meet another man like me. In my experience, most guys feel very little at all.

"You can be a bit more heavy-going with mine."

"You mean you want pinching and biting?" I wince inwardly. I can't think of anything more painful.

"No! No at all. Just a firm suck, or a bit of a roll between your fingers."

I'm glad for these instructions. If this thing between Bruno and me is just a one-off, I want to blow his mind. Moving my other hand around, I find his left nipple and get a small surprise. "This one's pierced?"

"Yeah. But it hurt so fuckin' much I never let them near the other one with that bloody needle."

I laugh quietly as I massage both of his little chest nubs, and Bruno moans exactly the way I did. It's automatic and it resonates with base, animalistic desire. I'm gonna send this big bear to heaven tonight if it's the last thing I do.

Bruno grasps the back of my head again, pulling me against his lips for a desperate reprise. Our kiss is fast and intense, ending when the door bursts open suddenly.

"Get a room!" Drunken sniggers come from behind us, but they barely register.

"Take me home with you, Bradford," Bruno mumbles *sotto voce*. "Or we could try my place. There's a good chance Brendan won't be there."

At the sound of his name, my trusty canine companion stands to attention, making me laugh out loud. "This 'Brendan' thing is gonna be a problem." I reach down and grab *my* Brendan's harness. I have no idea about the domestic dynamic between Bruno and his partner. Right now, all I want is for the two of us to enjoy ourselves without any awkwardness. "My place will be completely free. I can guarantee Jarrod will be out partying for the rest of the weekend."

Guess he knows my boyfriend's name now too.

CHAPTER 3

"How did you get here?" asks Bruno as we emerge from the pub.

"A bus and two trains. It's a bit of a pain, but I'm an expert these days." I'm feeling impatient. More than a little eager to get this man somewhere I can ravage his body. "Let's just take a cab. I've got a taxi card, so I get them for half-price." I glance over at Bruno, shrugging my shoulders. "Unfortunately, I had to be ninety percent blind in order to qualify for it." I really don't want to go into how much I've lost. I don't want him to pity me in any way.

Stepping forward, I signal to a passing taxi. The driver slows down, then takes off again. I follow the cab with my eyes, noticing how it stops to pick up people further down the block.

"What the hell did he do that for?" Bruno is frowning.

"This happens sometimes. They have to take guide dogs, but some of them don't want a bar of it." I keep my voice even. It's not worth getting upset over.

"Fuck that. Arsehole." Bruno strides forward, flagging down another passing taxi. He doesn't speak to the guy, just opens the back door and climbs in, then waves for Brendan and me to join him.

Whether the driver is pissed off or not, I don't know. "Where to?" he calls over to us.

"Bondi, thanks." I'm still standing at the open rear door with Brendan, and the driver leans across to adjust the front passenger seat as far forward as it will go. I breathe a sigh of relief—he's clearly well-educated on right-of-access for blind people with service animals. After I've climbed into the back seat and shuffled across a bit, Brendan hops into the rear footwell like he's been trained to do.

I'm now squished in the middle, but it's perfect. I have no choice but to be pressed up against the warm, masculine body of the gorgeous bear to my right. As the taxi takes off down King Street, I feel Bruno's hand slide into mine. This small gesture of intimacy softens my heart, and a rush of pure heat storms through my body.

"Bondi, eh? Fancy," says Bruno. The warmth of his breath caresses my ear. The melodious tone of his low mumble resonates through my soul. God, I need more of this.

"It's an old apartment in the *bowels* of Bondi. Really, I was incredibly lucky to get it."

"How so?"

I take a breath, launching into the super-short version. "I was paying a fortune to rent a tiny studio in Bondi when I suddenly lost a ton more of my sight. My doctor got me onto Housing Pathways, and they quickly found one of their places. Apparently some elderly person had passed away, and I was considered a high priority."

I'm embarrassed by this. Government housing is notoriously hard to get, and I've always felt like there were other people more needy than I was. At times like these I have to remind myself: *I lost my sight.* Just because I've adjusted and learnt how to cope, just because it's been over five years and I've nearly forgotten what it was like to be 'normal'—it doesn't mean things are easy.

"That's bloody fantastic," says Bruno. I can't hear any judgement in his voice. Maybe I'm being too paranoid about all of this. "Were you with your partner back then?"

"No, I met him a year or so afterwards. Before that, it was really hard. I was blinder than I am now and I had months before it improved a bit with more surgery. By the time Jarrod moved in about four years ago, I was a lot more independent. I didn't need quite so many visits from support workers."

"Must have been great having him around all the time to help."

I try to stifle a snort, but I fail spectacularly. "Jarrod may have been a lot of fun, but if anything, *I* was the one looking after *him.* Domestic duties are not his forte." I'm trying my best to sound lighthearted. Bruno doesn't need to hear me whinge about my trials and tribulations. He doesn't need to know that Jarrod hasn't been paying his share of the rent—rent that was raised back when I told the Housing Commission someone else had moved in. He doesn't need to hear how I'd be better off alone. I've been trapped in a relationship that's continuing out of habit, vainly hoping for a return to the way things used to be, back when

Jarrod loved me. But I can see now that that's never going to happen. I hate myself for believing too long.

Things fall silent between Bruno and me. I begin to worry that I've lowered the mood, but I feel him squeeze my hand. His thumb starts to stroke along my knuckles again and I relax into his touch. Familiar music wafts into the rear of the cab. I lose myself in the eerie orchestration, the melancholy drama of the accompaniment.

"You know this?" Bruno's voice sounds surprised as it buzzes near my right ear. I hadn't realised I'd been humming along. I've been caught out in a candid moment.

"Yeah, Beethoven. *Fidelio*. I sang this role in a minor production in Germany."

Bruno shifts slightly, turning towards me. "Really? You were an opera singer?"

I laugh quietly. *Another thing I lost*. "Only a small-time one. I did my music degree at the Conservatorium here. Sang professionally in the chorus at the Sydney Opera House from time to time. The odd principal role for small opera companies too. Then, when I'd saved up enough money, I spent a few seasons in Germany, singing in minor productions for modest performance fees." I grin across at Bruno. "So I wasn't exactly a star."

"But you did it for a living! That's so impressive!"

"Nah. I just got paid here and there from it. After my degree I also did my education diploma, so teaching music part-time was my bread and butter."

"You were *heldentenor*?" A voice sails across from the front seat of the cab. Our driver must have heard every word of our conversation.

"Well, I had the heavy tenor voice. It was easier to get work if you were loud." I shouldn't minimise my former skills, but I've always been bad at self-promotion.

"You sing! You sing for me!" The driver's European accent is insistent.

"Nah, I'm very rusty." I laugh, suddenly bashful.

"I want to hear!"

"Yeah! Go on, just a little bit?" Bruno squeezes my hand.

The aria playing on the stereo has moved well into the final section. Conceding defeat, I take a huge breath. The sound of my opera teacher's voice rings in my ears: *"Take the air right down to your balls!"* Throwing caution to the wind, I launch into the closing lines of Beethoven's masterpiece.

"Der führt mich zur Freiheit, zur Freiheit ins himmlische Reich,
Zur Freiheit, zur Freiheit ins himmlische Reich."

"Wow, that's incredible!" Bruno laughs, as whistles come from the front of the cab.

I guess the residual alcohol has liberated more than my sexual inhibitions. Despite no warm-up, my crunched-up sitting position, and my lack of technical and musical polish, I've managed to generate a large sound. "Thanks, fellas. It's definitely not up to scratch, though. I'm lucky if I can afford to see my opera teacher once a month these days."

"Jesus," says Bruno. "I was about to bring up my amateur attempts at singing, but it's nothing like that."

"Really? Tell me more." I'm fascinated to hear we have this in common.

"It's not really worth mentioning, honestly. My dad always wanted me and my twin sister to sing. Mainly Italian songs." I can see Bruno's cute little blush making another resurgence. "I never turned out to be the Mario Lanza he hoped I'd be. Gabriela's a lot better than I am. She just played the lead in *Mamma Mia* for Miranda Musical Society."

"Really? That's pretty damn impressive. They've gotta be the most competitive amateur company in Sydney."

I'd prompt Bruno to sing a bit for me, but the taxi has now pulled up and I can spot my daggy sixties apartment building to the left of us. "Thank you for the performance!" the driver says, after I've put my taxi card through and paid for the remainder.

"No, no—thank you for listening." I'm grateful for the validation. I feel better tonight than I have in ages.

Bruno and I stroll up the street a bit so Brendan can stretch his legs and do his business before bedtime. There's a slight ocean breeze making its way through Bondi, tempering the worst of the steamy late January heat. I go through the motions with Brendan—finding a grassy area, removing his harness, then holding his leash as he dutifully circles around me, searching for exactly the right spot.

"My God, there's such an art to it," says Bruno.

"It's all part of the routine. Brendan knows what's expected of him and exactly when it will happen."

"What, like crap-on-demand?"

I erupt into loud laughter that turns into cackling as Brendan looks up at me in confusion. "Beats having him squat in the middle of the food court at Westfield."

When Brendan is all taken care of, we head back to the apartment building. Passing by the bin, I ditch the offending doggie bag before leading Bruno inside and along the corridor to my front door. "Ground floor, eh?" he says. "That's handy."

"I know, right? And the back door of the apartment leads to the common area behind the building. Perfect for Brendan."

"You have a garden?" says Bruno, following me through the narrow hallway entrance.

"Nah, just a concrete area with clotheslines and a strip of lawn. Nothing fancy here." I wave towards the open bathroom door. "See? Handrails and open shower, courtesy of the previous tenant's disabilities." I lead Bruno through to the small lounge room. To the right of us is the main bedroom, but we won't be going in there tonight. It just seems a bit weird. Open relationship or not, it's a line I won't cross. Plus, I have a sofa bed in the spare room. "Take a seat, Bruno. Can I get you a beer?"

"Thanks, but only if you're drinking too," he says, settling onto the couch.

I could definitely do with a boost of Dutch courage. Jarrod and I agreed to this extramarital arrangement well over a year ago. Really, it was just a technicality, because I knew he was already screwing other guys. To date, though, I've only exercised my freedom a scant few times, and never back here at my flat.

Brendan follows me to the laundry and I free him from his harness. He knows the drill and his thick tail swishes as I fill his bowl with dog biscuits. Then, I dash to the kitchen, grab a stubby of Cooper's for Bruno, and rummage around in the top cupboard for my bottle of Bundy. The best thing about my penchant for dark rum is that my alcoholic boyfriend hates it and *usually* won't touch it.

Back out in the living room, I furnish Bruno with his beer and place my oversized tumbler on the coffee table. Then, I pause for a moment so I can lose myself once more in Bruno's dark puppy-dog eyes. God, he's so bloody beautiful. "Are you gonna be right if I leave you here for a few minutes?"

"Yeah, sure. I'm fine." Bruno smiles up at me. I can tell what he's thinking. Time to go and wash *down there.* But there's no need, I'm primped and preened already. I knew what I wanted tonight.

Instead of taking off to the bathroom, I pass by the linen cupboard near the laundry and stock up. Then, I head to the spare room and switch on the portable air conditioner. Given how stuffy and warm it is in here tonight, I know we're gonna need it. After that, I set up the sofa bed. It's no rickety grandma fold-out—it's a super-comfortable upmarket number that I got for a bargain. I throw on the sheets and blankets, then stand back and admire my handiwork. It'll do. It's not nearly as big as the queen-sized ensemble that Jarrod and I sleep on in the main bedroom, but I kinda like the thought of forced proximity with Bruno. I have high hopes for a long and drawn-out cuddle session.

The last thing I do is take two hand towels and tuck them under the edge of the sofa bed. Shutting the door to the spare room behind me, I pass by the lounge room sound system, firing it up to resume the renaissance playlist I'd had on before I went out tonight.

As I grab my drink and take a seat next to Bruno, I suddenly feel inhibited. It's silly—we've already had a comprehensive make-out session in the men's toilets and a cosy cab ride home, but now we've broken the rhythm. This change of scenery has me feeling like I need to start all over again for some reason.

"Is this more opera?" asks Bruno.

"Uh, it's a motet," I answer, snapping out of my wandering thoughts. I catch Bruno's inquisitive expression. "A choral piece, kind of like a song with multiple vocal parts." I don't like to ramble on about these things to people who aren't students. For all I know, Bruno might just be feigning polite interest, but he seems attentive. "It's from 1603. *Ave Dulcissima Maria* by Carlo Gesualdo."

"That all sounds very cultured and elegant." Bruno grins, and the light dances across the surface of his eyes.

His description makes me snicker. "He was a bad man, by all accounts. An Italian prince who murdered his wife and got away with it because of his social status. But musically, he was a genius. Hundreds of years ahead of his time."

"It's beautiful," mumbles Bruno. "So soothing." He relaxes back, taking a swig of his beer and closing his eyes. I wonder if he's nervous like me. We sit there for a while, letting the angelic sounds wash over us. Between the alcohol and the music, I'm starting to ease into the moment again.

I smile as I watch Brendan quietly pad back into the room, lie down on his bed in the corner, and start hoeing into his favourite chew toy. He's so attentive, so in tune with me, it's like he can sense that he needs to keep a low profile.

Bruno makes the next furtive move, sliding his fingers over to interlock with mine. It's the precise segue I needed. Ditching my now-empty glass, I pull his hand to my mouth and place a line of soft kisses over the back of it. The skin is warm and the hair covering it dances across my nose and moustache. My response pays off and Bruno leans forward suddenly, locking his lips with mine. It's a much more gentle prelude than the one we'd enjoyed in the toilets at the pub. His voice hums as he moves, his mouth softly nipping away at me. Our moustaches brush together as our noses nudge side-by-side. The combined heat of our skin lingers in the air, driving the urgency inside me up another notch. I clasp my hand to the back of his head and we begin to move faster. He's kissing my cheek, moving further back towards my neck. As his humid breath wafts across my ear, I begin to moan. At once, his strong arms are around me, clutching me tight in a secure embrace. His gentle kisses rain down behind my ear, then trail along my neck. A rush of energy climbs its way up to my scalp, ripples of heat that reverberate through every hair follicle. His tongue traces my throat and I let out a small cry. This kind of sensuality is something I'm not accustomed to. I can't believe I've gone through so many years without it.

"Oh, God," he whispers. The shaking in his voice, the potent sense of passion in his tone unleashes something wild inside me and I clamber onto his lap, my knees straddling his hips. I launch myself at his lips again, delving my tongue in deep, fighting with him in a burst of desperate need. My hands clutch at his neck, his shoulders, the back of his head, as I battle to get further into his mouth. Bruno grips me tight, his fingers kneading at my back, one hand working its way down till it slips under the waistband of my shorts. I feel his fingers travelling hastily along my bare arse crack and my groans hurtle into a sudden crescendo.

My rampant lust is spiralling out of control. Our faces are so profoundly entwined that I don't ever want to let go. Bruno kisses with such intensity, it's like his whole mouth is dying to own me. Our tongues are thrusting, tasting, swallowing, our grunts are coming at a rate of knots, our arms are grabbing at each other in a frenzy. Somehow, one of his fingers has found its way to my arsehole. It's pressing eagerly, working its way just inside. My entire body tenses. I can no longer restrain the urge to move into the second act.

"Jesus!" I moan, tearing myself away from Bruno's lips. "Let's go." No further explanation is needed as I shuffle off his lap and drag him towards the spare bedroom. After shutting and locking the door behind us, we find ourselves in a mad scramble to try and undress. I stagger around, unzipping my work boots while I watch Bruno fairly flinging his t-shirt over his head. I can't get rid of the bloody steel-caps fast enough, stumbling as I prise them off at the heel, immediately followed by my footy socks. With one manic shove, my running shorts and jockstrap are down at my ankles and I kick them to oblivion. The very last thing I do is rip off my t-shirt before I allow myself to look at Bruno again.

Taking a small step back, I ogle him in wide-eyed wonderment. He's absolutely breathtaking. A searing vision of naked, bearish beauty. Bruno is the perfect mix of broad stockiness and cuddly curves. I advance towards him as if I'm hovering on a cloud. That first touch is pure magic. The softness of the forest on his chest, the tactile delight my fingers experience as they move through it—I'm breathless all over again. Bruno's hand roams my pectoral, brushing my nipple as I whine openly. Over and over my dick flexes, consumed by an ache so sublimely intense it's like I'm about to come already.

This is the eye of the storm for us. Sliding his arms around me, Bruno kisses me gently on the lips and we move in tandem towards the sofa bed. It's still a bit warm in here, so I throw back the covers. Bruno climbs onto the mattress, holding his hand out to guide me down beside him.

I don't think I've ever enjoyed snuggling up to a man this much. I can recall one or two wonderful instances when I was a lot younger, and they've lodged themselves in my memory firmly enough that the feelings are now rushing back to me. But there's something about the way this man is touching me that blows those other men out of the water. His hands traverse the fur on my torso with such reverence. His dark eyes stare deeply into mine, a concentrated mass of tender yearning. I could just about drown.

My fingers trace the lower curve of his belly, raking softly through the hair above his cock till I feel the warmth of his shaft against the back of my hand. It's standing at attention silently, waiting for me. And it's bloody magnificent. I don't grasp it; I stroke my fingers along the length, till the tip of my pointer lands on the puckered end of his foreskin. The opulent hood is still in place, covering the prize underneath. I trace the edge of it, the tiny folds and furrows just detectable under the pad of my finger. I'm savouring this discovery. Bruno breathes heavily when, at long last, my hand closes around his substantial girth. I'm fascinated at this throbbing warmth I'm holding. I can't wait to find out all the wonderful things it can do.

I know how to work a dick like Bruno's. Slowly, I begin to move his foreskin up and down, letting the underside of my index finger brush against the back of his unsheathed knob each time. Bruno shudders and moans, and I'm well aware this is my cue to increase the pressure slightly. I can feel the lower ridge of his knob through the rolling hood, and I bump the curve of my fingers over it every time my hand goes up and down. "Oh, man," Bruno pants. "You're so good at this."

His warm fist wraps around my own shaft and begins to mirror the movements I'm making on his dick. "I don't have a foreskin, so you're gonna need some kind of lube with mine," I whisper.

"Oh, sorry, of course. And what about this?" He tickles his finger over the rear of my knob, jiggling the Prince Albert ring and making me squirm with pleasure.

"Best thing I ever did. I had to change my… erm… wanking technique, but it adds this extra come-blasting dimension."

This clearly amuses Bruno, who laughs as he brushes his hand lightly up and down over my knob, driving me crazy as his fingers strum against the titanium jewellery. "Well, it seems kinda weird asking for instruction on something we've been doing since we were twelve, but maybe you'll fill me in on this technique?" Bruno's face is right next to mine and his playfully-raised eyebrow makes me snort with stifled laughter. It's probably not the right thing to be doing in the heat of passion, but I love how comfortable we seem to be with each other.

"Um… just kinda come at it from underneath while you're stroking. Nothing to it, really."

"Well, I want a taste of this dick of yours first, and I'm not keen on a mouthful of lube." In no time at all, Bruno's flipped over to lie in the opposite direction and my cock is submerged in the wet heat of his mouth. His tongue swishes all around my glans, frantically teasing the piercing, making it twist and turn and set off the nerve endings inside. When my heavy panting turns into stifled moans, he sinks down further onto my shaft, taking every inch of me into his mouth, then sliding back up to once again lavish my knob with every blessed movement he can muster. My back arches in ecstasy, my arse clenches, my balls draw up tight. I need to amplify this. My fingers move up to stroke my nipples. Somehow, I've begun to cry out. He's incredible. Nobody has ever blown me with this kind of skill. Nobody has ever sucked me off till I've come, but I could see it happening right now. A sudden surge of pleasure has my hips thrusting upwards. At the same time a moist finger finds its way into my arsehole and I practically wail.

With lightning speed, Bruno leans over me, pushing my legs right up and burying his tongue where his finger has just been. Jesus Christ, I can barely remember the last time someone rimmed me. Jarrod's certainly never been into it, despite how much I love it. My rampant groans are tempered only when I turn sideways and see Bruno's fat prick just inches away. Reaching underneath him and grabbing his hips, I hoist him over me into a sixty-nine. Instantly, my mouth is filled with his colossal member. I work back his foreskin and feast on the flavour of him. He's bloody delicious. His knob is thick and firm as it drags up and down against my tongue. I start to suck and swallow and thrash around, devouring him with all my might.

Everything about this is glorious. A tongue is being thrust deep inside my arsehole and I'm gorging myself on the most heavenly dick I've ever had the pleasure of tasting. I'm starting to feel giddy. I slide my hands up the back of Bruno's thighs and discover heavy, hairy balls. *Oh God, I need some of these too.*

Bruno's penis springs free of my mouth as I push upwards on his butt cheeks. Pulling him back down towards me, I shift my face up and bury my nose in his manly crown jewels. Bruno is well-showered, I can tell. But his musk is there in spades. It's sending me completely feral. I slather my nostrils all over his scrotum, drawing in as much of his scent as I can. My tongue follows suit, tracing around each big, beefy testicle. A large vibration rocks against my arsehole as Bruno groans. *Oh? Have I discovered something special here?* I repeat my move, dying for an encore. I want to hear him bellow. I want to feel his tongue thrum deep inside my anus again. *Bugger me, this is pleasure overload.*

As Bruno's second vocal vibration strafes my sphincter, I run my hands inwards across his arse cheeks and straight into his furry crack. One of my thumbs lands smack-bang on his perfectly-puckered little quoit. I stroke up and down over it, desperate to discover every detail. Now, I'm bloody *ravenous*.

Craning my neck up as far as possible, I clutch onto his buttocks and pull them apart. I need to eat Bruno's beautiful arse in the worst way. I'm trying my utmost, but he's so much taller than I am. The best I can manage is to slather my tongue over his taint while my nose is pressed against his hole. His masculine aroma storms into my nostrils, driving my libido through the roof. "Turn over!" I gasp.

Bruno hears the urgency in my voice and his tongue vacates my arse immediately. Scuttling out from beneath him, I push him down onto his stomach. There, in all its hirsute naked glory, is that sexy butt I'd lusted after back at the bar. *"Big fat arse",* my Aunt Fanny. Sure, it's beautifully cheeky and chubby, but it's also rock solid with muscle under that padding—a prime picture of bearish grandeur. Straight away, I shuffle into position, sinking my face inside. I am engulfed in manly bliss. I breathe deep, rewarded with another heady pheromone rush. *Oh, my God. Heaven.* I can't hold out. My tongue gets to work straight away, licking hard at his succulent pucker, getting it nice and wet as I salivate at the sapid taste. I'm pushing inside his hole as fast as he did with mine. I just can't get enough. I'm growling, losing control. My fingers join the exploration, sinking into hot, velvety depths, massaging against his tight ring of muscle. "Fuuuuuck!" Bruno wails.

As I diligently pump my digits into him, loosening him up, I recall what he told me at the bar tonight:

"I don't even get a look-in, because the second I'm naked with a guy, their legs are straight up in the air."

Well, now he's met me. He hasn't seen what I'm capable of. I scurry up his body, lying on top of him and leaning forwards to rummage in the small chest of drawers next to the sofa bed. I know there are supplies in here. I'm pulling things out and plonking them on top of the drawers, groping around for the condoms. Finally, I locate a strip.

"Um, I'm happy to use those if you want," Bruno's voice calls out from beneath me. He reaches across and picks up something I've tossed onto the top of the drawers. "But if we're both on this…"

He's holding my bottle of PrEP, the one I hide from my thieving partner. I'm certainly not bankrolling Jarrod's extramarital lifestyle.

My erectile muscles tense hard. "Are you sure?"

"Yes, I'm sure. I'm a good boy and get all my tests done."

"Me too." *Well, plus the fact I'm a homebody who rarely has sex these days.* I wiggle my flexing erection against his wet, well-fingered hole. "You do feel amazing like this."

Bruno laughs as I push a little more firmly. His anus is starting to open up. He squirms a bit and thrusts his arse upwards just as I apply even more pressure. Suddenly, my knob is inching into his hole. It looks like I've done so well in getting him ready that we don't even need lube. Further and further I sink. The moist warmth envelops my cock. The metal ring in my piercing rubs inside my shaft as it presses deep up Bruno's arse. I'm plunged into white-hot nirvana and I'm absolutely lost for words.

Bruno's moans morph into whimpers when I start to thrust in earnest. My arms are braced on the bed, my knees are pushed against his widely-spread legs, and my abdomen is jammed against his furry butt cheeks. With this great big bear beneath me, his soft cries coming in a steady stream, and the searing sensation of being buried in his most personal place, I don't think I have ever enjoyed topping a man so much.

"Jesus *Christ*," Bruno groans. "I swear I can feel that ring grinding right into my fuckin' g-spot."

Keen to pick up momentum, I lean forwards and wrap my arms around him, plastering my nose and lips against his shoulder blade. He's such a *man.* The smattering of fur lining his back makes my cock flex even harder as I pump more forcefully into his arse. I clutch him tightly, breathing him in deep, rocking my hips up and down. *I'm giving him exactly what he craves.* This thought spurs me along even more.

My excitement shoots skyward as I feel his hips raise off the bed. I lift myself up again and notice that he's snaked a hand underneath himself. It's shuffling hard on his cock—I can see the frenetic movement in his arm, I can hear the brushing sound against the sheets. Bruno's vocalising grows louder as I pound him into submission. *I'm going to make him come. I'm going to send him to the goddamn moon and back.*

My head is in a whirl. I wonder whether I can orgasm at the same time as him. It certainly seems like it's possible. My God, he feels *so*—

"Stop!" Bruno gasps, wriggling out from under me. "I'm not gonna be happy unless you get a turn with *my* dick." His face comes close to mine. It's flushed, it's euphoric, and it means business. Bruno pushes me down onto my back and clambers between my legs, shoving them right up in the air. "Jesus, this mancunt of yours is so fucking *hot,*" he growls.

I kinda love his dirty words. They don't come so naturally to my own lips, but it's like I've ignited some kind of filthy fire in him and he can't restrain himself. One of his fingers is already rubbing against my anus, insistently working its way inside. As he probes, Bruno reaches across to the bedside table and grabs the bottle of baby oil I've plonked on there. I'm glad he's doing this. I doubt I could take his fat penis with just spit and fingering. I feel a large slippery stream hit my taint, then a flurry of digits begin rubbing it into my pucker. A couple of these fingers thrust straight inside me, seeking out my prostate. My moan turns to a roar as another moist hand grips my cock and begins to slide up and down over my knob, bumping into the PA as it goes.

"Just hold on a moment," whispers Bruno. "I'm gonna make it even better." His fingers slide out of my hole and a big, thick knob presses on it. I counter his move, pushing my sphincter out against his cock while I look up into his eyes. His salacious grin verges on evil. I feel a wonderful stroking sensation on my dick and realise he's still holding onto it. His surprise distraction does the trick and the tip of his cock is suddenly inside me. In quick, tiny thrusts he advances into my arse, watching the expression on my face with each move. I'm amazed. I'm stretched to oblivion but it doesn't hurt. It's *unbelievable.* He's managed to get that massive dick right up me with exquisite technique.

I can't even contain my whines as he begins to drive slowly and steadily in and out of my hole. I could cry, it's *that* good. And when his hand starts sliding up and down over my knob again, I know it's all getting past the point of no return. I'd almost reached a monumental climax when I'd been pounding his beautiful arse. Now, I'm arriving way too fast.

Should I stop him?

Jesus, no! Are you mad?

My eyes roll back as my body begins to stiffen. Suddenly, Bruno's stomach presses against me and my right nipple is sucked into his mouth. As soon as his tongue starts to swish over it, I bellow. I can't even tell him that I'm coming. I'm too busy hollering at the top of my lungs, giving in to the delicious agony in my arse, my balls, my cock, as an almighty tension seizes me. I'm lingering at the apex for an eternity. Tension gives way to a mind-bending explosion, and the sweetest pain of all rocks me to the core. My prostate goes into overdrive and I feel every spurt of come projecting out of me, punctuated by Bruno's tongue bombarding my nipple, his hand squishing over the end of my dick, his cock ramming up my back passage. The holy trinity of orgasms.

I'm dizzy with euphoria. I gaze up at Bruno, who grins back down at me. Without a word, he pulls out of my well-sated rear end, climbs over me and sinks my residual erection straight back into his arsehole. He's straddling me frog-style, jerking fast on his cock, panting as he thrusts his hips back and forth. I watch his face as it morphs into a pained state of bliss. "Nnnnnnnngh!" he groans, bouncing hard as his hand slows down on his penis and thick jets of spunk begin to skim across my torso. His anus squeezes my dick with every shot as he rubs out his orgasm. His body continues to jolt in the aftermath, shocked by the intensity of it all. It's a marvel watching this man at the peak of his pleasure. Truly breathtaking.

Bruno closes his eyes, releasing a long breath with a serene smile on his face. I'm immensely proud that I played a pivotal role in making him feel this way. He's certainly just sent me to places I've never been before. Leaning forward, he lets my still-firm cock slip from the warmth of his arse. "That was fucking *incredible*," he chuckles.

"Absolutely, Bru." I'm grinning like a total dork. I want to gush and tell him it's the best sex I've ever had, but there's no way I'm gonna embarrass myself like that. Instead, I focus on just how much come is painted all over my chest and stomach. Rummaging on the floor under the sofa bed, I locate my strategically-placed hand towels and pass one to Bruno. After rubbing it all over his cock and balls, he reaches behind himself and grinds it up and down inside his arse crack, smiling at me the whole time. It's such a divine spectacle that I barely pay attention to my own clean-up efforts.

Once I've thrown both towels over near the door, Bruno lies down and scooches in against me. I purr with contentment as he nuzzles my neck, his hand sliding across my chest. Maybe if I don't move, he'll stay right here like this all night.

I'm not an idiot, I'm well aware our intimacy isn't real. He's just a nice man. Insanely good in bed. Sensual and tactile and gorgeous as hell. But we don't really know each other. We have our own lives, our own baggage. Right now, though, I want to pretend. I want to imagine that all these good things I'm feeling are here to stay. Reality can bugger off. I need this little glimmer of happiness.

CHAPTER 4

It's so peaceful lying here in the dead of night. The moonlight dances through the gap in the curtains, casting an ethereal glow around the room. The air conditioner gives a comforting hum, its steady stream of coolness allowing me to sink into Bruno. His breathing is slow and even against my neck. I could fall asleep, but I want to be present for every moment of this.

"It's a decent size," mumbles Bruno.

"Sorry?"

He gives a barely audible laugh, sliding his hand down to cup my dick and balls. "Well, *this* is a given. But I was talking about the room. I'm just noticing how much you've got in here."

"Oh, right. Yeah, the big bedrooms in this place kinda make up for the small dark living room."

Bruno raises his head slightly. "The piano, for instance."

My piano. There's a story there. "I've had it since I was a kid. My dad left it for me when he shot through. The last nice thing he did, really."

"I'm sorry to hear that, mate." Bruno relinquishes his hold on my crown jewels, raking his fingers through my chest hair and planting a kiss on my neck. "It must have been hard on you."

"He wasn't all bad. He was a music teacher and gave me piano lessons from the time I was old enough to understand. But when I turned ten he ran away with one of his postgrad students. Took off up north and started a new family as far as I know. Hardly ever heard from him after that."

"Oh, geez, that's just awful."

"Nah, it's fine. Ancient history. Anyway, I kept playing. Mum was adamant I shouldn't lose my skills. She scrimped and saved and I continued having lessons with other teachers. By the time I was in my mid-teens I was teaching my own piano students. So, when I eventually took up singing lessons I was able to pay for them myself."

"Gee, you're so talented. Do you still play? I mean, with your sight, you know…" His voice trails off. I can hear the uncertainty in it. It's incredibly sweet.

"I can play stuff by ear or things I remember, but I tend to mess them up. Piano playing is all about muscle memory, but you still use your eyes. Of course, I can't see a music score anymore." I know what comes next here. I've had these questions many times over recent years. "I mean, we all know there are world-class musicians like Stevie Wonder who have no trouble. But he's learnt that way all his life. And the kind of music he plays is heavily improvised. Classical scores are full of intricate notation and precise directions."

"It should be different with opera though, shouldn't it? I mean, your voice is part of your body."

"Sure. But you've got a ton of other things to follow. You've got the music notes and all the markings. Then you've got the lyrics running underneath and they're mostly in Italian, German or French. And underneath all of that you have the other singers' vocal lines and the orchestral accompaniment which you also have to follow.

"Then, you have to add in dramatic and musical interpretation. On top of that, you're wrestling with vocal technique and voice production. Then, when you've learnt the music and you start doing stage rehearsals, you need to think about movement and the physicalities of acting."

I feel like I'm rambling, but there's no short version here and I don't want him to think I'm some kind of self-pitying cop-out. "So, that chapter of my life is now pretty much over since I lost the sight. I mean, I *could* sit down and memorise a score if it was blown up to a large enough size. But running around onstage and climbing up and down rickety scenery is out of the question."

"Oh. That's such a shame. I loved hearing you sing." Bruno snuggles in closer, his beard caressing my pectoral, his belly pressing against my hip.

"You're gonna make me start blushing now." I nudge him with my shoulder. "I haven't given up on music entirely. I've done a few concerts, things where I could stand with other soloists in front of an orchestra. And I still do some part-time online teaching." I gesture towards my desk against the opposite wall, with my laptop and massive fifty-inch TV monitor. "This spare room is actually my study."

I'm tired of dominating this conversation. I never want to look like one of those people who goes on about themselves non-stop. What I *do* want is to know every detail of Bruno's life. I'm fascinated, but I would hate to look like I'm prying. *No, bugger that. It's worth showing him that I'm interested.* "Anyway, Bru, that's enough about me. I wanna hear about you now." Bruno gazes up at me, eyebrows raised. I fix him with my cockiest grin. That oughta manipulate him.

He shuffles around a bit, bending his elbow and propping his head on his hand. "This is where I tell you how boring my life is by comparison." His dark eyes twinkle as he grins back at me. The creases at their outside edges are beautiful—the true mark of a man who's lived a life of happiness. "Grew up in Maroubra, not too far from the beach. My parents are still together, still in the same home they bought over fifty years ago. My only sibling is the twin sister I mentioned, and she lives with her family just a couple of blocks from mum and dad. She and I go over and help them out when we can. They're getting on a bit and they have a few health issues."

"So, you live near there too?"

"Not far. Brendan and I bought an apartment in Randwick in the noughties when the prices weren't so insane. We definitely wouldn't be able to afford it these days. It's great, because I work at Prince of Wales Hospital and I can walk there."

I study Bruno's face. It's bizarre to think that he and I have lived within a few suburbs of each other for so many years, yet our paths have never crossed till now. But then, I'm not exactly a social butterfly. We're also both ensconced in our respective domestic situations. Maybe it's not so inconceivable in this big old city.

"Psych nursing," he says, answering a question I've been too distracted to ask. "I was in management for ages. These days I just work in the casual nursing pool. Less stress, better penalty rates and I can pick and choose the shifts I feel like doing."

I take in the scope of the hefty man pressed alongside my body. "Bet there aren't many psych patients willing to take you on."

"Oh, believe me, they try."

"That's what Jarrod does. Casual and agency nursing. I don't ever know about his schedule. He comes and goes, works when he wants to."

Bruno just looks at me quietly, a slight smile on his face. I regret bringing up Jarrod's name immediately. *Jesus, what the hell was I thinking? Have I gone and destroyed this blissful little bubble we've been in? He's probably trying to work out how to execute his escape right now.*

"Who's that?" Bruno says. I follow his finger to see it pointing towards the photo on top of my piano. "May I?"

He's already shuffling off the sofa bed, making his way over to it. I'm far too mesmerised by my first real look at his naked backside to think of answering. I mean, yeah, we've just been all over each other close up, but there's something truly magical about watching a sexy naked man walk away. Bruno turns and comes back towards me, showing me his other side. I can feel a stirring in my loins again already. I'm kinda chuffed at my stamina, till I remember the half a Cialis I swallowed before going out earlier tonight.

Sitting down on the edge of the sofa bed beside me, he tilts the photo my way, but he needn't bother. I know that picture like the back of my hand. "That's me at seventeen, my sister Summer when she was four, and our mum."

"Such a cute little kid! She's much darker than the two of you."

"Yeah, we have different dads."

"And your mum looks so lovely."

"You're right, she was."

Bruno glances sideways, hesitating. "Oh. Is she no longer with us?" He screws his eyes up and chuckles nervously. "Sorry, I'm being nosy."

"No, not at all. She was a real saint. Worked her fingers to the bone to make sure we had a good life. Finally got to retirement age and died of cancer not long after." The painful memories of my mother's slow demise aren't something I want to entertain right now. Coming back from Germany to look on helplessly as she slipped away from me. Barely able to comprehend the grief before I was plunged into permanent near-blindness. Somehow, I made it through. Maybe I'm stronger. Or maybe I'm delusional. Maybe I've just buried it all. In any case, I'm not about to start digging to find out.

Bruno reaches across and starts stroking the fur on my belly, still studying the picture. I admire his discretion. He's sensitive enough to know that no further words are needed, but his physical caress tells me everything he wants to say in a much gentler way. "You were just as handsome back then, Bradford. I'll bet you were popular."

I want to laugh bitterly at this, but I dare say it wouldn't be appropriate right now. "Thanks, but that wasn't the case. I was right down near the bottom of the barrel. The boring little boy who hung out with the geeks and misfits. The kid who got called 'poofter' and 'homo' long before he even knew what it meant."

Bruno looks surprised. "Really? Why would they say shit like that to you?"

"I dunno. I don't recall being flamboyant or anything. It's like they were just generic insults. Boys who play piano instead of rugby do tend to cop it, though." I'm starting to sound really negative and I don't like the impression I'm giving off. I need to paint myself in a better light. "I suppose other kids had it much worse than I did. I'd see them getting bullied badly. New kids, kids who were a bit different. It used to really upset me to see them all alone at lunchtime and I'd always try to befriend them. But, sooner or later they'd see my kindness as weakness. Work their way up the food chain, then *they'd* be the ones calling me 'faggot' whenever they saw me."

Jesus, Bradford! How the hell did we get here? I'm desperate to change the course of this conversation. My childhood wasn't peaches and cream. So much of it, I hated. It was something I was glad to be rid of.

"I'm sure you had a ton of attention when you got to this age, though." Bruno holds up the photo slightly. His eyes are fixed on mine and they radiate warmth and compassion.

I so dearly want to tell him something positive and affirming, but I can't lie—it's just not in my nature. I decide to colour my response with as genuine a smile as I can muster. Bruno's generosity deserves that much. "I've always been a short guy with a baby face. When I was fifteen or sixteen, I looked about twelve. Tween girls in Year Seven would flirt with me. Find out my home number and call me at all hours. Nobody my age would have looked sideways at me. Certainly no guys."

Bruno's eyes twinkle in the moonlight, encouraged by the smile I'm still managing to keep in place. "I find that hard to believe, mate. Surely there were boys secretly checking you out with longing glances."

"Not that I ever knew of." *This isn't entirely true.* "Well, maybe there was one."

Bruno's looking at me intently. One hundred percent focused. Gee, he's good. *Bloody psych nurses.*

"I was getting pretty good at singing and piano by the time I finished Year Ten, so I changed schools to one with a much better music program. There was this kid in a couple of my classes who hardly ever spoke. Thin guy with dark floppy hair. I gathered he was kind of an outcast because nobody had much to do with him. We were all a bit older then, so the bullying wasn't so overt. But to me it was pretty apparent.

"Somehow we became friends. I can't remember, it just sort of evolved. The school was on a small clifftop next to the beach. And if you walked around the edge of the grounds and across the student car park, you could make your way through the bushes and down a dodgy pathway to this little cove. It was supposed to be out of bounds for students, but we didn't give a toss. We'd take off at lunchtime and go and smoke on the rocks at the base of the cliffs.

"Like I mentioned, this guy never said much. I could hear he had a bit of a stutter. He must have done a lot of work on it, because it wasn't that bad, he was just kind of hesitant when he spoke. None of this mattered to me. It was like our quiet company brought us closer."

I take a huge breath. *This doesn't have to be hard. It was forever ago.* "Anyway, at the end of the year, he said his family were moving to some town up in Queensland. I felt extremely sad, but I didn't know how to talk about it with him. We didn't have that kind of verbal friendship. I just remember sitting there smoking with him down at the cove on his last day, neither of us saying a word to each other. I wanted to reach out and touch him. I wanted to hug him, tell him how much his friendship had meant to me. But I wasn't equipped with the right tools.

"I remember walking back up with him, past the school and along the road to the bus stop. I know we said goodbye, I can't really recall any details. I just remember when he'd climbed onto the bus he made his way right down to the back. And he propped himself up against the rear window and waved vigorously. There was no expression on his face, just this urgent final signalling goodbye. Right then, I was hit by this overwhelming regret. I'd left it too late. I could have taken that risk and let him know how I felt, but I was too bloody gutless. I just stood there and watched him go as I tried not to cry.

"The next year on the first day back at school we were all gathered for the initial assembly, sitting on the ground in this big concrete undercover area waiting for the teachers. I remember I was there all alone, feeling more exposed than I'd ever felt in my whole life. There were these gossiping girls creating a frenzy and I was trying to listen in. I heard them mention his name, then a whole lot of overexcited yabbering, then some girl shrieked, 'No way! He *killed* himself?' I remember the sudden jolt of shock that went through me. But I didn't believe what they were saying. They were just malicious rumour-spreaders who'd latch onto anything and try to own the drama.

"It wasn't till we were sitting in our assigned homeroom and the teacher got all sombre and started spouting stuff like 'tragic loss' and 'if you ever need to talk, my door's always open' that it finally sunk in. I have vague memories of standing up and barging out of the classroom, banging into chairs as I heard the word 'faggot' snickered behind me. Somehow I found myself down at our spot at the cove and for the first time it struck me—I'd never, ever seen him smile. Not even once."

I have to stop there. I'm a pigheaded bugger and I can hold it together at the worst of times. But right now, I'm seriously worried I might lose it in front of Bruno. *Why the hell did I even say all of this stuff?* I need to round this off, stat. "I never went back after that. I enrolled in one of those adult dropout programs at TAFE college and did Year Twelve there instead."

Bruno's staring at me with a kind of bizarre intensity. I've just dumped a ton of heavy crap on him. Definitely not first-date material, let alone something to unleash on a poor hookup. But his reaction doesn't seem quite right. His expression is off, somehow. *"Craig?"* he says.

I'm confused. It's like I'm in an alternate universe. "My middle name. Nobody's called me that since school."

"Craig Reilly from design class at St John's High in Little Bay? Before they knocked it down to make apartments?"

I guess that's enough detail, he certainly couldn't have mistaken me for anyone else.

Bruno's eyes are wide. He taps his chest. "Matt Borelli. I was a year ahead of you, but there was only one combined design class. Remember? I used to come up to you and tell you off for smoking because I knew you were a singer?"

"Jesus! Big solid Matt with all that curly hair?" I'm staring at his nearly fifty-year-old features and there's a slight familiarity coming into focus.

"You weren't the only one who hated his first name," says Bruno. "When I was in primary school, they used to call me 'Browneye' and bend over and stick their arse out at me."

"God, kids are horrible, aren't they?"

"They were a bunch of little cunts. It was easy to change when I went to Catholic High School and they all went to the public one. Nobody knew me, so Bruno Matteo Borelli just became Matt Borelli."

"I started calling myself Craig after my dad left. I didn't want to have the same name as him anymore."

Bruno climbs over me and lies beside me on his stomach, propping himself up on his elbows. "Well, Bradford Craig Reilly, you're wrong about one thing. There *was* a guy shooting you longing looks. I didn't give a flying fuck about you smoking. I just wanted any excuse to talk to you, but you never seemed interested."

Four, five times he must have walked up to my table and spoken to me that year. I can barely get my head around the fact he even remembers this. "Um, you were a big burly Year Twelve and I was a pathetic little Year Eleven. There was no way I would have even *dreamt* you'd want anything to do with me."

"Oh, fuck, mate," Bruno huffs. "I would have given my left testicle to know you better back then. You were such a sweet little guy." He's still staring at me in wonderment. "And I'm pretty sure you haven't changed one bit." He shakes his head incredulously. "Can't believe I just got to shag my teenage crush."

"...*and* be shagged by him." I grin at Bruno. This turn of events is so bizarre. The past of more than thirty years ago has come hurtling into the present and smacked me so hard in the face I can hardly get my brain to catch up. "You know, even though I'm pretty freaked out by all this, you just gave me the biggest retrospective validation. I spent my entire teenage years feeling like I was worth absolutely nothing."

Bruno's brow wrinkles and he launches himself at my mouth. Without his lips leaving mine, he shuffles on top of me, his heft pressing me into the plush memory foam mattress. I'm completely encapsulated in potent masculine affection, surrounded by the kind of fervent, animalistic desire that I haven't realised until tonight how much I've been craving.

His tongue roams my mouth with every ounce of the verve he showed earlier. The fire inside me begins to rage as I realise nothing has evaporated between us. Our intimacy hasn't ended with our orgasms; there's more to come. *Oh, God, please let there be more.*

Softly he withdraws, placing sustained, tender kisses on my lips. "Sorry," he whispers. "I must be squashing you."

"Squash away, Bru." I tighten my arms around his huge barrel chest, raising a facetious eyebrow. "You're like a big furry wombat."

Bruno guffaws at my ridiculous comparison. "Well, I guess 'wombat' is no more ridiculous than 'bear' if you really think about it." He leans out a bit, looking me up and down. "And if I'm a wombat, then you're a koala." His lips curl up in a smirk. "*Blinky Bill.*"

"Are you telling me my ears are hairy?"

He lowers his head and nuzzles my lobe, running his nose upwards along the curve of my pinna. "They seem pretty well-groomed to me, *Blinky.*"

"Good. Because I just paid the barber twelve extra bucks to wax them. And if we're gonna start talking about children's books, then you're definitely *Harry.*"

"What? *Harry the Hairy-nosed Wombat*?" He brushes a finger and thumb underneath his nostrils. "Who's casting aspersions about excess facial fuzz now?"

The pressure of Bruno's bulk has me giggling like a kid instead of laughing like a man. But the sound is infectious, and Bruno joins me, cackling away, clutching my body and rolling us onto our sides as our childish mirth dies down. It's a sweet moment. The kind of comfort I'd expect with a lover I might have known a lot longer than a few hours. Of course, we both know we're just being silly, just mucking around. We've met, we've shagged, we've chatted, but that's it. Still, it's nice to be relaxed enough with each other that we can share a dumb joke or two.

The reality check kicks in when Bruno's expression changes slightly. His eyes search mine, flicking from one to the other, two big pools of gentle warmth. "Should I take off and give you a bit of peace now?"

"No." My response isn't planned. It's automatic, emphatic. Probably far too needy for a hookup situation like this. My first instinct is to wince, but the way Bruno has just delivered his words gives me hope. It sounded like he was fishing for an invitation to stay, not seeking an excuse to leave.

Should I say more?

Yeah, I'm gonna go for it.

"This is nice. Do you *have* to leave?" *Oh. Was that manipulative? Should I have given him an out?*

Bruno allays my fears, cuddling even closer. "I don't have to go *anywhere*, Bradford."

CHAPTER 5

The first thing I hear is a lengthy groan. Through the dense fog I realise it's come from me. My eyes open as I slide into consciousness and I'm suddenly aware of my surroundings. I'm also now aware that I'm alone. Maybe he's in the shower. I stretch myself out, undoing the kinks of a heavy night's rest. I'm lucky like that, I always sleep like a bloody log.

I touch my lips and immediately remember I'm not wearing the mouth splint that stops me snoring like a fuckin' walrus. *Oh God, did I disturb him? Did he go and sleep in another room?* This thought jolts me further into awake mode. I'm racking my brain. No, I remember things now. I remember wrapping myself around him—I remember him pulling my arm tight across his torso as I spooned him from behind. I remember his palm stroking over the fur on my chest. I remember soft kisses, I remember brushing his fringe off his forehead. I remember my hand slipping inside his furry arse crack as we slept face to face—fuck, I loved touching him there. That beautiful spot is like the epicentre of his manliness. I remember the powerful connection I felt as I stroked his tight little hole. I don't reckon I took my fingers off it the whole night. Yeah—we were definitely together. He never went anywhere.

Sitting up, I scan the room, seeing it in the light for the first time. It's still pretty dim in here. There's a small window, but it's partially plugged up with the air conditioner's exhaust hose. My eyes land on Bradford's office chair. He's neatly folded my clothes and placed them on it, putting a fresh towel on top. It's so bloody sweet of him.

Oh, does this mean something else? Is he prompting me to get ready and fuck off?

No, surely not, he was so keen for me to stay.

Shaking these stupid thoughts out of my head, I haul my weary arse off the bed and wrap the towel around my waist. When I open the study door, the warm, humid air from the rest of the apartment hits my body at exactly the same time the smells of cooking invade my nostrils. *Fuck, I could eat a horse right now*. I pad quietly in the direction of food. Cos this is an old apartment, the kitchen isn't open plan—it's in a cramped little room of its own. I stop in the doorway and spot Bradford with his back towards me, diligently working on several pots and pans at the stove. Morning sun's blaring through the window above the sink, casting a completely new kind of light over the man I've just spent twelve fuckin' amazing hours with.

Bradford is topless, wearing nothing but a sexy little pair of shorts. They're different to the ones he wore last night. The flimsy blue fabric chews right into the crack of his bearish little bum. Fuck, I'm such an arse pervert. I'm absolutely obsessed with them, and Bradford's is no exception: two chubby squares of firm muscle, enough to make my mouth water just looking at it. God, it was awesome with my face down inside there last night.

Behave, Bruno. You can't fuck him over the bloody stove.

Yes, I could... Jesus, that would be so hot! Fuck, my cock is starting to swell. I'd better stop touching it.

Bradford's short hair is neatly brushed to the side, kinda like how it was at the bar last night. He's got a few grey hairs at the temples and they blend really nicely with his natural dark blond. I spend a few moments looking at the profile of his thick beard. It's full and bushy; all nicely shaped with greys sprinkled through it. His back is smooth, except for a fuckin' hot hairy welcome mat. It's spread over his lumbar region and it creeps down below the waistband of his shorts. *'Look what I've got hidden under here,'* it says, like it's advertising for his arse.

Right now, I'm turned on to instant wank-level by his manly beauty. But I'm also touched as all get-out that he's obviously in here doing this cooking for *me*. I mean, there's no other explanation for it. Not unless that arsehole boyfriend has come home. I duck my head out and spot the other bedroom door open. Craning my neck a bit, I can see the bed is empty. Nup, this hot little bloke is in here making *me* breakfast. *Me*. Leaning back in the doorway, I watch him there, still working like a bloody Trojan, still completely oblivious to the fact I'm standing here.

"Fuck!" I groan. I'm surprised by how intense I sound, but I'm just not used to this.

Bradford jumps a bit, then turns around, spatula in hand. I see a huge flash of fear cross his face. “I’m sorry, is this too…” he glances back at the stove. “Um, do you need to leave?”

The uncertainty I see in him crushes the fuck out of me. I go to him straight away, pull him tight against my body and kiss the top of his head. His hair is still damp from the shower, rich with the smell of coconut shampoo. “No, I don’t. I’m just—” I tilt my head back and look into his eyes. For the first time I’m fully hit by their vivid steel-grey colour. It’s like there’s a storm brewing inside them. “No man’s ever done anything like this for me, Bradford.” It’s not too far from the truth. Definitely no bloody hookup has ever managed more than to kick me out once they’ve blown their load and wiped the lube off their arse.

Bradford smiles at me, and the gratitude in his expression crushes me all over again. It’s so out of place and I need him to realise this. I lean down and kiss his lips, letting my hand slip from his shoulders to his welcome mat. Working my fingers under his waistband, I discover he hasn’t got any underwear on. *God, he’s So. Fucking. Hot.* I stretch my hand down further, running my palm over the soft furry surface of his butt cheek, squeezing it in a way that my fingers delve right inside his crack.

Bradford moans instantly. “I’m gonna wreck breakfast if we don’t stop now,” he murmurs. “It’s your call.”

“Fair point. Can’t have me ruining all this hard work of yours.” I give his arse a final squeeze, letting my fingers get another prod at that sexy little hole of his. Coming back up to stand, I stretch out my weary arms, neck and shoulders. “Breakfast it is, then. I’m happy to stay here and help you, but you’re all nice and showered and I’m bloody rank.”

Bradford chuckles, leaning forward and burying his face in my armpit. It takes me by surprise, triggering an awesome throb in my dick. Tingles shoot down my spine as Bradford begins to sniff deep and hard. The rush of air and the gentle brushing of his nose against my bushy pit have me shuddering. “Oh, fuck,” I gasp, as he begins to lick in long, firm strokes. Bradford seems to like my reaction and he snickers quietly as he moves across my chest. Back and forth he goes, slowly sucking each of my nipples into his mouth. “Oh, shit. Oh, my *fucking God.*” I’m moaning like a bitch and I don’t care. The nicest fucking feeling is raging through my body as his tongue expertly works each hardened little tit. It’s so fucking amazing that I nearly protest when he suddenly stops. The rude shock disappears when I feel his beard, lips and nose submerge in my other armpit. I’m panting. My dick is now starting to ache.

“You’re all *man,*” Bradford mumbles, as his nose sniffs in huge lungfuls of my scent. The second his tongue starts to lick up and down, my dick flexes and my arsehole clenches tight. I want to jerk myself till I paint his entire body with my come—it's that fucking good.

Bradford finally stops, rubbing his beard and mo around my pit, then grinning up at me. "I could do this all day, you know. But go wash off your beautiful musk if you think it'll make you feel better. I'm gonna be another five or ten minutes here."

"Uh, I'm assuming we're still alone?" I tilt my head in the direction of the lounge room.

"Oh, yeah. No sign of him. He'll be passed out in some other apartment with whatever guy he went home with. I can guarantee it."

"Good." With that, I pull my towel off and tug down on my foreskin, stretching out my firm prick. Bradford's eyes fixate on the spectacle between my legs and he lets out a loud growl. It's time for me to behave, I know. As a parting move, I reach over and fondle the ring in the end of his dick through the fabric of his shorts. He's well and truly reaching a full and fabulous stiffy, and as I wiggle the jewellery he gives a sexy little whine. "That's exactly what I wanted to hear from you," I mumble. "I'm never gonna be able to keep my hands off this, you know."

While I'm making my way down to the bathroom, it dawns on me what I've just said. It's fuckin' cocky of me to expect a repeat performance of last night. I'm well aware of both our situations. Waltzing off into the sunset is not on the cards with Bradford. But I definitely want to fuck him again. *Many* times.

I go to shut the bathroom door once I'm in there, but then I think twice and leave it wide open. It's an invitation—I'm imagining how hot it would be if Bradford put breakfast on the back burner and joined me. But I also kinda like the thought of that boyfriend coming home and seeing me here—standing in the open shower, my big bear body and thick cock on full display. I don't want to fuck him, not in the least. He just rouses the protective alpha lurking beneath my calm exterior. I don't like him. I don't like his smarmy, self-righteous attitude. I definitely didn't like the way he pushed Bradford around. Yeah, of course I'd been listening to their whole bloody confrontation—how could I not? How could my attention *not* have been captured when I spotted that gorgeous little bear sitting there all by himself last night?

As the hot water pelts down on my back, I feel the tension in my shoulders give way. My body relaxes completely and I allow my cock to blast a heavy stream of piss against the shower floor. *Oh, fuck, I forgot where I was. What if Bradford walks in on me? Would he be disgusted? Maybe he's a kinky little cunt and he'll be all turned on. He certainly couldn't take his eyes off my dick when we were standing at the trough in the dunnies last night. I fucking loved the way he got hard as he watched me.*

My hand is working my foreskin up and down as I piss, and my cock is getting hard really fast. I feel like I'm marking my territory, staking my claim on that sexy fella out in the kitchen. My fantasies are running wild. I'm so fucking horny. There's an ache in my prostate and it's travelling right up the inside of my dick. I would fucking *love* to come right now, but I'd better stop. This wank has gone way too far. Bradford's put so much hard work into making breakfast, and I can't be in here spraying the shower with my spunk.

Fuck it, I am *definitely* going to con him into another night of hot sex—A.S.A. Fucking P.

Back out in the cosy little lounge room, a beam of light pierces through the small window, shining a weak glow over the dark space. I hear a thumping sound and spot Brendan lying quietly on his bed, his wagging tail hitting the cushion underneath him. Crouching down, I give his neck a ruffle and he nuzzles against me. More pats turn into a furry hug and I'm instantly in love. It's no wonder he and Bradford have such a strong bond. "Hey, matey," I whisper in his ear. "You keep looking after that fella for me, OK?"

I waste no time getting back into my clothes. I'm not the kind of man who likes putting on yesterday's tighty-whities, but I was hardly in a position to bring an overnight bag. After I've tidied up the room, I walk over to turn off the aircon, then hesitate. *Should I be doing this? Is it overstepping the mark? I doubt he'll want to come back in here, will he?* After thinking about it for way too long, I decide that Bradford's power bill is more important and I hit the switch.

Out in the living room again, I spot Bradford ferrying plates to the small dining table. He glances towards me and a shy smile forms on his lips. His eyes flick from my fully-clothed body to his near-nakedness. "I guess I'm a bit underdressed now," he says.

"I think you look fuckin' woofy, mate." And he does. Bradford is the perfect teddy bear—chunky, chubby, hairy and solid as fuck. When he turns to go back to the kitchen, I slide my hand over his arse once more and give it yet another squeeze. The little grunt he gives makes me wanna rip those fuckin' nylon shorts right off him.

"Take a seat, Bruno," he calls over his shoulder. "Just grabbing the coffee." As I settle at the table, he comes back in with a small stovetop percolator. "I'm assuming you're a proper Italian and you like it strong."

"You'd be right, there." I watch as Bradford empties the entire contents into the mug in front of me. "Aren't you having any?"

"Nah," he says, taking a seat. "I never drink it." I notice he has a teapot next to him. "I buy it for Jarrod." He winces visibly, then immediately starts shuffling dishes heaped with food. "There's beans and mushrooms and *pane di casa*. Oh…" He stands back up and runs into the kitchen, returning with another plate, which he places in front of me. "And these. Italian sausages from the continental butcher."

"Coincidence?" I say, smirking and raising an eyebrow as I take one of the snags and offer the plate back to him.

"Oh, no thanks. They're both for you. I don't, um, eat meat." There's an uncomfortable expression on his face. "I buy the sausages for…" He dips his eyes and hangs his head slightly.

A fast picture forms in my mind. I'm seeing a man whose confidence has been beaten down so far that his self-esteem is shot to pieces. Sure, Bradford's well aware of his sexual appeal—he was like a fucking tiger last night. But in the harsh light of day, it seems to me that his sense of worth doesn't extend much further than the bedroom. I fucking hate to see him like this. He's more amazing than most guys I've ever met, and I've found this out in only a matter of hours. I don't want to patronise him. I'm agonising over whether to say something.

In a snap decision, I grab his hand and squeeze hard. "Mate, we both have partners. You should never feel you have to apologise for mentioning his name. And I really am so fuckin' stoked that you've gone to all this trouble." I rustle up the warmest smile I can manage. I want to tell Bradford I hope that cunt of a boyfriend I almost met appreciates everything he does for him, but I stop myself. I'm not sure I could deliver that line politely.

Bradford's clearly a whiz in the kitchen. His mushrooms are slathered in olive oil, garlic and fresh herbs. His beans aren't bog-standard Heinz, they're the giant Greek variety and he's added chopped fresh red chilli to the tomato sauce. And outside of an Italian cafe, I have never had coffee this good. As I help myself to the beans and mushrooms, Bradford passes me a small dish of shaved fresh parmesan. I sprinkle a ton of it over my piled plate, then notice Bradford does the same. "You still eat cheese, do you?" I do a quick double-take. "Sorry, just curious. I don't mean to pry or anything."

"Oh, no. you're fine. Ask away." He smiles up at me eagerly. He seems so keen for my approval, and it's sweet as fuck. "I'm not a full-on vegan," he continues. "My boots are even leather. I have a lot of guilt over that, but it's been impossible to find synthetic steel-caps that aren't only in online shops." As he pushes the food around on his plate, I see a blush forming on his cheeks. "My stupid wide feet. I have to try on a whole lot of shoes before I find the right ones."

"Mate, your feet are so fucking hot I nearly sucked your toes while I was ploughing that arse of yours last night."

Bradford looks up at me, a huge grin plastered over his face. "I would have moaned hard enough to crack the walls if you'd done that."

Mental note taken for future reference. I'd carry on this dirty talk a lot longer, but I'm too busy gulping down every skerrick of food Bradford's putting in front of me. I feel like I have to pace myself in case I look like the pig I really am, but Bradford is holding his own. He's scoffing down hearty serves and chomping on thick slices of crusty bread and butter. Clearly that's why he's not a stereotypical skinny vego, but I love that about him. All the while, he's encouraging me to have seconds and even thirds. *My God, this is a man after my own heart.*

"What's that?" I say, pointing to a plate of weird scrambled eggs that Bradford seems to be hogging to himself.

"Oh. You won't want this. It's, um… scrambled tofu. I would have made us some eggs, but I" — he pauses for a fraction of a second — "didn't realise I'd run out of them."

Hmmm. Let me guess why. "Mind if I try a little bit of it?"

Bradford looks surprised and immediately passes the dish over. "You might wanna sprinkle on some of this." He hands me a bottle of something called Maggi Seasoning. "It's like soy sauce on steroids."

I admit that in nearly fifty years, I've never had scrambled tofu. It's nothing like I expected. Bradford's cooked it with heaps of herbs and spices and shredded spring onions, and with the sauce added, it's amazing. "Jesus," I say with my mouth half full. "You're a top-shelf cook, mate. How long have you been vego?"

Bradford smiles shyly. I wonder if it's something he avoids talking about with people. I wonder if he cops shit for it. But surely he can see I'm genuinely interested. "I've always been a huge wimp when it comes to animals," he says. "I'd never really thought about what meat actually *was* till I was nine and I read a book called *Aldo Applesauce*. The boy in the story was a vegetarian and his parents were really supportive about it. So, I told mum and dad I wanted to do the same thing."

"And were they? Supportive, I mean?"

Bradford's ribs jiggle with a laugh that I can't really hear. "My mum and dad were bourgeois types who worked in the arts. They thought it was quite cool. Or amusing, at least. They never imagined my diet would last, but it did, and then my sister followed suit. She wanted to be exactly like me when she was little. God knows why." He stops a moment to skol down the last of his tea. "I've tried being vegan a few times, but it always plays havoc with my guts." Breaking eye contact, he stares down at his empty plate. "Sorry, that was a really boring story."

"You don't bore me in the slightest, Bradford. I could listen to you all day." *Well, at least when your mouth wasn't stuffed with my cock.*

It's almost like Bradford is reading my thoughts. He grins as he stands up and lazily adjusts his cock and balls, even though we both know he's not wearing underwear. "Well, I'll give you a bit of respite before you think twice and change your mind."

Bradford protests when I get up to help clear the dishes, but I'm not having a bar of it. As I watch him busily stacking everything at the sink, I find myself hoping that our time hasn't come to an end. The last thing I want is for him to feel like I'm wearing out the welcome mat, but we're at a crucial point now. I have to act fast. "So… what are your plans for the morning, mate?" *I hope that sounds vague enough.*

Bradford turns to me, wiping his hands on a tea towel. "Um, I was going to take Brendan out for a *stroll*." I see him glancing over my shoulder. "We don't use the 'W' word till it's actually happening." He grins, then pauses before continuing with less certainty. "You're more than welcome to come, if you don't have to rush off."

The way he bashfully delivers his offer goes straight to my soft spot. "That's exactly the invite I was hinting at," I murmur. Gathering him into a bear hug, I breathe deeply, sniffing in as much of his scent as I can get. The warmth of his skin soothes me so fucking potently that I want to drag him back to our little nest in the study and spend the entire day there.

Instead, I let go of him, then plant a kiss on his lips. It's just a brief kiss, but the tenderness of it speaks loud and clear. I need more of this. I need a *shitload* more. Leaving Bradford to go get himself ready, I wander back out to the lounge room and plonk my arse on the couch.

After a couple of minutes, Bradford comes in wearing a t-shirt and holding running shoes and socks. As he rounds the couch and takes a seat, Brendan hops off his bed and disappears down the hall. He's back in an instant, tail wagging, carrying his harness in his mouth. I watch with fascination as he circles the coffee table, drops the harness and sits tall in front of Bradford.

"Wow," I say. "Do they teach him to do that at guide dog school?"

Bradford grins at me. "No, I trained him. As soon as he notices me come in here with my shoes, he knows it's time."

Once Brendan is all ready, Bradford takes off down the hall and returns with a backpack. He stops when he gets near the closed door of the spare bedroom. "I can't hear the aircon. Did you turn it off already?"

"Uh, yeah. Sorry, I didn't think you'd be going in there again."

"Oh, no need to apologise. That was really thoughtful of you." He turns around and begins darting from the kitchen to the master bedroom and back down the hall again. It's amazing when I think about it: all last night, all this morning, he's been doing stuff with so much ease that I've almost forgotten about his disability. He doesn't hesitate or seem unsure about anything. I've noticed how he holds his hand out a bit as he moves, brushing against surfaces to judge distance. Now and then, he looks down at the floor when he walks, not just with a flick of his eyes, but with a full movement of his head. It's never really occurred to me how someone with tunnel vision might need to do this. I want to ask him a ton of questions, but maybe it's a discussion we should leave for another time.

"You'll have to forgive me," he says, reading my mind. "I've got to stick to these routines. It's impossible for me to get things done otherwise."

"Mate, I'm beyond impressed. You don't pissfart around half as much as most of us and we've got no excuse."

"Believe me, I'd take ten times longer if I had to try and find stuff. If something's not in its place, I've got a frustrating search on my hands. It's certainly a hassle liv—" he cuts himself off. I look at him intently. I want him to finish his thought. After a moment, I see a flicker of trust in his eyes and he smiles. "A hassle living with someone who leaves the place in a bloody mess."

I can't even imagine what this poor man goes through.

***

Bradford and Brendan know this suburb inside out. As we make our way through the streets of Bondi, I notice the little things Bradford does—how he pauses with Brendan to listen for oncoming traffic, how he crosses streets at quieter spots, how he follows Brendan's lead if there are any obstructions, how he manages the ground when it becomes dodgy. "Isn't it much harder getting over these surfaces without a cane?" I ask, after we've passed a bad section of footpath.

"You know, I really thought that would be the case. But right from the start I had no trouble connecting with Brendan's movements. If the ground isn't even I'll feel it through him. Plus, if I'm desperate, I've got enough vision that I can tilt my head down and squint."

It takes us about twenty minutes to reach the southern part of Bondi Beach Park. Bradford leads us straight through, then down the steps and the ramp onto the beach. "Fancy a wade in the surf?" he says as he squats and unties his shoes. "You might wanna roll up your jeans."

I can sense the excitement in Brendan as the two of them charge forward. I walk a few steps behind, admiring the way they pretty much skate across the wet sand till the waves begin lapping at their ankles. Bradford looks over his shoulder and smiles at me, his expression as sunny as the weather beating down on us. Even if I never get to see him again, this moment is something I'm always gonna remember.

As I sidle up to Bradford, my feet soothed by the swirling water, he takes off Brendan's harness. Straight away, the yellow lab starts to romp through the shallows with unbridled enthusiasm. "I'm not supposed to do this," says Bradford, "but he loves it so much and he always stays really close by."

I slide my arm across Bradford's shoulder and I feel him lean against me. The pure and simple joy that grips me is all the courage I need. "Bradford?"

"Yeah?" He turns towards me. The sunlight floods his face and for the second time today I find myself lost in his stormy grey eyes.

"Do you reckon we could take a stab at being… you know… good friends?"

"I dunno, Bruno," he says coyly. "Would it involve occasional benefits?"

"Shit, yeah."

"Well, then I'd like that a lot."

"So, you'll swap numbers and let me call you?"

I study Bradford's smile. It hasn't faltered once since we got to the beach. Gone is the fearful person I saw earlier this morning, and in his place is a man who is open and unguarded and totally sure of himself. Bradford's gaze drifts back out to Brendan, and he watches fondly as the lab clowns around in the surf. "So long as you remember this isn't some Jennifer Aniston rom-com," he replies. "I don't want to be left on tenterhooks all week waiting to hear from you."

Not a bloody chance, mate.

CHAPTER 6

I'm floating on air. It's like my feet don't touch the ground the whole journey home from the beach. I know I shouldn't feel like this. It's ridiculous. Right now, though, I couldn't care less. I am going to enjoy my little bubble of happiness. God knows it's been in short supply lately.

Getting home just cannot happen quickly enough for me. Once I'm inside my flat and I've dealt with Brendan's harness, I head directly to my study. I need a hit of that magic again. When I barge through the door, I immediately notice the neatly-made bed. Nobody ever makes my bed for me. But *Bruno did.* I'm all choked up. I wish I'd come in here and spotted it before we went out. I wish I'd been able to make a great big fuss over it. Now, Bruno will never know how utterly moved I am by his gesture.

It's warm in here, so I switch on the air conditioner, draw the curtains and shut the door. After kicking off my shoes and peeling back the covers, I slide onto the mattress. I can smell Bruno's scent. It's definitely there—powerfully masculine and comforting. Pulling the pillow he slept on against my nose, I breathe in deep and fall softly into Eden. I'm a teenager once more and this is my fantasy.

"It's nice to see you with a smile on your face again, Bradford."

I startle at the sound of her voice. "*Mum.*"

My God, it must have been four years since she's visited. The first time it happened, I'd not long lost most of my remaining eyesight. My life had reached a level of desperation so intense that I was strangely calm. The magnitude of everything I'd been hit by was too much to take in, so I didn't. Then suddenly one day, I did. Spectacularly. I was in a heap on the floor bawling my eyes out when her voice swooped into my consciousness like some kind of supernatural salve.

It wasn't like those silly movies where the character does a pantomime freakout when they first see something that shouldn't be there. Her appearance was natural and organic. I wanted to believe in her presence so much that she made herself even *more* present. My sheer will strengthened everything I saw and heard.

Mum was there through the worst of that first year. Not all the time—she dropped in briefly and at random. *"I can only show up when I'm needed,"* she'd tell me. *"I have no say in these things, otherwise I'd never go away."*

And one day, when I truly believed I'd found happiness again with Jarrod, she did.

I turn over on the mattress, trying to adjust my eyes in the dark room. There sits my mother, perched on the top lid of my piano, her feet dangling down to the keyboard.

"He's gorgeous. *Very* sexy," she says, with a coyly-raised eyebrow. Her voice doesn't resonate externally. It echoes only in my head, but it's clearer, like it's not tainted by anything going on in the real world.

A sudden thought hits me. "Jesus! You weren't here last night, were you?!"

Mum chuckles, a deep throaty laugh. "Darling, I may have changed your nappies when you were a baby, but there's no way I'm barging in on that sort of thing."

Well, her sense of humour is still intact. I look at her there, poised on the edge of my upright, wearing her favourite painting smock. She's not the same woman who wasted away in front of my eyes. Sure, she's still a sixtysomething. But she's every bit the vibrant, esoteric art teacher I knew all my life—and not a day older than she was when she used to come and see me several years ago. "You left," I whisper. "I never got to say goodbye. *Again.*"

Her face furrows and her eyes radiate sadness. "Oh, darling. I really have no—"

"No say in these things. I know." I can't hide the weary resignation in my tone.

"We're not really talking about anything as nebulous as the last time I appeared before you, are we, Bradford?" I don't answer, so mum presses on. "You can't keep beating yourself up. It's senseless. I don't want this gnawing away at your soul forever. *Please.*"

That night still haunts me. I was exhausted. The palliative care nurse convinced me to go home and get some sleep. I sat beside mum as she lay in her hospital bed, holding her hand, and I sang *Che Gelida Manina.*

It was always her favourite. I knew she couldn't respond, but I hoped she could hear every note—every crack and wobble in my heartbroken voice as I tried to get through that aria like it was a lullaby. At the end, I held *'Vi piaccia dir'* as long as I could, till the last strains of the imaginary orchestra died down. Then I kissed her forehead and I left. Less than thirty minutes later, on my way home, I got the phone call to tell me that she'd passed.

"If only I hadn't gone, mum. If only I'd stayed half an hour longer, I could have said goodbye."

I'm fighting back some kind of deluge. It's odd. I should be immune by now. Mum and I have discussed this before, years ago when the wounds were fresh. And I still think about that night all the time. But right now, I'm not just thinking. I'm actually saying it out loud and it's so much more painful.

Mum's now on the edge of the bed. She doesn't float over like some cartoon apparition. She doesn't climb down and walk over like some anthropomorphic ghost. It's like a jump cut—she's just here instantly, exactly where I need her to be. "Bradford," she says softly, "*listen to me.* You blessed me with the most wonderful send-off I could ever have asked for. Your voice… it gave me permission to leave. *Never, ever* doubt how perfect that was." Something in her expression soothes the pain in my chest. Just as in life, this has always been the way with her. "But if you're really intent on making it up to me, there's something you can do, you know."

"Yeah?"

"Don't waste a day, Bradford. I can see how things are for you here with Jarrod. You don't have to stay in a relationship that doesn't make you happy."

I give mum a look. She knows what I'm going to say. "Sadly, you could apply that same principle to my bloody dad, couldn't you."

"Different situation entirely. I thought we were happy. It came out of the blue." She fusses with her top, primly smoothing it down. "Anyway, he didn't just walk out on *me.* He walked out on you too, and for that I will never forgive him." Her eyes meet mine in defiance. "Yeah, yeah. I know I'm supposed to be all angelic and fluffy, but I still have my quirks and I'm not apologising for them."

The look on her face has me in stitches. I start to cackle, releasing the rush of emotional energy that's been building inside me. After I've wiped the tears from my eyes, I glance up again and she's gone. Nowhere to be seen. "Oh. Goodbye, Endora."

Ever so faintly, her reply rings in my ears. "That's *not* my name."

***

Bruno comes through with the goods. After spending Saturday evening catching up with Summer and Nathan, then ploughing through online teaching work on Sunday, my phone buzzes with a text at seven p.m. that night.

BRUNO: OK, mate. I reckon this is the right amount of time, don't you?

God. Could this man be any more in tune with me?

BRADFORD: I'd say you were pretty spot on, there, Bru.

BRUNO: And you're still interested in meeting up again?

Ha. Am I ever.

BRADFORD: I'm keen as mustard.

BRUNO: How do you feel about soccer?

BRADFORD: I know next to nothing about it. I can bone up if necessary.

BRUNO: Jesus, mate... all I've thought about the last two days is you boning up.

Yeah, that was deliberate. And I have more.

BRADFORD: Sorry. Ask me about cricket and I'll definitely be able to chew the fat with you.

BRUNO: Bloody hell, I'm gonna need to have a wank now.

BRADFORD: Been there, done that already.

This is the truth. But I'm so turned on right now I'm sure I could manage it a second time.

BRUNO: Mate, you are a torturer. Next time I want evidence!
BRADFORD: That can be arranged. But before I whip it out again, maybe you'll tell me what you were gonna say about soccer?

BRUNO: Sorry, got sidetracked with all that talk about your beautiful dick. I play for a gay social team on Saturday afternoons. It's our final game next weekend, so I thought maybe you might wanna come and watch me make a fool of myself?

BRADFORD: Mate, I'm sure you're brilliant. It's all in the Italian genes. Count me in.

I know I'll just spend the whole time squinting at small blurry figures running around a field, but I don't care. Any excuse to see this man again is fine by me.

***

The week drags by like any other. Jarrod's return on Sunday night is uneventful. We don't talk beyond the necessary household exchanges. He comes and he goes and I don't question it. I'm used to this pattern and I don't care to cause any waves. I just get on with my daily routines: walking Brendan, running errands, working online, listening to audiobooks. When Jarrod's not home, I watch TV. I know he can't stand the audio descriptions I have to have switched on, so I generally make myself scarce when he's around.

Running in the back of my mind is my next meetup with Bruno. Every detail of our weekend together is emblazoned on my memory. I'm trying not to show any excitement in my day-to-day mood; I don't want Jarrod to get suspicious. Of course, our whole open arrangement is old news now, and if Jarrod can fool around, so can I. I'm just mindful about giving him any ammunition, any reason to send snide comments my way. So, as far as the topic of Bruno is concerned, I'm keeping mum.

Bruno stays in contact throughout the week. I notice his text messages are sent under the pretext of making arrangements for the weekend. I know what he's up to and it's a charming little game. He's letting me know he's keen without trying to look too obvious, and it makes me feel like a giddy adolescent all over again. The fact that his texts always lead to a stream of flirtatious SMS banter gives me the best kind of butterflies. I'm trying to be guarded and not get my hopes up, but dammit, I *need* this. I can't help the way I feel, and I don't want any of it to stop.

***

Saturday afternoon rolls around and not a moment too soon. Thankfully, Jarrod's at work, or at least I think he is. I'm dressed in my Nike trainers, a tight Puma polo and another of my many pairs of slutty little running shorts. I almost look as if I'm gonna be playing in today's match, which would definitely be a sight. I take my hat off to those low-vision people who do blind sports, but it's a skill I've never even looked into, let alone learnt.

Brendan is all ready, having brought me his harness as soon as I appeared in the living room with my shoes. He's sitting there patiently, most likely wondering why we haven't left yet. I'm hoping Bruno isn't running late, because I can sense the anticipation emanating from my four-legged friend. I don't feel too guilty, though; we've already been for a long morning walk together.

Bruno is bang on time. There's no intercom in my little apartment building, so he knocks directly on my front door. I wonder how I should greet him. It's silly, given the fact we've already enjoyed each other's bodies so comprehensively. But a week is a long time, especially in *gay* time.

Once again, my anxiety is quelled as soon as I open the door. Bruno and I move with magnetic speed towards each other, wrapping our bodies together in a big bear hug. He's so warm, so strong, so solid yet so soft and cuddly. I let out an audible breath as relief overtakes me. Wave after wave of it bombards my body, running from my scalp and straight down my spine. I'm shocked to realise the amount of tension I've been carrying around.

Bruno growls as he nuzzles against my cheek, coming around to kiss me gently on the lips. What starts off as innocent quickly escalates when his tongue barges into my mouth. He tastes of mint. He grunts softly as we begin to spar. *Oh, God, I've been dying for this all week.*

Pulling away from my lips, Bruno lowers himself to my height, pressing his belly close and grinding his crotch against mine. I can feel the hardness of our erections bumping over each other. "As much as I'd love to take you into that study and fuck you till you scream, we'd better press pause and get going," he says with a smirk.

I study his face, watching the glint in his eyes. What I wouldn't give to be able to turn the clock back a couple of hours right now.

Brendan and I follow Bruno out of the building to his car. I'm expecting some bog-standard kind of recent-model SUV, like everybody seems to drive nowadays. What he leads me to is a beautifully-restored

Holden Kingswood HQ sedan. It must be as old as I am. "Wow, these are worth a fortune!" I say, as I walk around it, admiring the gleaming metallic duco.

"Upwards of forty grand. But I bought it a long time ago for a fraction of that. It was a real labour of love getting it into this condition."

"So, you're one of these butch blokes who knows all about cars?"

"Ha! Not at all. Gab's husband Claudio handled most of it. I just did what he told me to."

I notice his HQ is one of those ones with a front bench seat. I also notice the immaculate cream upholstery. "I might just duck inside and get the car hammock for Brendan." I'm not sure how far we'd be able to push the bench seat back so Brendan could sit in the front footwell. In any case, he'll be perfectly happy sitting behind us. With Bruno's help, the thick dog hammock is secured and Brendan is strapped in place. I swear I can see him smile as he pants away, staring regally out the window.

We head west along Oxford Street, through Moore Park and Alexandria, then down past Sydenham to Fraser Park football club. On the way, Bruno tells me about his morning, how he's been to his parents to give them some help around the house. "Dad had a stroke a while back, but he's recovering well," he says. "He has a carer come in a few times a week. Mum definitely isn't pleased about that." He gives a little snort. "Typical proud Italian mamma. But it's really too much for her to handle on her own. Me and my sister do whatever we can, but we both work and Gabriela has her boys to look after as well."

Bruno's devotion to his family speaks volumes. It seems the picture of him I'm forming in my mind is turning out to be pretty accurate. I like this man. I want to know everything about him, and I hope he sticks around, in whatever capacity.

The main sports field at Fraser Park has stands on one side, next to a low building which I assume houses the changing rooms and showers. Brendan and I follow Bruno as he leads us right around to sit in the front row of seats. He looks so damn sexy in his soccer getup. His jersey hugs his broad shoulders and shows off his padded physique and belly. His floppy soccer shorts mould around his big buttocks, wedging right in between them. God, the way that arse talks to me as he walks along is driving me mental. I'm already erect and leaking into my shorts. I can safely say I'd have no qualms about grabbing him and ravaging him right here, right now.

Once Brendan and I are settled on our bench, Bruno jogs out onto the field nearby to join his team mates. Everyone is dressed in their own gear, they're not wearing any kind of team uniform. I remember Bruno saying something about this being social soccer, so I suppose that's why, but I wonder how they tell the teams apart. Then I spot the guys putting on those coloured bib things. *Of course, silly me.*

While they all do their pre-game warm-up, I take in my surroundings. There are only a few other people in the stands, plus the odd group dotted around the outside of the field. Looks like it's just a friends-and-family situation, but it's kind of nice how relaxed and low-key the atmosphere is.

The game gets underway and I try my best to see what I can. As I'd anticipated, the boys are just blurry figures—I can't make out any detail. I do, however, spot a bald head with a big black beard every now and then. Bruno seems right into the whole thing, and I can't help feeling some misguided sense of pride. There's no way I can tell who's kicking what, but I like to think he and his team are thrashing the others. Right now, I could really do with a sighted person to give me a running commentary.

Half time arrives and the team go off to their respective areas. I crane my neck and squint till I spot the big bald bear. My heart jumps a little when I notice him turn my way and wave to me. It's such a simple gesture, but it fills me with a kind of hope that I know I'm not entitled to. I wish I could see him better. I wish I could see the expression on his face. Instead, I'm left to imagine these nuances as I wave back at Bruno's blurry form.

I only know the match is actually over when I hear cheering and see guys running around and jumping up and down hugging each other. I'm so clueless, I'm not even sure who won until I see some of the men jogging towards the stands and spot Bruno in amongst the joyous melee. Breaking free, he makes his way to me and I stand up just in time to get a big sweaty bear hug.

"I don't know how much you could see," he pants, "but that was fuckin' awesome!"

A couple of guys jostle up behind Bruno. "Hey, big boy! Drinks in the green room," one of them says excitedly.

Bruno shakes his head. "Nah, we might just take off now."

"No bloody way! You're coming." He grabs Bruno by the shoulder, then looks squarely at me. "You too. Hop to it."

Bruno seems momentarily uncomfortable, but gives a small smile of defeat. "Just a quick one?" he says to me.

I don't really have time to assess his reaction, because me, my bag and my dog are seemingly whisked towards the building behind the stands. The "green room" that the guy mentioned turns out to be just the changing room, where teammates are laughing and rough-housing. Some of them are on benches pulling off their shoes, so Brendan and I slink off to the side and have a seat near them, taking in the general flurry of excitement. I startle as I hear a loud pop, then another. Champagne sprays through the air as two men circle the room, doing their best to drench us all. They certainly get me a good one. I'm summarily saturated with sparkling wine, though I can't help but laugh along with everyone else.

"Jesus, you're soaked!" Bruno appears through the tangle of men and stands in front of me, offering me a plastic cup half-full of whatever they haven't managed to paint everyone with.

"All part of the experience," I grin, as I'm showered by more droplets from a shaking Brendan.

A number of rousing, shambolic speeches are up next. I can't really make out much of what they're saying, given the amount of ribald interjections and cheering. I notice some guys are now stripped down to their underwear or wrapped in towels as they join in with the merriment.

Soon, the speeches dissolve into general chatter. A few men start to file into the adjoining room and I hear the cascading sound of showers being turned on. Bruno makes his way back over to me. "We should get going," he urges.

"Not a chance," booms a voice behind him. A towel flicks Bruno, and as he swivels around in protest, a hairy otter stands there naked, dick swinging happily between his legs. "You fuckin' stink, Bruno. Get in there!"

Bruno grimaces and shoots me an apologetic look. I can't help but feel amused at his shyness as he starts to undress. *You've got nothing to be ashamed about, mate.* I stare in admiration as he shucks his shorts and undies and that big package of his comes into view.

"Hurry up!" barks a voice to my left and a hand tugs at my arm. I look sideways to see a furry young cub in a towel grinning at me.

"Oh, no, I wasn't even—" A towel lands across my face and I'm jostled to my feet by multiple sets of hands. Everyone's laughing. It's all in good fun. I guess I can go along with it, it's not like I haven't showered naked in front of other men before.

It takes me seconds to kick off my shoes and strip out of my sticky champagne-soaked clothes. Maybe a shower will do me good after all. I leave my rogue towel with Brendan, and I'm swept with the few remaining guys into the next room. My errant eyes are suddenly feasting on a sea of naked bodies. This is clearly an old amenities block—there are no cubicles, just a multitude of open shower nozzles along three walls. Sexy, hairy arses, swinging penises, dad bods, chunky cubs, burly bears, slim otters, a muscly dude or two… my own dick is betraying me. I've deliberately abstained from masturbating for days, anticipating a big horny reunion with Bruno. But now I'm rapidly becoming hard. *Jesus Christ, Bradford. Look away. How embarrassing!*

Scanning the room, I spot Bruno's rear side and gravitate towards him. He's down near the corner and the shower head next to him is free. As I turn on the hot water, he looks my way and does a double take.

"Yeah, I know, Bru—I was coerced. I didn't have much say in it." I grin at him, reaching across to the shelf and helping myself to what I assume is his body wash. I quickly lather myself up, making sure to stroke my cock while I look at him. If I'm going to be hard and horny, I want it to be because I'm taking in the sight of the sexiest man in here.

Bruno growls, following suit. His right hand slides his foreskin back and forth, his semi quickly working its way to full mast. My own penis is throbbing now as I quickly rinse the body wash off myself. I hope no one has noticed our surreptitious little mating dance. I'm sure they're all busy doing their own thing, anyway.

A wanton moan sails through the air and I look over my shoulder. As I squint around the room, I'm shocked and intrigued to find some kind of orgy happening. I spot a guy on his knees giving an enthusiastic blow job. A few other guys are clustered together, groping each other. Another guy is pressed up against a wall with a man behind… *fucking him?*

Oh, my God, it's like half-price Tuesday at Sydney Sauna.

"This is why I didn't want us to come back here after the game." Bruno takes a step forward and pulls me into his arms. I can feel the thickness of his penis as it flexes hard against me. "I've only played at this ground once before, and with all these open showers, things inevitably ended up like, you know..." He keeps one arm across my shoulder as he steps back and turns to take in the full spectacle. "We should be able to slip out of here and take off now, though."

"Too late," I choke out. A mouth has just clamped around my penis and I look down to see the young cub who'd practically dragged me in here. He's sucking me with incredible proficiency, pressing his tongue up against the underside of my knob, busily wiggling my PA ring. It's bloody exquisite. Without missing a beat, his hand reaches up and grabs Bruno's erection, pumping it rhythmically as he continues slurping away at my dick.

"Oh, God," Bruno sputters, after Young Cub's mouth suddenly pops off my cock and presumably suctions straight onto his. *Yep, there he goes.* "I guess we could…" Bruno leans closer to my ear. "I realise I have no right to ask this, but I'd be more comfortable if we didn't… um… actually *fuck* anybody else here."

I move my head back out to gaze at his earnest expression. "You read my mind, Bruno. I want to save that for just us."

A bashful smile ghosts across Bruno's face and he presses his lips to mine. Our tongues start to dance while the cub toils away below, his hand expertly working my cock. *Yeah, this is nice.* Bruno's deep growl against my mouth raises in a sudden crescendo and he breaks our kiss. "Oh, fuck!" He shudders and pants, and I peer around to see a man squatting behind him with his face buried in Bruno's arse.

I grin up at Bruno. "Mouths working you from both sides, I see?"

Suddenly, it's my turn to groan as the cub's mouth slips back onto my cock again. Bruno grabs hold of my head and we lean into each other, kissing more hungrily this time. "Oh, mate," he groans, "What I wouldn't give to take you away and pound that tight hole of yours right now."

As Bruno finishes his sentence, the phantom rimmer slides up from behind him, his grinning mug appearing above Bruno's shoulder. "Eating that big hot arse of yours is fuckin' amazing," the man growls. "I'll bet it's even more amazing with my cock inside there."

Bruno's face goes all sheepish. "Uh… thanks, but maybe not, Jim. I only really do the fucking thing with one guy in here."

"You mean this fella?" The man steps out from behind Bruno to get a good look at me. I cast my eyes up and down his figure. He's a furry man in his forties with a sexy dad bod and a long, hard dick that he's rubbing slowly and firmly. "He's one hot little bear," Jim says to Bruno. "I wouldn't mind watching him pound your hairy manhole."

The cub down below disengages from my dick with a lip-smacking sound. "Me too," he chirps. "Then maybe you'll switch?"

"Turn around and face the wall," orders Jim, spanking Bruno fair on the arse. "Let's see what your boyfriend here can do." While I stifle a giggle at the 'B' word he's just used, Jim holds up a bottle to me. "Conditioner," he says. "I've loosened him up with my tongue, but he's gonna need a little more lubrication before he takes that cock of yours." A wolfish grin tugs at the corners of Jim's mouth as he squirts a large amount of the creamy liquid into his hand. Reaching down, he rubs it into my dick with studied expertise. It feels incredible; I'm a sucker for a skilled hand. But I'm considerably more desperate to sink into Bruno's delectable arse.

He's already in position, facing the wall with his legs apart and his bum thrust right out. Now, he's the perfect height for me. Gathering some of the conditioner from my dick, I rub two fingers against his hole until he allows them entry. In and out of his tight ring I pump them, stretching them apart as I go. Bruno moans quietly, turning up the volume as I work in a third finger. I know he's ready now. After placing my knob against his well-probed pucker, all it takes is a slow and steady push till I'm buried to the hilt.

God, I remember how good this was. Grabbing onto Bruno's hips, I start driving into him with gradual acceleration. "Fuck, that's hot," Jim growls. I glance across to see his hand sliding up and down his lengthy penis. In one quick motion, he's on the floor and shuffling beneath Bruno. From what I can make out, I'm pretty sure his mouth is now servicing Bruno's fat dick.

But Bruno isn't the only one getting a little extra help. A finger—no *two* fingers—are suddenly slid into my arsehole, and they make their way straight to my prostate. Another hand is resting on my buttock, gauging the movement of my hips. The fingers inside brush systematically and gently over my g-spot, not missing a beat as I groan and begin to ram hard into Bruno's arse.

Bruno's moans turn into bellows, and I find myself joining in chorus with him. I'm suddenly glad for every mile I've walked up and down all those hills with Brendan. My arse is working overtime, my glutes are burning, my quads are flexed within an inch of their life. My anus tightens each time the guy behind me thrusts his fingers into it, which in turn causes my cock to flex hard inside the heat of Bruno's rectum. It's pleasure overload. I'm almost dizzy with how good it feels.

Over and above all this, I'm beyond excited to think I'm going to make Bruno come. I want him to bloody explode. I'm using every bit of strength in my brawny butt to pile-drive him into oblivion. Bruno's legs begin to tremble and he stifles a wail. "Fuck, I'm gonna shoot," he blurts. I feel his arse constricting wildly around my dick as he lets out a guttural roar, and I know I've done my job. "Oh, Jesus," he whines, his body continuing to convulse. As his spasms slowly subside, I feel him starting to relax, and I slowly edge my hard cock out of his warmth.

The fingers vacate my hole and a body slides up behind me. "Your arse is fucking hot as hell," I hear the cute cub whisper. "And so are you."

I'm still trying to catch my breath as I turn my head sideways. "You can talk. And you're bloody talented to boot."

Cute Cub slaps me on the rump. "I'm off," he whispers. "Thanks for the fun, sexy."

Glancing down, I spot Jim shimmying out from under Bruno, looking like the cat who got the cream. Well, I guess he *did* get it, didn't he. "You fucked one delicious load outta this bastard," he says to me.

I'm chuckling and panting as I stand there stroking my cock. I desperately need to blow. Bruno's turned back around now and he moves in close to me. Sliding his hands over my pectorals, he begins to caress my nipples. "You were fuckin'…." He shakes his head, lost for words. "You were a bloody *animal.* I came even harder than last week."

His thumbs are gliding over the hardened nubs on my chest, my fist is speeding up on my cock, and—*God*—there are hands pulling my arse cheeks apart. A long tongue wastes no time spearing right into my arsehole and I nearly hit the roof. *Jim.* I can see now why Bruno was so impressed. I'm close, so very, very close…

There's a bit of a commotion happening across the shower room, a flurry of voices. I'm right on the edge of orgasm and I'm far too thrilled to care. My hand is rubbing hard over my slick knob. The ring in my dick is twisting and turning, working me from the inside. My nipples are on fire. The tongue inside my anus is burying deeper and deeper.

A man rushes right over to us just as I tense up. I'm a live volcano and I'm about to—

"Fun's over, guys," the man mutters with urgency. I holler as my cock begins to pulsate. Thick missiles of spunk shoot out of me. One after the other they come in an exquisite barrage while my arsehole fights with the tongue that's jammed inside it. My head is in a whirl as I gaze down and notice my load has landed in long, splattered lines on Messenger Man's wrist. I look back up at him, wide-eyed. Slowly, he raises his arm and licks it all off. "Thanks for that," he says with a wink.

***

After Bruno, Brendan and I have beaten a hasty retreat, we drive back through Sydenham. "You reckon Brendan might fancy a romp around the dog park?" says Bruno, as he takes a right turn and heads down to Tempe. "He was such a good boy, waiting there for us while… you know."

I crane my neck around to look at Brendan in the back. His tongue is lolling out in the air conditioned comfort, a big smile on his doggy face. He knows what's going on. "He's definitely keen on that idea. And so am I." Bruno and I might have got our rocks off back there, but I'm nowhere near ready to bail on a date that I waited a whole week for.

Bruno drives down a small street flanked by Tempe Recreation Reserve to the right, and some urban bushland to the left. Turning up a steep side road, we make our way through the trees to a car park. Just over from us towards the east is a huge fenced area. Bruno pulls up the sedan, letting the engine idle. "Bradford," he says after a short pause, "is it too forward of me to say the only man there today I really wanted to be with was you?"

"Not at all." I grab his hand and give it a squeeze. "It was definitely fun. Like a hot porn scenario. But I'll take our one-on-one intimacy over that any day." It's the truth, but I'm being careful here. I don't want to make a wrong move. I clear my throat and fix my gaze out the windscreen. "I don't know the rules. I just know I want more of this bloke sitting beside me right now." I steal a glance at Bruno, who reaches over and undoes my seat belt. Pulling me across the bench towards him, he wraps his arms around my shoulders and hugs me tight. Our upper bodies are twisted towards each other and our legs are awkwardly entangled, but this hug means so much more than we could possibly articulate at the moment.

Brendan is in his element in the dog park. He doesn't visit them very often, he's normally walking by my side. Plus, you hear all kinds of stories about aggressive dogs at these places. And dogs getting fleas. Fortunately, my little mate is in tip-top shape and has all his regular treatments.

At the moment, there are only a few others here. Squinting hard, I spot a couple of people over in a far corner with their dogs close by. Somebody playing fetch with a large black dog on the southern side of the park. Two people with what looks like fluffy little pooches frolicking happily near the northern edge.

Bruno produces a tennis ball from his pocket. I'm instantly touched as I realise he's planned this whole outing. He launches into a spirited game of catch with Brendan. My lab is in seventh heaven, jumping and diving to grab the ball, then dutifully returning it to Bruno every time, eager for more. God, I wish I was able to do this properly. My attempts are always clumsy and slow. Ball sports and me parted ways after high school; my sight was already getting far too bad. Right now, though, I'm more than content to just watch these two. It warms my heart to see the way they interact.

***

By the time Bruno pulls up outside my apartment, it's early evening. It won't be dark for hours yet, so it doesn't even feel late. It's an odd time to end a date, but today seems to have reached its conclusion. I catch Bruno's eye and he smiles at me. "I really want to invite myself in and spend the night," he says. "Unfortunately, I'm working at seven a.m. tomorrow." I watch his barrel chest rise and fall as he inhales and lets out a long sigh. "I hate day shifts, but they pretty much begged me to come in and I can't say no to the Sunday penalties." Grabbing my hand, he intertwines his fingers with mine. "Please don't think I'm giving you the brush off. That's the last thing I'd want."

"Of course not," I say. "We can catch up again anytime." I'm trying to sound like so many things at once: patient, understanding, relaxed, yet keen. Yes, I'm *really* keen, but I don't know how much I can let that show right now.

"You reckon we can do it one night this week?" Bruno ventures.

"Yeah, for sure. Anytime you want is fine by me." Blatant, stupid happiness is seeping from every pore in my body. For once, I make the first move and shuffle over the bench seat to kiss Bruno goodbye. He slides his arm around my back and grips my shoulder as our lips meet and a blaze ignites.

Oh, God. I see it now. Bruno kisses without reserve. There's no barrier to his heart. His innate and instinctual display of trust knocks me sideways. I've never been able to do what he does; I need that buffer, that layer of self-protection. But as we're joined here tonight, as the electricity storms through our bodies and collides where our lips and tongues and clutching hands meet, something important becomes apparent. I have no layer this time. I am exposed. Bruno has opened a door and I've walked right through it.

The sound of our rushing breath fills the car as our lips finally part. Bruno's head sinks forward and he nuzzles into my neck. His beard is a soft pillow against my skin. "Today was really nice, Bradford," he mumbles against me. It's not a grand statement, but it's genuine in its simplicity. And it resonates with me more than I want to let myself believe.

Brendan and I stand at the kerb and watch Bruno drive away. I don't know what's going on, but amidst the bleak outlook of my day-to-day existence, I finally feel like there's something to look forward to.

Back inside the apartment, I notice Jarrod has been home again. The lounge room that I'd carefully tidied has now been messed up. Jarrod's dumped things on the couch and thrown cushions on the floor. On the coffee table, there's a glass with dregs in it and a used ashtray. This pisses me off—we have a smoking area outside. It's not raining, it's not cold. Jarrod's just lazy and selfish.

In my clean kitchen, there are now dirty dishes in the sink. The butter has been left out of the fridge, a smeared knife plonked on the bench next to it. The bread is sitting there open, slices tumbling out of the unsealed bag. In the bedroom, clothes have been strewn all over the mattress, and my nicely-straightened linen is crumpled.

I'm so bloody sick of this. A deep sigh rattles from my chest and I collapse onto my side of the bed. As I reach across to tap my talking clock, my hand bumps against a notepad. *I didn't leave this here.* Picking it up, I see a message crudely scrawled with black Sharpie in Jarrod's handwriting:

Gone away for a couple of weeks.

That's it. Nothing else. I mean, I'm used to Jarrod taking off to visit family and friends down the coast. With his agency work, he's able to get nursing shifts anywhere. Usually there's some mention of these trips in advance, though.

You know what, Bradford? Who bloody cares. Don't look a gift horse in the mouth. He's gone. You can breathe easy for a little while.

CHAPTER 7

"Darling, it's been *aaaages*. What time are you finishing? I need a good bitch session."

"Gina G! Well, aren't you a sight for sore ears." I glance at my watch. "I'm on late shifts at the moment, but I'm nearly due for dinner break."

"Fabulous. Meet you in the cafeteria in ten." That's my friend Regina, bossy as ever. We've known each other for decades, since we studied nursing together at uni. It's one of those enduring friendships, the kind where we only catch up on occasion, but we know it's always gonna be there. Regina tends to flit around, living in different cities for a few years at a time. After breaking up with her latest "*bastard*" husband, she's now back in Sydney for a stint as manager of the neurology ward here at the hospital.

The first time Regina left Sydney, she wasn't Regina. Back then, she identified as a very effeminate gay man and occasional drag queen. I remember her return after several years in Melbourne. The transformation was a knockout—it was as if she'd become who she was always meant to be. Her slight Asian build made her look like an exotic princess, though she was one hundred percent raucous Aussie every time she opened her mouth.

"Jesus, what a clusterfuck of a weekend," she says, kissing me on the cheek as we meet at the cafe. "I'm starving. Let's talk and walk."

It's one of those seventies-style cafeterias with a long metal counter where you slide your tray along and get what you want from the displays. I trail behind my bossy friend as she tells me all about her Saturday drama.

"So, I go to this women-only event with my lesbian mates. And these bitches on the door won't let me in. Can you believe that? Apparently, I don't count as a woman. This young scrag stands on her TERF soapbox when I demand to know what her damn definition of a woman is. 'Well, having a *cunt* for a start,' she sneers at me. And I tell her, 'I've had a *cunt* longer than you've been alive, honey.'" Regina points to a piece of fish at the exact time she drops the C-word. The cafeteria lady behind the counter gives her a shitty look and Regina smiles sweetly back at her.

"You're fucking kidding me. What happened after that?"

"Nothing. I left," says Regina. "The night was pretty much ruined."

Stuff like this makes my fucking blood boil. I know Regina hates anything that looks like pity, so I'm more than happy to show anger instead. "I remember reading a column in the Star Observer where something like this happened to one of their journalists. Fuck, I miss the days of the gay papers. You could have hounded them to write this up. People need to know this shit happens."

Regina gives me an indulgent smile. "Bruno. *Sweetie*. You're so 2005. You need to get your grandaddy arse onto social media one of these days. I've plastered it *everywhere*."

"Ugh. I have enough going on in my life without becoming glued to those bloody sites."

"Doesn't seem to have stopped you whoring around on Growlr," she chirps.

"Growlr isn't social media, it's just a place to find dick." I have to stop myself grinning like an idiot. "Anyway, I gave up all that shit."

We've finally reached the cash register, so I'm saved from blurting out too much. After paying ridiculous prices for our basic food, I find myself following Regina once again, this time to a secluded table up the back. "Well, that's my bitch forum used up," she says as we take a seat. "What's been happening with you?"

I'm in two minds here. I'm dying to tell her about Bradford. He's all I can think of. But then I have to tell her about so many other things. And do I really wanna be keeping someone informed about my private affairs—even someone who just skirts on the edges of my life like Gina does?

"You're fucking someone," she says with a raised eyebrow. "Spill."

Well, I guess the decision's been made for me, now. "Yes," I sigh. The relief running through my body now I've admitted this is a complete shock. Suddenly, there's a shit ton of word vomit trying to barge its way out of my mouth. "For a few weeks. This beautiful, stocky little bear called Bradford."

Regina looks up from her plate, curious as hell. She's never heard me say anything like this. I've been with Brendan forever. Of course, she knows all about our open relationship, but I've only ever had random hookups. Nothing more. "Oh? And what does this *Bradford* do?"

"He used to be an opera singer, then he had to retire when he lost a ton of his eyesight. These days he gets around with a guide dog and he does some kind of online music teaching."

"Hmm. And can he actually *see* you?" Regina eyes me up and down with a smirk.

"Yes, he most certainly can. And he's made it very clear that he enjoys the view."

Regina waves her fork at me. "Ooh, I like this smug thing you've got going on now, Bru. Kinda suits you. So what does Brendan think about this new boy-toy?"

"Ha! Well, for a start, this boy-toy is almost *our* age." I let that sink in for a moment. Unlike me, Regina's looming half-century is a bit of a sore point, even though she looks ten years younger. "And no. I haven't said anything to Brendan." I sit up defiantly in my seat. "Brendan has had fuckbuddy after fuckbuddy for years. I've never stopped him and I've never been jealous, not even once"

"But you don't want to tell him about *your* fuckbuddy."

"Those were the rules we made. We know we fuck others, but we don't share details. It's always worked for us." I'm feeling defensive, but I'm trying not to show it.

"Fair enough," says Regina. "Your relationship, your rules." She gives up on her limp-looking fish, plopping her fork down on her plate and dabbing at her lipstick with a napkin. "Tell me more about this Bradford, then."

A rush of childish energy hits me and I wanna squeal like a little girl. "I literally jump out of bed in the mornings, Gina. I can't wait to see him. Pretty much every day this last fortnight I've been walking for miles, up and down hills with him and his dog. I tell you, my arse has never been so perky, and I haven't had to do leg day in weeks."

"Ha! 'Leg day'?" Regina scoffs. "You're trying to tell me you've been going to the gym?"

"Cheeky bitch! I'll have you know I'm at the private hospital one *all the time*."

"How often?"

"Um… twice a week." I say it quickly, but it doesn't stop Gina laughing like a bloody hyena. "Screw you, look at these!" I hold up my guns. Yeah, I'm not remotely ripped; my body has an all-over chubby comfort layer. But my arms and pecs are nice and muscly underneath it.

"Lovely. What about your gut, though?"

"Hey! Men love my belly, thank you very much. Bradford can't keep his hands off it. He uses it as a pillow every bloody night."

"*Every night,* Bru? Just how serious is this affair?"

"Well, on my nights off, at least. I go and stay over at his place in Bondi. He's a fucking *firecracker* in bed. He's so eager and so adventurous and so bloody affectionate."

Regina smiles thoughtfully and her voice goes all delicate. "And what does Bradford think of your domestic situation?"

"Oh." I'm laughing now. "I haven't explained this properly. Bradford's in an open relationship too."

"And his partner…?"

"Is a fucking prick from what I can tell. I don't think he treats Bradford very well at all. Anyway, he's been away for the last few weeks."

"Mm-hmm." Regina looks doubtful. I suddenly realise how bad all this shit sounds.

"No. There's no sneaking around. Bradford's partner fucks more guys than *Brendan.*" Regina doesn't need me to say any more here. She knows bloody well that I'm the boring homebody and Brendan's the social butterfly. I take a deep breath. This is the part I really didn't want to get into. "Brendan's gonna be house sitting for this rich couple he knows while they're in Europe in March and April. Big terrace in Surry Hills complete with two cocker spaniels." I stare down at my awful coffee, which has now gone cold. "Things have been distant between us lately. I'm wondering if there's a lot more to this than just a change of scenery for a while."

I gaze back up at Regina, trying to work out her reaction. "You don't need me to tell you anything, darl," she says finally. "You already know what you have to do."

***

That night, Brendan's watching some bloody awful action thing on TV when I get home at ten p.m. "Hey, Brie!" I call out over the ruckus. I really should tell Bradford about this nickname, especially given the confusion with his dog. But Brendan doesn't even like *me* calling him by his old drag moniker. He was funny as hell onstage, but he's also a hairy otter of a man. He looked fuck-ugly as a woman, I can tell you.

"Oh, hey," he says, glancing up from where he's sprawled on the couch as I enter the living room. "There's leftover pizza in the fridge if you want any."

"Oh, thanks. That's really nice of you." We're speaking all kinda detached, but it's become the norm for us. We sound like flatmates. We act like flatmates. Brendan even sleeps on the daybed in the study a lot of the time. He'll stay up late watching TV, then go and pass out in there while I'm sleeping down the hall in the only bedroom. Sometimes he crawls into bed with me in the early hours of the morning. I don't know why he does it, I've never asked him. But there's no kissing. No cuddling.

After zapping the pizza in the convection oven, I wander into the lounge room and take a seat in the recliner next to the couch. I watch Brendan as I eat. He really is the loveliest man. Fun, happy, a decent person all round. We have a lifetime of history together. But we really are just friends now. All the sex and romance is a distant memory. I don't miss it and neither does he. I'm absolutely sure of that.

Brendan reaches for the remote, stops the program and rolls over to look up at me. "So, Bru… I notice you've been going out a fair bit. Are you seeing someone?" He doesn't sound like he's pointing the finger. It doesn't seem like he's remotely jealous or upset, either. How could he be, really? He's hardly the type to be a bloody hypocrite.

"Um, yeah. Just made a friend. Casual, you know." I can't hide how uncomfortable I sound. I feel like I've been caught out.

"Hey, it's fine. You don't have to say anything. No details, remember?" He swivels on his arse to sit up and looks at me for a few seconds. "Maybe…" His eyes shift a bit. It's like he's struggling with the weight of his thoughts. "Maybe all this stuff is happening at the right time. Maybe we should look at this house sitting thing as a trial separation."

I nod carefully. This is exactly what I was suspicious of. And now that it's out there, it can't be taken back.

"What are you thinking?" he prompts. "I mean, we both know this has been coming, don't we."

Thoughts are racing around my head too fast for me to catch them. I'm feeling so many things at once. I agree with everything Brendan is saying. One hundred percent. But part of me is fucking terrified.

Brendan tries one more time. "Bru, you've gotta agree that there's no relationship here anymore. There hasn't been for years."

"I know, but I don't want to lose my best mate," I blurt. I barely manage to stop myself breaking down like a fucking sook.

Brendan's expression twists up in some kind of pained sympathy. It's not a look I'm used to seeing from him. But then again, this isn't a situation we've ever found ourselves in. "Oh, Bru," he says softly. "After twenty years together we're not gonna stop being mates. I couldn't bear that."

I look at Brendan long and hard. I believe him. I've always trusted him completely. The absolute fucking chaos in my head suddenly comes to a screeching halt. This whole confrontation has been awkward as hell, but I can see it now, clear as day. *We're holding each other back.*

Late that night, after Brendan and I have given each other a long and uneasy hug, after he's gone to sleep in the study and I'm tucked up in bed, I cry. I cry because I know things will never be the same again. I cry because I built my life around this relationship. I cry because I'm shitscared of what will happen to me tomorrow, the next day, and every day after that. I cry because now that I've finally been cut loose, I no longer know who I am.

CHAPTER 8

Wake up! shrieks my subconscious. My eyes fly open and my hand automatically hits the big button on my talking clock.

"*Nine thirty-two.*" Its chirpy voice is irritating, especially after my late night and lack of sleep.

Oh, God. Brendan will definitely be in need of his morning dunny run; he must be busting right now. First things first, though, because I'm busting too, and I don't have the option of hoiking my penis out in public to hose down the communal lawn.

Dragging my weary body to the bathroom, I lean over the toilet bowl and let go. I just love the way pissing and coming looks now that I have a PA. If I'm being completely honest, I would watch other pierced men do it in kinky porn videos and I'd always blow the biggest loads. This was what finally drove me to get the ring in my own penis. Just knowing it's there, knowing that I'm like those guys—combine that with the other sexual perks and I'm as horny as I was at thirty.

I'm weighing up whether to have a cheeky shower, but I turn my head to spot Brendan waiting patiently by the open bathroom door. "Sorry, buddy. I'll take you out now." A quick glance in the mirror reminds me I wore stretchy gym shorts and a t-shirt to bed. That'll do; I won't scare the neighbours.

Normally, Brendan follows his strict guide dog toileting routine to the letter. For a long time, though, I've flouted these rules in the morning at home. Today—like every other day—I remove both his harness and leash as soon as we get outside so he can have some freedom. But as always, Brendan pauses and his big brown eyes look up at me expectantly.

"I know, buddy," I say, as I take a seat in one of the nearby plastic chairs. Way back when I was smoking, this was the spot where I'd have my first cigarette of the day. Brendan waits till I'm settled, then gently touches his nose against my leg before bounding off. It's a routine he's always followed, but it's not something he's been trained to do. He knows when his harness is off it means he's not working and he's allowed to be a regular dog. But it's like he's so concerned about me, he won't go anywhere until he's sure I'm OK.

I consider myself lucky that there's one soul in this world who's truly got my back.

After breakfast and a long shower, I stand naked in front of the IKEA clothing racks next to the bed. When Jarrod moved in, I got rid of all my furniture from this room. I gave away my double bed, moved my bedside drawers to the study, and vacated the built-in wardrobe so he could use it. At the time, I wasn't too worried—I can see clothes a lot easier on racks than inside a dark wardrobe, and Jarrod's queen-sized bedroom suite was bigger than my little double. Back then, I saw what I did as a welcoming gesture. These days? It's like I'm a guest in my own space. I try not to feel resentful. After all, I offered. I have no right to be upset that Jarrod took me up on it.

Pulling on one of my brand-new pairs of Bonds tighty-whities, I turn and peer over my shoulder, doing my best to admire my bum in the mirror. I am hugely turned on by bears wearing this kind of underwear, especially Bruno. Every time he strips off in front of me, that's what he's got on. I'd always worried that they'd make my arse look fat, but Bruno's buns are so tasty in them that I just had to go out and buy some for myself. And they look pretty damn good on me, even if I do say so.

My phone trills just as I'm doing the final adjustments to my cock and balls. *Summer.* Geez, it's been a few weeks.

"*Daaaarling*," she says, as soon as I answer.

"Hi, sweetie. Whatcha up to? Aren't you working today?"

"My client isn't home," she sighs. "Not answering her phone, either. So I'm sitting in my car waiting for her to show up. I'll give her ten more minutes, then I'm off."

"That sucks. Will you still get paid?"

"God, yeah! You bet we're gonna bill the NDIS for no-shows. Anyway, why aren't *you* working?"

My chuckle is almost a chortle. "Sweetie, I get eight hours of teaching work a week if I'm lucky. Oh! Have a listen to this—" I grab my iPad off the bedside table and click open one of the essays I stayed up marking last night.

"'*It never fails to perplex me that so many ensembles treat the first chorus of Bach's 'Wachet Auf' like some sort of pompous dirge. Their sluggish tempi and muddy, oversized choirs are misplaced romantic interpretations that do no justice to Bach's vision. The whole thing should move forwards at a snappy pace, and the semiquaver passages in the strings need to be crisp and crystal clear, as do the melismas in the vocal parts. The latter cannot be achieved if the piece is weighed down by all and sundry in the choir stands—it needs a tight, small chamber ensemble of voices for maximum agility. Far from this merely being a subjective view based on my own selfish listening pleasure, these requirements are essential to fully realise the precise and deliberate intricacy of Bach's masterful word painting.*'" I'm beaming with pride. "This is why my job is so great. How could you not love teaching students like her?"

"Ha! Yeah—she sounds exactly the same as you."

"Oh. Pardon me for being passionate about what I do." I toss my iPad onto the mattress indignantly, even though I know she can't see me.

"Speaking of passionate," says Summer, "are you ever going to actually start singing again?"

This is a sore subject. I'm so out of practice, I doubt I'll ever be back in professional shape again. But I'm not going to get into that with Summer. "I'm still seeing the opera teacher once a month. Maybe I'll do some more performing when all this crap with Jarrod is sorted out."

Summer pauses for a moment. "How are things going with him?" She's being cautious. It's not like her and it unsettles me. I cringe as I picture her sitting at home with Nathan talking about her sad old brother and his sad old life.

Do I even have the insight to give her any kind of coherent answer? Do I even want to open Pandora's Box right now? There's a sudden surge of pressure in my chest. Realisation smacks me hard in the face—I'm *dying* to tell someone. "Jarrod's been away for a few weeks and it's been *so nice* with him gone."

I think about how much I've loved having Bruno here anytime I wanted. I should feel at least some semblance of guilt over this, but I refuse to. Jarrod has never made any bones about the amount of men *he's* shagged in the last year and a half.

My phone beeps in my ear. "Hang on a sec." I switch Summer to speakerphone and have a look at the text message that just came through. "Well, talk of the devil..."

JARROD: Hey Brad, I'm coming back today. Be home by six. Is there food in the house? Do you want me to get stuff for dinner?

"Wow." The word pops out before I remember Summer's still on speakerphone.

"What? Come on—tell me tell me tell me!" Now, *that* sounds more like the Summer I know.

"I haven't heard from him the whole time he's been gone. Now he's coming back this evening and even offered to shop for dinner."

"What do you mean?" says Summer. "Doesn't he do any shopping?"

I can't even manage to stifle a rueful laugh. "Jarrod doesn't really do anything. I look after the apartment. He just comes and goes and I clean up after him. Brendan and I do the shopping, I just lug home whatever I can fit into a backpack."

Summer groans with audible exasperation. "I don't understand, Braddy. Why don't you just do it online and get it delivered?"

Bless her, always looking for practical solutions. As if I haven't already considered this a million times. "The website is such a strain to see and the order takes me so long, I only do it if I need to buy too much stuff to carry home. Otherwise, it's easier to just walk down to the shops and squint along the aisles using a magnifier."

"Sweetie…" Summer starts. "Um, are things really that bad with Jarrod?"

Here we go. "Yeah, they're not great. He's been drinking a lot for months. I know he's hitting the party drugs too, because he's so bloody erratic. I—" Ugh. I've never voiced this out loud. "I think sometimes he's on meth."

"Oh, God," gasps Summer. "You have to get out of this, darl. Really. Do you… do you still love him?"

"No." I don't even need to think about this, my body just expels the answer. "I prayed for so long that things'd go back to how they were at the start. It was so stupid of me; of course they weren't going to. And frankly, I don't care anymore, especially since I've started seeing—" I cut myself off. As desperate as I am to tell Summer about Bruno, I just can't bring myself to do it. I don't think anyone's going to understand what's happening between us. Maybe I'm getting ahead of myself. We're both with other partners, for God's sake. But in my head, this whole thing with him has gone way beyond sex and friendship.

"Started seeing what?" says Summer.

"Ugh. Nah, don't worry about it."

"No! Screw you, Braddy! You can't leave me hanging like this!"

I let out a long sigh, trying to think of a save. "Especially since I've started seeing him in a new light. Jarrod treats me like a doormat. I can't remember the last time he spoke to me like a human being. That's why this text he sent is so strange."

"You know, maybe it's an olive branch."

I consider this for a moment. "Possibly. Oh, what the hell." I start to text Jarrod a reply, reading it out to Summer as I type. "'*Thanks, Jarrod. Don't worry about shopping though. I'll organise dinner. See you at six.'* You think that sounds alright? Should I say 'Welcome home', or do you reckon that'd be too much?"

"Nah. Just leave it as it is."

With Summer still on speakerphone in my left hand, I hop around, trying to get into my new three-inch Puma running shorts. "Anyway, all I've done is go on about myself. What's happening with you? When are you all coming to Sydney?"

"Still a couple of months away. It's gonna be disruptive to the girls having to change schools, but they're only in kindy and Year Two, so they'll be OK."

"Gosh, they weren't even *in* school when I was last over there. How old are they now?"

"Turning six and eight. You haven't laid eyes on them in three years, Braddy. They still ask about you all the time."

Way to make me feel bad, Summer. "I'm so sorry. I'll be seeing all of you again really soon, so I promise I'll make it up to them."

The line goes quiet for a second. "Oh, gawd," Summer moans. "Here's the community transport bus. Guess she's decided to show up after all. I gotta go. But Braddy…"

"Yeah?"

"Really think about this shit with Jarrod, OK? And call me anytime. I'm worried about you."

"Don't be. I'll sort it out."

Well, that's a lie, Bradford, isn't it?

To complete my brand new outfit, I slip into a tight sky-blue Cricket Australia polo I've just bought. I'm such a fraud. I haven't played cricket since I was a schoolkid. But, damn, doesn't it look great on me. Once upon a time, I would hide myself behind baggy shirts. The uneasiness I felt at having any kind of love handles seeped into every cell of my body. It was my silent shame; a constant undercurrent of inadequacy pervading my entire existence.

Nowadays, I look in the mirror and I see a man with physical appeal. Yeah, I'm a bit of a porker, but it works for me. All that opera singing has given me a big barrel chest. Couple that with my tree-trunk thighs, and I'm the best kind of bear. Anyone who doesn't like it can kiss my hairy arse.

The second Brendan spots me emerging from the bedroom carrying my work boots, he snaps to it. I listen to the click-clack of his feet on the tiled floor in the laundry, hear the jingling sound as he collects his harness and leash, then grin like a twit at his little dance routine when he returns. How the hell could I *not* take my precious boy for a decent walk after that kind of performance dedication?

I'm so glad I stayed up late and finished marking those assignments. With no teaching work hanging over my head, today's walk is so much more relaxed. It's sunny and hot, but there's a persistent breeze rolling in from the ocean. When my legs, my butt and my dog have had their required workout, I stop in at Woolworths. Brendan knows his way around this place better than I do, and he's very happy to steer me directly to the meat section. I haven't really thought about what to make Jarrod for dinner, so I scan the shelves. My eyes are immediately drawn to a pile of pink, shrink-wrapped packets. *Corned silverside.*

I remember making this for Jarrod several years ago, way back at the beginning. He'd raved about how it was his favourite, so I spent a good few hours cooking the whole shebang one evening when he was coming over for dinner. I simmered the beef for two hours with onions and turnips and carrots and vinegar and brown sugar. Then, I served it up to him smothered in parsley sauce.

I remember Jarrod's reaction. He wasn't just blown away, he was visibly emotional. I could see his eyes glistening in the candlelight as he quietly spoke. "You made this exactly like my nan used to before she died," he said. The vulnerability in his smile cut right to my core. Later that night, he held me in bed, stroking my beard. As he studied my features, the same vulnerability he'd shown at dinner came over him. "I love you, Brad," he whispered. It was the first time he'd ever said those three little words.

Yes, things *were* good between us once. I'd just look at him and I'd feel truly alive. Desirable. Like I was of some value as a person. I don't know what happened. I don't know where those feelings went. I certainly don't know what I did to deserve his animosity.

As I'm rummaging through the display to find the smallest piece of pickled beef in there, I can't help but wonder if it's a wise move trying to dredge up a memory like this with Jarrod. I know it won't rescue the love we once shared, but maybe it'll give him pause to think. Maybe he'll consider being a little kinder to me. That's all I'm asking for.

Brendan's been sitting there patiently, his furry doggy butt parked on the cold floor next to me as I've been staring at the hunks of meat. I dump the silverside in my basket, then spot some large soup bones on the bottom shelf. "You want one of these this arvo, buddy?" *Ha. Stupid question.* I plonk the meatiest one I can find in the basket next to the beef, then realise I'll need to get something for myself. I want something easy, something that doesn't require too much fuss to make while the beef is cooking.

This is one of the things I found the most frustrating when I lost my vision. All of a sudden, things in the kitchen became way more difficult. I could still see well enough to cook simple dishes, but with tunnel vision, poor clarity and slow visual reflexes, I could no longer dart my eyes around willy-nilly. Tending to a host of kitchen tasks all at once was out of the question. These days, I have to carefully plan and predict pitfalls. I have to have everything set out and ready, as if I was on a TV cooking program—one of the proper old-fashioned ones, not those stupid modern reality-show ones where they all run around bitching at each other.

Steering Brendan to the vegetable section—he doesn't seem quite so enthusiastic about this leg of the journey—I pick up the carrots and turnips and onions. Next stop is the bakery, where I grab a crusty grain sourdough, followed by the cheese section, where I pick up a wedge of imported pecorino. My final stop is in the grocery aisles, where I buy some thick spiral pasta and a few jars of antipasto goodies.

On my way home, with my stuffed backpack weighing down my shoulders, I feel a sudden pang of doubt. I'm waiting at a crossing light and I reach down to ruffle Brendan's head. "You reckon I've gone overboard here, buddy? Do I look desperate?"

Desperate. A shudder goes through me. I'm certainly not desperate to rekindle anything sexual with Jarrod. It's not just because I've got a hot new Italian… Italian *what*? What do I call him? I hate that 'f'-buddy word. It makes it sound like all we do is cop each other's dicks up our arseholes. Bruno is my… *paramour.* Yes, I like the sound of that. It's illicit, it's *verboten*, but it's sensual.

"No, this definitely isn't about Bruno, OK?" I say.

Brendan glances up at me with his best *'What the hell are you waffling on about?'* expression.

"Jarrod just doesn't like us anymore. But we're cool with that, aren't we?" I reach down and ruffle Brendan's neck.

He snaps to attention as he hears the crossing light go off. To my left, a woman comes into view, turning her head and shooting us a bemused smile. Gee, I must look like a complete madman having these detailed discussions with my labrador in public.

"Why on earth do I put up with his crap, buddy?" I say as we round the next corner. "Why do I keep him around? Am I really that pissweak? Why can't I confront him, eh?"

Brendan doesn't respond; he's too busy concentrating. But I know the answer: Yes, I am weak. I know I won't tackle this right now, I'll just let sleeping dogs lie. When the time comes, I'll make my move. At least that's what I always tell myself.

***

Back at home, Brendan and I have a couple of hours to spend out on the lawn—me lying on the picnic blanket listening to my audiobook, and him annihilating his bone. I watch him there as he attacks the grotesque item. The joy it brings him is priceless. I wouldn't swap these little moments for anything.

I'm the first to admit I'm a shocking gardener. I have zero talent for keeping plants alive. However, I have managed to successfully grow several herbs in the box outside my kitchen window. My parsley is thriving right now and it comes in handy tonight, tossed through Jarrod's meat and veggies, and thrown in liberal amounts into the thick white sauce. While the meat is busy cooking, I rustle up my all-time favourite vego pasta dish, with onions, garlic, green chillies, artichokes, sun-dried tomatoes and kalamata olives.

I've organised it so everything's all done by six-fifteen. There's no way I'd ever expect Jarrod to be home on time, but I wanted dinner to be well underway in the event he did actually show up when he said he would. It feels pathetic, worrying about things like this. But I've put in a lot of effort and I don't want that to be tarnished if he gets back here and it looks like I'm nowhere near ready.

I sit there at the nicely-laid table, and I wait. Much longer than I should. It gets to the point where I know dinner will be ruined if I don't eat it. So, I do. I dish myself up a king-sized bowl of pasta, shave tons of pecorino on top, and eat till I'm stuffed full. In between mouthfuls, I help myself to sourdough with lashings of Lurpak butter. It's decadent and I'm determined to enjoy every bite.

When I'm done, I stare at the table, at the napkins and cutlery and glassware and side plates and breadboard. And I feel embarrassed. Gathering as many things as I can, I make my way to the kitchen. There in the low oven, I spot the silverside, still clinging to life.

Why did I bother? What's wrong with me? What did I expect? Am I really surprised? It's my fault. It's definitely my fault. I'm an idiot and I should have known better.

Pulling out the casserole dish from the oven, I grab a knife and hack the beef to bits. All it amounts to in the end is a couple of handfuls of sad slices.

"Hey, buddy," I call out. Brendan's there in a flash, sitting tall in front of me. One by one, I hand-feed the morsels to my best friend, smiling at the way he beams after every bite.

Seeing as Jarrod's not home, I decide to put on a movie after dinner. Brendan's not allowed on the couch, but I deliberately bought one with removable seat cushions. I arrange a couple of them on the floor in front of the couch and sit down on them. As soon as I'm in position, Brendan lies next to me and rests his head on my lap. It's our little cinema ritual and it's something we only get to do on occasion. Jarrod won't be pleased if he sees it. I can just hear him now: *"You treat that bloody dog like it's a child."* At this late stage, though, I couldn't care less. I've gone above and beyond for him today and he can go to hell.

There's still no sign of Jarrod when I'm getting ready for bed. Once upon a time, I used to sleep naked. I loved that sensation of complete freedom; it made me feel sexy. But after a while living with Jarrod, it started to make me feel shame. More specifically, Jarrod made me feel shame. These days, I wear boxers. I guess I'm not as confident as I thought.

Brendan wanders into the bedroom, just like he does every night. He gives the space a cursory check, then comes up and gently touches his nose on my leg. Satisfied that I'm OK, he trots off back out to the lounge room to his own bed.

I am loved. This is my final thought before I fall asleep.

***

It seems like hours later when I'm woken by Jarrod barging through the bedroom door. There's not a hint of consideration for the fact I'm in here sleeping. He's clearly in a foul mood, tossing his bag down and swearing at God knows what. At times like these, I'd normally keep a low profile. But his careless entrance adds insult to injury after his no-show tonight.

"Where were you, Jarrod?"

"Caught up with Davo. Not that it's any of your business." Jarrod's rifling through his bag. I can see his dark form hunched down. I can hear zips being wrenched open. I can also hear objects being tossed all over the floor. The floor that I tidied when Jarrod left.

"So, what was that text about being home for dinner at six?"

Jarrod lets out a huff. "What are you? My bloody keeper? I don't have to answer to you. It's my life and I'll do what I damn well want."

I'm trying my best to control myself. "After I got your message, I went shopping. I bought a ton of food and lugged it all back here. I made silverside and veggies exactly the way you like it, then I sat there for ages waiting for you to show up."

"Well, I never asked you to do that." Jarrod's using his arrogant sing-song voice. "Stop your bitching. I'll fuckin' eat it tomorrow."

"Too late. I fed it to Brendan."

Jarrod stands up, turning on me. It's dark in here, but I know him so well I can sense the way he's leering. "Jesus, you and that *fuckin'* dog of yours." I watch his silhouette as he throws whatever he's holding on the floor. "Anyway, why are you always around? Can't I get a bit of peace and quiet without you lurking in my fuckin' space?"

"This is *my* bedroom too, Jarrod."

"Oh really? Well it's *my* bed!"

"Because I got rid of mine when you moved in!" This is escalating fast. My heart is racing and I'm starting to wish I'd never said anything, but I don't seem to be able to stop myself. "Why don't you go and sleep in the study if you want some space?"

Jarrod rips the blanket and sheet off the bed, throwing them across the room. "No, *you* go and sleep in the fuckin' study." He switches on the light, exposing me as I'm cowering on the mattress in my underwear. The look of repulsion on his face robs me of any self esteem I've been able to rekindle in his absence. "In fact, you can take all your shit with you. I don't want you in here anymore."

I've never felt more pitiful, more lame, more *worthless* than I do right now. With my tail between my legs, I grab as many things off my bed-side table as I can and slink out. In the lounge room, I feel a cold nose against my leg. Brendan's been waiting. He's heard what was going on and he's worried about me. I could just about cry right now.

"Come on, buddy," I whisper, and lead him into the study. After plonking down my salvaged items on the desk, I shut the door behind us. Bruno and I have slept in this room every time he's been over, so I have sheets and blankets folded underneath the sofa. Brendan sits quietly as I make up the bed and slip under the covers. "You wanna get up?" I pat the mattress.

He seems confused for a minute. This is something that never hap-pens. He *always* sleeps in his bed. But I'm not about to go out there and drag it in here. I can hear Jarrod moving around making noise and I don't want to run into him again right now. When I pat the mattress once more, Brendan suddenly twigs. This is a *treat.* With lightning speed, he hops up to settle on the end of the sofa bed. "This is just for *one night*, OK?" I may as well be speaking Swahili, but Brendan can read my tone. I'm sure he understands. Settling back, I hope like hell I can recapture the remainder of tonight's sleep.

There are all kinds of sounds going on out there now. I don't think Jarrod's trashing the place, it's not loud enough. *He wouldn't be moving furniture at this time of night, would he?* I close my eyes and try to tune it out. Whatever it is, I'll deal with it tomorrow. Somehow, I manage to bring my focus onto my breathing, listening to the sound of my body inhaling and exhaling.

The door bursts open and something slaps against my face. Light is streaming in from the lounge room and Jarrod's standing at the door, hands on his hips. I grope around and pick up the item that hit me. It's a dildo. It's *my* dildo. He's clearly been going right through my stuff because I have it well-hidden. I should be mortified, but it's hard to keep a straight face as I hold the big eight-inch dong and look back at Jarrod. I never actually cared about the fact Jarrod's dick is nothing to write home about. But I know it's a sore point with him. And he knows this is exactly what I'm thinking as he slams the door.

My sleep is turbulent and I wake up early. I don't want to go out there if Jarrod's around. It seems quiet. Maybe he's still asleep. No, no—maybe he's doing an early shift. He hates working those, he only does them when he's desperate for the money. *And he has just been away for weeks*. That would explain last night: his supposed intention for dinner at six, his foul mood when he got in late. *Please, please let him have left already.*

I decide to chance it. Brendan needs to go outside for his dunny run, anyway. When I open the study door, I'm met with mayhem. All my stuff has been thrown on the floor or tossed over the couch. The shelving unit that held my folded clothes has been dragged out and unceremoniously dumped on its side. My shorts and t-shirts and underwear are now spilling out of their baskets in all directions. My hanging rack is upended; pretty much thrown from Jarrod's doorway. *Yes, it's Jarrod's doorway now.*

The impact of this scene is too much for me to handle right now. A wet nose tentatively brushes against my hand. I glance down to see Brendan standing beside me, his usual morning enthusiasm replaced by a quiet and sombre countenance. "Oh, buddy. I'm so glad I didn't leave you out here last night."

Slowly and carefully, I pick my way through the mess, looking closely at the floor to avoid stepping on anything. The only time my eyes leave the carpet is to check for signs of Jarrod. Squinting into the bedroom, I'm relieved to see that it's devoid of human occupants. Down the hall in front of me, I spot the open bathroom door and note the lack of any noise coming from there. *Thank God.*

After I've pulled on some clothes from the mess, Brendan and I make a pit stop through the laundry for his leash and harness and doggie bags, then we're straight out the back door. It's such a relief to escape the apartment and all that bad energy in there. Sinking down into one of my dilapidated plastic chairs, I stare at the blurry figure of my dog. I envy the simple joy he finds in things. You'd think he'd been taken on a special outing, the way he roves across our meagre strip of grass.

"It doesn't seem like it right now, but this is for the greater good, Bradford."

My mother's voice makes me jump for a split second. It shouldn't, in all honesty. This is exactly the kind of moment she might have shown up for in the past. "Nice of you to drop in, mum. It's been a little while."

"You were doing really well, Bradford. There was no need for me to hang around."

"Tell me, mum—in all this time, have you ever visited Summer like this?" It's only now that I turn around and spot her there, lounging back in the chair next to me with her right leg casually slung over her left. She has a kind smile on her face, that warm expression that always made me feel better as a child, no matter what.

"Summer has Nathan and her girls. A career she loves. She's truly happy."

I know what mum's trying to say, I really do. But I feel wretched. Loser Bradford with his lame excuse for a life. She can't even escape me in death.

"Darling, don't *ever* feel like I'm here out of some begrudging sense of pity. I know I always tell you I can only show up when I'm needed, but you know what?" She pauses till I make eye contact with her again. "I'll take it. *Any* chance that I get to see you again is a blessing, you understand?"

"It's the same for me, mum." My voice is the faintest whisper. I feel like I should speak up, but I can see in mum's eyes that the message has got through. It's like this connection is… *otherworldly.* That word is just a little bit too obvious, though. I can never be sure if mum is actually here. As this thought runs through my mind, her image begins to fade. "Don't go!" I cry out. The knee-jerk desperation in my voice shocks me, but it's exactly what the doctor ordered: slowly, her form becomes more opaque again. "You're right. I need you, Mum. I don't even know how to move on from here."

She reaches out to me. Her right hand tries to touch my cheek, but it stops short and I notice the pain in her expression. I notice the way she draws in a deep breath. I notice the effort she's making to hold herself together. It takes her a while, but eventually she begins to talk. "Bradford, this is the first step. This is the beginning of the end for you and Jarrod. And you didn't even have to lift a finger—Jarrod did it all for you. The next move should be yours. And you'll know when it's time to make it." As her image fades again, she mouths the words: *I love you.*

"I love you too, Mum," I whisper to the empty chair beside me.

Back inside the apartment, I survey the damage once more. *This is for the greater good. This is for the greater good.* Mum's words buzz round in my head like a mantra as I bend down and begin to pick up the pieces of my life.

CHAPTER 9

BRADFORD: Brendan and I are all packed and ready for the trek over there. See you within the hour!

Bradford's text comes just as I'm switching on the aircon in the bedroom. I've already got the one on in the lounge room, because the temperature outside is rising fast. Spring stuck around for a long time last year—things were pretty mild, even in December. Now, the late arrival of summer means we're still paying the price in March.

BRUNO: Hang on a minute, you're not walking here are you? It'll take you forever and it's gonna be a bloody hot day.

BRADFORD: Relax, Harry. It's only ten a.m. and it's not gonna hit the high temps till this afternoon. Plus, Google tells me your place is only forty-one minutes' walk from mine.

I love that he's using the little nickname he gave me. *'Harry'* and *'Blinky'* may have started as a silly joke on that first night we fucked, but it wasn't long before the cutesy monikers kind of crept into our banter here and there.

BRUNO: If you or Brendan get too hot or tired or anything at all, you make sure you call me, OK? I'll be right there.

I'm embarrassed to admit that we've been rooting each other for like, a month and a half, and Bradford has never been to my place. The kinda 'Don't Ask, Don't Tell' arrangement that *my* Brendan and I had together made it impossible to bring hookups here to the apartment. But if I was to put myself in Bradford's shoes, the fact that I've never invited him over could easily make him think I'm just screwing around behind my partner's back. I would hate it if he ever got that impression of me.

Brendan and I gave it a really good shot before we admitted we weren't happy sexually. At the time, deciding to open the relationship seemed like the best way to move forward. I never publicised it beyond my closest friends—I've found that outside of other gay men, very few people seem to understand. Most of them are too busy having secret affairs while they tell the world they're in a happy monogamous marriage.

I did talk about it all with Gabriela, though. Obviously, as twins, we've always been thick as thieves. There was no way I would have been able to keep my situation with Brendan a secret from her. In any case, she's no cishet conservative; she's like a gay man trapped in a woman's body. Her camp sense of humour and raucous theatrics are much more drag queen than middle-aged mum.

So, I'm hoping to clear the air with Bradford when he arrives today. I've whipped him up a huge salad and antipasto platter for lunch. I've also bought four-legged Brendan a big rawhide chew bone—something I hope keeps him occupied while I fuck the hell out of his owner. I'm in a particularly cock-horny mood and I've been craving that hot little manhole of Bradford's for days now.

Me and my hard dick are standing in front of the open fridge, trying to decide whether to take the antipasto platter out, when I hear a discreet little buzz in the hallway. It's so polite, so very *Bradford.* And he's really prompt—he definitely didn't dawdle on the way here.

I slide the platter back onto the shelf it came from, then shut the fridge and scurry out to the intercom next to the front door. "Hey, sexy! I'll come down and show you the way." I wince as soon as I've said it. I'm such a fucking clumsy dickhead. When it comes to Bradford, I have no idea how to offer help without looking like I'm patronising him.

"Nah, that's OK—I'll be able to find you no worries.
Thanks, though."

I can hear the cheery smile in Bradford's voice. He's like this all the time. Sweet and upbeat and eager to please, as if he's lucky I'm paying him attention. If only he knew how much I've come to rely on the kind of happiness I feel when I'm around him.

"Gee, it's nice in here," says Bradford, as I bustle him and four-legged Brendan into the hallway. Bradford looks super hot, in both senses of the word. Of course, he's sexy as fuck. But I suspect the walk was a little more taxing in the heat than he'd bargained for. Brendan, for one, is panting like a trouper. Before Bradford does anything else, he stretches up to kiss me. It's long and soft and gentle, and a synergistic sense of relief crackles between us. God, this little bloke knows exactly how to make me feel like priority number one.

"As much as I wanna ravage you, I think you'd both better come in and cool off first." My lips buzz against Bradford's as I speak and he gives the tiniest little grunt, enough to let me know he'd have preferred more. I hold my hand out for Bradford's backpack, which he passes to me before squatting down to undo Brendan's harness. I size up the heavy bag. "What on earth have you got in here?"

Bradford chuckles as he stands up and takes it back from me. "Standard baby bag. Everything I need to keep a bored labrador occupied." He looks around him. "Are you gonna give me the grand tour?"

"Ah, there's not much to see. The bathroom and laundry are back here." I point to the end door. "This is the bedroom here." I show him the doorway in front of me and Bradford pokes his head inside. "And if you follow me, I'll take you through to the lounge room and kitchen."

"Is this a one bedroom place?" asks Bradford, as he follows me into the lounge. He's sounding chirpy and friendly, not suspicious or judgemental, but I still can't stop myself cringing.

"Uh, kind of." I show him through to the small study. "Brendan use—" I stop myself saying *'used to'* just in time, covering it up with a little cough. "Brendan *usually* sleeps in here, but as you can see, it's not really a room, just an alcove."

"Oh, right." Bradford seems mildly surprised. "I… um… didn't realise you two were kind of like Jarrod and me."

I look at him for a moment, trying to work out what he's referring to, but there's no obvious parallel here. There's certainly no way he could be referring to the emotional abuse I'm sure he's being subjected to. He's always been a bit vague around the topic, but I'm hardly surprised. People in his situation are embarrassed. They feel like they're at least partly responsible. I'd love it if Bradford opened up to me; I could offer him so much support. But, other than listening openly and somehow letting him know I'm on his side no matter what, all I can do is wait patiently till he feels comfortable enough to share.

Bradford smiles weakly at my pregnant pause; at my baffled expression. "I haven't really had a chance to tell you this, but there was a bit of an ugly confrontation and I was sort of… uh… banished to the spare room on a permanent basis."

My hackles are immediately raised. "What the *fuck?* Are you OK?" I reflexively look him over, hoping and praying there are no physical marks.

Bradford notices and his hand shoots to his cheek. I've never seen someone look so mortified. "No, nothing like that. Jarrod's just a bit of a prick. There's never been anything physical."

It's my turn to look mortified now. "Jesus, I'm sorry, Bradford. I didn't mean to—" I cut myself off. There's nothing I can add here that will make my assumption look any better. Hauling him into my arms, I pull him tight against me and kiss his sweaty brow. I love how short he is. I feel so powerful, so protective when I hold him like this. "And to answer your question, no. Brendan and I have been lucky in a way. The relationship just kind of morphed." I glance over Bradford's shoulder at the neatly-pfaffed day bed. My partner is impeccably tidy. It's one of the things that's always helped us get along so well. *Got along, Bruno. Past tense, remember?* "He's a bit of a night owl and generally crashes in here. Occasionally, I might wake up and he's in bed next to me."

This is starting to make me squirm. Bradford deserves to know at least some of what's happening here, but I'm not sure how far to go with it. Before I can open my mouth again, he breaks our embrace with a smile and slides his backpack off. Unzipping it, he pulls out a plastic disc and some kind of folded canvas thing. "Do you mind if I fill this?" He pops out the plastic disc and it turns into a dog bowl.

"Oh, God! Yeah, of course." I look down at four-legged Brendan, patiently waiting as I've been waffling on about my domestic situation.

"That all sounds a bit stressful for you," says Bradford as he follows me through to the kitchen. "I mean, you never really know where you stand, do you? At least I have a spare room to move into. It kind of gives me a boundary that Jarrod can't cross. We've gone from sharing like a couple to living like flatmates." Bradford looks up at me as he's filling the bowl in the sink. "I've still ended up vacating the living room whenever he's been around, though." He seems resigned. Beaten. I wish I could do something to help him.

"Bradford…" I falter, almost choking on my words. He's looking at me attentively, eyebrows slightly raised. "I'm so sorry I've never had you over here. I *swear* it's not how it looks. Brendan and I are like brothers. We're not physically involved, and we *are* open. He really does have more than his fair share of sex with other guys. It's just…" How the hell do I explain this? "We agreed that we wouldn't tell each other any details about our hookups and fuckbuddies, if that makes sense."

I really want to tell Bradford about the separation, but I don't think I can bring myself to do it. It's all too early in the piece, and Bradford has enough to cope with. If I mention I'm going to be single again, he might feel pressured into making a decision he's not ready for, and I don't want to stress him out. Even though it's only been a whirlwind six weeks, I don't want to lose what we have together. If all we're ever going to be is fuckbuddies, I'll take it. Hands down, I will.

I decide to just give him the necessary details. "Brendan's taken off to house-sit in Surry Hills for the rest of March and most of April. I would have mentioned it, but he only told me a few days ago. It all sounds a bit suspicious, I know."

"Why?" Bradford seems genuinely confused.

"It looks like I'm just inviting you around because he's gone away. But Bradford—" I cup his face in my hands and stare into his stormy eyes. "He does know about you." *Bloody hell, I'm making a right dog's breakfast of this.* "I mean, I've told him I'm, um… seeing a guy on a casual basis."

Bradford grabs my hands, pulling them from his cheeks and placing a gentle kiss on each one. He looks up at me earnestly. "Bru, I believe you. I know this isn't an easy situation. I'm just glad we'll be able to spend more time together."

"We will, *Blinky*. You got my word on that."

With a bashful little grin, Bradford turns away and retrieves the canvas item he brought with him. "Well, *Harry*, I'm in danger of ripping off those clothes you're wearing, so I'm going to have to take care of this right now." He undoes a valve and starts inflating what turns out to be some kind of dog mat. With his colossal opera-singer lungs, he has it pumped up in no time. Placing it on the carpet, he whistles to Brendan, who dutifully lies down on it.

"Gee, you certainly do come prepared." I grin over at Bradford, who's fishing out a packet of dog treats from his bag. "Oh—I got your little mate a present." Darting over to the kitchen counter, I retrieve the rawhide bone I bought and hand it to the handsome lab. I swear his face lights up as he immediately clamps his jaws over it.

"Wow, buddy, aren't you lucky? What do you say to Bruno?" Brendan doesn't even look up when Bradford speaks, but his tail thumps repeatedly against the dog bed in acknowledgement.

I catch Bradford's gaze. He's been smiling at me, observing the way I was beaming down at his dog. Bradford looks at me like this often. It speaks volumes, but it never fails to send a jolt of pain through my heart. It's because of what's written all over his face. Loud and clear, his expression says: *I can't believe there's someone who's being this nice to me.*

There's so much I want to tell him. I want him to know how much lighter my life seems since he came into it. I want him to know how his positive energy works its way into every aspect of my existence; every day there just seems so much more to be happy about. I want to tell him how he's made me feel truly hot for the first time in years: like I'm not just a big cock, I'm not just a bear who's sexy enough for one fuck and that's it. I am a man who deserves to be appreciated completely. I'm a man who deserves the same kind of unadulterated affection and sexual worship that I freely give out. I thought I was done. I thought this kind of confidence was gone for the rest of my life, but Bradford and his generous heart brought it all back to me.

For now, though, I'm not going to open my big fat trap. This isn't the time and place. I can't say I'm too worried—I'm pretty certain it'll soon be all over with that arsehole boyfriend of his. Now that they're in separate bedrooms, the countdown has begun. I'll be there for Bradford when they split. I'll wait until that precious heart of his is mended, and then he'll see that I'm worth taking on.

This is my fantasy. I know it hasn't been long. I know Brendan and I have only just agreed to break up. But I need to believe, and I don't give a flying fuck what anyone else thinks.

I'm riled up now. I grab Bradford by the shoulders, steer him around and push him against the wall. Yanking the hem of his t-shirt, I pull it straight over his head and bury my face in his armpit. "Oh, Jesus *fuck,*" I moan as the fresh scent of his musk invades my nostrils. Without conscious thought, my thumb finds its way to his right nipple and begins to stroke the tip of it. Bradford's immediate whine makes me vacate the heady pleasure of his hairy pit so I can latch my lips onto his other nipple. I'm an expert at this now. He likes it sucked fast and light, he loves my tongue darting over the end of his little teat, he goes crazy when I gently flick it against my teeth as I feed on him. I can feel his arm moving slightly and I know exactly what he's doing. It's like his pre-masturbation technique—he's just running his fingers over his knob, jiggling the hot little PA ring. God, I'm so envious of the mileage he gets out of that thing. If I wasn't such a wimp with pain, I'd have one of them too.

All this thought of Bradford's dick has me grabbing at the lower edge of his little jogging shorts. With one sharp tug they're down. I'm fully expecting underwear, but Bradford's hard cock springs straight out, slapping against his abdomen. Glancing at the fabric now pooled at his ankles, I see they're those kind of running shorts that are so skimpy they have the briefs sewn into them. "Jesus, Bradford! You and your slutty pants… you are so *fucking hot.*" I'm on my knees in an instant. Grabbing his penis and holding it upwards, I bury my nose in his sweaty balls and breathe deep. "*Fu-u-u-u-ck*," I half-laugh, half-whimper. "How do you smell this good?"

Bradford's panting, his hands running over my scalp, stroking it with reverence. "*Harry*," he chokes out. "*Your* scent is so bloody hot it turns me into a filthy, desperate whore."

"I fuckin' love it when you talk like that," I growl, swinging him around and flinging him onto the couch. It takes less than two seconds to have his legs pushed high in the air, his arsehole fully exposed and my nose and lips grinding right against it. "Jeeeesus… and I *love* your hairy cunt."

"You're so dirty," Bradford giggles, his hips squirming as I rub my face in even more vigorously.

Oh, I can do much worse than that. "Dirty? What? Because I'm turned on by this hot little shitter?"

Bradford laughs so hard his arse thwacks against my chin. "'*Shitter*'? You've been watching far too much porn."

I slather my tongue broadly across his taut pucker. "Nah, porn's total bullshit. I learnt it all from magazines like *Honcho* and *Bear* and *Inches*."

"Really? God, I haven't seen one of those since the nineties."

"They were my staple wank diet all through my late teens and twenties. Those stories in them were fucking filthy. I'd work my dick into a frenzy reading them and then flick over the pages to a hot naked bear when I was about to come." I push the tip of my tongue just inside his ring, teasing it open slightly, then move my head back to admire the view. "Preferably a man in the same position you're in right now. Legs over your shoulders, showing me your cock and balls and cute hole."

Bradford's dick stiffens, flexing against his belly at my description. "Tell me more."

His lusty tone makes me chuckle. "And here I've been, dying to get as nasty with you as possible, but holding back because you're so sweet and lovely."

"Sweet and lovely? No bloody way!" Bradford chortles as I grin up at his face, my lips so close to his hole that it's brushing against me with every joyous little laugh. "Haven't you noticed how I worship every hotspot on your furry body? I've practically taken up residence in your crotch."

"Oh? So you're telling me after all this time that you're super fuckin' kinky?"

"Um, maybe." He sounds all coy. "I'd say I'm… 'vanilla bear with extras.'"

I slide a finger into his tight little back passage, making him grunt. "And what exactly does 'vanilla bear with extras' mean, Bradford?"

"You know, like all the bear stuff I do with you, and even a bit kinkier. But no whips or chains. No cock cages, no nipple clamps, no bossing me around."

"Hmm. This is getting interesting." My stiff prick is still all cooped up in my thin shorts and underwear, and I rub it against the edge of the couch as I push up Bradford's legs a bit further. His finger is jiggling against the ring in his knob, making his dick leak visibly. "So… 'even a bit kinkier', you reckon? What else does that involve?"

Breaking into a smug grin, Bradford wraps his hand around his girth and begins to stroke. "Let's chug down a few beers and you'll see what a pig I can be."

My shaft tenses hard and I grind my knob into the couch again. "Watersports? You're driving me up the fucking wall! So I'm guessing you have a thing for boots and sweaty jockstraps too, then?"

"Actually, I prefer your tighty-whities, Bru. Something that spends all day nestled between your arse cheeks. Haven't you noticed I stole a pair from you last week?"

"Oh, I wondered where they went. You filthy little bastard."

Bradford looks pleased as punch with my assessment. "Yep. I pilfered them from your pile of dirty clothes."

"And how were they?"

"Not musky enough," he chirps. "I want you to wear them for a lot longer."

"Right. That's *it.*" I spread Bradford's legs wider and scooch around a bit. Just as I'm thrusting my tongue into his hole again, I spot four-legged Brendan out of the corner of my eye. "Uh, do you think he minds?" I jerk my head in the direction of the labrador, who's still wholly absorbed in his rawhide bone.

"Nah. He's facing the other way. But we'd probably be more comfortable in your bed, you reckon?"

That's all the encouragement I need. "Come on." I'm up on my feet straight away, ripping off my clothes and tossing them aside. Bradford stays there with his legs in the air and watches me. Slowly and deliberately, he pulls his arse cheeks wide apart and slips a finger inside his little brown hole. The cheeky grin on his face brings out the animal in me, and I grab his hand and yank him off the couch with urgency. Clasping his shoulders with one of my big paws, I try and steer him in front of me, but he ducks and moves behind instead.

"You first," he says. "I want to watch your arse while you walk." Aware of his eyes boring into my buttocks, I puff up like a peacock.

I'm thrilled that he likes my hairy bum. He shuffles up close to me as I reach the hallway. Immediately, I feel fingers sliding into my arse crack, hitting my bullseye and rubbing insistently. Bradford just can't leave my arse alone. After countless years of men who only ever wanted me to fuck them, it's a refreshing change. In fact, I'm well and truly addicted to the amount of anal attention he lavishes on me.

The bedroom is dark with the blinds drawn. I'm far too anxious to be all over Bradford to bother going and tackling them, but I still want the best view possible. Climbing onto the mattress, I bend right over and reach out to switch on the bedside table lamp. I feel Bradford's face slam right into my arse and he rubs his beard and nose and moustache around vigorously. "Jesus, you're perfect," he growls, before he jams his tongue right up my arsehole. Fuck, it's fast becoming my favourite thing. Resting on my shoulder with my face buried sideways on the mattress, I reach down and roll my nipple piercing between my fingers. My other hand finds its way straight to my cock. I breathe a sigh of relief as the familiar pleasure causes my erectile muscles to throb. Pulling my foreskin back, I wrap my thumb and forefinger just below my knob and pulse hard. Bradford is going at my arse like a lion at a carcass, grunting and thrashing and poking his tongue in as deep as it can go. I could easily start flogging my dick. Just a tiny shift of my hand and I'd fall straight into the pattern I've been using all my life. And I would come so fucking hard and fast. Any other time, I wouldn't be able to resist it. But today, I need to be inside his hot arse. I need to feel his muscly little ring strangling my rigid prick. I need those blond furry buns of his slapping against my groin with every thrust I send up his fucktunnel. I need to hear him scream.

Just when I'm about to scoot out from under him, Bradford's fingers slide inside my hole. I'm sure there are two; the stretch is so fucking good. And they are straight onto my prostate, carefully strumming it as he twists and pistons them up and down. My hole tightens over and over. It's intense. Exquisitely intense. I can't believe the things this man can do. I can't believe I've been drifting blindly through life without experiencing this kind of utter fucking bliss.

I'm moaning hard. I don't even consciously realise it at first, but the second I do, I flip over and tackle Bradford to the bed face-down. "You are *not* gonna make me shoot my load just yet, mate," I snarl. "Your arse needs a good hard pounding first."

Bradford turns his head and I can see the side of his grin. His teeth are showing and his right eye is twinkling and I just want to devour the little bastard. "You won't get any complaints from me," he coos, and thrusts his arse upwards.

I can't wait a moment longer. My cock is so hard it's sore as fuck. I collapse onto his back, stretch over to the bedside table, and grab the lube, pumping it manically into my hand. I'm getting it everywhere, but I don't give a flying fuck. So long as it's all over my dick and his hole, we're set.

Bradford backs up onto my fingers as soon as I start rubbing his little pucker. He's rutting against me, whining, desperately trying to consume my hand with his arse. *God, I wonder how many digits I could get up there?* My cock throbs hard, reminding me it needs attention. Slipping my fingers from Bradford's wet hole, I position my knob against it.

Bradford's hand reaches around and grabs my hip, yanking me towards him. "I need it, Bruno," he pants. "Please. Now."

I try to be gentle, gradually applying pressure. But Bradford bucks his backside against my cock the same way he did with my fingers. Only this time, he does it with the force of a fucking rhino. Every inch of me drives right through his hot little browneye, plunging me straight into heaven.

"YES!" he yells. "Oh God, yes!"

Obviously, he's not hurt. He's made his desires pretty clear, so I don't waste a second. My fat Italian schlong needs friction *right fucking now*, and his arse is gonna cop it sweet. Straight away, I begin to ram into him. Fast, furious and hard as I can. And Bradford cries. Ecstatic moaning sobs rumble up from deep within his chest. I see him fumbling for the bottle of lube, then he drops his top half onto the mattress and reaches underneath himself to rub his cock. I *fucking love it* when he does that. I look sideways into the mirrored wardrobe. Angling myself slightly, I can see my thick inches sliding in and out, disappearing between his chunky butt cheeks. And I can see his hand moving up and down his rock-hard shaft, rubbing firmly over his knob in that beautiful way he does it.

Jesus, *fuck*, I'm not going to last. By the sounds of it, neither is Bradford. He looks so hot there on the bed, this dirty little bearslut with his fuckin' beautiful arse thrust right up, greedily seeking whatever pleasure I can give it. I gather more speed. Faster, harder. I'm clutching onto his hips, walloping them against my groin as I jam my cock up him. My butt muscles are burning in the best way. My cock feels like it's gonna burst. Bradford's manhole is so fiery, so wet, so muscular.

"Harder!" he wails.

"Harder *what*?" I growl.

"Harder, *please*," he whines. His arm is speeding up underneath him.

"No. *What do you want me to do harder*?" I'm gonna get this little fucker to show me how filthy he can be if it's the last thing I do.

"Pound me," he whimpers.

I slow down my thrusts, grinning like a wolf. I know he can't see me; his face is ground into the bed. But this is fucking *fun.* "You're gonna have to do better than that, mate."

Bradford groans, bucking his hips back onto my cock. "*Fuck* me!" he hollers. "Fuck me hard!"

Jesus, I love hearing that language coming out of his polite little mouth. With a roar, I pick up the pace, but I'm not giving it my all just yet. "Fuck you hard *where*?"

"Unnnnngh!" he chokes. "My *arse*! *Fuck my arse*!"

"Nup, not good enough." I stop dead in my tracks and Bradford bellows in protest. He's panting hard. His arsehole is squeezing my dick and I really want to fuck it into oblivion. I can't resist pulling out and slamming into him just one more time. That's all it takes for Bradford to get the hint.

"Fuuuck!" he screams. "My CUNT! Fuck my fuckin' hairy CUNT!"

Oh, my fucking GOD. The filthy way he says it pushes me over the edge. I batter that fucking little cunt as viciously as I can while Bradford shrieks at the top of his lungs. "Fuck, I'm gonna come!" he howls. A strangled, high-pitched caterwaul makes its way out of his throat and I feel his sphincter seizing up like a garrote. *Oh, Jesus, fuck me sideways with a chainsaw.* I can barely stand it. I'm going to explode. This is gonna be a deluge.

My knees tremble as my cock reaches its painful zenith. I'm bellowing as loud as I can. My arsehole clenches hard, my balls draw up tight, and almighty relief surges forth as I send my load shooting deep inside him. It's utterly fucking divine. I linger there a moment, relishing the last waves of my climax. I've driven a fucking torrent of come up his beautiful mancunt and I have never felt quite so powerful, so masculine, so bloody *invincible*. This little bear has raised me up so high. He's given me new hope. *He's given me a new lease on life.*

A wave of emotion overtakes me and I lower myself onto him, kissing the back of his neck. I feel like I could cry, but I'm saved from embarrassment when Bradford giggles and wiggles his arse underneath me. "Did I do good?" he says.

"You did fucking *incredible*," I croon into his ear. "You were dirty as fuck, and you gave me the best dickgasm I've had in I don't know how long."

"Dickgasm? You mean as opposed to an arsegasm?"

"Well, yeah. Those are different." I sniff deeply across the back of his head, taking in the scent of his sweat. "You send me to the bloody moon when you fuck my arse."

Bradford chuckles. "Where do you think I've just come back from? My hole has never been so well serviced." He wiggles his hips again. "And I would really love it if your dick stayed inside there a bit longer."

"Well, it depends. I made lunch. And it's all totally vego."

Bradford cranes his head around, turning his body underneath me. My cock slips out of his warm arse as he moves, and I miss it instantly. He's staring up into my eyes. Genuine surprise is written all over his face, and it claws at my chest. "You did that for me?"

My God. He doesn't think he's worth it? I run my hand down his cheek, cupping his beard. "Of course. You've cooked for me loads of times, it was the least I could do."

We shuffle onto our sides and lie there quietly face-to face, our hands lazily roaming the fur on each other's chests and arms. The world is silent, bar the low hum of the air conditioner. I'm spent and sated, my muscles sighing with relief as they sink into the mattress. My rounded belly is ergonomically pressed against Bradford's, allowing my back to straighten and relax completely. It's a bear thing—we're built for this sort of comfort.

From time to time, Bradford smiles up at me. The bashfulness of his expression warms my heart with its earnest glimpses of joy. I need to see him like this all the time. I worry so much about what's going on behind closed doors at his place.

"Are things really OK, Bradford? I mean, with Jarrod?" My thoughts just slip out as words. I probably should feel mortified, but to my surprise, I'm not. Maybe we're at the point now where this line of questioning is fine.

"Um, yeah. I guess we've reached a kind of stalemate for now. That whole showdown we had at the weekend was really stressful, but I spent the day setting myself up in the spare room and I realise I'm much happier with my own space. I feel like I can avoid him more easily now."

"You don't know how relieved I am to hear that." Of course, Bradford's safety is something I worry about and it puts my mind at rest to know he's taken this step. But I want so much more for him. I want to tell Bradford how I really feel. I want to spill my guts, appeal to him, beg him to give me a chance. I'm not going to do it, though; it isn't fair to him.

Taking a breath and burying those feelings as deep down as I can, I let just a sliver of them escape. "You deserve to be happy, Bradford. You deserve the world."

And one day, I'm gonna give it to you.

CHAPTER 10

Once again, the late onset of our summer has proven to be the gift that keeps on giving. After a few weeks where the heat has slowly abated, we're now blessed with a patch of super-sunny warm beach weather. I'm sure it's a final fling before summer says its last goodbye; it's not often we have these kinds of days at the end of March.

I've got up early and tidied the apartment, my efforts leaving me in a sweaty mess. After a long shower, then a good ten minutes sprawled naked in the aircon to cool down, I'm now dressed and ready and excitedly waiting for Bruno's arrival.

With the blue waters of Bondi a mere walk away, I haven't been to the Northern Beaches in many years. Right now, Bruno is coming to take me to his favourite spot up there. "It's a different experience to the eastern suburbs beaches," he told me when he called to suggest the outing. "There's more space, less crowds, bigger waves."

This man—I want to gush about him to everyone. Things between us have barrelled ahead so rapidly that my heart is in serious strife. I've never had a friend with benefits like this. In my experience, they've basically started with great sex, then the law of diminishing returns kicks in. You're lucky if you get a few good shags in before the whole "friendship" fizzles out altogether.

With Bruno, however, what began with a bang has moved in the opposite trajectory. My need for him is so all-consuming, so dire, that I constantly have to remind myself it can't go beyond what we have. These regular reality checks hurt more and more with every passing week. Two and a half months, it's been. Two and a half months with nothing but bliss. I don't know how that can be possible. Common sense tells me it won't last, but I'm going to ride the wave nonetheless. I'd be stupid not to.

Brendan's at the door whimpering long before I hear a knock. I swear he can detect the sound of Bruno's Kingswood all the way out the front of the building. The moment I open up, he's all over Bruno. He knows not to jump on people, but that's not good enough for Bruno, who crouches down and lavishes him with big neck rubs and hugs. "Hey matey," he croons. "You gonna give me some doggie love?"

Brendan responds enthusiastically, bombarding Bruno with rapid-fire licks behind his ear. I can only admire the way these two have clicked. After spending years with a man who has never really liked my dog, it's a refreshing sight to see this kind of open affection.

Bruno stands up, giving Brendan a final pat. "Off you go, matey," he says. "Time for me to say hello to dad." Bruno smiles at him as he trots back off to the lounge room, then turns his focus to me. Wrapping his arms around my shoulders, he presses his head against my neck. "Coconut," he mumbles.

"Yeah. Reef tanning oil."

"What, you don't use sunscreen? You'll get cancer." He brushes his nose playfully up my neck, sniffing hard as he goes.

"I use the SPF15 version. I'll be fine." My hands, as usual, have found their way under the waistband of Bruno's shorts to his arse. "What's this?" My palms brush over bare, furry flesh.

Bruno moves his head back, a wicked grin on his face. "Easy access swimwear. Loose little running shorts with no undies."

I move my hand all over Bruno's arse, relishing the way the hair on it caresses my palms. As I go, I work against the stretchy fabric of his shorts. I could easily slip my hand or cock up the leg of these. Jesus, just the thought of it is getting me super-horny. "So, you'll let me molest you in the water?"

"That's what I'm hoping for."

"You're a genius. Gimme a sec." I break free and push my work shorts and speedo to the ground. My semi-erect penis bounces out and Bruno's eyebrows shoot up.

"Are we having a quickie or something?" he says.

"I've just remembered I have some shorts a lot like the ones you're wearing. I expect to be molested too." Swivelling around, I bend down to pick up my discarded clothes. As I stand up again, shaking them out to fold them, my cock is suddenly immersed in warm wetness. Bruno's on his knees, his tongue pressing and massaging on the underside of my knob, his lips pulsing up and down my shaft, while he simultaneously sucks me like a Hoover. His technique is so intricate, so attentive, so bloody impressive that I'm at full mast immediately.

When his finger makes its way through my legs, past my balls and lands firmly on my arsehole, my cock surges and flexes. Bruno and I both moan in unison. Me? Well, that's obvious. Bruno knows exactly how to make me squirm and whine and even scream. And I know precisely why *Bruno's* making these noises. I've just flooded his mouth with precome, and he's sucking and swallowing extra hard now.

I'm steeped in a blessed state of euphoria. My thumbs are stroking my nipples and Bruno's finger is sliding into my arsehole, seeking out my prostate. With his beautifully-honed oral technique, I think there's a distinct possibility I may erupt inside his mouth and bombard the back of his throat with the load of spunk I've been storing up. Given the fact he's also playing with my arse, I'm closer to this goal than I've ever been.

Still, I'm gonna save it. Gently pulling away from him, I run my hands over his smooth scalp as he looks up at me quizzically. "Am I doing it wrong?"

"Ha! You're the best I've ever had by far," I tell him, "but I'm gonna stretch my come-budget as far as it'll go today." Bruno grins, and when he stands up, I land a playful slap on his buttock. "Giving this arse of yours a whole lot of love is number one on the agenda."

He follows me into my room, and I look back at him, noticing the bulge of his firm dick pushing against the floppy fabric of his shorts. This is dangerous. We're in our little sex den and we're both horny as hell. At this rate we will never get out of here.

"New sheets," chirps Bruno as he sprawls decadently across the sofa bed, the wrinkled end of his penis poking out the leg of his shorts.

"Um, no, actually." I turn and bend right over, rummaging through the bottom shelf of my clothes rack, pushing my arse out as far as I can because I know he's watching. "You just haven't been here in a few weeks."

"You know, it's been so nice having you come over to my place since I've had it to myself," says Bruno. "Knowing we're completely free to do whatever we want. Fucking this sweet arse of yours" — he reaches out and rubs my exposed anus with his finger — "whenever and wherever I choose to do it."

The bulk of March whirls through my mind. Regular nights with Bruno where we have shagged all over every surface of his apartment. Jesus, it's been wonderful. "Here they are." I stand back up, slipping into the shorts. "They look OK?"

"What do you reckon?" says Bruno, grabbing at his crotch.

"That's a good enough answer for me." I gather my wallet and keys and phone, then have a sudden thought. "What's the parking like at this place?"

"It'll be pretty terrible, but it's worth it," says Bruno. "We'll most likely snag a one-hour spot. Maybe stretch it to two hours without copping a fine."

"We'll take my disability permit. There's no time limit, so no fine." I duck out to the lounge room and rifle through the basket on the bookshelf where I keep it. I'm groping around, trying to locate the plastic suction-cupped windscreen card, but I can't feel it. Pulling the basket right out, I sit on the couch and dump the contents on the coffee table. No, it's definitely not there.

Bloody Jarrod.

I'm dialling his number before I even think it through. If he's taken the damn thing, I'll be so pissed off that I won't be able to keep a lid on it. When he answers, all I get is a terse "Yeah? What do you want?"

"You wouldn't happen to know where my parking permit is, would you?"

"I've got it." He says this like it's totally normal.

"Why?" I can't hide the annoyance in my tone.

"You don't fuckin' use it!" Jarrod's voice has doubled in volume. "Davo needed it."

"Jarrod, it's *my parking permit.* Blind person, remember? Anyway, who's this 'Davo' you keep talking about? Am I supposed to know him or something?"

"Just a guy I'm seeing," Jarrod snaps. "None of your fuckin' business. You're clearly off getting rooted by any dick you can get your fuckin' hands on."

Spying my bedroom door still open a crack, I take a huge, calming breath. This is embarrassing, and Bruno can obviously hear it all. I move the phone closer, growling right into the mouthpiece. "Jarrod, I couldn't care less about who you have sex with. And I don't give a toss whether your mate '*needs*' my disability permit. It's *mine.*"

"Fuck off." The phone goes dead in my ear. Jarrod's not used to me standing up for myself. I'm not used to it, either. I'm trembling with rage. And even though I'm doing my best to control it, my efforts are only making things worse.

Bruno emerges from the bedroom wearing his best jolly smile. I know he's trying to reassure me, trying to lighten the mood, and his generosity makes me want to cry. I'm so mortified. "Sorry about that," is all I manage to squeak out.

He joins me on the couch, pulling me tight against him and kissing the top of my head. "*Blinky*," he murmurs into my hair. "You don't ever need to apologise for him, remember?" We sit there for a moment, allowing the tension to simmer down. The warmth of Bruno's breath against my scalp is soothing. Waves of energy course down through my neck and suddenly nothing in this world seems to matter anymore.

"I've got an idea," says Bruno, shifting and sitting back to face me. "You know Wombat Valley?"

I ponder this for a second. "You mean that gay B&B in the Southern Highlands? With all the camping grounds?"

"Yeah, that's the one. The owner's sister is a friend of mine from work. It's right near a river. We could go and swim there instead. "

I pull out my phone and glance at the clock. "Have we got enough time?"

"It's a bit over an hour and a half's drive away. We'd make it by two, easy. That'll give us all afternoon."

***

Time flies as we cruise down the M5. Bruno and I chat in the front on the bench seat, while Brendan is strapped into his hammock in the back. Every time I glance around at him, he's sitting tall, grinning as he stares in wonderment at the scenery flying past him out the window. Before long, we're pulling up at a service station somewhere along the Hume Highway outside of Sydney. Bruno jumps straight out, unlocks the old manual fuel cap and begins to fill up. After fishing for my wallet, freeing Brendan from his seatbelt in the back and putting on his harness, I round the car towards Bruno.

"I'll get this," I say, trying to adopt my firmest tone.

"No, you won't," says Bruno. "I invited you here, and I'm paying." He hangs up the nozzle, kisses my cheek and starts off towards the shop.

I'm not going to argue. Bruno is generous to a fault and I wouldn't want to insult him by pushing too hard. Scanning the surrounding area, my eyes land on a fruit stand underneath a big tree off to the side. "You wanna go and check that out, buddy?"

Brendan pants up at me, then instinctively turns to head off in that direction. I swear, this dog can understand me in ways people would never expect.

There are stacks of strawberry punnets on the stand. Deep red and luscious, they're screaming out for me to buy. I've packed sandwiches and drinks in my cooler, but these will definitely make a nice dessert. To their right, I spot some honey with homemade labels on the containers.

Not just jars, but those large half-litre buckets. "From our own bees," says the man behind the stand. Bruno will love it. I've seen the way he wolfs down the muffins with mascarpone and Tasmanian Leatherwood honey I put in front of him.

"It's the perfect gift," I tell the man, handing him the bucket and two of the large strawberry punnets.

"Do you like my flowers?" A small voice sounds beside me, and I look down to spot a little girl there, pointing at bunches of what look like wildflowers. "I helped pick them." Her large earnest eyes gaze up at me as she speaks. That's gotta be a foolproof sales tactic.

"They look really, really beautiful," I tell her. "Do you reckon I could buy a bunch?"

"Yes!" She bounces on her toes and takes one from the front. "These ones?"

"Oh, yeah. They're *definitely* my favourite." I take the small raffia-tied bouquet and hand it to the man along with my credit card.

"What about me? Can I buy some too?" A man has sidled up next to me in my blind spot.

Just as I turn to make way for the new customer, I spot Bruno walking up towards us with a wide smile. "Hey, Henry!" he calls out.

"Bru! It's been a while." Henry pulls Bruno into a bear hug. "How's Hannah? Tell the lazy cow to give her brother a call sometime."

"I'll make sure I hassle her at my next shift," Bruno reassures him, before holding his arm out and cupping my shoulder. "Bradford, this is Henry. He owns Wombat Valley."

I focus in on Henry. He's a pleasant-looking grey-haired bear in his fifties with a ready smile and, as evidenced by the way he clasps my hand, a firm and sincere shake.

"Your mate Bru here just missed the last gay camping group weekend at our place." He nods over to Bruno, who shrugs his shoulders.

"Yeah, I know. I was too busy spending my free time with this handsome bugger." Bruno pulls me into a half-hug as he talks. I'm struck by how open he's being about our whole arrangement. It feels nice, like it's being given a new level of legitimacy. "I definitely want to get back there again soon," he tells Henry, then turns to me. "Maybe I can convince you to join me?"

I chuckle as I look back at Henry. "Isn't he a charmer? As if I'd need any convincing." Yeah, I'm definitely loving this sickening-new-couple act Bruno and I have going on right now.

"We're actually heading out your way to go swim in the river," says Bruno.

"Nice day for it," chirps Henry, dumping his pile of strawberry punnets on the counter. "Looks like the last of the swimming weather before we start freezing our tits off."

After goodbye hugs, Bruno, Brendan and I stroll back towards the car. "This is a bit sappy," I apologise, presenting Bruno with the bouquet, "but a cute little kid talked me into buying it for you. Oh, and this" — I hand him the bucket of honey — "is because you wouldn't let me pay for the fuel."

Bruno's brow wrinkles as he looks at my presents, and he scratches the back of his neck. I've seen him do this before. It's like a nervous gesture. No, it's like he's touched or overwhelmed. He reaches over and wraps his arm around my head, pulling me close and kissing me on the brow. "You're the sweetest man I've ever met, you know that?"

***

After travelling down the Hume Highway a bit further, we make a right turn and head west. Before long, we're driving around the side of steep mountains, the car weaving through the curving road as it makes a slow descent. I've never actually travelled to these parts and I had no idea this sort of landscape was here, right on my back doorstep.

Eventually, we reach the floor of a valley. We continue to duck and weave, arriving at a rough car park. In the near distance, over a large, grassy open area, there's a substantial river. Not just a little creek, but a waterway big enough to accommodate the blurry speedboats I can see skating across the deep green surface.

With Bruno carrying the Esky full of food and drinks, and me balancing the backpack and Brendan, we make our way through the parkland and right along the edge of the river. At one stage, Bruno points to a walking track that winds through the trees and bushes from the river bank. "Wombat Valley homestead's just down there." He grins at me over his shoulder. "One day I'm gonna take you for a dirty weekend in their master suite."

I get a thrill every time he talks like this. I don't know what our future will involve. I don't dare analyse it too much; I just want Bruno to be part of it.

The bush thickens as we make our way further down the river. Bruno stops when we come to a little alcove—a tiny grassy area tucked between some trees. The sun is beating down and dappled shade frolics across the grass in the warm breeze. "Perfect spot, eh?" he says as he plants the Esky on the ground.

Together we set up the picnic blanket and towels. I pull out the large ham bone I've brought to occupy Brendan and he gets stuck into it straight away. Peeling off my t-shirt, I grab the Reef tanning oil and start to apply another layer.

Bruno scooches closer and takes the bottle from me. "I'm not gonna sit idly by watching you stroke your body like that," he growls. "Let me put it on for you."

I lean into his touch as he massages the oil into my back and shoulders. The strength and sensuality of his hands has a direct effect on my dick, which starts to grow with hardening throbs. Involuntary moans rumble from my throat as he works the oil into my chest, rubbing his fingers across my nipples. Pretty soon my cock has grown to its full seven-and-a-half inch length. With no room for it in my slutty little shorts, it's now sticking right out the leg opening.

"Oh, fuck," groans Bruno, spying my wayward erection. "That is so hot!" Pushing my shoulders till I'm lying down, he straddles my chest and sucks my knob straight into his mouth. The delicious shock of his hot, wet tongue is eclipsed only by the fact his arse is right in front of me. The stretchy fabric of his shorts is no match for my prying hands as I yank on the waistband till his buttocks are fully exposed. I don't even need to pull on Bruno's hips, he knows exactly what's going to happen. In one swift move, he's shuffled back and his arse has descended onto my face. The thick fur and heady scent engulf me and I can barely comprehend how wonderful it is.

The fact that I'm a whore for a beautiful manly arse is nothing new; I've been that way since the first signs of puberty. And sure, until Bruno, I'd been deprived of my obsession for years. But what makes it so magical with him is the way he responds. It's not just me being a horny bugger selfishly drowning myself in pheromones—this man absolutely *loves* what I'm doing. He's vocal and it's one hundred percent primal. Every moan is a sincere acknowledgement of gratitude and extreme pleasure. This—*this* is what drives me wild. I need to please him. I'm hardwired that way and there's no point fighting it.

Just as I'm busy revelling in this heavenly state, smothered by Bruno's butt while his hand is gripping the base of my dick and his mouth is bombarding my pierced knob, we hear an outboard motor whirring in the near distance. Bruno's lips pop off my dick with a wet squelch and he sits up slightly, his furry hole grinding against my face. "Fuck," he says, scuttling off me, tucking my dick away and hiking his shorts up with seamless choreography. Instantly, he's lying on his stomach alongside me, while I prop myself up on my elbows. Now, we're just two men innocently sunning ourselves as a speedboat soars past.

Bruno glances back over his shoulder, grinning at me. "That was close."

"I was having so much fun with your arse it didn't even occur to me that we might have had spectators."

We lie there for a quiet moment, following the blur of the speedboat. "You never come when I blow you," says Bruno, his gaze still fixed out on the river. "I need to ask you again—am I doing something wrong?"

I'm immediately confronted by this. It's one of my biggest inadequacies. "No. Not at all. Truly, you're brilliant. Your mouth moves in so many ways and I get really close. It's just… something that never happens to me." My explanation sounds ridiculously lame. I don't really have an effective way to reassure him, so I start to babble. "I used to try and fool myself and blame it on not having a foreskin, but I've been proven wrong by a whole lot of cut guys." *Jesus. Now I'm sure I look like a total slut.*

Bruno finally looks around at me again, his face twisted into an amused smirk. "Never say never." His gaze drops to my crotch, then back up to my eyes. "Challenge accepted."

I'm relieved at having dodged a bullet. I'm also blown away at how understanding Bruno has been yet again. It's a powerful aphrodisiac, and my cock is still hard. Fumbling around the picnic blanket, I locate the bottle of Reef.

With the coast now clear, I sit up properly and slather my hands with the oil. Straddling the top of Bruno's thighs, I crouch forward and start massaging his back. My fingers knead into his bearish padding, pulverising the thick muscles below as Bruno moans appreciatively. I want to give him the best rubdown, I really do, but it's not long before I've worked my way south and my eyes land right on his big beefy bum.

After dousing my hands with more oil, I slide my fingers up the leg of his shorts and delve between his cheeks. Bruno's breathing heavily, waiting to see what I'll do. "This little hole of yours is the most beautiful thing I've ever laid eyes on," I growl, as I rub oil over the puckered aperture. My motion grows more insistent, and two of my fingers are immediately granted entry. Bruno's breath catches when they head straight for the firm lump of his prostate. I don't press hard, just brush lightly over the surface, and Bruno thanks me for it with beautiful little whines. I listen to him intently, guided by his body's pattern of tension and release.

The motion of my fingers morphs into a rhythmic pumping and Bruno's voice gets a bit louder. I don't know what's thrilling me more—the warmth of his arse as it tightens around my digits, or the rapturous noises resonating in his throat.

Bruno hasn't spoken a word, but he's well and truly tuned in to my body's movements. He arches his back as soon as he feels me shift into place and pull the leg of his shorts up. While I prep my engorged knob with firm, greasy strokes, I thank whatever God there is that they gave me a decently long penis. Given the position Bruno's in right now, my extra inches enable me to manoeuvre between his hefty buttocks and push straight into his hole.

Oh man, I love that feeling, that first slide into fiery dank warmth. I love the fact that Bruno whimpers every time I thrust into him. I love how he pushes his hips up, dying to be filled with as much of my dick as possible.

I've now sunk in as far as I can go. Sure, I could tell Bruno to get up on his knees and stick his arse right out. I could make him pull apart his cheeks so I'm able to drive into him till his tight ring is pressed against the base of my shaft. He's done that before, and the view was so beautiful I almost passed out with sheer lust. But for now, I just lay my belly against his back and slowly plunge five or six inches in and out of him.

"Bradford," Bruno mumbles, speaking at last. "Can we do this forever?" He sounds dead serious. A wave of emotion hits me. I feel the pressure behind my eyes, I feel my sinuses start to swell and I feel the ache deep within my chest.

Don't I have the right to be happy?

Giving in to the moment, I lean my head forward and kiss Bruno behind the ear. As I rock my hips, pushing into his warmth, the only safe thing I can think of to say is, "We can do it for as long as you want, *Harry.*"

Our special little bubble is rudely burst by the sound of another outboard motor. This time, it's much easier to disengage. In two seconds flat, I've slid out of Bruno's hole and plopped onto my stomach beside him, obscuring my raging hard-on underneath me. When the boat has careened off into the distance, Bruno turns to me. "Maybe we should go for a dip?"

It takes effort and concentration for me to get down the embankment into the river. There are reeds and tree roots and tripping hazards galore, but I make sure I memorise the terrain for when I get out. I feel like a helpless old person, but Bruno is undeterred, holding my hand and guiding me with a firm grip on my shoulder. The water is cool as we swim out into the shallows, and I'm pleased to find there is a solid sandy riverbed underneath my feet.

"Brendan seems pretty content," says Bruno, wading towards me and wrapping his arms around my waist.

I squint up at our little alcove to spot a blurry, furry form lounging on the grass. I can't make out any detail, but I've seen him in this position so many times I can picture it in my head: he's lying on his side, propped up with his front paws out like the sphinx, his head turned towards the sun. When he was younger, I would have had to keep a much closer eye on him with all his puppy-like exuberance. These days, he's quite content to kick back and chill out until it's time for a walk.

Satisfied that my boy is happy, I turn my focus to Bruno once more. His damp beard glistens in the sunlight, the black curly hair with its patches of silver steadfastly holding shape. I can't say the same for mine—when it gets wet, the wavy hair weighs down and I look like a drowned rat.

The kindness in Bruno's eyes cuts through me as I watch him study my face. Slowly, he moves forward and joins his lips to mine. Our kiss is gentle, sustained. His mouth is soft and his tongue lazily explores inside me, rubbing over and under my own tongue in a luxurious shuffle. Warmth spreads throughout my chest and travels through my body, shattering into a supernova of tingles at the surface of my skin. The sheer sensual beauty of it all is only disturbed by the incessant throbbing in my crotch.

Grinding my hips forward, my erection brushes over Bruno's. He pushes back, grunting into my mouth as we both find a new urgency. Bending down, Bruno grips my thighs and draws my legs up and around his waist. We're buoyed by the water, and it feels like we weigh nothing. Gravity doesn't exist; only the strong pull of Bruno desperately trying to get me as close as possible. "You know, I could easily fuck you right here," he pants, grinding his penis against my taint.

"Do it," I moan. It's an emergency. I can't even hide how much I need him right now.

Reaching down below my leg, Bruno frees himself from his shorts and I feel his hard cock pressing up into my crack. After one more fumble, he's pulled my shorts aside and his rigid knob is butting hard against my bare hole. I'm desperate for him. I know I'm not lubed, but I can't bear to break this rhythm we've got happening. Spending the next few days with a sore arse is a price I'm willing to pay. I close my eyes, groaning hard as I try to expand my arsehole to accommodate him. I can feel the burn as he starts to enter a little, but he's just too big and thick.

"Hang on a moment," I gasp, shooting Bruno a smile and wriggling from his embrace. I wade back to shore and scramble up the embankment, bending forward to steady myself with my arms. The picnic blanket is mere steps away and I spot the sun glinting off the brown plastic bottle of Reef oil. Emptying a huge squirt into my palm, I pull my hard dick from my shorts and coat it well. I need it as slick as possible, because I am determined to shoot like a rocket. Glancing back out to the water, I spot Bruno facing my way. I turn my back to him, yank down my shorts, pull one arse cheek out and bend right over. Shoving two fingers up my hole, I pump them in and out, giving Bruno the best little show I can manage as I grease myself up good and proper.

"Jesus!" shouts Bruno. "Stop torturing me and get back in here!"

Quick as I can, I make my way down the embankment once more. I look at my feet the whole time, concentrating as hard as I can. I have to get to him *now.* I'm barely back in his arms before he's hiked my legs up high again. I wrap them around his thick body, then lean back in the water, tilting my hips to give him easy entry. Bruno grips me under the arse and pulls the fabric of my shorts aside. Straight away, he's pressing his huge knob against my anus. This time, it's a lot easier. I push hard against him and feel his girth as it stretches my hole in the most sublime way possible. It hurts so good I have to stop myself crying out. Pulling against his buttocks with my ankles, I draw him towards my arse as he thrusts headlong into me.

I'm absolutely elated. I feel so incredibly manly right now. So potent, so virile. The ache in my arse has travelled right up through my taint, my balls and along my shaft to my knob. In one deliberate move, I've reached into the leg of my shorts and pulled out my throbbing penis. "I'm sorry, Bruno, I'm going to blow so bloody fast," I pant, as I begin to rub hard over my knob. "But you keep fucking me as long as you need to. You know I'll love every second of it."

Bruno's white teeth glint as a lascivious grin overtakes his entire face. Without a word, he starts shafting me as hard as he can. "Yeah? Like this? Fuck you like the hot little bearslut you are?"

My brow is wrinkled with ecstatic pain. "Yes. Fuck me so fucking hard, *Harry.* I'm begging you. Please, my arse is dying for it."

Bruno roars and tightens his grip around my hips. His colossal dick is punching my prostate with such vigour that I know there's no use trying to hold off. I can feel it happening already. "I'm gonna come," I wail, my voice breaking into what almost sounds like embarrassing sobs. But I'm powerless. My whole body convulses as my orgasm fights hard against the massive rod ploughing into my g-spot. For one brief, blessed moment, I'm on the verge of bursting, before my body finally detonates. Squinting down, I see the perfect arcs of sperm catapulting from my raging red knob, skidding across the wet fur on my belly.

"Oh, fuck!" yells Bruno, barrelling forward and licking hard at my stomach, trying to catch every drop of my load. His rigid cock slips from my arsehole as he pulls me upright against him and thrusts his tongue into my mouth. He thrashes it around, rubbing it hard over every surface, eagerly feeding me the load he's pounded out of me. It's like we're madly indulging in something forbidden, something only two men as close as we are can possibly share.

With his mouth still pressed against mine, Bruno swallows hard. I let the spoils of our intimacy linger a moment longer as I look deep into his dark eyes. Slowly, I feel his hand slide between us and begin to move on his penis. I know what to do now.

Without breaking contact, I slide around his warm body and cuddle him from behind. With one hand, I reach up to his pierced nipple and begin to roll it between my fingers. I slide my other hand into his arse crack and push my thumb straight into his hole. By the time the pad of it hits his prostate, Bruno is moaning every second, barely stopping to breathe. I can feel his anus tightening and releasing every time I stroke over the hardened g-spot. "I have never been fucked so well in my life, Bru," I croon into his ear.

"Yeah?" he gasps. "Tell me how much you loved it."

"You sent me to fucking heaven. You pounded my fucking hole so good I nearly fainted."

"Oh, God." Bruno's voice is wavering. "Keep going. Please."

"You mean this?" I move my thumb a bit more forcefully, thrusting it in and out of his tight ring, butting it against his prostate with every shove.

"Yes. Harder. Oh, fuck. Yes… harder!"

I begin to slam it into him at double speed, rolling his nipple more firmly. His prostate is swelling fast. "You're coming, aren't you? I can feel it. Do you know how much I love this hot, sweet little cunt of yours, Bru?"

"Euh! Euh! Euh! Oh, FUCK!" Bruno's arsehole clamps tight, squeezing out my thumb when his body starts to shake. I ram it back up inside just in time to feel the wild spasming at the front of his rectal wall, prime evidence of the huge load he's blasting out into the water. I'm wrapped so tight around him, joined to him in the most intimate way possible, living this entire experience with him. Every jolt of his body. Every rise and fall of his ribs. Every pulse of his anus. Every vibration in his chest. We are one.

We are one.

CHAPTER 11

I slowly come to, my eyes rapidly adjusting to the surroundings. Trees. Gentle water lapping nearby. Grass. Clean air. I'm on my side, my head propped up on Bradford's backpack and my hand across his chest. Glancing over him, I see Brendan snuggled into the crook of his arm. Bradford's still sleeping sweetly, his eyes closed, a pile of clothes nestled under him as a makeshift pillow. The atmosphere is filled with an all-consuming sense of peace. We're suspended here in a soft cloud and every part of me wishes we could stay this way forever.

"Hey." Bradford's voice is a husky whisper as his eyes open and he turns to look at me. "I was having a wonderful dream, then I woke up and it was all true."

Reaching over to brush the hair from his forehead, I lean into him and kiss him gently on the lips. "It is. Every bit of it." I'm dangerously close to blurting out too much. I need to get a hold of myself. Gazing back out at the sky, I see the sun setting through the thick canopy of trees lining the far side of the river. Brilliant shades of orange, yellow and pink pierce through the leaves and branches, casting their glow in our direction.

"You know, we'll never have this moment again," says Bradford.

I look at him as he lies there staring at the view, the dying rays of sun flickering across the shining surface of his eyes. He doesn't seem wistful. He's truly finding joy in such a small but magical point in time. My heart swells and an ache builds behind my eyes that I almost don't manage to contain. Bradford's world has shrunk down to tiny proportions, yet he's still grabbing shreds of happiness wherever he can.

"Your life is gonna be full of these," I whisper, placing my hand against his cheek. The softness of his beard caresses my palm and Bradford follows the featherlight pressure, turning his head till his eyes meet mine. "I'll make sure of that, *Blinky*."

As the sun begins to take its final bows, a chill works its way into our warm valley paradise. Before long, we're up and dressed and packing our mess into the Esky. Every single sandwich is gone, every single strawberry was dipped in honey and savoured with a smile. I've never had such a perfect day.

After retracing our steps to the car, Bradford lets Brendan off his leash and we jog around the open parkland with him. Brendan runs back and forth, jumping with excitement at the prospect of two burly men joining him in this romp. I watch Bradford with a mixture of concern and curiosity as he runs along beside me. He seems to be doing fine, though. He's taking it very carefully, glancing down at the ground at regular intervals, making sure there's nothing to trip him up. And the look of freedom on his face tells me it's all worth it.

Darkness has fallen by the time we're driving our way up out of the valley. My high beams scan the road ahead of me, alerting me to every twist and turn. Soon, we're onto a stretch of open bush road and I'm able to gather a bit of speed. The windows are open, there's a fresh breeze circulating, and my spirits are soaring.

Just as I'm leaning into my buoyant mood, a dark object runs straight out in front of the Kingswood. There's an almighty thud against the bumper and I jolt up in my seat. I'm so shocked that my body doesn't react and the car keeps speeding along.

"Oh, God!" cries Bradford. "Please stop. *Please*." There's a gut wrenching panic in his tone which snaps my body into action. Squeezing on the brakes, I bring the car to a quick halt and pull off to the side of the road.

We've barely stopped when Bradford's out the door. In the rear view mirror I see him running as fast as he can, stumbling, falling over and getting up again as he rushes towards whatever it was I hit. I jump out of the car and take off after him, feeling sick to my stomach. By the time I reach him, he's crouched down in front of the object at the side of the road. Bradford has his phone out and the torch shining on it. There lies a great big wombat. It's not all bloodied, but it's definitely not moving.

"Oh..." Bradford's voice breaks into sobs. "I'm sorry I'm sorry I'm sorry," he chants as he begins to cry openly. His shoulders shake and I'm standing there, useless. All I can think of to do is squat next to him and rub my hand over his back.

Bradford makes a visible effort to slow down the deluge pouring out of him. "It's just…" he's beginning to hyperventilate. "He had a life… and now it's over."

That line is a stab in the guts. It's so much more than a wombat; I can see all too clearly that it's a reflection on Bradford's own situation. I have never needed to try and save someone so desperately. I don't care whether it's right or wrong, I am driven by a force I can't control.

Shuffling closer, I wrap one arm around him and pull his head against my chest. "Oh, God, *Blinky*. I can't believe I was so fucking careless." I want to throw up. Between the poor wombat and Bradford's distress, I'm in grave danger of starting to bawl myself.

"No. It's not your fault," sniffs Bradford. He begins taking big breaths, struggling to get himself on an even keel again. Leaning forward once more, he gingerly reaches out to the lifeless wombat, stroking the tips of his fingers on the furry creature's hindquarters. "No pouch," he says, "So no young. And really big. He's definitely a boy."

"What should we do with him? It doesn't feel right just leaving him here on the side of the road."

"No, it's fine," says Bradford. "He has to stay here. They come past and make a record of any wildlife that's been killed."

We remain there on our haunches for a short while, letting it all sink in. I feel so bloody stupid. Normally, I can handle any situation like this. It's my fucking *job*, for God's sake. But seeing Bradford in such a state hits way too close to home. I'm at a loss as to what to do. Finally, I have a thought.

Running back to the car, I retrieve the bunch of wildflowers and return to where Bradford's crouching, still stroking the poor wombat. "Here" I say gently. "I can't think of a more fitting use for these."

Bradford takes the bouquet, his tear-stained face looking up at me. "Thank you," he whispers. With quiet reverence, he places the flowers against the wombat's belly, then gives him a final pat. "Goodbye, little man. Somebody cared about you." Rising up slowly, he shudders as he stifles another sob, then wipes his eyes, takes a deep breath and does his best to stand tall.

With my arm around his shoulders, I follow his lead as he turns and we walk back to the car. I'm still deeply rattled, but I'm relieved that Bradford seems to have found some kind of closure.

He holds my hand as we drive back into Sydney. We don't really talk, but that seems to be the best course of action right now. I feel like I have so much to say. I just don't know how to go about saying it.

An idea comes to me as we pass by Sydney airport. Taking the exit to Wentworth Avenue, I head towards the lower eastern suburbs. Bradford watches out the window, glancing at me every now and then, but he doesn't ask questions.

I haven't been to Little Bay in absolutely ages. It's not far from where I grew up in Maroubra, only a ten minute drive south, but it's tucked away, nestled in its cove above the Botany Bay National Park. As we round the road to our old high school, we're confronted by large apartment blocks instead. The only thing telling me we're in the right place is the name of the road; everything else is so different to the way it was decades ago. I keep an eagle eye out for a parking spot while I edge the Kingswood down the crowded street.

"Wow, this place is so different!" says Bradford as we pull up. Stepping out of the car, he stands there a moment, scanning the buildings in front of him. I can see the edges of his eyes bunching up as he squints, a sight I'm now completely familiar with, but one which never fails to tug at my heart.

With Brendan all harnessed up, we walk down a small service road that leads to the back of the buildings. Landscaped gardens have replaced the school sports fields, and we make our way through them, trying to locate the path down to the cove. By instinct, Bradford seems to have steered Brendan to the exact spot. What used to be a rocky trail through the bush is now a railed set of steps. It's a shame all the rustic beauty I remember from my high school years has been replaced by this sterile development.

Down in the sandy cove, Bradford lets Brendan off his harness, keeping him on his leash. Brendan's sombre nature changes instantly; all of a sudden he's a normal dog. The moon is out in full force, lighting up the cove with a magical glow. It beams off the gentle waves, creating a silvery moving blanket that stretches across the bay.

"What was his name?" I ask Bradford, as we stare out to sea.

"Whose name?"

"Your friend. The one you used to come here with."

"Oh." Bradford nods slowly, a distant smile on his face. "Chris."

There's something about this place. The otherworldly moonlight filling every corner of the cove. The lazy breeze. The memories flooding back to me. Everything seems to be pushing me to make a statement, to open the door just a crack and let this amazing man get a glimpse of what's going on in my heart.

"You never got to tell him what you needed him to know." I'm on the edge of a precipice here, barely hanging on, but I feel an urge that I'm powerless to stop. "Sometimes we let opportunities pass us by and we live to regret it. I'm not going to do that, Bradford."

Reaching out, I take his hand and turn to him. The light behind his head fans out. It's mesmerising. Maybe it's just my mind playing tricks on me, but right now there's a halo around Bradford. "We've been connected for thirty years, *Blinky,* and it all started right here." The stark honesty of the moment makes me want to look away, but I keep my eyes focused on Bradford's. "The past few months have been the happiest I've ever known in fifty years. I want to keep our connection. I don't care how we define it, but I need to be in your life. Always."

Bradford doesn't say anything, he just averts his eyes and bows his head slightly. I immediately feel worried. I've gone too far. I've exposed myself, laid myself open, made myself vulnerable in a way that's making me shake.

Bradford's voice is so tiny I can hardly hear it over the noise of the ocean. But the words he says resonate in my head as loudly as if he's shouting them to the world. "Please don't ever go anywhere, *Harry.*"

CHAPTER 12

Aware that I'm going to have to deal with Jarrod, Bruno graciously drops me back at my apartment after we've left Little Bay. I'd much rather stay at Bruno's; I can barely face going back inside here. Putting one foot in front of the other, I make my way through the front door and along the hall. The place is dark, and as I approach Jarrod's bedroom, I see the door wide open. Thank God, he's not home yet.

I don't want to deal with any of this. Doubling back to the laundry, I stash all of Brendan's stuff and fill his bowl with food. Leaving him to eat, I make my way to the study. There, I strip out of my clothes, slip on a pair of boxer shorts, collapse onto the sofa bed and drift off.

It must be quite a bit later when I come to. I've never been one for naps. The superficial sleep I get is rife with bizarre and uneasy dreams, and I always wake up with my mind in a nasty fog. Lately, though, I've taken to having frequent naps with Bruno. These are different. I doze in and out, half-waking to find him close to me, and I cuddle into him and fall back to sleep. With his warm body touching mine, my dreams are still bizarre, but they're sexy and filled with intense loving overtones. After those naps, I wake up with a hard dick and a smile on my face. Like this afternoon on that riverbank.

Right now, though, I've just had that first kind of nap. The horrible one. Struggling to my feet, I decide the only way to deal with it is a long, hot shower. First things first, though; I'm parched.

Feeling my way through the darkness, I pad into the kitchen and switch on the light. The glare cuts right through my eyes and sears into my brain, so I stop a moment to let my shockingly sluggish pupils adjust. I almost wish I hadn't come in here, because Jarrod's left a trail of half-eaten food over my clean counter and a pile of dirty dishes dumped in the sink.

These days, my reaction is automatic. I could get upset about the fact he's messed up my tidy kitchen. I could get angry about his flagrant disregard for my feelings, his utter lack of appreciation for anything I do for him. But I've learnt that it's not worth the stress it causes me.

One by one, I pull out all the dishes from the sink and turn on the hot tap. Glancing upwards, I notice my near-naked body reflected in the kitchen window. I don't want to give the neighbours a show, so I wind down the blind, then get to work on Jarrod's mess.

As I'm scrubbing, I'm also taking stock of what's been going on here recently. It's no wonder I've napped twice today; the quality of my sleep has been terrible. Jarrod and I are barely cohabiting. He also doesn't seem to be doing many nursing shifts at all. And now the weather's cooler and I'm not running the air conditioner in the study, I can hear people out in the living room at all hours. These people come and go; they don't stay long. I can hear the rise and fall of their chatter, I can follow the pattern of their tone that signals their departure. Sometimes, when I'm in the kitchen or the living room, there's a furtive knock at the front door. Jarrod always darts straight down the hall to answer it, and the random person's brief doorstep visit is always punctuated by a short amount of secretive mumbling.

It's plainly obvious that Jarrod's dealing. It's also clear that he's well and truly sampling the merchandise. He's become all gaunt and tetchy. He has facial tics and he sniffs and scratches at himself. Over the course of a few short weeks, I've been banished to the spare room of my own apartment and the rest of the place has been turned into a sordid drug den. How the hell did I get to this point? How did I let it happen?

I'm still up to my elbows in suds when the front door opens. I don't even bother turning around, it's not like we ever greet each other.

"Here's your precious fuckin' parking pass," Jarrod's voice snaps. I hear plastic slap and skid on the kitchen counter, but I don't turn around just yet. I'm too busy taking a deep breath. I know it's time to have this out.

Wiping my hands on the tea towel I have across my shoulder, I turn round to face the music. Jarrod's all wired and jumpy, like some kind of aggressive insect looking for a fight. My heart is beginning to thud in my chest, but I can't back down now. "Why do you hate me so much, Jarrod?"

"Oh, fuck. Here we go, playing the victim. *Poor little fucking Braddy*," Jarrod snorts.

"No. I wanna know. What did I ever do to you to deserve this?" My tone is firm. Harsh. I'm determined.

Jarrod takes a step forward, leering at me. "Isn't it obvious? You're pissweak. You've got no balls. You're boring as fuck. You're always *here,* you and that bloody dog. And all that fucking singing? I mean, *give up* already. *Nobody's* listening anymore."

I hold off on my response to let that last bit sink in. He's gone about as low as he can go. The trouble is, I know he's right. And this pause of mine is giving him all the validation he needs.

I cannot let him win. Steeling myself, I deliver the line I've been dying to voice for months. Years, even. "Why do you stick around then, Jarrod? Why don't you just leave? There's nothing here for you anymore."

Jarrod's eyes blaze. "No, *you* can fuck off out of here! I'm not going anywhere."

And right there, my worst fear is laid out in front of me. I'll never get rid of him. This is where logic would have me back down, but I've got so little left to lose. "This is *my flat,* Jarrod. You live here by *my good grace.* And it appears you don't think you have to pay FUCKING rent anymore!"

The shock on Jarrod's face at hearing me swear is so brief it may as well have not happened. But I saw it. Straight away, he's on the attack again, moving another step closer and slapping his hand against the counter. "You miserable penny-pinching little *cunt*. You're the one who owes *me* money."

I'm so aghast, I actually laugh at this. "How the hell did you come to that conclusion?"

"I should have been getting a Centrelink allowance all this time and YOU never bothered to organise it. So *there's* your fucking rent," he snarls.

I draw air in through my nose, trying to stabilise my voice, but I can't quite manage to contain the incredulity dripping from every word. "You think you deserve government money for looking after someone with a disability? *I'm* the one who runs around cleaning up after *you*!"

Jarrod has no answer to this. He knows it's true, but he can't possibly let me get the upper hand. Baring his teeth, he grinds his finger into my breastbone and moves into full belligerent mode. "*I am entitled to the carer's payment*!"

I take a step back. I'm truly worried this might get physical. Bringing my voice down a few decibels, I finally allow myself to point out the obvious. "You don't *care* for me, Jarrod. Not in any sense of the word."

In the blink of an eye, a hand connects so hard with my face that my neck wrenches sideways. I'm not even sure what's happened. It takes moments for me to realise I've been slapped.

"Why the *fuck* did I bother coming home?" Jarrod yells. "I'm going back to Davo's." As I cower against the sink, near-naked, hand pressed against the sting on my cheek, he looks me up and down with a palpable sense of disgust. "And put some *fuckin'* clothes on, for God's sake."

Jarrod turns away, but that's all I manage to see. Suddenly the light is out and the kitchen is plunged into darkness. I want to open the window blind, but Jarrod's still here. I can hear cupboards rattling, then a whole lot of clinking. All of a sudden, there's smashing. One after the other, glass tumblers shatter against the floor. I can hear the tinkling sound of the broken pieces spreading everywhere. I can feel shards hitting my legs. Standing there frozen to the spot, I hold my breath till the smashing stops. Till I hear Jarrod storm down the hall and leave, slamming the front door behind him.

I have no idea what to do. My head is spinning so fast I can't slow it down long enough to form any kind of logical thought. I'm standing here barefoot in a pitch-black room and no matter where I step I'll slash my soles on jagged glass.

The window blind. I reach behind me, keeping my feet glued where they are on the floor. Feeling first for the wooden edge of the window frame, I move my hand inside it, groping for the chain pulley attached there. It takes a dozen small tugs till I hear the blind reach the top. But it makes no real difference. All the apartment buildings and trees outside are blocking the moonlight.

The cupboard under the sink. There has to be something in there to help. I slide down slowly onto my haunches, fumbling around to find the door knob. There's a basket in here where I keep a little dustpan and brush. I feel for the wicker sides, then the handle. I'm trying to pull it closer at an angle behind me while I'm twisting my back and swivelling slightly on the balls of my feet. At last it's sticking out far enough for me to rifle through its contents, but the bloody brush isn't there.

I want to scream. I feel like flinging the whole basket across the room, but instead, I slide it back. Patting randomly around the cupboard, I knock a few aerosol cans and bottles over, then my hand lands on bristles. Carefully extracting the brush, I twist my back around again, wincing at the cramp I've got from the awkward search.

First, I brush my immediate surroundings. Any direction I can, so long as it's away from me. Delicately running my palms over the floor, I check it for random stray bits of glass, but I've done a thorough job. Now I can lean forward on my knees and brush towards the entryway.

It takes me a while, but I make it to the far side of the kitchen. A wet nose snuffles against me and I instantly want to sob. Brendan's been waiting for me, keeping guard. I'm so relieved that I forget about switching on the light for a moment while I hug him, nuzzling into his furry neck.

After I've put on shoes and returned to clean up all the glass, I go down to the bathroom, strip naked and stare into the mirror. The adrenaline has all but dissipated now. I feel numb. Sickened. I can't even face the magnitude of what's just happened, so I don't. I shower, dry off, then open the bathroom door to find Brendan waiting there pressed against it. He follows me back to the study, touching his wet nose against my leg every now and then, reminding me he's close by in case I need him. I pull on a t-shirt and boxers, shut the study door and get into bed, calling Brendan to come and lie next to me. He knows it's one of those occasions right now. He knows how dire things have become, so he scoots further up the bed and lays his head against my body.

"Bradford, do you remember when you were thirty?"

Mum's voice is quieter than usual, but it startles me nonetheless. She's perched on the foot of the bed with her hair pulled back and a paintbrush stuck out of it. "I should really be used to you popping up every few weeks by now, shouldn't I, Mum?"

"Do you remember?" she presses.

I cast my mind back. I was so young, so green. Horny as hell, having great sex. Oh, Jesus, some of those men… I still masturbate over the memories. Shaking my head of those thoughts, I recall how much hope I had for the future. An opera career, a loving relationship—these things were all in front of me. "Yes," I reply through my distant smile.

"Eighteen years ago, it was. Doesn't seem that long, does it?" In a quick jump cut, mum's right by my side looking down at me. "I was eighteen years older than you are now when I died." She lets this sink in for a moment, before proceeding in her most gentle of manners. "That could be all the time you have left. Eighteen years, gone in the blink of an eye. Please don't waste a second of it." I look at her freakishly crystal-clear image. I haven't seen anything crystal clear since I was a kid, but it's like this rule doesn't apply to my mum. Slowly, she begins to fade. Just before she disappears entirely, I hear her faint last words. "Promise me."

I promise, Mum. I promise.

CHAPTER 13

"The flu? Really, Bradford?" Mum's voice startles me, coming out of nowhere as usual.

"Well, I had to tell Bruno something, didn't I? I couldn't let him see me like *this*." I'm staring in the bathroom mirror, checking the bruise Jarrod left on my face—the one that has only now just faded after seven days. Craning my head to the side, I move my tunnel of vision till I spot my mother's reflection in the doorway.

"Have you left the house at all this past week?"

Her question makes me wince. I'm never sure how much mum knows or doesn't know. Maybe she just wants me to say it out loud, like it's of some kind of therapeutic benefit. "Only to take Brendan for his walks. Even then, I had to wear dark glasses and they messed with what little sight I have left. Brendan was all confused because I was being so slow and careful when I walked."

Mum's reflection cuts to directly behind my shoulder. The reprimanding look on her face is tempered only by the worry I can see in her eyes. "Darling, you can't make problems disappear by simply ignoring them."

"I know. You're right, but Jarrod won't leave! I have no idea what I'm going to do." A guttural groan charges out of my body. "I suppose I should consider myself lucky he didn't punch me. With all those hipster rings he wears, I might've ended up with a nasty gash instead of just a bruise." I can't believe I'm actually voicing all this stuff. Sure, it's only to mum—alive or dead, I've always been safe with her. Nevertheless, it's still grossly uncomfortable. I'm racking my brain to try and find a positive angle. "At least Jarrod's avoiding me. He's been out a lot of the time and I hide in my room whenever he comes home."

Mum reaches out to touch me, but as usual, her hand stops short. I see the flicker of frustration in her expression before she turns it into a kind smile. "Where does Bruno fit into all this?"

Bruno. My one ray of sunshine. "He's been amazing, Mum. He even pushed to come over and play nursemaid. I told him I'd ordered all my groceries online and I had everything I needed. I only convinced him to stay away by pointing out he'd catch whatever virus I had."

Mum studies me for a moment, choosing her words carefully. "He'd help you, you know. He'd be here in a flash if he had any idea what was going on."

"No. It's far too humiliating. There's no way I want my private shame and embarrassment to be compounded by anyone else knowing about it." I turn around, sucking in a deep, fortifying breath. "I'm aware that I need to do something about Jarrod, but I just don't have the energy to fight right now. I haven't seen Bruno in a week. Honestly, that's the only thing I want to do." *Yeah, Bradford, that's right—bury your head in the sand.* "I'm pathetic, mum. Weak as piss."

"I won't hear that kind of talk," she says, moving closer to me. "*You are not pathetic.*" I avert my eyes. I can't even meet her gaze, it's too intense, too knowing. "Look at me, Bradford." It takes some effort, but I do as I'm told, and her expression pierces right into my soul. "You've been going through all this alone and you don't have to."

"Mum, Bruno has his own life and his own partner. He doesn't need to deal with all my dramas as well. I certainly don't want to give him any excuse to run."

"Don't underestimate him. He's a lot more present than you might realise," she says cryptically.

"What do you mean?"

Her left eyebrow raises ever so slightly, but her face is giving nothing else away. And without another word, she vanishes.

***

"So, this Italian club, it's kind of like an RSL or a footy leagues club, is it?" I ask Bruno, as our taxi heads west through the Cross City Tunnel.

"Well, maybe not quite that huge." Bruno grins over at me. He's absolutely gorgeous tonight—dressed up for his big fiftieth celebration in an expensive-looking button-up shirt and dark jeans that make his arse look more toothsome than ever. I'm glad said arse is now planted firmly on the back seat next to me, otherwise—taxi driver or not—I'd be groping it for the whole journey. "Gabriela's booked out a function room with a dance floor and karaoke, and we've nutted out a full three-course dinner menu. A lot of people are coming, so prepare to be swamped with overbearing Italian family members."

It's fair to say I'm more than a little nervous tonight. I haven't met a single member of Bruno's family. In fact, other than our fleeting chat with Henry and that debauched afternoon with his soccer team, I haven't met anyone associated with Bruno at all. For more than three months, we've been operating on the down-low.

Twenty-three days have now gone by since that awful night with Jarrod. I'm still doing my level best not to run into him. Shunting back and forth to Bruno's apartment several times a week has certainly helped.

I still haven't said a word to Bruno about what happened with Jarrod, though maybe he's had his suspicions. Since our reunion, he's been extra protective of me—always holding me close, always reluctant to see me leave. His quietly-concerned expression has become a mainstay. There's a desperate urgency in the way he has sex with me. Maybe I'm reading too much into it. Maybe he's just in hyper-passionate overdrive, making the most of the time he has left while his partner is away.

All good things come to an end. Bruno will go back to his old routine and I'll have to settle for the role of Friend With Occasional Benefits. I'm trying not to panic; I just have to remind myself that he wants me in his life for good. I need to believe in this.

"You're very quiet tonight. Is everything OK?" Bruno reaches over and squeezes my hand, his voice cutting right through my thoughts.

I've been so busy stewing over my situation I've forgotten to put on my cheery face. I've had to be vigilant about this with Bruno. I don't want to find myself in a situation where I have to answer difficult questions. There's no way I'm going to taint a single moment that we get to share together. And right now, the last thing I'm keen to do is put a dampener on Bruno's big night.

"I'm great," I say, flashing him my best smile. *No, Bruno. I'm crawling on the edge of a knife, scared stiff over what Jarrod might do next.*

"How are things with… you know…?" Bruno's being as delicate as possible. I can hear the trepidation in his tone. He knows it's a touchy subject, but he still checks in with me every time I see him.

I'm not going to lie to Bruno. But I'll only ever offer him the side of the truth I can cope with. "Still tense. Still trying to keep right out of his way," I concede. "I'm really glad I've been able to escape and come spend time at your place." As soon as the words have left my lips, I kick myself. "Not that I ever need an ulterior motive to see you." *God, I need to get a bloody grip.*

Bruno fixes his big dark eyes on mine. "I'm always here, OK? *Anything* you need. You got that?" His tone is emphatic. He definitely knows more than he's letting on.

I'm dying to say something. Mum was right—I've been staggering blindly through all this crap with Jarrod on my own. But it's my punishment for being such a pushover. I got myself into this nightmare and it's my job to get out of it again. Of course, Bruno would rush to me and do anything he could if he knew the gory details. His heart is as big as Tasmania. But do I really want him saving me like some damsel in distress? Do I really want that dynamic between us? Absolutely not. More than anything, I want Bruno to see me as a whole person. Someone who's strong and capable and can meet him as an equal.

"Thank you," I tell him, putting on the most confident, manly air I'm capable of. "That means a lot, it really does."

You're the only thing that's keeping me sane right now, Bruno.

***

The Italian club does seem a bit like an RSL, with its patterned carpet, sign-in booths, and various bars, restaurants and gambling rooms. Pokies, Keno and all manner of sins clearly play a large part in financing the impressively-sized venue. Bruno, Brendan and I navigate a wide carpeted staircase to a foyer, which leads us through double doors to our function room. Before we even enter, I can hear the ear-splittingly tuneless sound of some dear old matron warbling away in Italian.

"The joys of karaoke," mutters Bruno as we scan the scene in front of us. It's like a wedding, except where the bride's table should be is a low stage next to a DJ booth and huge video screen. Tables full of guests are chatting raucously in that distinct Mediterranean style—shrieks, laughs and overdramatic campiness permeate the air-conditioned atmosphere. The whole place is garishly sterile, like one massive plush office floor, yet it's strangely comforting. Somewhere I could sink into with ease. I think I'm going to enjoy this.

"There you are!" Squinting into the low-lit yonder, I spot a woman rushing towards us. As she nears, I can see her masses of dark curls—the kind of hair women paid a fortune to have permed that way in the eighties. Her slender, curvy-hipped figure is hugged by a tight dress, and she's skilfully whisking across the carpet in strappy heels.

I take a step back, allowing her some personal space to hug Bruno, but she comes right for me instead, wrapping her arms around my upper body in a Chanel-soaked cloud. "I'm glad you could make it, sweetie! Bru's told me so much about you."

He has? "Um, all good things, I hope." I'm busy trying to shake off my initial surprise and act all charming and confident. Let's face it, insecurities are boring.

She pulls her head back, clasping her hands to my shoulders. "Are you kidding? He *raves* about you." She glances over to Bruno. "You're right, Bru. He's absolutely gorgeous. Come on, you've gotta meet everyone." Instantly, she's grabbed my hand and I'm being carted off across the function room floor.

"So, I guess you've now met Gabriela," Bruno murmurs in my ear.

"Well, I could see the resemblance." I shoot Bruno a grin, noticing the way his eyes twinkle back at me.

"Mum, Dad—you gotta meet Bruno's new man," Gabriela calls out, as we approach a table of several people.

Bruno's new man? I'm a little stunned, but I love the sound of it. If Gabriela is going to exaggerate in the name of theatrics, I'm all for it.

"Bradford, this is Valentina, our mum, and Giovanni, our dad."

Valentina is a stately, grey-haired Italian matron, impeccably dressed with a calm air about her. She smiles primly and offers me her hand, which I shake delicately as we exchange pleasantries. I then turn to Giovanni to do the same, but he chortles and struggles to his feet. Rattling off something in Italian, he pulls me into a hearty hug. "No bloody formality, please," he says in a heavy accent. He's well-dressed in a blazer and tie, with an open, ready smile and a fedora still on his head even though we're inside. I watch as he carefully sits down again. Bruno has painted a pretty accurate picture; he does seem quite frail.

Once again, I'm steered by Gabriela towards a tall, imposing-looking man in his fifties. He's flashily-dressed, wearing a sharp-looking suit with an open-necked shirt, a thick gold chain, and chunky rings on each hand. "And this is my husband, Claudio," says Gabriela.

Claudio's grip on my palm is bone-crushing and he claps me on the shoulder with his free hand. "Good to finally meet you, brother," he says, with more than a hint of that Aussie-Euro tough-guy inflection in his voice.

I'd better butch it up. Filling my lungs, I drop my voice a tone or two lower than usual. "Pleasure's all mine. I'm honoured to have the invite."

"Oh, don't be silly." Gabriela playfully slaps the shoulder that Claudio's just pummelled. "We've all been dying to see who's been putting that spring into Bruno's step lately."

I glance over to Bruno, who's been standing meekly in the background with a bemused grin. Getting this kind of feedback is more powerfully validating than I could have imagined. I really had no idea Bruno had said much about me at all—to *anybody*. Turning to Gabriela,

I square my shoulders and pile on the charm. "Is the rest of your family here? Bruno always talks about his nephews."

"Oh, no." Gabriela guffaws at my gaffe. "They don't wanna be around all us oldies. We set them up with pizza and ice cream and their favourite babysitter. Plus," — she tilts her champagne glass against her lips and drains it — "we're gonna have quite a bit of this." Wiggling the empty flute between her rouge-noir polished fingers, she scans the table, presumably seeking more.

"Birthday boy and girl at the head of the table," announces Valentina, in an accent as pronounced as her husband's.

"Mother has spoken," sing-songs Gabriela, before grabbing my hand and fairly dragging me and Brendan around to sit next to her.

Brendan dutifully lies on the carpet between my chair and Giovanni's. The elderly man leans down and begins making a fuss over him. I can see that Brendan's trying to behave as best as he can, but his exuberant personality is bubbling below the surface as he happily soaks up the attention.

"We have *so much* to talk about," says Gabriela, clutching onto my arm with one hand while holding her glass out to her husband for a refill.

I squint over at Bruno, who's taken the seat between the two of them. His face is a bit of a blur, but I know it well enough now that I can see the muscular raise of one cheek as he winks at me. Everything about his expression says, *I told you she was overbearing.* What Bruno isn't aware of is just how familiar I am with this scenario. I'm in my element: all the gorgeously camp sopranos I've sung with adopted me as their cute little gay tenor friend during performance runs. Next to those Amazonian divas, a stocky short bear like me was the ideal accessory, and it was a role that I relished.

Gee, how life has changed. I didn't realise how much I missed it till now, with Gabriela chatting away at me, telling me all about her family. "Dad *never* takes off his fedora," she chirps. "He's always been embarrassed about his baldness. I wasn't the least bit surprised when Bruno's big head went exactly the same way."

I glance over at my gorgeous paramour, who's chatting animatedly in Italian to Claudio. "I'm obsessed with Bruno's bald head," I say dreamily. "I literally cannot stop kissing it." I think of the nights I spend with my lips pressed against Bruno's smooth scalp as he's sleeping snuggled into my chest.

Snapping out of my reverie, I look back at Gabriela, whose face is piqued with amusement.

"Sorry," I say. "TMI? I mean, you *are* twins, after all. Don't you guys share everything?"

Gabriela throws her head back and whoops with laughter. "Darling, *nothing* is off limits with us."

My mind races to imagine exactly what Bruno has been blabbing to her about. I turn scarlet as I think about the kinky shenanigans the two of us men get up to. What on earth is Gabriela picturing right now? *Never mind, she's moved on...*

"Marco's nine. He's still very much a little kid. He was the surprise, really. I mean, *me* with a second baby at *forty*? It was already a miracle having Stefano when I was nearly thirty-eight. Mum was the same way. She and dad were in their early thirties, which may as well have been a hundred in an Italian family. Her pregnancy was a shocker, which she's reminded us of practically every day of our lives. That's why they never had any other kids." She stops to take another gulp of her champagne. "Stefano's twelve and already starting to go through puberty. He's definitely developing a bit of a teen attitude. God help me. I'm just glad I didn't have a daughter, we'd be screaming at each other for a whole decade."

I love how she's spilling all this to me. Her energy is infectious. I'm just sitting here with my Cheshire cat grin, nodding and giving encouraging responses, doing my best to be as charming as possible.

"Bru tells me you also have just one sister?"

"Oh, yeah. But not twins. Summer was from mum's second marriage, so she's thirteen years younger than I am."

"Oh? And is she just like you?"

I can't help but laugh to myself. *No, Gabriela. She's actually more like you.* "She's got long dark hair and she's a total extrovert. Also a bit of a hippie. She and her partner Nathan are moving to Sydney soon; maybe you'll meet them."

I'm always careful when I talk about future plans with regard to Bruno. I don't want to jump the gun and jinx everything. Our connection is precious and I'll do whatever I can to hold onto it. It's a delicate balance, trying to show him how interested I am without letting him see how much I've come to rely on his love.

Oh, JESUS! How the hell did that word just pop into my head?

With my thoughts deviating, I've missed Gabriela's response. She's pushing a folder under my nose. "I've signed all of us up. So you'd better flick through this."

"Sorry? Signed up for what?" I open the folder and hold it close to my face. I have to squint really hard and scan at a snail's pace, which is why I never read print. In the space of a minute I'll end up with a huge headache. I'm confronted with list after list of songs, all in Italian. My attention tunes back to Gabriela.

"... of course you're going to sing! Bruno never stops talking about your talent." Gabriela thrusts a pen and small piece of printed paper at me.

Mild panic rises in my chest. "Oh God, no. I can't. I… don't know anything. I was an opera singer. I don't think Wagner is going to go down too well in this place."

In amongst Gabriela's protests, I can hear some young girl screeching out an off-pitch rendition of Umberto Tozzi's *Ti Amo*. My mind goes into problem-solving overdrive. *Umberto Tozzi.* I remember dancing around the living room when I was eight to Laura Branigan's version of his song *Gloria*. Later, as a party-hard opera student, I drunkenly taught myself Umberto's original Italian lyrics. But that was, what? Over twenty-five years ago?

Snapping my head around, I search for the huge video screen I'd noticed earlier. The lyrics projected onto it seem quite big. If I squint hard, maybe it'll help. "OK," I say, filling in the piece of paper with my song choice. "But I'm going to need a couple of stiff rum and cokes first."

"Of course, darling. We can't have you going in there *dry*. I'll get you a double." Gabriela snatches the piece of paper and disappears. By the time she's come back, the MC is calling out my name. "Looks like I'm too late," she trills, plonking my drink on the table and waving me off. "Don't worry, it'll be here when you get back."

Bloody hell! My heart jumps as I realise what I've just been railroaded into. Rising to my feet, I make a conscious effort to put on my theatre persona. *It's just an act, Bradford. You've done it countless times before.* Nobody wants to see a lack of confidence, so I just have to shove it right down and pretend like it's nothing.

"I look after your boy," pipes up Giovanni, as I cast a sideward glance at Brendan.

"Will you be OK?" This comes from Bruno, who's starting to get up.

"Nah, it's fine," I say in my most reassuring tone. "I'll just look down."

My trip to the stage involves me keeping my eyes glued to the floor in front of me. That's the greatest hazard right now. My hands brush against chairs, warning me in advance of their proximity. The dance floor is easy, there's nothing in the way. And the two steps up to the rostrum will be OK, so long as I watch where I put my feet.

It's only now that I notice the music has well and truly kicked in, having started at the beginning of my journey. I've barely had the mike shoved in my hand before I have to sing the first "*Gloria*." There's literally no time to stew over how I'm going to sing this, so I launch into it with the gusto of a seasoned seventies variety TV performer.

As I prattle off the first verse, reciting the part I know best, it dawns on me that I can't just stand still onstage. This is where my penchant for daggy seventies and eighties music kicks in. I've danced around mimicking to the video clips of countless disco songs—when I was a kid, when I was a drunken uni student. I used to be fun once upon a time.

Right—it's time to go full-on camp. Bugger it, I can't see anybody anyway, so it's not like I'm going to be put off by their reactions. I make my best effort to channel John Travolta and add his swagger to my act.

I'm impressed at how my voice has automatically adjusted. Without conscious thought, I've thinned out my tone, reined in my operatic vibrato and added a raspy edge to my phrasing. I can't believe what a massive buzz this all is.

The Italian gets a little hairy at one point and my pulse rises sharply. Squinting to my right, I realise the lyrics on the video are *almost* visible. I can't really see them, but the general shape of the words gives me an instant reminder of what I might possibly have forgotten.

As soon as I'm back on track, I turn towards my blindest spot on the left of me and I'm hit by the amount of people on the dance floor. I've been so busy coordinating my little act that I literally had no idea. There in the middle is Gabriela going wild, twirling around on her heels, with her big bald bouncing bear of a brother thrashing rhythmically beside her. It's so damn cute that I nearly forget what I'm doing.

As I start belting out the home stretch of chorus repeats, other people raucously sing along. The dance floor is now throbbing with animated verve. I'm gobsmacked. I'm also gyrating like a refugee from the Village People, but it seems to be working. As the synth trumpet toots the outro, people start whistling and clapping, and Gabriela rushes towards me.

"My God, you were *fabulous*!" she shrieks, flinging her arms around my neck. "You *have* to get up again later."

I'm almost hyperventilating, coming down from my intense performance high. "Nah, they'll be well and truly sick of me. Someone else's turn."

I don't really hear Gabriela's reply, because Bruno's lips are suddenly mashed against mine. His big hands clasp the back of my head and air rushes from his nose. "Jesus," he pants, his lips buzzing against my moustache. "I never wanted to fuck the living shit out of you more than I do right now."

Back at our table, Brendan has firmly transferred his affections to Giovanni, who is not-so-surreptitiously handing him morsels from the appetiser platter. Valentina catches my eye, claps her hands together and launches into an ebullient tirade of Italian. I nod and smile politely, unsure of what's going on.

"Oh, Mum," Bruno calls across the table. "Bradford doesn't actually speak Italian."

Valentina's eyebrows shoot skywards. Her eyes bore into me with confusion. "But you sound like natural!" she says. "What you mean you not speak Italian?"

"We had to learn to pronounce it properly when I was an opera singer," I say, with a sheepish shrug of my shoulders. "I still have to use a dictionary to translate."

Valentina looks back at Bruno with a dubious expression. "Well, *you* teach him, you hear?" She follows this up with a coda in her native language, something that makes Claudio, Gabriela and Bruno all laugh.

A couple of heavily-laden waitresses sidle up to the table. "*Vitello tonnato*," says one of them, placing large plates of what looks like cold meat salad in front of Gabriela and Valentina. "Chi è vegetariano?"

"Over here, Melina," says Gabriela, patting my shoulder. A huge caprese salad is slid graciously in front of me. I look over at Bruno, who's grinning across the table. Trust him to take care of the menu—he knew exactly what I'd like.

While everyone is talking and tucking into their veal, I marvel at the vibrant tomatoes, the piquant basil, the smooth virgin olive oil dressing and the decadent buffalo mozzarella adorning my plate. It's hard to pace myself politely and not just wolf it down. There are huge baskets of crusty bread and I'm getting stuck into that too. God, I love Italian food. None of these teeny-tiny elegant serves. We are expected to *eat.*

After we've finished our entrees, while Valentina is involved in a lively cross-table discussion with her twins, Giovanni motions for me to come closer. "How long you know my son?" he says.

"Um, we met in January." I'm not quite sure where this is going, but I don't elaborate. I just watch quietly as Giovanni mulls this over.

"He been very happy this year. I not seen him like that in a long time." He grins at me and I spot a twinkle in his eye—the same one I see in Bruno sometimes when I'm lucky. "*You* do this," Giovanni continues, patting me on the shoulder. "You make my son smile again."

I'm so taken aback I almost feel choked up. All this—everything I'm seeing tonight—has been happening behind the scenes. I had no idea anyone really knew I existed. I'm still processing this when the thought of Brendan pops into my mind. *Bruno's* Brendan. Nobody here seems to mention him. Maybe they're being polite, given I'm at this party as Bruno's sort of surrogate date.

My mind flicks back to a week or two ago. I'd originally planned to take Bruno out to dinner tomorrow—April twenty-first, his *actual* birthday—knowing he had his proper family celebration tonight.

***

"I'd really, really love it if you could come to Gab's and my fiftieth," Bruno said. "I want you to meet everyone."

"Me?" I was so surprised I almost spat the word out. "I mean, what about Brendan? He wouldn't want me tagging along, would he?" At the sound of his name, my dog suddenly appeared by my side, touching his wet nose against my leg.

Bruno looked down and laughed, wiping his hand across his face. "Oh, God. I have to tell you this. Brendan will kill me, but we can't go confusing your poor dog any longer. I actually call him 'Brie.'"

"'Brie?' Like, as in triple cream?"

"Yeah. 'Brie-Ann Jatz', to be exact. He used to do drag at Annie's Bar in the noughties and that was his stage name. He hates it, but he's stuck with it as far as I'm concerned. Anyway—" Bruno grabbed my hand and squeezed it. "Brie has other plans."

"Really? Plans more important than your fiftieth?"

Bruno looked visibly uncomfortable. I wondered if he and Brie had had some kind of falling out. Surely not? Bruno hadn't seemed upset or rattled lately. He'd been his usual affable self. "Brie has never really got involved with my family much. He's been to the occasional thing, but..." Bruno's voice trailed off and he closed his eyes. "Well, we've led our own separate lives for a very long time now."

I already knew this. But the way Bruno said it right then gave it a lot more gravity. I didn't want to pry, though. It was none of my business and Bruno already seemed upset. Instead, I just leaned forward and kissed him. "Thank you. I'd be honoured to be your guest."

***

With the tables cleared of entrée plates, it's open season. People come left, right and centre to our little group, congratulating the birthday boy and girl, paying their respects to the parents, and—surprisingly—gushing to me about my performance. "He was an opera singer for many years," chimes in Bruno. The pride I can hear in his voice makes my heart swell. It's deliciously possessive of him, and my mind floats off to a world where I can truly be his. One day I would love that more than anything. It's my fantasy and I don't give a damn what anyone else thinks.

The MC calls Gabriela's name and she guzzles the last of her champagne before swanning off to the stage. I stand up and turn to try and get a good view. After all Bruno's said about her singing, I'm dying to hear what she can do. A warm arm slides over my shoulder and hugs me close just as *Love is a Battlefield* begins to blast through the speakers.

"I didn't know there was an Italian version of this," I say to Bruno.

"There isn't, as far as I know," he replies, just as Gabriela launches into the spoken intro in English.

"What do you mean? All the songs in that folder were Italian."

Bruno breaks out into guffaws.

"What?"

"Only the ones at the *beginning* of the folder."

"Oh, God! You mean I gave myself a panic attack trying to sing the only Italian pop song I even *partially* know, and it was all for nothing?"

"Well, you were a hit, weren't you?" says Bruno. He grabs my hand and yanks on it. "Let's go and dance.

"No, no, no no no…" I sound like a whining child. "I don't dance."

"Rubbish," he chortles. "I just saw you do it onstage, remember?"

I resist Bruno a moment longer, seizing my rum and Coke. "I'm gonna need some more Dutch courage." Tipping my head right back, I swill the whole damn lot in a couple of gulps.

"That was a double, you know," says Bruno.

"Oh. No wonder I'm getting pissed." I can feel my head spinning as he steers me into the crowd on the dance floor.

By now, Gabriela has launched into the opening chorus and—as I expected—she's a powerful belter who gives Pat Benatar a run for her money. Not only is she singing with so much clout she has to hold the dodgy mike away from her face, she's also dancing frenetically—heels and all.

I have been paying such close attention to her singing, I haven't even bothered to be inhibited about my own dancing. Bruno and I are bopping about with gay abandon, grinning like idiots at his sister.

I can hear the instrumental section approaching. Bruno leans closer to me and speaks loudly in my ear. "Gab and I used to practise the dance routine for this bit in the lounge room when we were about ten. We got it down to a fine art."

"You mean like this, *Harry*?" Right on cue, I fling straight into the quintessentially eighties boob-shimmying.

Bruno takes one look at me and laughs, joining in perfect sync. We turn to face the stage, grinding around like total twats. I can just imagine the sight of it—two chunky, chubby bears humping the air like we're jazz ballet queens from 1984.

"Oooh!" squeals Gabriela into the mike. Straight away, she's clacking down the stairs towards us. She barges in between Bruno and me, swivels to face the same way, and suddenly it's three of us in our own little *Solid Gold* display. We do every attitude walk and air punch, getting so carried away that Gabriela has completely forgotten to return to the stage by the time she has to sing again. She doesn't even miss a beat, though, turning back and singing into the mike right there on the dance floor while she continues the routine one-handed.

Like the pied piper, everyone follows Gabriela on the final strut till we get to the fist pumps at the end. It's shambolic—I can only imagine the alcohol-fuelled spectacle we're all making, but the whole place is rumbling with electric energy. There's a palpable sense of unity here that I haven't felt in as long as I can remember.

Amidst all the whistling applause, Gab throws her arms around Bruno and me. "Bloody hell, Bradford," she laughs. "You were amazing… we have to do this more often!"

Back at the table, they're already serving the mains. "I'll just go find Claudio," says Gabriela, and saunters away. With both her and her husband *in absentia*, Bruno commandeers the spot next to me.

"Claudio's been off on his phone all night," I observe. "Is he a workaholic or something?"

"He's got his fingers in all sorts of pies," says Bruno. "I gather he's been more on the straight and narrow since he became a dad, but he certainly seems to know a few shady people, if you catch my drift."

"So… don't get on his bad side, eh?" I'm being a cheeky little bastard, but Bruno knows it's all in good fun. He chuckles, reaching across and brushing his thumb up and down over my nipple. The sensation shoots straight to my dick, flooding it with a delicious, tingling warmth.

"He's actually a really great bloke," says Bruno. "He loves my sister, he loves his boys and he's been like a brother to me."

With perfect timing, Gabriela waltzes back to the table with her husband in tow. Come to think of it, he *does* look like he just stepped off the set of *Goodfellas.*

"What did we miss?" chirps Gabriela.

"*Pollo Ripieno*," Bruno replies, as he stuffs a hunk of polenta-crusted chicken in his mouth. "Hurry up, it's getting cold."

My own main course is a decadent mushroom ravioli in parmesan cream sauce. It's so divine I'm pretty sure I might even lick the plate clean. Of course Bruno was behind all this. There's not a drab roast vegetable in sight; none of the usual humdrum fare that clouds menus put together by people who neither know nor care about catering to vegetarians. I want to gush and tell Bruno how touched I am, but I don't trust myself in my semi-drunken state. After Bruno's little nipple caress, my dick is now hard and I can feel the pre-come oozing through my shaft.

Too much rum, too little recent masturbation, and a sexy man within groping distance mean my inhibitions are fast flying out the window.

After dessert—and a dreadfully-warbled tribute ballad courtesy of some septuagenarian aunt—the MC addresses the room. "For our final song tonight, we have a very special couple coming to perform. But before we get them up here, let's sing them both a huge Happy Birthday!"

With that, he launches into a cringey rendition of the hackneyed dirge, scooping and ad-libbing like he's some sort of modern-day R&B crooner. The entire room joins in, but their tuneless mirth is a hell of a lot more fun to listen to.

"What the fuck? No bloody way, Gab! I am *definitely* not singing." Bruno's face is one part amusement and three parts panic.

"You bloody well are!" Gabriela retorts, grabbing his hand and tugging hard. *Gee, she certainly seems to do that a lot.* "You know the song, you'll be completely fine."

"Oh, fucking *hell*," Bruno grumbles to me under his breath.

I vaguely recognise the introduction which plays as Gabriela's carting Bruno onto the stage. The second she opens her mouth, I know exactly what it is. *Sarà perché ti amo*.

It's a much simpler song for Gabriela to sing, because it covers only a small range right in the middle of her vocal register. Still, she gives it her professional polish, committing to every word.

The real revelation is Bruno. When he gets to his verse, he's skilfully thinned out his tone so he can belt as high as Gabriela did. It's raw and untrained, but he's *good.* And after one or two lines, he's settled in and he turns to look directly at me.

"What'd I miss?" Claudio's gruff voice is directly behind my right shoulder.

"Just the agonising Happy Birthday rendition." I smile and glance sideways, but he's still out of my sight range. "You must never stop working."

Claudio chuckles. "Gotta make the big bucks. Gab has expensive tastes."

My eyes are still fixed on Bruno, waiting for his second solo verse. Sure enough, he turns to me and grins, once again directing the whole thing my way. I may have had more double rums than I can remember, I may not actually speak Italian, but I can pick out enough words to know what he's singing about.

By the time Gabriela and Bruno reach the final choruses, the entire room is shout-singing along with it. Bruno is positively beaming, and when he gets to the very last line, he points right at me. *"Sarà perché ti amo*," he sings, and I know exactly what he's saying. *Maybe it's because I love you.*

I can barely see Bruno now because of the tears welling in my eyes. As they begin to spill down my cheeks, Claudio leans in from behind and mutters into my ear. "He's fuckin' nuts about you, you know?"

***

Back at my apartment, Bruno and I stumble through the door, rip our clothes off and fall into bed. There in the dark, he draws me close and nestles his head into my chest. I sling my leg over his hips, pulling them towards me till his cock presses against my taint. I slide one arm under his pillow and cradle his head with the other. Resting my lips against his smooth scalp, I breathe in his special scent. The room spins gently in my drunken state of happiness.

And this is how I fall asleep, with the collective joy of tonight radiating through my soul.

Sarà perché ti amo
Sarà perché ti amo
Sarà perché ti amo

CHAPTER 14

My first thought as I'm struggling to wake up is *how bad is my hangover?* I'm still groggy as hell, but I'm instantly recalling how much champagne I swilled with Gabriela. Bradford and I were legless when we got back here to his place, well past the ability to fuck. I run my hand down to my dick and find it's hard as a rock. Looks like I've passed test number one. Lifting my head, I discover it's not aching. I guess it pays to only drink the good stuff. Test number three—I run my hands over my belly. No nausea. In fact, other than my fuzzy head, I seem to have got off lightly.

Moving the sheet down, I turn my attention towards Bradford. He's lying on his side away from me, his upper leg bent so he's almost on his front. There's a beam of light creeping through the window and it's casting a glow right over his back and arse. The hair over his buns is almost luminescent. There's no way I can resist this.

Leaning forward, I run my nose over his lumbar region, letting the fur tickle my nostrils. Slowly, I move further south, feeling that point where his back morphs into the cleft of his arse. One of my hands is already stroking his right arse cheek. I pull it outwards, separating the two burly mounds so I can have a good look inside his crack. I never fail to get a thrill when I see this. I love the thickness of the hair in there. I love how his skin tone gets darker at the deepest part. His puckered brown hole drives me fucking mad. And there's little else in this world that gets me going more than the scent of Bradford's morning arse. Every time I see him, he's showered within an inch of his life. At moments like these, though, I manage to catch him unawares.

Lowering my face towards his little paradise, I sniff hard and begin to lick in slow, sensual strokes. Savouring the taste of him, I try my best to work out exactly what it is that I love so much. He's not sweet or salty, he's *umami.* That indescribable quality that gets me salivating. And the pheromones rushing into my nostrils are sending me fucking dizzy. I'm having way too good a time to go all animalistic on him. I want to wallow in this sensory fucking overload.

Bradford moans and moves his hips slightly, pressing his arse up against my mouth. "If you keep doing that, I'm going to have to jerk off," he mumbles.

Oh, fuck yes. As much as I adore foreskins, uncut guys like me tend to jiggle our cocks too fast to get a really good look. Bradford's technique is full visuals, though—the sight of him slowly rubbing his well-slicked hand up and down his cut cock instantly makes me want to come.

Pulling my tongue from his succulent pucker, I slowly massage it with my thumb as I reach over to the top drawer next to his sofa bed. There at the front is the bottle of Johnson's Baby Oil we always use. "Get cracking," I say, handing it to him.

Shuffling down the bed again, I fling his leg over so he's on his back, grab him behind the knees, then push upwards till his feet are high in the air and his little cunt is smiling at me. *Now I'm gonna go in for the kill.*

"Jesus!" gasps Bradford, as I jam my tongue straight into his taut ring. I'm all done with that delicate licking now. I am gonna eat the absolute fuck out of this hot arse. In and out I thrust, grinding my face hard against him, twisting this way and that to try and get in even deeper. Now and again I deviate to his arse cheeks and his taint, biting, licking, and sucking, all the while keeping his wet little cunt in a holding pattern with my probing thumb.

Bradford's hips are squirming and his arm is speeding up a bit. "You're gonna make me come way too quickly, you know," he pants.

There's nothing that'll spur me on faster than hearing those words. I live for that sort of thing. Every muscle in my body aches to give Bradford pleasure. I've been ramming my own hips into the mattress, coaxing my foreskin back and letting the friction against the sheets keep me in the horniest state possible. But now that's not enough.

Letting go of one of Bradford's legs, I reach down and grip myself where it feels the best. I am absolutely desperate to blow my load, and if I time it just right, it's gonna be spectacular.

As I jerk my foreskin with increasing speed, I delve my tongue even further into Bradford's hole. I'm jackhammering it now and he's whining with even more intensity. "Keep going," he rasps. "Please… Oh,

God, I'm gonna blow…" He lets out a stifled screech as his body starts to tremble. When his arsehole clamps around my tongue and goes into a throbbing seizure, I hit the point of no return. My dick has never felt this good before. I could finish myself off right here, but there's one more thing I have to do.

Clambering up and over Bradford, I stretch my foreskin back as soon as I feel that beautiful soreness deep inside me. I almost don't make it, but I drive my cock into Bradford's mouth just in time to let it rip. Throwing my head back and screwing up my eyes, I float off to a happy place as heavenly sensations wrack my body. A sublime ache is running from my arsehole all the way to the end of my dick. Every colossal squeeze of my prostate is propelling come right down Bradford's throat and he's swallowing rapidly in a series of gulping nasal moans. I can feel his tongue rubbing hard against the most sensitive part of my knob, making each spurt more exquisite than the one before.

After my balls are completely drained, after my shuddering subsides and I'm left utterly breathless, I finally look down again. Bradford is quietly staring up at me with his lips still wrapped around my dick. I feel like a fucking *god.* The devotion in his eyes tells me everything I need to know. I could never, ever give him up.

***

Once I'm out of the shower and almost finished drying myself, I hear voices outside. Wrapping the towel around my waist, I quietly open the bathroom door to eavesdrop.

"Nah, Davo. Don't worry, we can use Brad's pass, I'll just go get it." There's a short pause. "Oh. What the hell are you doing here?"

"It's my home, Jarrod. And it's also my parking pass."

Jarrod's voice shoots right up. "Jesus, you're such a petty little bitch!"

Incensed, I march out of the bathroom and right down the hall.

"Well, this is *my* fucking towel," I hear Jarrod snap. I reach the living room just in time to see him ripping the offending item from around Bradford's waist, leaving him cowering there naked.

Right. It's *on.* Yanking off my own towel, I yell out at him. "Hey! You'd better have this one as well, then." I throw it at Jarrod and it lands right on his face as he whips his head around in my direction. "Careful, it's covered in come stains."

Jarrod throws the towel on the floor in disgust, just as a familiar face walks out of the bedroom and stops dead in his tracks. "Bruno?" he says.

"*Brendan?*" I can hardly believe my eyes.

"'Brendan'? What do you mean, '*Brendan*'?" Bradford's face contorts with confusion as his attentive dog rushes up to his side. "Isn't this 'Davo'?"

It takes a split second for the penny to drop. "Brendan *Davey*," I sigh. Jesus, fuck. What a farce.

Jarrod's head is flicking back and forth. His nostrils are flared and his teeth are bared. "*This* clown is your partner?" he snarls at Brie. "What the FUCK is going on here?" Turning to Bradford, he lunges forward and shoves him hard, sending him stumbling into the bookshelf behind.

"*Jesus*, Jarrod!" gasps Brie.

With my face in kill mode, I fly at Jarrod, crashing into him with my chest. Like a typical bully, the scrawny bitch scurries backwards till he's in the kitchen doorway. His eyes immediately drop to my naked crotch.

"Go on, get a good look!" I bark, flipping my cock and balls up and down with my hand. "Haven't you *got* one of these?" I'm right up in his face again.

"*Braddy*," Jarrod snipes, his eyes not leaving mine. "Tell your big fat *boyfriend* he can go *fuck* himself."

"Hey. Come on," Brie interjects, calmly putting his hand on Jarrod's shoulder. "Let's just get out of here, OK?" *Good old Brie. Ever the peacekeeper.* He shoots me a bewildered look as he steers Jarrod towards the hallway. Jarrod's still bitching and moaning, but he's led firmly down to the front door and suddenly they're gone.

It's only now I realise that I've ignored the most important person in the room. Turning to Bradford, I grab him by the arms and look him up and down. "Fuck, *Blinky*, I'm so sorry. Are you OK?"

Bradford looks rattled. Embarrassed. But he makes a painfully visible effort to smile. "I'm fine. I'll live."

"I really didn't mean to interfere. I know it's none of my business, but I just saw red." I'm trying to work out how to say what I really need to. I don't want him to feel any more emasculated than he might already be. "Please don't think I was patronising you by stepping in."

To my surprise, Bradford chuckles. After all the shit that's just gone down, he actually *laughs*. "It was kind of hot, really. You're my man and you came to my aid."

The gentle glow in his eyes speaks volumes. *You're my man.*

***

"Thanks for letting me stay last night," says Bradford, as we sit down to the shabby breakfast of Eggs Florentine I've just made. He shifts uncomfortably in his seat, staring at his plate. "I really hate that you had to see all that drama yesterday morning."

He hasn't broached this topic till now and I haven't pushed him. He's been as affable as ever, and I'm well aware his permasmile is hiding a lot more than he's willing to let on. I'm torn, though. I don't want to cross that line where caring concern turns into pushy intervention. He's clearly a proud and independent man. I mean, just look at how he's coped with the huge changes in his life. On the other hand, I'd hate for him to think I'm not showing him enough support.

"Hey," I say as gently as possible, reaching out and taking hold of his hand. "I know it's only been a few months, but we're way past this, yeah? Don't feel you have to put on a brave front with me. I'm here for it all."

Bradford looks at me for a moment. "Bruno, I'm going to say something, and I don't want you to think I'm trying to lay any heavy expectations on you." He's fiddling nervously with his fork, but he doesn't break eye contact. "I don't know how I'd make it through all this if I didn't have you around."

Throw all your expectations at me, I want to say. *I will do anything to try and make you happy.* However, I don't think bombarding him with my desperate desires is the most helpful way to respond right now.

We're suddenly interrupted by the sound of the front door bursting open and heavy items being dumped on the floor. "Jesus, someone needs to teach straight men about the Neapolitan code." My wayward ex-partner saunters into the room and stops short. "Oh, sorry! Didn't know you had company."

"Bradford, you've met Brie, haven't you?" I shoot a smarmy smile across the room.

Brie screws up his face in distaste. "Ugh. Are we *really* using that name now?"

"Uh… maybe I should clear things up," says Bradford. "Brendan?" Bradford's dog is up lickety-split, trotting over to stand at his side.

"Your dog is called *Brendan?* So, what else? You have a cat called Lisa?" Brie's in full sarky drag mode, and Bradford laughs dutifully.

"No. Brendan would go mental if I brought a cat into the house."

"Well, at least *Brie's* better than *Davo*." Brie pulls out a chair and collapses onto it with dramatic flair. "Sorry about all the shit that went down yesterday, Bradford. Jarrod's a bit out of control, but I've never seen him behave like that before."

"Oh, I'm used to it." Bradford's smiling, but I can see his cheeks are flaming red.

Time for me to change the subject. "There's coffee in the pot, Brie. I'll get you one." Hopping to my feet, I walk round the breakfast bar into the kitchen, and spot the suitcases Brie's plonked down the end of the hall. "Oh, are you back now?"

"Yep. The house is tidy, there's a quiche in the oven, and the landlords are on their way home as we speak. Last night's hookup with the stinky straight guy was my swansong."

"So… what's this 'Neapolitan code'?" I hear Bradford ask, and Brie and I burst into childish sniggers.

"Well, darl," chirps Brie. "Think of the ice cream. Mister Straight Guy was *desperate* to be rimmed."

"I'm confused," says Bradford. "You mean you spread ice cream on his arsehole?"

I try to suppress a laugh, but it comes out as a snort.

"Not exactly, sweetie. Here, have one of these while I explain." Brie picks out and unwraps one of the mini Snickers bars from the candy bowl in the middle of the table. Thrusting it at Bradford, he continues, ticking off each point on his fingers as he goes. "Vanilla means *'I'm not going near that arse unless you've just stepped out of the shower'*. Strawberry means *'I like my men to have a little musky manscent down there'*." He fixes his eyes on Bradford, whose gob is still stuffed with Snickers. "But *nobody* wants chocolate. *Capisce?*"

Bradford heaves and coughs as he swallows. "Oh, God. I'm never gonna look at a pack of Fun Size the same way again." He pops down his cup and gets to his feet. "Well, on that note, I'm gonna leave you two to catch up. Brie—thanks for the entertainment. Bru—thanks for the great brekky."

"Let me give you a lift." I'm already lunging to get my keys.

"Nah, really, it's fine. Four-legged Brendan needs a good walk and we love this autumn weather."

I follow Bradford along the hall, then admire the glimpse of his hairy bum crack as he squats down to harness Brendan. Standing up, he turns to face me. "Thanks for everything," he says shyly. "I've really loved this time with you while Brie's been away." The smile on his face is tinged with a kind of sadness I don't think I'll ever be able to forget.

"*Blinky,*" I whisper, wrapping my arms around his neck and pressing my cheek hard against his. "It's not over. The cat's out of the bag, now. We can see each other whenever we want and it doesn't fuckin' matter." I ease my vice-like grip on the back of his skull and gently kiss his forehead. "And that cunt's not gonna come anywhere near you whenever I'm around, alright?"

I urgently want to spill the beans about Brie and me breaking up, but there's a good chance it'd come back to bite me in the arse. Sure, it might prompt Bradford to finally ditch that fucker, but logic and Oprah tell me that he'll need a long break from relationships afterwards. And my dick and my heart are not gonna stand for that. I can't stay away from him, so fuckbuddies it is for the moment.

With Bradford gone, I rejoin Brie at the dining table. "So… *Jarrod*," I start. "You know I've never cared who you rooted round with. But *that* dickwad?"

"He's cute and he fucks like a jackrabbit," shrugs Brie. "But you're right. He's a hot mess. We've only hooked up here and there, but I've noticed him getting a lot worse lately. One of his friends actually let something slip yesterday." Brie eyes me for a moment, tight-lipped.

"Come on. I can see you're dying to tell me."

He leans forward secretively, as if the walls have ears. "He's been suspended by the nursing board. They're investigating him for supposedly sticking his fingers into the Oxy cupboard."

"Really? Shit."

"You know what those meth heads are like. Anything for a comedown."

My head is swirling with this revelation. "Meth? And you overlooked this because… why?"

"He always told me he was on E," retorts Brendan. "And I'm hardly gonna be a hypocrite after all the trips I took in my youth. Though you'd think at thirty-nine he would have woken up to himself by now."

"Well, *fuck* me. I wonder if Bradford knows about all of this."

"Tell him. Use me as the fall guy." Brie stands up, gathers the cups and plates, then heads round to the kitchen. "After all the shit that's just happened with him, I'm definitely keeping my distance, anyway." Turning his back to me, he begins to stack the dishwasher.

"Leave that, Brie. It's my mess."

"Don't be stupid. I'm already here, I may as well. Oh, and we should talk." I look over to him, but he's bobbed down out of sight. "Maybe we should think about putting this place on the market."

It strikes me as a bit of a cop-out that Brie's not saying this to my face. Then again, maybe it's the only way he can bring himself to broach the topic. I feel grossly uncomfortable too, so I hope we can kill it off quickly. "Sure. Why not. Let's get the wheels in motion. I can even move into Mum and Dad's rumpus room for a while if it comes to that."

With a final clink, Brie shuts the dishwasher door and turns to face me. "Well, that was a lot simpler than I thought it would be."

He's right. I feel at peace. A warm smile spreads across my face as I see my lovely best mate standing there, wiping his hands on a tea towel. "It doesn't need to be a drama. We're good, Brie. We're always gonna be."

CHAPTER 15

I'm on a high. This usually happens after a great lesson with my opera coach. Besides the fact that singing is good therapy, and besides the fact it gives me hope that I may not be wasting whatever talent I have, it's the air that does it for me. All those great big lungfuls I've been sucking in for an hour and a half make everything seem lighter. I feel like I'm about to take flight.

"That's thirty-two sixty," the cab driver calls over his shoulder. I'd normally take the bus and light rail to my teacher's posh place in Pyrmont, but I've got a ton to do today. Fishing my wallet from my messenger bag, I hand over my taxi card and Visa, then stuff the wallet back where it was. Gathering up the pile of massive opera scores on the seat next to me, I open the door for Brendan and grab his harness.

"Here you go." The driver hands the cards back to me, but my arms are full. Dropping Brendan's harness, I shove the cards into my pocket, then thank the driver profusely as I shuffle myself and my dog out of the back seat.

***

"We're gonna get you ready first, buddy," I tell Brendan, dumping my messenger bag on the coffee table in the lounge room. He's easy; I already keep most of his stuff in a backpack. I, on the other hand, have a lot more mucking around to do. Firstly, it's May. I'll probably freeze my tits off, but there's also a good chance I could be sweating buckets when the sun's at its peak. So, I have three days' worth of all-weather clothes to nut out.

When Bruno mentioned he was gonna take me back to Wombat Valley, he was true to his word. This evening, I'll be meeting him for dinner at Thai Nesia in Darlinghurst, then we're gonna spend the night at his place before heading down to the Southern Highlands first thing.

"Won't it be a bit awkward for Brie having me crash in your bed?" I'd asked Bruno when he'd suggested it.

"Not at all," Bruno had said. "He set himself up in the study the night he came back. It's actually worked out well for us the last few weeks."

"OK. But I think we should abstain from loud raucous sex."

"I'm pretty sure I can tie a knot in it for *one* night. But we are gonna fuck like horny teenagers the whole time we're in Wombat Valley. Ya got that?"

After packing my clothes and toiletries, I strip out of my jeans and fold them carefully to wear later tonight. Reaching down to the bottom shelf, I pull out the running shorts I wore yesterday and double check for the emergency twenty dollar bill I stuffed in the little waistband pocket. Brendan's been waiting patiently during this whole flurry of activity, knowing he's been promised the Bondi to Bronte beach walk. After my opera session, I have nervous energy to burn, plus I want to wear him out so he's happy to just chill tonight.

The whole journey with Brendan takes us a couple of hours, including little breaks at Tamarama and Bronte. When we arrive back at the apartment building, he's well and truly ready to settle down for a rest, and so am I. My legs and arse ache after hiking up and down all the coastal steps and ramps. However, I'm vain enough to know they need the upkeep.

Walking through the apartment, I can tell Jarrod's been home. My stuff has been taken off the coffee table and unceremoniously dumped on the floor; the place smells of cigarette smoke; and there's a half-empty coffee cup with two cigarette butts floating inside it. It doesn't look like he's stayed long, because that's about the extent of the mess he's made. I'm not going to call out his name. I don't ever speak to him now unless it's absolutely necessary. A quick check of every room confirms the place is empty, so I settle on the couch for a short nap.

After showering and dressing, I do a final whip around to tidy the apartment. It seems pointless; Jarrod's going to funk it up again while I'm gone. Retrieving my messenger bag from the floor, I rummage around in the zipped pocket to grab my wallet, but it's missing. Panic sets in as I tip out the entire contents onto the coffee table. No, it's not in there at all. *Oh, Jesus Christ.*

Darting from room to room, I check everywhere I can think of. A dreadful feeling forms in the pit of my stomach. I may as well face the fact—Jarrod's stolen it. In a last-ditch attempt, I push open his bedroom door and venture inside. Picking through the mess of clothes and crap everywhere, I scan the floor around the bed, eventually spotting a bright green article poking out. Thank God—that hideous colour has helped me find the damn wallet countless times.

I take a look in the note compartment, but I already know the cash is gone. Even though there was only a hundred bucks, I'm still fuming. My heart rate shoots sky-high when I check the card slots. My Visa is gone. I want to throw up. What the hell am I going to do? I have to work this out pronto or I won't make it on time tonight.

Right. I should call Bruno. I need to get online and block the card. I need to transfer money to Bruno for our holiday expenses. My head is swimming as I dart back to the study, making a detour to the lounge room to grab my iPad. I plonk my arse down on the sofa bed and sign into the banking app. Thank God, it doesn't look like Jarrod has used it yet. Just as my finger is hovering over the "block" button, I have a thought. *In the cab.* I'd stuck my Visa and taxi card in my front pocket. Bloody hell, I'm such a dickhead. I'm even wearing the same jeans *right now*. Tossing my iPad aside, I dig down into the pocket, retrieve the offending articles, then shove them back in my wallet. While I'm at it, I also rescue the emergency twenty bucks from the tiny waistband pouch in my running shorts.

By the time my cab has turned up, I know I'm gonna be late. As we drive, I send Bruno a text, then shove my phone underneath my crotch. It's a bizarre little trick I learnt—it means I don't have to fish through my bag or try and wriggle around extricating it from my jeans. This quick-retrieval system comes in especially handy tonight, because every ten seconds I'm checking the phone for Bruno's reply, which never comes.

When the taxi pulls up on Oxford Street, we're in a no parking zone. I offer a lame apology as I pay the driver, then quickly slide out of the back seat after Brendan. And then I hear the smash. I cringe as I look down at the bitumen and spot my phone. Even with my terrible sight, I can see the silvery matrix of a shattered screen.

"Wow. Looks completely buggered, mate." The taxi driver deposits my overnight bag on the pavement and fishes the offending device out of the gutter for me.

I could let out a barrage of expletives right now. It'd be unlike me, but what the hell else could go wrong tonight? Thanking the driver, I hoik the huge bag over my shoulder and hurry into the restaurant. Up and down and around the tables I hobble, squinting hard as a confused Brendan ambles along beside me. I should be following the rules, not overriding my dog, but I'm way too flustered now. I head to the bar and flag down a waiter. "Sorry," I pant. "I'm meeting someone here and I can't find them. Borelli. Table for two?"

The waiter glances down at my dog. Sometimes it pays to appear a little bit helpless, because rather than giving me directions, he comes around and leads me towards the back. There, at the end, is a small empty table. Settling Brendan first, I collapse onto the chair and instinctively check my phone. Yes, it's a total write-off.

Another twenty minutes goes by and there's still no sign of Bruno. This isn't like him. He couldn't just be stuck in traffic for this long, could he? Maybe I should have done the old-fashioned thing and actually *called* him when I had the chance. It's only now that I have a sudden brainwave. *My iPad.* I can log into my Google account to find his number and call him from a payphone or something.

Leaning down, I ransack my messenger bag, then my overnight bag, blanching as I remember tossing the iPad aside on the sofa bed to get the cards from my wallet. My hands scrunch in my hair as I groan out loud. What the hell is wrong with me? I'm not like this. I'm always organised. I have to be. All this *shit* with Jarrod is taking its toll.

I spend a further twenty minutes sitting at the table, my head churning over all the possibilities for Bruno's no show. He can't be upset with me, can he? We've never had any semblance of an argument. I mean, I would just cry and cry and cry if that happened. My guts wrench as I consider the possibility he might be having second thoughts. Maybe he's texted me to call off our little holiday. Maybe he's prepping the stage by degrees so he can let me down easy. Or maybe—*Oh, God. Please, no*—maybe something terrible's happened to him.

That's it. I can't take any more of this. Standing up, I fish the last twenty bucks out of my wallet. Just as I'm about to slip it under the napkin holder, the waiter who's been hovering over me for three quarters of an hour returns. "Sorry, I think I've been stood up," I mumble, handing him the cash.

The taxi ride home takes forever. I'm working myself into a frenzy. I need to pull my head in. There's bound to be a perfectly good explanation. After rushing a confused Brendan back into the apartment, I'm relieved to find the place silent with all the lights off. Thank God Jarrod's not home. I'm so agitated by now I would probably tear strips off him.

In the study, I dig through my desk drawers and find my old phone. Switching on the ridiculously expensive bright lamp I got from Vision Australia, I curse repeatedly as I try to execute the frustrating task of switching over the nano SIM card. By the time I'm scrolling through for Bruno's number, I'm so riled up I have to deliberately slow my breathing. I need to remind myself that it's *Bruno*. There's no way I want to sound like I'm snapping at him; he's only ever been kind and loving towards me.

While I'm waiting for him to answer, I can hear the incessant beeping of delayed messages coming through. They must have been from him.

"Oh, God, Bradford. I've been trying to call you for nearly an hour." Bruno sounds absolutely frantic. "Dad's in surgery. He's had another stroke. I'm at Prince of Wales with mum and Gab." He chokes on his words. "Sorry, we have to cancel our trip."

"Jesus, Bru, don't worry about *that*! I'm on my way." I hang up before he can protest.

After getting the run around at the hospital, I finally find the waiting room they're in. First, I spot a blurry Gabriela on the couch with two young boys. Nearby is an even blurrier Claudio, whom I only recognise because there's a phone glued to his ear. Valentina is pacing up and down, her arms clutched over her chest. And Bruno appears from nowhere, running right into me. "Oh, baby," he whispers, throwing himself into my arms.

"I'm sorry I missed your calls, Bru. My phone smashed on the road and it's totally wrecked and I didn't even have my iPad so I had to go home and find my old phone so I could ring you—" I need to shut up. I'm babbling like an idiot about dumb things. I know I should be asking after Giovanni, but that might be too intrusive right now. Bruno can tell me about it when he's ready. For the moment, I'm just going to hold him as long as he needs me to.

Lifting his head off my shoulder at last, he grasps the strap of my bag. "Let me take this," he says, then leads me into the waiting area.

"Hi, darl." It's Gabriela. Her mascara is running. She grasps my shoulders and gives me a small kiss on the cheek. "Dad's still in surgery. That's all we know so far." She turns to Bruno. "I'm gonna have to take the boys home soon."

I glance over at the two sleepy kids slumped on the couch. "I'll take them." The words come out automatically.

"Thanks, but we can't ask you to do that." Gabriela forces a weak smile, but I'm not giving up.

"We'll just get a cab. Don't worry about anything. You stay as long as you need to."

She glances back at her kids, then sighs in defeat. "Thank you, Bradford. I'll make sure I don't stay too late. They've got school tomorrow, anyway."

"I'll sleep over and drop them off there too. I'm sure the kids know where to tell the cab driver to go." I can see Gabriela trying to churn the logistics through her mind. "Let me take care of this," I press. "You just focus on what's happening here."

Valentina's voice sails out from behind Bruno in a rapid-fire barrage of Italian. She ushers him away from us, her staccato voice continuing its emphatic delivery.

"Don't be silly, mum," says Bruno. "He's a school teacher. Of course he can look after two kids."

Valentina peers over and notices me watching. I swear her face turns crimson for a split second, then with a lofty lift of her chin, she turns back to Bruno.

I'm distracted by what's going on behind me. "You boys promise to behave for Bradford, OK?" Gabriela's in full-on don't-mess-with-me parent mode. The boys roll their eyes and slide off the couch. "Stefano, Marco, say hello to Bradford."

Their responses are barely muttered, and I have to work hard not to smirk. The poor kids must have very little idea what's going on.

"Come on, fellas. Get your things." Bruno's standing there with my overnight bag already slung across his shoulder.

As we're making our way down to the taxi rank, he loops his arm over the back of my neck. "You sure you'll be OK tonight?"

"Relax, Bru. A couple of tweens are a piece of piss compared to a classroom full of hormonal sixteen year olds."

Bruno whisks the boys into the waiting taxi with no-nonsense efficiency. He turns to me, grabs my shoulders and presses his forehead against mine. "Thank you for doing this," he mumbles.

"Don't mention it. Honestly, I'm here for you, *Harry.* Anything you need, OK? I'm dead serious. Now, get up there and be with your family."

After kissing Bruno on the lips, I settle Brendan in the rear footwell, then slide in around him to sit next to the boys.

"Can I pat your dog?" Marco's in the middle with his arm already stretched out.

"Yeah, he'd love that."

Brendan's busy lapping up the attention when Stefano's voice pipes up from the far side of the cab. "So… you and Uncle Bruno, eh?" He pauses for a second. "Who gets on top?" He starts to snigger, quickly followed by Marco.

Cheeky little brat. He's clearly hoping he'll get a rise out of me, but it's not happening. He's gonna get the most cryptic response I can think of. "Well, Stefano, you'll learn in life that things aren't always black and white."

Stefano snorts. "That's *racist.*"

"We haven't had any dinner," chimes in Marco. His tone is reprimanding, as if I've been neglectful in my duties.

"Neither have I. What do you want?"

"Pizza," says Stefano. He's sitting there sullenly. I'm sure he thinks I'm going to say no.

"Good answer. I'll order some when we get back to your place."

"*And* chicken wings," he stipulates.

"No worries."

"Ooh! And ice cream too?" squeals Marco. Well, at least *he* sounds excited about it.

Thank God I didn't leave my credit card in my wallet for Jarrod to steal—it's definitely gonna get a good workout tonight.

***

I let them eat as much as they want. Meh, they're kids. They've got guts of steel; they'll be fine. I also let them stay up late and watch a movie. They've had a nasty upset today, so I'm not going to crack the whip. There will be plenty of time for rules later. The TV blasts away in the background while I struggle to mark some practice exams on my iPad.

At one stage, I glance down at the floor where Marco is sleeping curled up with Brendan, half on a cushion, half on Brendan's blow-up bed. Stefano's stretched out on the couch opposite with his eyes closed. *Ha! I knew they wouldn't last.* It doesn't take too much coaxing to shepherd both groggy kids to their proper beds.

One benefit of all this happening tonight is I'm well-packed for my aborted holiday with Bruno. I have everything I need, which is more of a blessing than it would be for a sighted person. This house isn't familiar, so finding anything would require a stressful and long-winded search. The only thing I have to look for is some kind of quilt to throw over myself.

Linen cupboards are a royal pain in the arse for anybody, but for an almost-blind bugger like me they're an exercise in pure frustration. Once I locate and open the telltale double doors near the bathroom, I breathe a sigh of relief. Gabriela has everything neatly stacked and sorted, so I don't have to rifle through and unfold all manner of Manchester to find out exactly what it is. Grabbing a couple of woollen blankets, I make my way back to the living room to set up for the night.

Claudio and Gabriela clearly aren't short of a buck or two, so their couches are long and luxurious. The throw pillows are expensive and fluffy and they'll do nicely for my head. Once I'm tucked in and warm, my mind wanders to Bruno. I hope he's OK. I really want to call him, but I'm sure he has more than enough on his mind. I'm in a bind, because I would hate for him to think I wasn't there when he needed me. I remember back when my mum died, people never knew what to say. They were all full of well-meaning platitudes and standard comfort lines, but when it came to their own comfort it was obvious they couldn't wait to get away from me.

In the end, my rumination is my downfall tonight. I don't even get to make a decision, because apparently I'm out like a light.

***

It's dawn when I'm woken by people coming into the house. Sitting up all bleary-eyed, I hear Gabriela and Claudio's voices. "Oh, sorry darl." Gabriela drops her volume as she rounds the corner to the living room and spots me. She walks over and perches on the edge of the couch near my feet. "Thank you *so much* for doing all this."

"Don't mention it," I croak. "We had a great time. How are things at the hospital?"

"Dad's in intensive care. He's still unconscious. Mum won't leave his side. Bruno says he'll stay a bit longer before he heads home. Claudio's gotta go to work, so I've come back to get the boys ready for school."

"No, I'm doing that. You need to go to bed." My statement is firm. I'm not going to just offer, it's a done deal.

Leaning over, she wraps her arm around my shoulders and gives them a squeeze. "You're an angel, Bradford. If you're *really* sure it's OK, I'll book an Uber."

"Of course it is." I reach over and check the time on my iPad. "Stefano said they get up at seven-thirty, so I'll wake them in an hour."

"The little shit!" Gabriela shakes her head. "*Seven.* He'll do anything to keep his lazy arse in bed a bit longer." She glances at her phone. "They've got another half an hour."

"OK. I'll have a shower and get their breakfast ready." I swivel to a sitting position and slowly stand up. I'm still in yesterday's clothes and I feel gross. "Please go and get some sleep, Gabriela." I stare at her with raised eyebrows. "And don't worry about picking the boys up after they finish, I'll do that too. *No bloody arguments.*"

Marco is surprisingly compliant when I wake him up and usher him into the bathroom. When I duck my head into Stefano's bedroom and call his name, all I get is a loud groan. *Lawd, I remember all too well how I was at that age.*

Next, I raid the kitchen fridge. Poking around in the door compartment, I spot a block of haloumi, which I cut into slices and pan fry while I rustle up a pot of scrambled eggs. As I'm setting the plates on the breakfast bar, I spy a note underneath a coffee cup with two twenty dollar bills.

For the boys' lunches. Thanks for this, we owe you one. C.

Wow. Mine used to cost three bucks. Kids are bloody expensive these days.

***

The boys' private Catholic school turns out to be a ten or fifteen minute drive away in northern Randwick. Taking a risk, I hop out of the Uber when we arrive and dial Bruno's number. Maybe he's back at his place by now, and I'm in the neighbourhood.

"Hey, gorgeous. I just got home." Even over the phone I can hear how exhausted Bruno is. "Mum's asleep in the recliner in Dad's room. She's refusing to leave. Gab texted and said she'll go back there early this afternoon. How were the boys last night?"

"They were fine. Stefano was determined to scope me out a bit, but it's nothing I haven't handled before. I've told Gabriela I'm going to pick them up from school this afternoon."

"Oh, man. That's so kind of you. Really."

"It's nothing, Bruno. I just want to help in any way I can."

"You reckon you could help me too?"

"Anything. Just say the word."

"Will you come over to my place? I could really use a cuddle while I get a few hours' sleep." He sounds so earnest, so emotionally fragile. My heart aches for him in the worst way possible.

"I'm already on my way, *Harry*."

With the help of Google Maps, it only takes a few minutes to get to Bruno's place. He answers the door in a towel, melting straight into me. His beard is damp from the shower, his breathing is slow and deep, and his body is heavy and warm. With gentle movements, I steer him towards the bedroom, supporting him all the way.

After settling Brendan, I take off all my clothes, crawl into bed next to Bruno and cuddle up behind him, spooning him tight. "Thank you," he whispers.

For once, it's me who's able to be the strong one. I can finally give Bruno back just a little of what he's given so freely to me.

CHAPTER 16

The next few days go by in much the same manner. Between Bruno, his mum and his sister, they've cobbled together a constant vigil at Giovanni's bedside. Gabriela's taken time off work, but I've beaten her down till she lets me look after the boys without protesting. "Like it or not, you're stuck with me as a babysitter for the moment," I told her.

I've been spending the daytimes at Bruno's apartment, curled up in bed with him while the boys are at school. The rest of the time, I've been at Gabriela's place. The boys have quickly become used to me, and I think they're pretty pleased with my chilled approach. This is a difficult time for them, so I'm not gonna behave like some arsehole disciplinarian. So long as they're fed and made to shower and go to school, it's enough for now.

Each afternoon I've helped them with their homework. Each evening I've dug through Claudio and Gabriela's fridge and pantry and cooked up something for dinner.

"Nonna doesn't make it like that," Marco will tell me.

"Well, I do. I'm sure your nonna is an expert, but there's lots of ways to cook things and I know how to make food taste good."

There doesn't seem to be any arguments about that when it comes to eating. I may not win any prizes for the healthiest cooking, but I always end up with empty plates.

Both Claudio and Gabriela have had it drilled into them that I am staying, so they are free to come and go as they need. The boys and I are happy to just hang out watching TV at night with Brendan. I'm sure I'm letting them stay up well past their usual bedtime, but I'm glad it earns me extra brownie points with them. There have to be some perks when you're a kid who's saddled with some rando babysitter.

Throughout this whole ordeal, Jarrod has been the last thing on my mind. My sole concession was to send a terse message that read, *"I'm gonna be away for a few days."* At this late stage, I feel like that's all he deserves.

***

On my third night with the boys, Claudio picks them up from school, then drops them home after taking them to visit the hospital. Leaving them with me so he can return to work, I go through our established evening routine. Gabriela and Claudio still aren't home by the time the boys are in bed, so I stay up and finish some more of my marking. I'm glad it's close to the end of semester and I'll be free of work for a while. It's been especially tedious having to get everything done on my iPad. Typing is much more cumbersome when you have to wedge the device inches from your face and tap away with one finger.

Just as I'm done for the night, I hear a faint sound from one of the rooms. Tiptoeing down the hall, I pass Stefano's bedroom. As he's twelve and pubescent, he always has the door firmly shut. *Ha. Couldn't possibly think of a reason why he does that.* When I get nearer to Marco's partially-open bedroom door, the sniffling is clear as a bell. My heart breaks for him. He's still such a little kid and this whole situation must be scary as hell.

Brendan is hot on my heels as I pad quietly into the room. Pulling up Marco's desk chair, I take a seat, then signal to my furry best mate. I know it's probably breaking a house rule, but the kid is distressed and I know how therapeutic Brendan can be. He's also very intuitive—at my command, he's hoisted himself onto the mattress with as much delicacy as possible. He immediately aligns himself with Marco and nuzzles against him. Marco flings his arm around him and begins to cry hard. I just wait there patiently, biding my time till the deluge slows.

I'm not going to ask Marco open questions, but I'll probe just a little. A few 'yes' or 'no' ones might prompt him to open up. "Are you sad about nonno?"

"Yes." Marco's hyperventilating, punctuated by broken sobs. "Is he going to get better?"

I've left this side of things to his parents. I don't want to step on anyone's toes, but Marco's distraught, and I'm not going to lie to him. "I really don't know, Marco. He's very, very sick. Maybe I can ask Uncle Bruno."

"He was still asleep today. Mum said he never woke up after the operation." Marco's voice breaks as he finishes his sentence. I can hear the fear and confusion in his voice. This is something so foreign to him. I sincerely doubt he has any point of reference.

"Sometimes people are so sick after they have an operation it might take them a long time to wake up."

"But what if nonno doesn't ever wake up? I never said I loved him. He might die and he won't know." Marco falls into a second and more powerful wave of sobs. Brendan nudges against his face, licking at his neck, and he eventually comes back to shaky breaths.

"Nonno already knows it, buddy. You know how I know that?"

"No." Marco turns his red eyes to me.

"Well, what stuff does he do with you?"

He thinks for a moment, still sniffling here and there. "He takes us to the beach. And he buys us ice cream. And he comes with us to swimming lessons and he watches when we play soccer."

"Well, Marco, sometimes when old people like us love someone, we do things like that. It's kind of a way to let them know that we love them without actually saying any words. And nonno can see how happy you are when you do fun stuff together. That's how he can tell that you love him too."

"Can he really?"

"Totally." I move in a little closer, leaning my elbows on my knees. "And you know another thing? Sometimes when sick people are asleep for a long time like nonno, they can actually hear everything we say. So when you were with him today, I reckon he definitely knew."

"OK." Marco takes a final sniff, then settles back, keeping his arm around my dog. "Can Brendan stay here with me tonight?"

I smile and slowly get to my feet. "For a little while. Just till you go to sleep, OK?"

"Bradford, can you babysit for us all the time?"

God, the kid's got me feeling all emotional now. "I'm here whenever you need me, buddy."

On my way out of Marco's room, I almost jump at a figure lurking in the hallway. It's Claudio. "You're gonna do me out of a job, mate," he says, patting me on the shoulder. His phone rings, and he disappears into his bedroom.

By the time I've reached the lounge room, my own phone is ringing.

"Hey, *Blinky*." Bruno sounds shattered. Given the amount of sleep he must have had, I'm not surprised. "Can I see you tonight?" He pauses for a moment. I can hear him breathing. "Dad passed away."

I don't even know what's going through my head. Somehow I manage to blurt out, "I'm coming down there now." Immediately I'm groping around in the bag for Brendan's harness.

"No. We're going back to Mum and Dad's. I'll come and get you."

The wait for him is the longest I've ever experienced in my life. Within seconds, I've gathered everything together in my bag. Then I sit there with Brendan, stroking his fur. Over and over I pat him, hypnotically focusing on the repetitive task, trying to alleviate how helpless, how utterly *useless* I feel.

Claudio emerges from the hall with his two sleepy boys in tow. He stops in the living room, digging out his keys.

"Bruno's picking me up," I say quietly. "You guys go."

Claudio nods. Words are difficult right now. Instinct has taken over.

Not long after they've left, Bruno arrives. His face is hollow. His eyes are blank. And as soon as I've reached him, he falls into my arms. For a good ten minutes, we stand there. His face is buried in my neck, and I feel his breath wafting over my shoulder in long slow bursts. His chest rises and falls as I clutch onto him, trying to shoulder as much of his burden as I can. I'm not going to say anything. Bruno's body is communicating everything I need to know.

Slowly, he lets me go. The smile he gives me is shot with a visceral sadness. He needs me to take control right now. I stretch up and kiss him softly on the cheek, then collect my bag and my dog. Grabbing Bruno's hand, I lead him to the door, turn the knob and switch off the lights.

I've never been to Bruno's parents' house, but it takes only seconds to drive there. We could have walked the distance in five minutes, but right now that's not important. It's one of those old fifties or sixties houses, with a flight of steps leading up to a front verandah surrounded by a white iron decorative railing. Bruno doesn't lead me that way, however; he unlocks the side gate and takes me down a sloping path.

The rear of the house is lower than the front, and at the bottom is a set of sliding glass doors. I follow Bruno through them and he switches on the lights, placing my bag next to a double bed in the corner. Squinting from left to right, I quickly try and orientate myself to the unfamiliar surroundings. It's a large tiled area, with a floral lounge suite towards the back and various cupboards lining the walls.

"This is the rumpus room," says Bruno. "It kind of doubles as a guest quarters. There's a laundry and a small ensuite bathroom through there." He points to a door on the other side of the room. Facing me, he places his hands on my upper arms. "Are you OK to stay here with me tonight?"

"Anything you want, Bruno. No matter what."

He smiles faintly, glancing towards the door. "I have to go upstairs for a while. Did you want to come?" He seems uncomfortable. I'm reading him loud and clear.

"Don't worry about me. You go and be with your family."

He leans forward and kisses my forehead, sniffing deeply in my hair. I know what he's doing. I do it to him too. Drawing in his scent like that reminds me just how lucky I am to have him in my life.

***

I wake bolt upright. I can't believe I passed out like that. I wanted to be one hundred percent present in case Bruno needed me. But the bathroom had been stocked with nice towels, the hot shower had been so soothing, and the neatly-made bed had been so comfortable that I'd fallen asleep with my iPad in front of me. Holding it up to unlock it with my face, I check the time. *Nearly three a.m.* Bruno must still be upstairs.

The tiles are cold under my feet as I pad across the floor to the sliding glass doors. There's a crack in the curtains, and a faint glow is filtering through. Poking my head between them, I try my best to make out where the light is coming from. To the right is a bright orange circle several feet off the ground. Underneath it is a white figure that seems slumped forward in a sitting position.

I slide the door open as quietly as I can and step out onto the freezing pavement. Slowly approaching the figure, I see it's Bruno. He's in a white bathrobe, sitting in a wooden outdoor chair with a towel draped over his neck. Above him, an outdoor gas heater burns away. The fingers of its radiating warmth flick at my cheeks as I approach in the frigid night air.

My heart twists in pain as I get close enough to see. Bruno is leaning forward, his shoulders shaking. And in his hands is his father's fedora. This is a private moment for him, but I can't bear to stay away. The second my outstretched hand touches the back of his neck, he leans into me and begins to howl. My reaction is unplanned, automatic. Immediately, my hands are around the back of his head, clasping it to my chest as I climb on to straddle his lap. I stay there, rocking him, my fingers stroking the back of his scalp as he falls apart in my embrace. *If only I can hold him tight enough, maybe I might be able to take some of his pain.*

My arms are burning, the towel around his neck is damp and clammy, and my legs are going numb, but it doesn't matter. I sit there and ride it out with him, trying to give him as much of my heart as possible. I'll stay here till dawn if it helps ease his suffering even one iota.

Long after the sobs have abated, long after his body has stopped shaking, long after his breathing has evened out, we're still sitting there. Finally, Bruno lifts his face from my chest. "Take me to bed, *Blinky*," he whispers.

Slowly, I slide off his lap and massage his legs. I want to apologise for weighing them down with my bulk for so long, but silence seems the best option right now. Helping him to his feet, I lead him across the garden and through the glass doors, which I lock behind us. Bruno is understandably shell-shocked, staying rooted to the spot till I gently guide him towards the bed. I take off his wet towel, slip off his bathrobe and hold the covers up so he can crawl underneath them.

I can't help becoming hard as I climb in behind him and cuddle up into the big spoon position. There's something so tragically beautiful in his vulnerability. My erection may be uncontrollable, but my actions aren't. I try my best to think of other things as my cock flexes against his arse crack.

"Fuck me." Bruno's voice is broken. "Please."

I want to ask him if he's sure, but there's a fragile urgency in the way he's pleading with me. Rolling over, I rifle through my bag, pulling out my trusty bottle of oil. Bruno moans quietly as I rub it around his anus, gradually pressing till I get two fingers inside. He only needs a cursory stretch before I can tell he's ready. I slick up my knob, move into him and push. He takes me fast. It's so warm inside him. His body comforts me as I draw myself against him, angling my hips while I thrust. He's breathing hard. His arm moves across mine, then I feel the thumping motion as he begins to jerk fast on his cock. His soft whimpers rattle me with their heartbroken timbre, but I know I'm giving him exactly what he needs.

Bruno's in a trance, barrelling forward with haste. He's grasping wildly for the finishing line and it's my job to help him get there. With three pained grunts, his body stiffens and his arse clamps hard on my cock. It's glorious, but the soaring intimacy I feel is tainted with a chest-crushing sense of melancholy. A long breath escapes Bruno as tension drains from his entire being. I hold him there, stroking the fur on his belly as I feel him go limp.

Slowly, I relax my hips and allow my cock to slip from him in tiny increments. He's sated. At least I've been able to help him in some small way.

***

FOMO has taken up residency in my life since Bruno burst onto the scene. This morning is no exception. It's nine-thirty and I've woken up with some awful ache in my chest, only to find Bruno isn't in the bed with me. He must be upstairs again with the family, but I can't get over the very physical feeling that I should be with him.

As my mental fog dissipates, I sense the pain behind my ribcage starting to ease. Maybe I have sleep apnoea. Then again, nobody ever complained about me snoring. Jarrod certainly would have hassled me if that was the case. *Deep breaths, Bradford. Oxygen is your friend.* Bit by bit, my rejuvenated lungs entice my thoughts to reorganise themselves into some semblance of logic.

The sliding door opens, and Bruno tiptoes inside.

"Hey, sexy man," I say in a surprisingly croaky voice. "No need to be quiet, I'm awake."

Bruno smiles, then strolls over to the bed, climbs on top of the covers and wraps himself around my body. He's freshly showered, I can smell the soap he used. I feel feral, all naked and unkempt after my unruly sleep, but Bruno seems to like it, burying his head into me and sniffing deeply. "I'm gonna have to go to Italy sometime soon," he mumbles against my neck. "Dad needs to be buried in the family plot in Calabria."

God. It sounds like the storyline from a Mafia movie. "Oh, OK. Won't that take a long time to organise, though?"

"I don't know. I imagine it will." He reaches down to my right nipple and idly begins to caress it. It reminds me that I'm still semi-erect with my morning boner. It also reminds me that I didn't come last night after I'd finished satisfying Bruno. I think I now have three or four days' worth stored up in my balls. I'm going to have to sneak in a wank at some stage. I'm not keen to bother Bruno about it. He has more than enough to deal with.

"What about the rest of the family here, Bru?"

He sighs. "Gab wants Claudio and the boys to come. She and Claudio are trying to organise things now. I guess it depends on the church. And the flights. And transporting Dad."

Bruno's being surprisingly pragmatic. Maybe it's the only way he can cope with it all at the moment. I'm just going to let him be. I need him to know that I'm a safe place.

There's a knock on the sliding door. Bruno glances at my naked top half, then his dark eyes meet mine as I pull the blankets up to cover myself. He's so considerate. "Come in," he calls out.

Gabriela glides into the room as Brendan walks up to greet her, tail wagging. She bends down and hugs him, ruffling his neck. "Claudio's doing whatever he can this end," she says. "We won't be able to get hold of anyone overseas till late this afternoon." Letting go of Brendan, she stands up, smooths herself down and graduates to the end of the bed, perching on the mattress. "I just came back to check on Mum. The boys are upstairs. I've kept them home from school." She glances at her watch. "God, there's so much to do. Are you around for a while later, Bru?"

"Sure, I can watch them." He sighs again, rubbing his hand over his face. "I'll have to go home and see Brie at some stage."

"I'll stay. Don't worry about any of this." I look from Gabriela to Bruno. "Really. You both do what you need to do. Bruno, you don't need me tagging along. Gabriela, you know the boys will be fine with me."

Gabriela smiles in defeat, reaching across and patting me on the leg. "Thank you for this, Bradford." She gets to her feet. "If you're sure it's OK, I'll bring them back here at lunchtime."

With Gabriela gone, Bruno pops back upstairs to see Valentina. After throwing on yesterday's clothes, I take Brendan for a short walk around the block, then pop into the small bathroom to freshen up. I almost feel guilty as my cock hardens under the cascading hot water in the shower. I'm thinking about how I held onto Bruno last night. The warmth of his furry body against my skin as I thrust my cock into his arse and brought him to orgasm. By the time I'm out of the shower and towelling myself off, my penis is standing at full salute.

Bruno's lounging on the double bed as I enter the rumpus room. "Did you just have a wank?" he asks, pointing to the tent in the towel around my waist.

"No. That shower's too small. I like to wank when I'm sitting or lying down."

When I've almost reached the bed, I pull the towel off my waist and allow my dick to spring out. "Of course I'd never say no to being pounded from behind while I'm standing in the shower."

Bruno sits up and suctions his lips straight onto my dick. The fiery heat of his mouth and firm rubbing of his tongue never fail to make me moan, and right now I'm louder than ever. In fact, I'm sure it's a little too loud. "Sorry," I whisper. "I forgot where I was."

Bruno lets my dick slip from his mouth with a wet smack of his lips. "Don't worry. We're safe. And while we're talking about you being pounded" — he slides his hand over my arse cheek and reaches in to stroke my hole with his finger — "I've worked you out now."

"What do you mean?"

He gives me an evil grin. "Why you slip your cock out of my arse after I've come. Why you never shoot in my mouth when I suck your dick."

I feel a little unnerved. "Yeah?"

"You like something up your arse when you blow. Like a couple of fingers. Or my tongue. *Or my cock.*"

I'm sure I'm turning crimson. I'm not some lazy bottom. I will happily drive my dick into my man's tight arsehole. I love it. But Bruno's spot on. "You make a good point there."

Bruno reaches under the covers and pulls out an object, holding it close enough for me to see clearly. "This oughta work a treat."

It's a big black vibrating dildo. I lean forward, squinting at the logo on the silver base. *Colt*, it says. "Is this yours?" My voice sounds incredulous.

"Um, yeah. Why… does that gross you out?"

My eyes go wide and I let out a raucous laugh. "Bruno, my tongue has barely left your arse for months. I just think it's… *fucking hot* that you lie there thrusting this up your hole when you're all by yourself. I would subscribe to *that* OnlyFans in a heartbeat."

Bruno growls and tackles me to the bed. Standing up, he yanks me over onto my back and pulls my legs till they're hanging over the edge of the mattress. Grabbing a pillow, he plonks it on the floor and kneels on it, pushing my knees outwards and upwards. Straight into my arse goes his face, and I feel the cold rush as his nostrils suck in air against my anus. This is immediately followed by the hot wet slather of his tongue as it probes hard, trying to get inside. He's rough and impatient and it's so damn arousing that I'm moaning like some filthy strumpet.

He breaks away from me, fumbling around the bed beside me. Producing a tube of lube, he squeezes some over my arse crack and tosses it aside. One of his hands gets to work rubbing it in as his other grabs hold of my erection. With perfect timing, his mouth clamps over my knob right as his fingers slide up inside my arse. Oh, Jesus, it's sublime. He's so bloody good. In and out of me he pistons, his knuckles bumping against my tight ring, his fingers twisting and brushing against my prostate, his lips sucking firmly along my shaft, and his tongue rubbing hard on my knob, jamming it against the roof of his mouth.

The supreme effort he's going to has me crying out. I'm trying to put a lid on it, but Bruno just keeps upping the ante. My toes are curling back and forth, my butt muscles are clenching and releasing, and now my thumbs are strumming my nipples. It's almost too much.

Bruno's fingers slip from my arse, but he doesn't let up with his mouth, pumping his head up and down, making my knob butt against the back of his throat. His hand leaves the base of my dick and I feel a probing against my slick anus. I know I have to work against it. As the large head of the dildo presses harder on my sphincter, I push outwards, grinding my hole onto it. Slowly, I feel myself expanding. If I bear down hard enough, I know it won't hurt much. Bruno seems to be well aware of how big this toy is, and the force he's using rapidly ebbs and flows, allowing the silicone monster to enter me by degrees. Jesus, the stretch is achingly euphoric, and it's all because he's busily bombarding my knob with his mouth and tongue as he works.

I'm hovering in a state of ecstasy. Just when I'm settling back to enjoy it, the buzzing starts. And increases. And increases again. Bruno begins to slide the vibrator in and out, pumping his mouth up and down the length of my dick. His pace accelerates till he's established a rhythm, then he adds in a swishing movement with his tongue, which rubs the PA ring inside my cock. This is where I begin to evanesce. It's like I've given in. I'm lying there, my fingers teasing the end of my nipples, while Bruno orchestrates a complex barrage of orgasmic manoeuvres designed to make me explode.

I can feel my arse trying to push out the dildo as I hurtle towards climax, but Bruno diligently counters it, building the tension till I think I'm going to split apart. "Oh, fuck, fuck, FUCK! I'm coming!" I wail. I feel the squeeze inside me, followed by the exquisite pulsating of my dick as it purges its seed into Bruno's mouth. I'm almost crying like a baby, it's that good.

Panting to the full extent of my lungs' expansion, I flop back against the mattress. Bruno's lips and tongue lap at the end of my cock, gathering the final vestiges of my sperm. Down below, I feel the huge dildo gradually withdraw from my arse. My breathing is slowing now, the residual hyperventilation sending me into a dizzy high. "My God, Bruno. That's never happened to me before. Ever."

His face rises from between my legs with a huge grin plastered across it. "Which part?"

"Lying back while someone sucked me off till I came."

He hoists himself up and over me so his fully-clothed body is pressed against my naked front and our noses are almost touching. "I thought so. And now that I've broken the seal, I'm gonna be doing this all the time." Lowering his face even further, he joins his soft lips to mine. Our beards converge and hot breath escapes our nostrils to create a warm cloud that cushions the closeness we're sharing. His tongue moves tenderly into my mouth, stroking, caressing, searching for the kind of gentle intimacy it needs. And I have it in spades for this man.

I reach up and cup my hands behind his smooth head, holding this precious part of him with as much reverence as I'm able to muster. I could never bear it if he slipped away from me.

Bruno nips against my lips with his, speaking to me while they're still touching. "Last night you were there for me, Bradford. Anything I needed, you gave it to me. I didn't have to explain myself, you just watched for the signs and you took care of them without question."

He lifts his head slightly, allowing me to stare directly into his eyes. I move my gaze from one to the other and back again, trying to disappear into them. *It's you,* I want to say. *There's nothing I wouldn't do, Bruno.* But I don't dare. All I can do is stroke the back of his head, trying my best to convey my thoughts by boring them deep into the dark irises looking down at me.

***

Gabriela brings the boys round at lunchtime as planned. Bruno's off at his apartment with Brie, so I take the boys out walking with Brendan while Gabriela drops in upstairs to see her mum. Marco and Stefano are quiet during the trek down to Maroubra Beach. I'm not going to try and prompt them to talk. I couldn't imagine anything worse than some adult poking their nose in and bombarding them with unsolicited questions and clumsy reassurances. As much as I remember what it was like to be their age, I'm well aware I'll just come across as an awkward dickhead.

"Are you allowed to take him on the beach?" says Stefano, pointing to Brendan as we stroll onto the sand.

"Yeah. Guide dogs can go anywhere."

"Does he play catch?"

"He loves it. I'm not very good at it anymore, though." We reach the sweet spot where the sand has firmed up but isn't wet. Stooping down, I undo Brendan's harness, then fish the tennis ball out of my backpack. "Try it if you want." I hand Stefano the ball, then unclip Brendan's leash. My excited lab has just spotted his favourite plaything and he flies into action. Sitting back on the sand, I watch as Stefano pegs the ball harder and higher, with Brendan matching each rise in energy. There's so much anger and frustration behind every one of Stefano's throws, but Brendan's enthusiasm is wearing him down. I can feel it. The joy that emanates from that dog is contagious.

Marco's sitting beside me, drawing in the sand with a stick. I watch him quietly. Here is where some meddling grown-up might consider it their duty to conduct a patronising interrogation. But I know he'll say something when he's good and ready. Soon enough, he stops and drops the stick. "How do you know that nonno could hear me when I was at the hospital?"

"Nonno was in a coma, Marco. And lots of people wake up from their comas and they say they could hear everything people were talking about."

"But nonno didn't wake up. He'll never be able to tell me if that happened."

"We just have to believe that all those people who did actually wake up aren't lying. Nonno knew you and Stefano were there. He just couldn't tell you."

"I gave him a kiss and a hug. Did he know that too?"

"When people are really sick like that, sometimes they hang on long enough to make sure everyone is OK. They wait till we're there, and when they've seen us all, they know it's alright for them to let go."

Marco turns to me, his brow furrowed. "How do you know all this?"

I can see the battle going on in his mind. It's written all over his innocent little face. It's leaping out at me through his large eyes, pleading with me to give him the answer he needs.

"I know cause it happened when my mum died. She was really sick just like nonno."

Marco nods slowly, then turns back to his sand drawing. After a few moments of scratching, he pipes up again. "So you think nonno is happy?"

My mind flashes to mum. Her intermittent reappearances. Those cherished glimpses of her loving presence I get when I need them the most. "I'm absolutely positive that he is, buddy."

***

Back at the house, Valentina has laid out milk and some kind of homemade cookies in the lounge room for the boys. From my vantage point near the couch, I can see her hobbling around the kitchen, slowly and painstakingly washing and stacking dishes. I'm in a bind here. Any other adult would rush to her and insist she rests while they take over. From what I've seen of her, though, she's a staunch matriarch. Her home is her pride and joy, and the last thing she'll want to be told is to go and lie down—especially at this moment. I know how important these mundane household tasks were after Mum died. Anything to keep busy, to avoid the incessant churning in my mind.

Once the boys have had their fill, I collect their glasses and plates and head to the kitchen. I stop in my tracks as I see Valentina braced with her arms against the counter and her head bowed. She's perfectly still, taking slow, deep breaths. This is the point where I intervene. I need to choose my words wisely. Tone of voice is going to be paramount.

She hears me walk behind her to the sink. "I have headache," she says primly, moving back to resume her dishwashing.

"I can do these if you'd like to go and spend a bit of time with the boys." It's an offer. She can say no and I'll back off.

A few moments go by before she answers. "Yes. Thank you." She leaves it at that, folding her tea towel and shuffling out of the room. I turn around and watch her leave. Her gait is heavy and slow. She's carrying the weight of the world and I can see the pain in every move of her body.

Turning back to the task at hand, I finish the last of the dishes, dry them and hunt round for their place in the cupboards. I take the opportunity to look over the beautiful articles she has on display: decorative earthenware platters, some antique china, a large intricately-cut glass bowl. I think of the perfectly-made bed I crawled into last night. Valentina *cares* about these things, and they're slipping from her grasp. The ravages of time are taking what's been precious to her all her life.

What do we have left when we no longer feel useful?

CHAPTER 17

As it turns out, the family only has to wait a week before they fly out to Italy. Apparently, they could either do it now, or they'd be waiting months. It's a mad scramble for them, but they seem to cope. Gabriela and Bruno are both back at work for a couple of days, fitting in the travel plans and preparation whenever they have time. They never fail to lavish me with gratitude for everything I'm supposedly doing, but it's nothing, really. I look after the boys. I tidy up here and there. I try not to step on Valentina's toes. She's very gracious, and I like to think it's because I know my place. Her family and her home are her *raison d'être*. Nonna holds her head high with good cause.

On the final morning before their evening departure, Valentina is out with Gabriela and Bruno. Everything is packed and ready to go. Stefano and Marco are bored, having come for Brendan's morning walk then watched TV for an hour or so. I wander into the kitchen and rummage through the cupboard for some flour and baking powder. I know there are eggs and milk and butter in the fridge. There's also some cream and sour cherry jam.

"What are you doing?" It's Marco, loitering by the breakfast bar.

"I'm going to make scones. Maybe they'll like some when they all get back."

"Nonna doesn't make scones," he says.

"That's good then. Nonna makes all her things so well that I'd never be able to match up. At least if it's something different, maybe it'll be OK."

"Can I help?"

Well, blow me down with a feather. "Sure." I check behind the pantry door, but there are only frilly aprons on the hooks there. Glancing back at Marco, I decide that would be cruel. I'm wearing the only one that doesn't look like it belongs on a granny. "We won't make you put on one of these. A little flour won't hurt. But wash your hands first, because we have to do this all with our fingers."

While he's at the sink, I crouch down and try my best to see the temperature dial on the oven. At home, I have little raised nub things glued at 180 and 200 celsius, put there by an occupational therapist. No such luck here, so I have to squat and squint. "We need to cook these fast with the oven really hot."

"Why?"

"So they don't end up all rock hard and flat."

Setting up two bowls, I show Marco how to scoop and scrape the measuring cup for the flour. "That's good mate," I say, even though he's getting more flour on the counter than in the bowl. "Now we have to rub in the cold butter."

"Can I have a go?" I glance up to see Stefano standing nearby. I nearly have to physically restrain my jaw from dropping.

"Yeah, sure. Here, have mine." Passing him my bowl, I turn back to Marco. "OK. Plop the chunks of butter in the flour, just like this." I drop in a few cubes, letting the boys do the rest. "Now, I'm just gonna show you how to mix it properly. Only a little bit, though. You can do the rest." Digging my hands into Marco's bowl, I demonstrate the rolling technique. "Try not to do it too much. We just want to squoosh the butter into the flour till it looks like crumbs."

Both boys look so engrossed in the exercise, I overlook the chunks of butter still left there. "That's excellent. Can you guys fetch the eggs and the milk?" With their backs turned, I'm able to quickly obliterate the residual lumps in their dough. After the boys have finished cracking the eggs and we've fished out the stray bits of shell, I talk through how to beat them with Stefano while I'm helping Marco measure out the milk. Once again, there's a sizeable mess on the counter, but they're both having fun. I can always clean it up later.

When both bowls have been mixed, I demonstrate how to pack the dough together. "Remember, we only want it to come into a ball. We don't want to knead it like bread, or the scones will be hard."

Rolling and cutting is the bit they like best. Stefano seems to be taking great care to make the scones as perfect as possible with the flour-dipped drinking glass. After getting the boys to glaze the finished tray with the pastry brush, I hold it with Marco as he slides it onto the hot oven shelf. "Nonna never lets me do this," he says.

"Yeah, well it's our little secret. It's OK, because I'm helping you." I wink at him, and Marco seems pleased with our clandestine little pact.

Turning around, I'm floored to see Stefano wiping down the bench, cupping his hand at the edge to catch the excess flour. I can't help but smile at the bits he's missing. I'm too busy bursting with pride to worry about the spillage. "OK, guys. They're gonna be baking for about twenty-five minutes. Do you want a drink or something? I'm gonna whip the cream while we wait."

"Can I do it?" says Stefano.

Wow. "Um, OK. I might have to tell you when to stop, though."

"Why?" This comes from Marco.

"Well, when we beat cream for too long, it turns into butter." Neither of them look like they believe a word I'm saying. "You're gonna have to trust me on this, guys. Someday, when we have a bit more cream, I'll show you how to make butter."

"Can we can we can we?" The excitement on Marco's face hits hard. It's so long since I've felt that kind of *joie de vivre.* Well, outside of the bedroom, at least.

We've just finished setting up the platter of scones when Bruno and Gabriela arrive with Valentina in tow. "Nonna!" Marco barges towards his grandmother, who looks momentarily surprised. "We made scones with Bradford. We even beat up the cream but we couldn't make butter today but Bradford's gonna show us how to do it next time."

Valentina looks amused but doubtful. Glancing over Marco's shoulder at our beautifully-fluffed creations, she stares at me with her eyebrows raised. "How you manage this?" she says. "They never do it for me."

***

Later on, as the family are waiting for their flotilla of taxis, Bruno and Claudio carry the mountain of bags downstairs while Gabriela is getting the boys ready. I'm busy doing dishes in the kitchen when I hear footsteps behind me. Wiping my hands on a tea towel, I turn and see it's Valentina. She's standing there all dressed up, clutching onto what I imagine is her best handbag. Her lips are taut as she studies my face.

"You know, Bruno is my only son," she starts. "I always wanna see him get married. Of course is not gonna be a girl, but he need a good man. I know he never gonna marry that party boy of his. But you..." She stops for a moment, her jaw tightening. "You know the meaning of family." Reaching out, she delicately pats my arm. "You think about it." After giving me a small nod, she turns and departs with regal poise.

Bruno and I get the last taxi. With my bag stashed in the back and Brendan stashed at my feet, I know it's time to go back home and face the music. After two weeks away, I'm dreading it. Bruno holds my hand the whole journey.

"I'm gonna miss you, *Harry*," I say, as we reach the international airport turnoff. "We've never really been away from each other since we met."

Bruno doesn't answer straight away. I turn and look at him. His face is in a visible state of turmoil. My stomach ties in knots. *Did I go too far?*

"Bradford, I need to tell you something. And I don't want you to get upset."

Oh, God. I feel sick.

Bruno squeezes my hand and turns to face me. "I didn't want to say anything to you because I know how hard all this shit is with Jarrod." He takes a deep breath, then launches into it. "Brie and I have split up. Nothing's wrong, we just know it's over. We've known it for a long time. As soon as I get back from Italy, I'm moving into the rumpus room at Mum's. Brie is already in the process of putting our place on the market." He looks into my eyes, his forehead wrinkled with intensity. "I know it's not a good time for you, but *I will wait*. As long as it takes."

I'm absolutely gobsmacked. It's an info dump, but it's like Bruno's handing it all to me on a silver platter. My brain is in overdrive. Thoughts are shooting around my skull, bashing into the inside edges and changing direction at the speed of light. *I have to get rid of Jarrod. I have to find the guts to kick him to—*

"You're gonna have to get out now." The taxi driver's voice pierces my stunned silence. Glancing around, I see we're in the congested dropoff zone. Traffic is banking up behind us.

"I'll text you as soon as we touch down in Singapore," Bruno says.

"Yes, yes. Please do." I'm gaping. I need to say so much to Bruno. I need to tell him how over the bloody moon I am, but it'll have to wait.

Leaning across, he mashes his lips into mine. "We'll talk soon," he whispers. I don't even get to reply. My hand feebly travels down his back to his arse as he turns and hoists himself out of the rear door. The moment Bruno slams the boot, the taxi's off again, leaving him behind. I try to see out of the back window, but it's in my blindest spot. Why the *hell* didn't I say something?

***

Back at my apartment, I'm faced with destruction. I stand there, slack-jawed at the wasteland around me. There's crap everywhere. The place stinks of smoke. Of rotten food. There are empty plates and beer bottles and cups full of half-drunk coffee with cigarette butts in them. There are cigarette butts scattered through the mountains of mess all over the floor. The kitchen is a bomb zone. I tentatively step into my bedroom and I'm hit with havoc. Someone has been sleeping in my bed. Drinking in my bed. Smoking in it. I nearly scream as I find my piano open, with drinks sitting on the bare wood next to the keyboard. Plates on top of it. *Cigarette ash and sticky wet patches over the damn keys.*

I'm beyond livid. Working from room to room, I take photos of everything, then send them one by one to Jarrod's phone number. There's no way that piece of trash is gonna deny any of this. It takes me all afternoon and well into the evening to clean it up. I don't even open Jarrod's bedroom door till I've finished. As predicted, it's just as foul as the rest of the place was. I'm *done* with him. He's turned my home into some debauched drug-addled hovel. A bloody *squat.*

Wrenching his wardrobe door open, I drag out two suitcases. I empty his drawers and pull everything off his coathangers, stuffing whatever will fit into one suitcase. I go to his bedside table and pack everything there into the other suitcase. In the bottom drawer, I see a metal box. I don't wanna touch it; I'm pretty sure I know what's in there. Searching in one of the suitcases I've just packed, I pull a clean sock over my hand. I carefully open the box, and lo and behold, it's full of the fruits of Jarrod's trade. I don't even need to rifle through it—fits, glass pipes, dozens of little bags of white crystallised stuff—they're all boldly on display.

When Jarrod's suitcases are full, I drag them out to the edge of the lounge room near the hall. Then, I sit on the couch with Brendan, staring at my phone, willing Bruno to call me. I don't know how long it takes to get to Singapore, but it can't be too much longer, can it?

Eventually, the door opens and Jarrod barrels down the hall, nearly running into the suitcases. "What the fuck is this," he snaps, glaring up at me.

"It's your stuff. Trashing my home was the last straw, Jarrod. Take the cases and get out of here." My heart is beating hard and fast, but I've never felt so driven in my life.

Jarrod laughs out loud. "I already told you. I'm not fuckin' going *anywhere.*"

I stand up, my face on fire. "I'm serious, Jarrod. Get the FUCK OUT!"

Jarrod momentarily reels. He's never heard me talk like this. I'm not sure *I* ever have, either. Quickly, he takes stock of his surprise and leers over at me. "Just try and make me."

"I found your stash. I've called the cops and told them where it is." I'm bluffing, but Jarrod's eyes go wide as saucers. "Go on, you better grab it and bugger off before they get here."

He darts into the bedroom, then reappears with his precious box, which he stuffs into one of the cases. Suddenly, the lights are out and the room is plunged into darkness. "You little piece of SHIT!" he snarls, his voice rising. There's a series of crashing sounds and something hard connects with my face, sending me falling backwards into the wall behind me. I don't even realise what's happened; it's like the pain takes a good second or two to register. Putting my hand to my face, I feel the warm slippery moisture of blood. It's my good eye. *He's punched me in my good eye.* And those ugly rings he wears have cut deep into my socket.

Over yonder, I hear my phone beep with a text message, then another. I'm scrambling to get up off the floor, but I'm in a daze. I feel Jarrod's fingers slide gently under my chin and tilt my head upwards. For one brief moment I think he's inspecting the damage he's done to my eye. All too late, I realise his caring touch is a trick when I hear the familiar sound of facial recognition unlocking my phone.

"Give it to me!" I yell, leaning forward and flailing my arms around in the pitch dark trying to grab onto his legs. But he's too quick for me.

"'*I never would have got through these last weeks without you.*'" Jarrod's voice is trilling away in its snarkiest sing-song tone. "'*Please give us a chance. I love you so much, Bradford.*'"

There's a huge smashing sound on the wall that can only be my phone. A swift kick hits me right in the middle of my guts, making me cry out and double over. At the sound of my wailing, Brendan starts to bark as loud as he can.

"Shut up," Jarrod roars. "SHUT THE FUCK UP!"

Brendan's barks change into gut-churning yelps. I can hear the thumping sound of Jarrod laying into him.

"NO! *PLEASE* DON'T DO THIS!" My appeal to Jarrod's sense of decency falls on deaf ears. The noises Brendan is making frighten the hell out of me. Groping around on the bookshelf to my left, I try desperately to find something. *Anything.* My hand lands on a hard object. It's a candle holder that Summer bought me. Thick crystal set on a heavy stone base. Grabbing it in my fist. I hurl it high in the direction of Jarrod's rage.

"YOU FUCKING CUNT!" he roars. It's worked. He's left Brendan alone. But another fist connects with my eye in exactly the same place as before. This time it's harder and my head smashes into the wall behind me. I'm briefly shocked by the dull clunking noise it makes, before the massive ache wells up inside my skull.

There's no time to think about that, though. I'm crawling on the floor, desperately reaching out to try and find Brendan. I can't see a thing at all, but I can hear rustling down the hall and the front door slamming. My head begins to throb hard. I'm becoming dizzy. I struggle to sit up. *I cannot pass out. I cannot pass out.* There's a scraping sound, and a furry head slides onto my thigh with a whine. *Brendan's been trying to get to me. He's been trying to help.*

The world caves in around me as I realise nobody is going to find us. We're going to die here. Filling my lungs, I start to scream. I think I'm forming the word 'help', but I'm not sure. Over and over I make the most ear-splitting sounds I can. My head is going to explode. *I have to stay conscious. I have to try my best, but I c—*

CHAPTER 18

Six days it's been. *Six days.* Six days of blindly moving through life. Presenting people with empty smiles and automatic chit chat. Ghosting through the machinations of this family circus with my heart ripped out of my fucking chest.

I don't know what happened. I don't know why. Or maybe I do know. Maybe this sick feeling clawing at me from the inside is the knowledge that I caused all of this. Why the fuck did I blurt out all that shit to Bradford? Why the goddamn fucking fucking *fucking hell* did I tell him I loved him? I've right royally screwed the whole thing up. Maybe I deserve it.

Every day I torture myself reading back over the text messages I've sent. The way they start out so hopeful, so excited. They way they morph into concern when I don't hear back from him. The way that concern turns into confusion. Then abject worry. Then sickening realisation. I'm now at the begging and pleading stage. I can't believe it's gone this far.

Why, Bradford? Why? You were so loving. You were so present. You gave me so fucking much. When Bradford looked at me, it was like he saw the whole world. And *he was mine*, before he ripped it out from underneath me. I'm not angry, I'm desolate. I'm bleeding. And I'm sitting here in this provincial cathedral barely able to compose myself.

I'm not even thinking about the funeral. My actions are rehearsed. I'm on autopilot. My body is numb, except for the mortal wounds that have desecrated my fucking heart.

The church choir stands up and begins to sing. The voices ring out, reverberating around the intricate structure of the cavernous building. It would barely register with me, except the music sounds eerily familiar. Glancing down at the funeral program, my eyes lock on the title. *Ave Dulcissima Maria* by Carlo Gesualdo.

Bradford. Our very first night together.

Some other force is in control of my body. A huge breath sucks itself into my chest, followed by a loud gasp barrelling from my throat. My façade has finally cracked. I urgently need to get the fuck out of here.

Shooting to my feet, I push my burly bulk past the raven-like form of my mother, who's sitting proud and tall in her best mourning garb. The cathedral's pews are a cruel squeeze. I'm losing precious seconds trying to extricate myself from their polished wooden jaws. Finally, I'm no longer able to contain the sobs tearing though my body. Out they gush; the precarious dam of my dignity bursting wide, laying my grief and devastation bare for all and sundry to gawk at. I don't care nearly as much as I should; my heart has been ripped to shreds and right now I don't even know if I'll survive this fucking agony.

After clumsily barging past at least four people, I finally manage to break free. Behind me, I hear my mother announce haughtily to everyone around her: *"La morte di suo padre lo ha veramente distrutto."*

Yes, Mum. My father's death may well have destroyed me, but it's not why I'm falling apart right now.

As soon as I reach the rental car, I lock myself inside it and pull out my phone. The Calabrese summer heat is fierce and I'm in a metal capsule wearing a black suit, but I don't give a flying fuck. My sweat mixes with my tears as I punch in Bradford's number for the very last time. "Hi… it's me again." I can't even curb my sobs. "I'm sorry, Bradford. I should never have said those things. Please don't cut me off, I'm begging you. I can't stand this. I'll do anything you want. *Anything.* Just call me. *Please.* Oh, fuck…" I gasp again and a colossal tirade of wails explodes out of my chest. I can no longer talk. Crushing my thumb against the red button, I realise it's all over. It's all too late.

***

Late that night, my phone rings. I shoot upright, groping over on the bedside table for it. My heart falls yet again as I see it's not from Bradford. It's a silent number.

"Hello?"

"Bru, darl, it's Gina." She sounds officious, dripping with professional concern. "This guy you were seeing? Bradford?"

"Yes?" My heart starts to thump. Panic is rising up to throat level.

"I've just come back from the conference in Canberra. I see he's been here in my ward for nearly a week."

"What? What the *fuck?*" I shake my head vigorously, trying to pull myself together as fast as I can.

"Domestic assault. TBI. LOC. ICH. PTA."

Domestic fucking assault? My mind swims with the abbreviations. Neuro was never my strong suit. *Traumatic brain injury. Loss of consciousness. Intracranial haemorrhage. Post-traumatic amnesia.* "How long was he out for?"

Gina takes a breath and sighs. "Well, I guess you're staff here and you'd have access to his records, anyway." She reads in a rushed manner, gleaning what she can from the notes. "'Consciousness returned the following night after emergency neurosurgery upon admission. Broken ribs… bruising… laceration to left eye socket… a tear to the left corneal graft.' They've had ophtho assess it and he's been referred to the eye hospital next week. But Bru…"

"Yeah?"

"They've told me he's still out of it. No recognition of family or personal history. Confused as fuck, darl. Let me look—" She pauses. "Yeah. Here it is. Occupational therapy have been working with him daily. Typical presentation. Agitated. Highly anxious. Prone to bouts of disinhibition and inappropriate behaviour. Psych have seen him and there's some talk of moving him down to them, under neuro. But he still needs to be here a bit longer."

Somehow, I manage to thank Regina while my head is already working on my escape. *Should I drive to Rome? I don't know. Could I even get a connecting flight from here? Fuck.* I'll work it out. I just need to get home *now.*

CHAPTER 19

There's a woman here. She's been here before. At least, I think she has. "Who are you again?" I'm feeling fucking tetchy as hell. Something is gnawing hard at me, but I don't know what the fuck it is.

"I'm Dianna, Bradford," she says patiently. "We're working together to try and get you better."

Better? Better? There's nothing the fuck wrong with me, is there?

I look from right to left. The room is a fucking blur. It's pissing me off. I stare at the woman. She has no facial features at all. The only reason I know she's a woman is because of her voice and her long flowing hair.

Jesus, why the hell can't I see anything? I claw at my face, but it fucking hurts. Who did this to me?

Suddenly, a rage erupts inside my chest. "That fucking CUNT!" I yell. "I'm gonna fucking kill the piece of shit!"

"Tell me who it is, Bradford." Apparently, that's my name. Dianne, Dianna—whatever the fuck she's called—sits there quietly. It's like she's not even taking me seriously. This is DIRE, fuck it!

"I. Don't. Fucking. Know." I'm growling. I wish I did know. I wish I could find him. "He took EVERYTHING. The cunt fucked up my whole fucking life. He took... he took..." I'm panting now, balling up the bedsheets in my fists.

What did he take? Who did he take? Sudden panic explodes beneath my ribcage.

"I've gotta call him. I have to—" I scramble out of bed and run to the window.

"Bradford, you need to put something on," Dianna says calmly.

"What the fuck are you talking about?" I look down. I'm naked. You know what? I couldn't give a shit. "It's my fucking dick. Who cares? Don't tell me you've never seen one before."

I'm pacing the room. Dianna hands me some kind of white robe. "Put it on," she says, a good deal more firmly than before.

"Fuck," I grumble, struggling into the ugly cotton monstrosity and yanking it over my front. "Happy now?"

I scan the haze of my surroundings again. There's a blue piece of furniture nearby. It's a chair. Well, I'm pretty sure it is. Striding up to it, I trail my hands over the surface, then collapse into the cold vinyl. All of a sudden, I'm exhausted. I want to cry. "I need to call him I need to call him I need to call him," I whimper. I sound like a pathetic child, but once again, I could give two fucks.

Dianna approaches me. "I'll find his number. You just need to tell me his name."

I squeeze my eyes shut. Nothing's coming. Try as I might, the gargantuan fuckup in my head won't let me remember. "I don't know."

***

I'm in bed. It's clammy. The mattress under me doesn't seem to breathe. The pillow behind me crunches. My neck is sweaty. The backs of my legs are sticking to the sheet underneath me. I feel gross. Heaving my sore body off the stifling foam, I walk over to what seems to be a chest of drawers. Opening one, I see a pile of clothes. How the hell did they get in there? I rifle through them and find shorts. Undies. A deep blue t-shirt. Clutching my selection, I turn and spot a large person sitting down near the entrance to the room. I stare long and hard. I think it's a woman. Yeah, she has massive tits. They're almost busting out of her dark blue clothes. Come to think of it, I'm sure I've seen other people in those same clothes a lot lately. It's a uniform. For what, though? The woman has her head bowed and she's fiddling with something. The sight is kind of familiar. A phone. Yeah. She can't take her bloody eyes off her phone. I really don't want anyone around me right now. I need to be free. Turning to my right, I see a small, angled room with an open door. Maybe I might go in there.

"Where are you off to?" A voice sounds behind me. I swivel back and see it's the big-boobed phone addict talking. I don't say anything, just gesture vaguely at the small room and head in that direction. "Keep the door open a bit, please," the woman calls after me. It seems like an odd request. What am I, a fucking child?

As I make my way through the open door, cold air whooshes over the wet fabric that's clinging to my back. It feels revolting. I want to rip it off me. I'm still clutching something, though. That's right. The clothes I found. Now I'm peering at a white object in front of me. It looks like a chair. Yes. It's plastic. I can feel the network of holes on the seat and the back. I dump the pile of clothes on it, then start to tug at the white cotton prison that's suffocating my body. Suddenly, I spot the large woman sitting in full view through the open door. For some reason, this stops me undressing. Why? Why should I give a fucking toss about her plonked out there on her bloody phone?

I take a step backwards and my arm hits some kind of flowy nylon stuff. I hear the sound of something jiggling against metal above me. Oh, it's a shower curtain. I think I'd be better off behind here. Ducking around, I pull the curtain across the rail in front of me and try to extricate myself from what I'm wearing. I'm wincing as I contort my arms, my torso, but eventually I manage to peel it from my skin.

Now I'm naked. I feel so... liberated. I want to be naked all the time. I run my hands over my stomach, my pecs. They're hairy. It's nice. My fingers strum over my nipples. Fuck, that feels good. It's weird; like I'm touching myself for the first time ever. I reach down and wrap my hand around my dick. It's firm. I'm rubbing it. God, I'd love to come.

I've forgotten why I'm in this room. My right hip bumps into cold metal. Fumbling around, I realise it's a set of taps. The kind with levers. That's right, I was going to have a shower. I yank on the levers and water cascades down on me. Fuck, it's fucking freezing. A yelp escapes me and I jump straight out. Sticking my hand under the water, I feel it heating up. It's better now. I heave a sigh of relief as I let the stream beat down on my back. My hand is around my dick again, but this time I'm hosing piss all over the floor. Oh, fuck me dead, I needed that. The relief rushing through my shaft makes me want to start jerking off. Yes, I have to do it right now. I don't know why I'm stopping myself. It's not like I ever did before. Or did I?

The water's off now, but I'm still in the shower. Why? I peek out from behind the curtain. The big woman in dark blue is still there. Oh yes—I'm naked. And I'm rubbing the towel vigorously over my dick and balls. Reaching behind myself and buffing it between my arse cheeks. I like it. I run my fingers over the puckers of my arsehole, pushing one just inside the edge of it. Even better. Fuck, how do I not know this about my body?

Dropping the towel, I grab the t-shirt and pull it over my head. It's tight. But it seems right. Maybe I like it that way. I look back over at the shorts and underwear dumped on the plastic chair. Do I really need them? My balls feel so nice like this. I'm not sure why, but suddenly the clothes are all on me. I'm dressed. I'm fresh and nice, but what I really want is to take everything off again. To go and lie down naked and find out everything that makes my body feel good.

I walk back out to the bed. It's damp. I didn't piss in it, did I? No. It's damp where my back would have been. I fumble around, running my hand over the sheets. There's one of those thick woven cotton blankets there. I can feel the waffly weave. It's like those ones in hospitals.

Hospital. Is that where I am?

I'm pulling the blanket up to cover the bed. Tucking it in. It's really neat. Am I good at this? I don't know. But I'm tired. My chest hurts on the left side. It's hard to breathe. I'm gonna lie down.

***

A woman comes into the room, followed by a man. I can't see their faces, but she has long dark hair and the man is tall. "Hey, Braddy. I told you I'd bring him, didn't I?" says the woman.

They're closer now. I think I might know them. Maybe. There's some kind of... familiarity.

"This is Nathan," the woman says. "Do you remember him?"

The man is leaning right near me. "Can you see me, mate?" he asks.

His features are blurry as hell, but they're there, at least. He's smiling.

There's a twinge of something in my head. "You're Nathan." My voice is resolute. "Yeah. You're Nathan."

"This could be a sign," the woman says. Her voice sounds kind of urgent. "Call the nurse, Nath."

He leans right over me. I think he's looking for the buzzer. He must be, but I'm not really paying attention. His sweaty armpit is right near my face. I can smell him and it's rousing something in me. Moving my head upwards, I sniff deeply and audibly. "Fuck, that's hot," I growl.

Behind us, the woman laughs. So does Nathan, who moves away.

"See, he *likes my macho scent," Nathan says, and the woman laughs harder. Now she's absolutely pissing herself.*

Something is twigging inside my fucked-up brain. I'm a teenager. Yes. At high school. All angst and self-hatred and constant wanking. But there's a little kid somewhere. A tiny little kid that I loved more than anything. A little kid who followed me round all the time. Who wanted me to play dolls with her. Who was so young and innocent and there was no way I could ever yell at her.

The woman's still laughing. She's in hysterics. Nathan's now pissing himself as well.

"You gotta stop, Summer," he says. "I can't fucking take it anymore."

Summer.

Summer.

SUMMER. My sister. My little sister. Oh, God.

"Summer," I gasp. Her eyes go wide. "What the hell happened? Where am I?" My head is spinning, but I'm looking around, trying my best to see things. I don't remember my eyes ever being this bad. I have a sudden thought. "Bruno!" Right then, a woman flies at my bed. Her eyes are tear-stained. "Mum!"

Mum's reaching out trying to touch me. She looks distraught, but she's smiling. That radiant beam of hers.

"No, sweetie. Mum died." Summer sounds deflated.

Oh, Jesus Christ. All too late I realise my gaffe. "Yeah. I know. Six years ago." Oh, God. Bruno. "I have to call Bruno. Now."

"Sweetie, you've said his name over and over. Who is he?"

"What do you mean? When did I say it?" Jesus, my head hurts. Right at the back. "Oh, bloody hell. Jarrod. *Brendan*!" I'm flying into a blind panic. "What happened to Brendan? Is he alright?"

Summer reaches for my hand and squeezes it. I feel sick. I can't see her face. Is she smiling or commiserating? "Don't worry. He's recovering with Susannah from Guide Dogs," she soothes. "He had to have surgery, but he pulled through fine. I've been calling for updates all the time."

Things are rushing back to me at a rate of knots. They're a complete jumble, but I'm trying my best to piece them together. "Jarrod smashed my phone when he found the texts from Bruno. *Oh, God, Bruno…*"

Summer's trying to be careful. I can hear it in her tone. But her hand is squeezing the hell out of mine. "Is this someone you're seeing? Is this why Jarrod did all this to you?"

"No." I'm firm on this. It's taking me a while, but I'm remembering the state of the apartment. The way that bastard destroyed my home. "Jarrod attacked me because I kicked him out. Told him I found his huge meth stash and called the cops on him. Bruno was just collateral damage. Jesus, Summer, I have to call him, but he's overseas and I don't have my phone and I don't know his number." I screw my eyes up. This is all getting too much. "Oh! My iPad…"

Summer sighs. "No, sweetie. The police didn't find any phone or iPad at your place. Jarrod must have taken both of them."

"Police?" I have so many questions, but I can't quite work out what they are. My anxiety is shooting through the roof. My head is splitting in two.

"It's fine, we can work this out," Summer soothes. "You know his name, so you could contact him on Facebook or Insta."

I'm racking my brain. This isn't ringing a bell. Bloody hell. I whimper in frustration as fragments come dancing in front of my eyes. "No. He's a technophobe and he hates social media."

"What about his family?"

Family. The whirling in my head speeds up, but I'm grabbing at bits as fast as I can. A woman. Boys. Gabriela. Cl… Claudio. Oh, God. Italy. "They're all overseas too. For the funeral."

Summer thinks for a while. "You've got an Android, haven't you? So those numbers will be saved on your Google account. I've got my old Samsung phone. We'll get you a new sim, get Telstra to port your number and you can call him. Do you know your Google password?"

I rack my brain. Surely I have it somewhere. I'm scanning my bedroom in my mind. My sofa bed. My piano. *Oh, Jesus. My annihilated piano.* My desk. *Yes, my desk.* Books on the shelf at the back. "Not off by heart, but it's in the back of the bright green folder on my desk. I write them all down there." I can just tell Summer's rolling her eyes. "Don't look at me like that. It's gonna help me right now, isn't it?"

***

After they've left, I come crashing down. There are blank spots everywhere. I can remember stuff that happened a while ago. But recently? So much is missing. It's like only the most pressing events have found their way into my head. I don't know what's going on. I'm so, so tired.

At some point, I'm woken by a doctor. I can't really concentrate on what he's saying. Head trauma, he mentions. Unconscious. Brain bleed. Emergency surgery. Post-traumatic amnesia.

Information overload gets the better of me. "How long was I out for? How did I get here?" I'm interrupting, but I can't help myself.

"You were brought in after a neighbour called the police. Following the surgery, you were unconscious for about a day. And Dianna has been helping you with the post-traumatic amnesia for nearly a week."

I blanche. "A week? I've been like this for a *week*?" I can't believe it. I've lost an entire seven days. *Bruno*. I want to throw up. Bruno hasn't heard from me in all this time.

The doctor continues in his officious manner. "The ophthalmologist has seen you about the tear in your left corneal graft. We've made you a follow up appointment with the corneal surgeon at the Eye Hospital on Monday."

Right then, a nurse enters. "Sorry, doctor. Bradford's drops are due."

"What is it?" I ask, as she pulls down my eyelid and deposits the cold liquid. "Maxidex?"

"Yes. Every hour. They're trying to reverse the graft rejection."

I want to scream. Graft rejection. I've been here before. Several times. More eye surgery. Another transplant. What the hell else could go wrong?

***

Summer returns with the phone, sitting inches from me so I can see her better. "I've set it all up. Do you want me to log into Google for you?"

"Thanks." Sudden realisation hits me like a ton of bricks. I must look like such a self-absorbed arsehole. "God, Summer, it's so nice of you to run around doing all this stuff for me. I'm really sorry I've messed up your da… hang on, when the hell did you and Nathan get to Sydney?"

"I flew over when I heard what happened. You'd listed me as your next of kin. Nathan and the girls just got here yesterday."

"Wait… you didn't come just for me, did you?"

Summer laughs. "Well, *I* did, at least. We were coming anyway. I had all these big plans about showing up and surprising you."

Showing up. My apartment. Oh, no. She's been to my apartment. "Jesus. Was Jarrod there just now? At my place? You didn't run into him, did you?"

"No, sweetie. He's gone. He's not coming back. It's been taken care of." She rubs my arm. *That's all you need to know for now*, she means.

Her attention turns back to the phone she's holding and she taps away at it. "Don't worry, Summer. There's no porn in my Google account. I keep it all on the iPad."

She scoffs and slaps me on the wrist. "I don't need to know that."

"Ha! Don't try and tell me *you* never perve at naked men."

There's a loaded look on Summer's face. "I have my own hot naked man." She stares at me for a moment. I can see she's trying not to snigger.

"What's so funny?"

"Nothing." She tosses her hair. "Anyway, I prefer to read smutty romance novels. So much more satisfying." She places the phone in my hand. "Have a look. Can you see it at all?"

I hold it right next to my eyes, tilting it in all directions. My face falls. "No. It's hopeless. Can you dial 101 for me?"

Summer taps at the phone again, then discreetly leaves the room. I slap the device to my ear. The first message plays. It's Bruno and he sounds happy. Sorry he missed me. Maybe I'm asleep. He'll try again when they land in Rome. I pull the phone away and squint hard at the keyboard icons. They're big, and I can't see the numbers, but I know where the four is located. Message saved. The next one, Bruno sounds concerned. One by one, the messages continue. I can hear the panic in his voice. He sounds baffled, bewildered. Eventually, he sounds sad. The devastation in his voice is a knife in the guts. Then I come to the worst of them all. Bruno is bawling. Unrestrained. Pleading with me. The agony I can hear is too much to bear.

I'm hyperventilating. All that's stopping me from falling apart is the insatiable urge to speak to him.

"To return this call, press two, two," the mechanical voice says. I squint as hard as I can, my finger shaking as I punch in the number. My head hurts so bad I feel like I might pass out. My chest aches. There are incessant sharp jabs in my fractured ribs, but it's the pain deep inside that kills me the most. When the call goes to message bank, it's the biggest blow of all. I can barely get any words out. "Bruno, I—"

That's all I manage to say before things fade to black.

CHAPTER 20

I've had a scan. There's no bleeding in my brain. I was most likely just overwhelmed, they told me. But I feel hollow. Everything is moving slowly. There are holes everywhere in my memory. Events flicker in my consciousness, but they're not complete. It's like a movie montage in fast forward. I'd try and work them out, but my thoughts all come back to Bruno. It can't be too late. I couldn't have damaged things beyond repair, could I?

"The connection is still there. Believe me, Bradford, it's too strong to be broken by all of this."

I'm in bed trying to nap. Opening my eyes, I spot her sitting on the edge of the mattress, clear as day. In a world as blurry as mine is right now, it's a wonderful thing to see this kind of detail.

Though the hope in my heart surges forth at her statement, I can't quite make myself believe it. "How do you know, Mum?"

She flaps her hand at me. "Oh, I don't have any magic view into his world. I just have this kind of… sixth sense, if you will." She sighs, long and loud. "Maybe I don't. Maybe I'm still just a regular mum. But ask yourself this, darling. Do you *really* believe that Bruno would be done with you? Honestly?"

I mull it over. "Now that you've put it that way—no, I don't. But sometimes people surprise us."

"He's stuck by you, Bradford. I mean, have you *ever* had a tense moment together? Doesn't that tell you something? Bruno—*and you*—will never find that sort of thing again. He's an intelligent man and he's well aware of this."

"You always make me feel so much better, Mum."

"That's what I'm here for." In her usual jump cut style, she's suddenly standing at my side. "I'm sorry about last time, darling. I should never have shown up like that, but I'd spent a week worried sick about you."

"Mum, don't apologise. You were here exactly when I needed you. You always are." I desperately want to give her a hug, but I know I can't. I'm just hoping she can tell what I'm feeling by the look on my face.

The door bursts open. Loudly. Blind hope tells me it's Bruno long before a big man throws his arms around my shoulders and crushes me into his chest. His scent is thick. I can't breathe him in fast enough. There are no tears I can offer him. I am completely numb. I am broken. And the only thing stopping me from crumbling into nothing right now is the man who's holding me together. Without him, I'd disappear. All I can do is draw him in through my nostrils, trying to make myself believe that he's here. *He's actually here.*

His body shakes and stifled sniffles resonate above me. "I'm so sorry, Bradford." The moment the words come out of his mouth, he breaks into sobs. "I was wrong. I should never have laid all that heavy shit on you the day we left."

I'm in such a daze it's taking me a while to process his words. A lightning bolt goes through my body as I realise what he's saying. "No! No, please! *Please* don't change your mind about me. I know my life is a mess but I promise I'll get it together. I'll do anything I can to show you I'm worthy."

Bruno grasps my shoulders, moving me outwards so he can look at me. "Of course you're worthy. I fucking *love* you…" His voice trails off as he ghosts his fingers under my eyes. "There's a storm raging inside you, Bradford. Things might be fucked up right now, but I'll stick around forever if that's what it takes. However long you need till you feel ready. I won't pressure you, OK?"

"No, Bruno! You're not… I mean I c…" In my abject panic to set him straight, I'm stumbling over my words. "I don't need time. I don't need anything except you. I would have told you I loved you months ago if I'd had the balls. And if that bastard hadn't smashed my phone and put me in a coma I would have called you straight away." I grab his face and pull it close, squinting as hard as I can. I'm sick and tired of all this blur. "When I found out I'd been off with the fairies for a *fucking week,* all I could think of was how I never got to say any of this to you."

"Oh, God, baby," he gasps. Now that he's so near, I can see the tears running rivers down his cheeks. Leaning even closer, he places his mouth softly to mine. Three gentle kisses. A simple, loving statement. Our lips brush together as he speaks in an urgent whisper. "I don't want us to ever be apart again. The second I can get you out of here, I'm taking you back to Mum's place and I'm gonna look after you."

He slides his hand behind my head and I flinch involuntarily.

"Oh Jesus, fuck." Bruno's brow screws up in horror as he looks me up and down, checking my wounds. "I've been mauling you to death and I didn't even think… did I hurt you?"

"No, Bruno. Maul away. Nothing else matters. I'm safe now." I try to focus my eyes on his, hoping like mad I'll be able to see them better again someday. "*Sarà perché ti amo*, remember?"

"I was singing it to you, Bradford. I wish I'd been brave enough to actually say it. Maybe then all this…" He screws his eyes up, turning his head to the side.

"Hey, it was gonna blow up sometime. My mess to take care of."

"You went through all this alone." He moves his face as close as possible. "Can you see my eyes clearly now?" I gaze into one, then the other. The sincerity in them is so potent I almost need to look away, but I've missed out on far too much lately. "You are *never* gonna have to do that again."

A familiar voice sails into the room. "I got us a park, but I might have to run soon—" Claudio stops short of my bed and his voice drops. "Oh, fuck, mate. That prick did a real number on you."

I instantly cringe with embarrassment. Amongst all this drama, I haven't even thought about how hideous I must look. "Nice of you to drop by, Claudio."

Claudio chuckles and pats me on the shoulder. "Good to see you, mate."

"Does this mean all of you are home now?"

"Nah, I got back late last night. Work, y'know. Gab and the others are there a bit longer."

A nurse bustles into the room spouting the usual pleasantries, then wheels the obs trolley up to my bed. "Doctors are doing rounds, they'll be here in a minute."

"I might go and see if I can find Gina," says Bruno. "Be back soon." He leans down and kisses my forehead.

"Fuck, Bru. That cunt's got it coming." I can hear Claudio talking under his breath as they walk away. "Want us to take care of him?"

Bruno laughs a little too loudly, then switches into a fast flurry of Italian as I hear their voices trail off down the hall.

CHAPTER 21

After I'm discharged from Prince of Wales on Monday, Bruno drives me straight to my appointment at the eye hospital in the city. "I could be here for a good couple of hours," I tell him as we round the corner towards the Domain. "Why don't you just drop me off and I'll get a cab back."

Bruno shakes his head. "I'm not letting you out of my sight. I've got a book to read. I'll be fine."

"Well, at least go to the cafe. Or take a walk in the Domain. I hate to think you'll be sitting there all that time on my account."

"You are priority number one, Bradford. I'm just sorry I won't be here for you this evening." He pulls up at a vacant spot on Hospital Road and reverses in. "Are you really sure you'll be OK without me while I'm at work?"

"I'll be fine. Honestly. I'm buggered and I'll probably just sleep all afternoon. It'll be so nice to be in a proper bed." I rifle through the big bag of stuff he's brought for me. "Thank you so much for grabbing these things." Stretching forward, I stick the disability permit on the windscreen. "And doing all this driving. And… *everything*." I feel like such a scab. Some pathetic loser who's completely reliant on the good nature of others.

Bruno leans over and buries his nose in my hair, breathing deeply. His hand gently clasps the side of my head, holding it against his face. "*Blinky,* I will never be able to thank you enough for everything you did when Dad… you know…" I can see it's a subject that's still too raw to be discussed freely. There's been that much turmoil lately, it's hard to remember it all happened so recently. Maybe it's the residual holes in my memory. In any case, Bruno and I don't need to say more. Words may not come easy at the moment, but the language of his embrace transcends any and all of them.

Once I've been seen by the consultant, I make my way down the hall with the cane Bruno brought for me. Yeah, it's like riding a bike, but I'm shocked at how much I've come to rely on Brendan. Every step I take is unsure. I'm trailing a hand on the wall, following the dark blue uniform of a nurse in front of me. If she's not crashing into anything, then so long as I'm right behind her, I'm OK.

Bruno's in the chair closest to the hallway and he shoots to his feet the second he sees me. "How was it?"

I try to smile, but it's a real effort. "Doesn't look like things will be getting better any time soon. They said the corneal transplant hasn't gone into failure yet, but it's definitely rejecting."

"So, what does that mean for you?"

"Bombarding it with steroids every hour while I'm awake. Weekly appointments. Coming into Emergency if anything changes. And if it doesn't get better, I'll be looking at another transplant." I sigh, long and hard. *Back down this road again.* "It's not the surgery I'm worried about; I've had so many of them. It's just… each time they transplant, there's a much lower success rate. And this one would be the third graft on the left side." I feel like tearing my hair out. "*Why* did he have to wreck my *good* eye?"

I'm more upset than I thought. Bruno takes my weight as we make our way through the hospital grounds to the car. The whole journey back to Maroubra he's holding my hand. He helps me into the rumpus room, undresses me to my underwear, and puts me to bed. I lay there with my eyes closed, my brain slowly churning with the magnitude of everything that's happened.

A soft kiss on my forehead wakes me from my daze. Bruno's there in his uniform. "I'm sorry," he whispers. "I wish I wasn't leaving you."

I reach up and stroke his beard. "Truly, you don't need to worry about me. I'm just gonna sleep." I trail my hand down over his belly and cup his crotch. His cock is fat and warm and I miss it dearly. "Obviously, I want you to stay for selfish reasons, but we have loads of time for that later."

My eyes follow his blurry frame as he leaves. I don't deserve his kindness. I'm one walking disaster after another. All I can do is hope and pray he doesn't realise this before I manage to redeem myself.

***

I love winter, I really do. After months of being in a continual sweat, it's always nice to be able to get around in cooler air. To snuggle up and keep warm at night rather than stick to the sheets. One thing I've never got used to, however, is the early darkness. I've woken up just now and it's pitch black. The sense of isolation is fierce. It's like it's torturing me down to my bones.

The hideous trill of Summer's loan phone splits through my psyche. There's no point in looking at it; I'd never see who's calling. All I can see on the screen is a green splodge next to a red one. "Hello?" My voice sounds like a cane toad.

"Hi, Bradford? This is Susannah from Guide Dogs. I've spoken to Summer and she mentioned you've been discharged."

My brain is lagging. Only one thought is galloping to the front of it. "Brendan. How is he? When can I see him?"

Susannah takes her sweet time answering me. Three seconds equals three years. "Brendan is recovering well physically. But…"

"Yeah?"

"There's a very real possibility he may be too traumatised to return to you."

Horror grips my chest and squeezes hard. "What do you mean? What's gonna happen?"

Susannah is clearly trying to be careful. "You may need to prepare yourself to work with a new dog."

In my messed up state, it sounds like this is a done deal. "No! You can't do that! *Please* don't." The words choke their way out of me like a whiny child about to burst into tears. "Haven't I already lost enough?"

I'm not even listening to what Susannah's saying anymore. My world is crashing down and someone else inside my head is finishing the conversation for me.

I'm absolutely parched. And freezing. Trembling. The blankets have made their way down to hip level. At some stage the call has ended, but I haven't noticed. I need to go upstairs, but I don't know this house well enough, especially now my sight is so much worse. The eight or nine percent vision I'd normally have is more than halved right now. And at this end of the scale, every percent lost means major changes to the way I live.

My back hurts as I swivel slowly to a sitting position. I feel like I've spent the past few hours in a state of complete tension while I've been asleep. Groping for my cane, I let it spring to its full extension and heave myself off the bed. I'm all giddy, but if I take it slowly, I'm sure I can make it upstairs.

There's a jumper at the end of the bed, which I pull over my head. Bruno has left me house keys on the bedside table, and I gingerly feel around for them. If I knock them off, they could skid anywhere. I certainly don't fancy lying face down on the cold floor tiles fumbling to locate them under the bed. Once they're in my grasp, it's time to work my way upstairs.

These first targets are large and easy enough—the sliding door, the pavement, the set of steps leading up to the back verandah of the house. The lock on the rear door is a matter of rubbing my finger over the keyhole, then inserting the key while I'm touching right next to it.

I know the kitchen well enough from the few times I've made lunch here. Of course, now I'm navigating it with virtually bugger-all vision. If things have been moved around in the fridge or on the counter, it's going to be an impossible search. I'd love to make tea, but I don't trust myself one bit at the moment: my head is aching and I'm too fuzzy to give it the extra concentration I'll need with my eyes this bad. I'll just fill a glass with whatever's in the fridge.

The cupboard with all the mugs and cups and tumblers is high up, second from the right. Stretching out, I pat my hand around inside it, feeling for the coldness of glass. I really should have turned the lights on. Then again, what bloody use would they be? It's not like I'm seeing anything more than blurs and shadows unless I shove something right next to my eyes.

After seizing a tumbler, I feel my hand bump whatever's next to it. The item falls out of the cupboard against my wrist, and my instant reaction is to flail around trying to catch it. It ricochets off my hand, causing the tumbler to slip from my grasp just as my elbow thwacks hard into something on the counter. There's an almighty smash as I lose my footing.

I'm down on the floor, struggling to get to a sitting position. Something hurts in my leg. As I feel the pain, the warm sticky wetness of blood, the jutting glass, a terrifying panic rises through my ribcage and closes like a vice around my throat. I can't breathe. The back of my tongue is blocking my pharynx. Images of Jarrod's hand bashing into my face for the first time. Falling to my knees amongst a pool of glass. Punches. Kicks. My dog yelping in agony. My poor little boy. My best friend who's being taken away from me.

I can't cope with this. I'm in a ball against the cupboard. Jarrod's words fly into my consciousness.

"Nobody's listening anymore."

He's right. I have nothing left to say. I am worthless. I am of no use to anyone. All of this, everything, *I deserve it.* I just want it all to end. If only I was at home, I'd have enough pills to do the job properly.

See, you can't even top yourself like a man, Bradford. You're an embarrassment.

***

Hours go by. Days. Months. I don't know how bloody long, but I'm still sitting here. My arse went numb long ago. The door opens and bright light pierces right through to the back of my skull.

"Oh, God, baby." Bruno's voice is a maelstrom of worry, relief, concern, pity. And I *am* pitiful, plonked on these cold tiles in the middle of a colossal mess I've created. I may as well have pissed and shit myself given how pathetic it all looks.

I can hear the crunch of glass under Bruno's boots, the sound of a door opening, the swish and clink of broken pieces being swept up. I feel weak. My hand falls to my side and lands on a huge shard. Running my fingers over it, I note the intricate patterns. "Oh, no," I whisper. "Your mum's beautiful glass dish." I want to weep. I'm sure I would if I hadn't already died inside. "Bruno, you didn't sign up for this. You can back out right now."

"No. Of course I'm not going to do that." His tone is gentle but firm.

"I'm deadly serious. I won't ever hold it against you. You don't need some lame millstone around your neck."

He squats down in front of me and grasps my shoulders. "It's far too late for you to kick me to the kerb now," he says. "I love you, you little fucker. You're getting all of me whether you like it or not."

CHAPTER 22

It's time to face the music. The last several days have been a haven for me. My memory is still patchy, I've had headaches, and I've slept a lot. It's been a blessing to spend every night with Bruno. He's held me constantly, treated me so well. And we've hardly been able to keep our hands off each other. The orgasms have been astronomical. However, Valentina and the others arrived back home last night, and they definitely don't need me hanging around like a bad smell.

While I may be feeling stronger every day, there's no way I'd be able to face going back to my apartment alone. Bruno has insisted on coming and staying with me. For once in my life, I'm going to push my guilt aside and be totally selfish. I want him there. I want his warm body, his hugs, his love.

"You know this is dangerous for you," I tell him as he loads his bags in the back of the Kingswood.

"What do you mean? What's dangerous?" He slides into the front with me and sticks the key in the ignition.

"You coming to my place. I might not ever let you leave."

"Who says that's a bad thing?" He reaches over and brushes his fingers through my hair. "You seem to be getting around a little bit easier these last couple of days."

"Yeah. I think I might be getting some improvement in my eye. Maybe the swelling's going down in the cornea. Everything's still a total haze, but I think it's not quite as bad as it was. It's just…" I let out a long sigh. "I've had this kind of thing happen before. The eye gets better, then it goes south again within a few months. So, I'm not out of the woods just yet."

I hate sounding negative. This is a good sign, a positive step. I need to allow myself to believe it. And Bruno is entitled to a lot more from me than constant drama. Adopting a brighter tone, I try for another subject. "How did everything go last night? Sorry I took off to bed early. Everyone was so nice to me, but I knew you all had a lot to catch up on."

Bruno smiles as he pulls up to the lights at Anzac Parade. "Don't ever think you're not welcome, *Blinky*. And don't underestimate how grateful they all are to you. Oh, and speaking of that, Claudio dropped this off." He reaches back and hands me a paper bag. Inside is a couple of folded pieces of paper with a box underneath.

Pulling out the paper first, I see it's a note that's been considerately scrawled in huge letters with thick black Sharpie.

"Mate, we will never be able to thank you enough for what you did for our family, but here's a start. Claudio, Gabriela and the boys."

The box has the familiar Samsung logo on it with a picture of a big-arsed phone. It must have been bloody expensive.

"Claudio tells me you're not to worry about the cost. He has friends in all the right places." Bruno glances over at me as he talks and I can hear the grin in his tone.

"Wow, this is amazing. I was dreading to think how much I'd have to fork out for a new one. It's so nice of them."

"Bradford," he says firmly, "you *deserve* it. And those boys think the sun shines out of your arse. So does mum."

I can't help smiling at Bruno's eloquent assessment. "How's she shaping up right now? I didn't want to look like I was prying, so I kind of, you know..."

Bruno chuckles at my awkwardness. "She's OK. Doing as well as can be expected."

"I really shouldn't be taking you away from her, Bruno."

"Nah, Don't worry about her. Gab and I will still be dropping in there all the time. Plus she has enough funding in her My Aged Care package for a lot more services. She knows she'll need to accept proper help if she's gonna stay at home on her own." He reaches across and slides his hand between my legs, squeezing my cock. "Anyway, how could I resist coming and staying with such a sexy man?"

The apartment is spotless when Bruno leads me through it. I walk around everywhere squinting hard, trying to get a close look at it all. The stench of debauchery is gone, there are flowers on the coffee table, and Jarrod's bedroom is completely empty. I'm absolutely gobsmacked. I thought I'd have another horrible panic attack, but it's like a different world now his presence has been banished. “I can’t believe you guys did all this for me.”

“You can thank Summer when she gets here. She’s the one who did most of it.” Bruno pulls me into his arms, reaching down and groping my arse. With a tilt of my head, I take his nipple in my mouth through the thin fabric of his t-shirt. “God,” Bruno groans. “It’s wonderful being completely free to touch each other like this.”

“I’m allowed to love you now.” My statement is simple, but the emotional rush packs a huge wallop. I look up at Bruno, who’s staring at me with a fondness that makes me want to cry.

“Yes, baby. We’re legit. It’s all you and me from here on.” He leans down towards me to kiss. It’s always his moustache I feel first. It’s a sensual, masculine blanket that merges with my own split seconds before his full lips touch my mouth. Bruno doesn’t pissfart around. He moans instantly as he presses against me, his wide, soft tongue surging straight inside. We’re like a Ferrari in this respect—nought to a hundred in no time at all. I desperately have to taste as much of him as I can. Every time we do this, my tongue fights with his, roaming wildly through his mouth, searching frantically, swallowing over and over. And every time it only gets better. It’s not just a reminder of the intense passion I’ve felt with all our previous kisses, it’s a brand new discovery. Each time, we reach a new plane and it’s higher than before. My moans become more desperate. My hands clutch at the back of his head. My beard grinds against his. My nose breathes him in. His scent, his wonderful scent, that blissful, intangible gift that I gorge myself on, no matter what part of his body I’m lucky enough to bury my face against. This man that I love so much it makes me want to bawl, to clutch onto as hard as I can lest he slips away from me. I need him with every part of my ravaged being. He is my life. My *fucking life.*

The doorbell rings and I’m almost glad. I’m so close to coming undone in Bruno’s arms that it rattles me. If I expose myself this much, if I lay myself bare and raw and bleeding, will I lose who I am? Can I thrust myself upon him completely, cracks and all? Would that even be fair to him?

Bruno doesn’t run off to answer the door straight away. For a few seconds, he stares at me, his brow knitted with intensity, his eyes shining. His heart is trying to say something to me and I urgently have to know what it is. *Anything, my beautiful man. Anything your precious soul needs, I’ll give it.*

When Bruno’s down the hall letting in our visitor, it’s not Summer’s voice I hear. “Hi, darl. You left all this stuff behind. Thought I’d drop it over.” Brie’s unmistakable tone projects through the apartment. He saunters in carrying an armload of items. "Oh, *darl*!" he gasps, quickening his pace as he approaches me. He tilts his head from side to side, surveying my face. I feel queasy. Like I should apologise for my grotesque appearance. "Jesus, look at you. That *fucking* trail of cat sick…"

Mercifully, he leaves it at that. He hoists up his delivery and I notice it's a pile of jumpers and jackets. "Looks nice and spacious in there," he says, nodding towards Jarrod's old bedroom and swanning off in that direction. "I'll hang Bru's fashion disasters in the wardrobe."

"Disasters? Ha! I could tell Bradford a story or two about *your* style fuckups over the last twenty years." Bruno ambles into the room behind Brie, and I hear the clink of hangers against metal. "Thanks for doing this. You didn't have to bring it all over."

"Well, you never know," sing-songs Brie. "You might *need* them." It's a loaded response and I hear him pause for dramatic effect. "Anyway, I wanted an excuse to come pay my respects to Bradford."

I've slunk into the room and I'm now staring at the empty four walls, the rejuvenated carpet. It's odd; nothing like I expected. There's a nice scent everywhere. A calming one. The place doesn't rattle me or even remind me of Jarrod's sinister presence. It's like all traces of him have been exorcised. All around me it smells like… like new beginnings.

"Speaking of Bradford," Brie continues, "come put the jug on, I have news."

I can't believe I've forgotten my manners. Jumping to it, I scuttle into the kitchen. It looks spotless, and my eagle-eyed Occupational Therapist of a sister has put everything back in its exact spot. I can't really see the items, they're just blobs, but there's enough detail to feel around and grab what I need. Bruno's next to me, fussing around with the coffee percolator at the stove. "Are you sure you're OK here?" His warm hand slides on my shoulder.

"Yeah, I can manage. I have this" — I hold up the little device that beeps when a cup is full — "and this." Grabbing the handle of the Uccello kettle, I demonstrate how it sits in its cradle and tilts to pour water.

"Is *that* what it does? I thought it was just some cordless kettle in a weird holder."

"Hurry the hell up with the tea, Martha Stewart," calls Brie from the dining area. "I'm dying to spill it out here."

At the table, Bruno and I sit opposite Brie, who slaps his splayed hands on the surface with a theatrical flourish. "So, Bradford… I got a call from one of Jarrod's cronies. It appears your ex got himself into a fight when he went out last night and ended up more than a little worse for wear."

"Jesus. How bad is he?" I inject my response with the requisite amount of concern, but I'm hardly shocked.

"Oh, you know. Black eyes, bruises, broken rib or two. He's been banged up pretty good, but apparently he'll be fine."

"Do they know who did it?"

"Oh, *darl.*" Brie swishes his hand dismissively. "With the amount of people he's been pissing off lately, it could be anyone."

The doorbell sounds, and Bruno stands up. "Well, it was only a matter of time." The tone of his voice is dark. Ominous. "Bad things happen to bad people."

While Bruno strides down the hall, foggy recent memories resurface.

"Want us to take care of him?"

Claudio's words ring through my ears, immediately followed by the terrifying memory of Brendan in distress. Oh, God, my beautiful boy. That gentle loving creature who would never hurt a soul. You know what? I'm just gonna count my blessings here. I will never, *ever* mention a word of this to anyone.

Summer bursts into the living room just as I'm standing up. Her arms are instantly flung around my neck and she squeezes tight. "Welcome back home, Braddy."

I feel like whatever I say is going to be grossly inadequate here. "All this stuff you've done for me, Summer. The hospital, this apartment… how the hell can I ever thank you enough?"

"Don't worry, sweetie, you'll be on uncle duties *all* the time once this is over."

"Oh, are the girls with you?"

"Not this morning, darl. They're out skating with cousin Oscar and Uncle Dominic." She looks at me for a moment, rubbing my arm. "I didn't want to bombard you too much. We'll bring them over next week. Promise."

I'm cringing at my stupidity. Of course she doesn't want to scare the poor things with the way I look right now. As usual, she's being discreet and I appreciate her all the more for it.

Summer looks across to the master bedroom. "Oh, I did a bit of a cleansing ritual in there. Hope you don't mind. Even after that pigsty was all spick and span there was so much bad energy left behind."

Man, I love my sister. "It worked, Summer. I could feel it straight away. Like a rebirth. The whole place was so tranquil." I give her a huge kiss on the cheek. "I really need to learn more about all of this from you."

A hand lands on my shoulder. I've been paying no attention to the voices talking behind me. "Hey, Brad. Good to see you." Nathan spins me around and his arms circle me in a tight manly grip, his hand slapping my back. The smell of his body makes me almost jump out of my skin.

"Oh, Jesus. Oh, *God.*" The horror in my voice can't even be masked as shards of memories rush back to me. "Did I—" *Yes, I did.* I whimper as I dig my hands into my face. "I'm so sorry."

Nathan and Summer are laughing like mad, and it only gets worse when a puzzled Bruno chimes in. "What's so funny?"

Nathan takes a breath out of his tirade. "Let's just say Bradford is a *pit* man."

There's a guy hovering silently behind Nathan. A bushy-bearded burly bear with long shoulder-length hair. I give him a tentative smile. I really should introduce myself, but I'm now all too aware of the angry scar on my left cheek. The complete redness in my left eye. The residual marks. The shaved patches and surgical wounds on the back of my head. My shame is right there in all its glory.

"Oh—Bradford, this is my big bro, Ryan," says Nathan.

I go to shake Ryan's hand, but he steadily pulls me into a warm hug. I'd normally feel awkward doing this unless it's someone I know really well. But Ryan is strong. Cuddly. Masculine. *Safe.* He doesn't say anything. He just rubs my shoulder blade as our hug ends, then smiles at me.

This quiet act seems to be Ryan's jam. He sits and observes everyone's raucous discussion as we have morning tea, only speaking when spoken to. His voice is gruff but unassuming. At one stage after we've finished gorging ourselves on cake, he taps me on the shoulder. "Is there anywhere I can go and have a cigarette?"

"Sure. I'll show you my old smoking area." I lead him down the hall and through the laundry to the back door.

"Wow, you have a yard?" Ryan follows me out onto the cracked concrete pavement.

"Well, I pretend it's mine. Most people only come out here to hang up their washing." I wave over towards the row of Hills Hoists as we take a seat in my plastic chairs.

Ryan pulls something out of his pocket and I spot the familiar sight of a cigarette being rolled. "You gave up?" he says.

"Yeah. About two years ago now."

He smokes without saying a word. I'm enjoying the calm. It's a surprise when I hear him speak again. "I'm gonna say something," he starts. "But it's really hard for me, so I want you to hear me out."

This does not sound good. Alarm bells are blaring in my head, but there's something about the earnestness in Ryan's tone that tells me I need to listen closely. Slowly, I nod.

"Um… I was assaulted too. It was different from what happened to you." He stops for a moment, taking a huge drag on his rollie. "At first, I wasn't ever gonna tell anyone about it, but I have a good friend who saw right through me." I see him stub his cigarette out, then watch as he begins to fidget with his hands in front of him. "I go to this, um, LGBT support group every second Thursday. Will you… come with me?"

Fear rises into my throat. Every muscle in my body is itching to run away and hide. The thought of being surrounded by strangers, of baring my soul, of being judged… I can feel the nausea starting already. But Ryan is looking at me intently. His brow is furrowed in the middle. The very essence of me can't bear to disappoint him. "Um, thanks. I guess so." Even as I say those words, I'm wincing inside. I'm doing it to please him—a man I don't even know—but part of me is aware that I've given the right answer.

***

When Thursday rolls around, Ryan comes to pick me up in a big old ute. I'd told him that I could get there myself and I didn't want him going out of his way, but he'd insisted. The subtext was clear—he was doing his bit to make sure I didn't squirm out of it.

I like the way he doesn't talk much. It means there's no obligation to engage in any sort of polite conversation, and I'm more grateful for this than I realise. Music is playing away on his car stereo, the kind of Aussie pub rock from when *I* was a kid. I wonder how old Ryan is. I know he's older than Summer and Nathan, but he'd definitely be quite a bit younger than me. It doesn't seem like the right time to ask.

We park in a back street somewhere in Newtown and I follow Ryan with my cane. The pavements are narrow and it's dark, but I focus on the back of him. He leads me into some kind of hall. It's an open place with a wooden floor and a circle of chairs. People are milling around at the side near some tables. I can feel my heart thumping in my chest. I am immensely relieved when Ryan bypasses the social chit-chat and ushers me straight over to sit down.

Channelling my opera technique, I breathe deep and low into my pelvic floor while the counsellor introduces the session. It seems to help straight away. Person after person tells their story. Some of them sound truly damaged. Some of them sound like professional victims. I know it's a front—we all do what we can to cope. Overall, I'm amazed at the similarities. These people are me.

By the time it's my turn, I have somehow developed a steely resolve. Words come out of me as if someone else is doing the talking. There's another Bradford in my body and he's taken over. I'm almost intrigued by my story. How Jarrod loved me at the start. How I loved him back even more, including his temperamental ways. How his fiery personality eventually turned itself onto me. How desperately I wanted things back the way they were. The drifting apart, the nastiness, the way he beat me down till I thought I was nothing but a piece of shit. Out spew the tawdry details, all the way to the bitter end—the end that is painfully visible all over my face. I'm almost rocked by how raw I must look to these strangers: the physical marks that demonstrate I've only *just* made it through. These are not memories, they're aftershocks that are still ringing in my ears.

I feel a visceral sense of relief—no, of *pride*—that I've made it through my retelling unscathed. It's helped that I can't see anything but vague human forms around me. I can't see their faces, their reactions. The visual anonymity of this is a blessing.

I'm snapped out of it by Ryan's gruff voice. He starts slowly, talking about the sudden and unexpected split with his partner at the time. The way he'd walked around in a daze for ages until a friend intervened. The way she'd mistaken his silent shock and heartache for a simple case of post-breakup blues. The way she'd encouraged him to get over it by going out for some casual fun. My morbid fascination turns to horror as he talks about his visit to a sauna. The trepidation he felt, the way he was just about to turn and flee when some big muscled man jostled him into a room. The way he'd thought the man wanted rough sex, but it quickly spiralled into something much more sinister. The way this man humiliated him, degraded him, beat and bashed him over and over, then repeatedly raped him into a bench. The way Ryan lay there and silently took it all because he hated himself so much he truly believed he had it coming.

I can barely breathe. This man—this lovely, quiet man—he did nothing to deserve this. *Nothing.* What happened with Jarrod was my fault. *My fault.* I could have got rid of him at any stage. I saw the signs. All of them. And I chose to ignore them. I was spineless. Gutless.

A massive cry erupts from me. I'm mortified beyond belief. I'm trying to choke it up, but a hand grabs mine and squeezes. Hard.

What? He's trying to console me? ME? After what he's been through?

I'm no longer in my body. I'm possessed. Sobs are ripping their way out from deep within my guts. They're ugly. The pitch goes higher and higher. I am no longer a man. I'm an embarrassing, screaming queen. A shrieking child. The pain is so searingly intense that I'm doubled over. It's so far down inside me that I can't even expel it. I can feel myself shaking violently, but I'm powerless to stop it.

Arms are suddenly around me. Somehow I'm on my feet, leaning against Ryan's sturdy frame. He's whisking me away somewhere through a door. Then I'm on a chair, writhing in agony as my body betrays me, strips me of any shred of dignity I might have had left. His hand gently rubs my back. Round and round. Firm and constant. Something about it hypnotises me. My terror is gradually ebbing away. Bit by bit, I'm grinding to a steady halt. I'm empty. I can hear the booming resonance in my head. There's nothing left. All gone.

It's a while before I can bring myself to sit up. Crushing shame sweeps right through me. I'm trying to speak. "I… I… I'm sorry. I can't believe I did that."

Ryan doesn't say anything straight away. He waits a moment till he hears my breathing even out. "We've all been there, mate. All of us. Including me."

It's dark out here. Ryan's fiddling round. He reaches over to me, putting something in my hand. It's a cigarette. I don't even think about it as I place it between my lips and he lights it. For some reason, it seems like the best thing right now. I sit there and concentrate on smoking. In and out. In and out. The headspin is helping.

When I'm finished, I spend a moment taking in my surroundings. I'm on a dodgy plastic chair in some kind of ramshackle courtyard. I can hear the traffic all around. The sound of people on footpaths. The noises of a dirty urban environment. Somehow, though, it's serene. Life is going on out there.

"I don't wanna push my luck, mate," says Ryan. "But I really think you should take this." He places something in my hand. It's a small card. "They're a counselling service I used to go to a lot. It won't cost you out of pocket. The one-on-one thing really helped." He slides his arm across my shoulders and hugs me tight. I lean into his embrace. It's so comforting. He's a big bear. Not as tall as Bruno; a slightly smaller version. His sincerity shines through in every move he makes. Once upon a time, long before Bruno, I might have fallen in love with this man. Tortured and unrequited love. The thought is so amusing, I even smile. *Shut the hell up, Bradford.*

CHAPTER 23

"Susannah called and she's running ten minutes late." I slump onto the couch and stretch the kinks from my back. "Guess I can catch my breath for a moment." To say I'm nervous would be an understatement.

I hear Bruno's footsteps behind me and his big, furry forearms loop around my neck. "I'm sure it's going to be fine," he soothes. "You know, she might even agree to let him stay if she thinks everything's OK."

"That's probably wishful thinking. But does the place look alright?"

"Baby, you've been running yourself ragged all morning. You've done everything you can and it looks perfect."

I know I've gone overboard trying to make the apartment look cosy and welcoming. But maybe she'll get a subliminal message and be more inclined to let me have my best friend back. If I'm being logical, though, I know it's much more a matter of whether Brendan responds well to our session today.

I try to sigh gently, but a tiny grumble of frustration works its way out instead. "I just can't stand not knowing. I mean, other than telling me Brendan's improved, she's been playing her cards pretty close to her chest."

When the doorbell rings, I hurry there so fast that I trip along the way. *Jesus Christ, I need to be more bloody careful.* I may have regained half the vision I lost when Jarrod put me in hospital, but the last thing my eye needs right now is more trauma.

"Hi, Bradford." Susannah is all cheery. It's a good sign. I'm not really paying attention to my own polite greeting. I'm too busy looking at my dog, who's sitting next to her, thumping his tail against the ground. All I want is to throw my arms around him and bury my face in his fur, but I have to be careful not to overwhelm him.

The moment I crouch down, he launches himself at me. His tongue slathers madly all over my face. His excitement skyrockets as I hug his neck, and he turns his head, trying to play-bite my nose with his back teeth. I haven't seen him this animated since he was a two-year-old rookie. I'm laughing my head off, toppling backwards onto my arse as he advances. When Susannah finally gets him to retreat, I'm left sitting there coated in loving doggie slobber. "Um, I think I'm gonna need to pack the baby wipes."

"So, have you had a think about where you'd like to go today?" Susannah waits by the bathroom door as I wash off Brendan's gift.

"Uh… Brendan really loves the cliff walk." I know I'm pushing it. "Only as far as Tamarama, though." Sinking my wet face into a towel, I wait nervously for her response. I need to show her we can conquer this situation. Brendan knows the challenging route down to the finest details.

"That might be a bit too far for him," she says. "I also have to go to another client after this."

Oh. That sounds promising. I mean, what would she do with my dog if she had to go and see someone else? She must be thinking of leaving him with me.

Bruno appears behind Susannah. "How about just doing the walk one way instead? You can call me when you get to Marks Park and I'll drive over and drop you back here."

Susannah seems happy with this. As she's fussing with Brendan, I follow Bruno to the lounge to grab my backpack. His arse looks so big and sexy in his flimsy Nike trackpants, and I grope it just the way it's been begging me to. "I love you, *Harry,*" I whisper, cuddling up to his back and kissing him behind the ear. "Thank you for this."

Bruno growls softly, wriggling his arse against my hand as I press my fingers inside his crack. "I'm sure you'll make it up to me somehow."

Brendan is on his best behaviour as I make my way down Bondi Road towards the beach. Not that he hasn't always been the best dog ever, but he's shifted into turbo right now. He's super attentive, walking crisply, stopping precisely, firmly guiding me around any obstacles. He has no hesitation navigating me past some new construction work we stumble upon. He even predicts the sudden moves of some rowdy teenagers that come barrelling towards us. There's no way he could know about my extra needs with my eyesight being worse than usual. A grin works over my face as I allow myself to accept the most obvious reason: *he's putting on a performance for Susannah.*

He knows exactly where we're going as he whisks us past the park overlooking South Bondi, guides us up the sloping hill to the change rooms, then helps me climb the crowded, curving stairs to Notts Avenue. These steps require him to be on the ball every time we come here, as tourists charge down them with no regard for anyone else. Usually they spot Brendan and have to spring aside quickly. Occasionally, they're just plain rude.

I'm dying to ask Susannah for feedback as Brendan fairly prances along past Bondi Icebergs, but I don't want to push things. I also don't want to push *Brendan.* I need to go easy on him, but I don't want Susannah to get suspicious. I'm gonna be a little devious here.

Deliberately slowing my pace, I descend the stairs down the cliff face with a lot more care than usual. Why wouldn't I? After all, my eyes are extra bad right now—of *course* she'd expect me to be lagging a bit. On top of this, I'm not in the kind of peak condition I was in before that bastard attacked me. With both these things in mind, Brendan can have a bit of respite. He loves this part of the walk best, anyway. The winding fenced path goes up and down and around the craggy rocks of Squid Bay as the sea frolics away to our left. It's breathtakingly beautiful. My own picturesque slice of nature mere moments away from the tight urban sprawl I live in.

Next, it's time to make the gradual ascent to the very top of Arin's Point. I take my time; I have every reason to be cautious with the various highly-blurred joggers and impatient people scrambling to get around me and my blind arse. If anything, Brendan seems to want to crank it up. He's staying in perfect sync with me, but I can feel his enthusiastic vibes shooting up through the harness. *See? It's me, not my dog, Susannah. I'm the one holding him back. He's coping fine.*

We stake our claim on a high point in Mark's Park. The view here spans from Ben Buckler Point in North Bondi all the way down to Cliff's Edge in Clovelly. To my eyes, these would normally be blurry built-up headlands jutting out into the ocean either side of me. Today, they're just smudged brown fingers in a haze of deep blue.

Pulling out the picnic blanket, I set it up on the grass as Susannah calls Bruno. Before I sit down, I pour half my bottle of water into Brendan's folding bowl. He laps it up with gusto, then sits primly and waits.

"He's done well," says Susannah. "I'm really pleased." I know she's not an idiot, but I'm hoping I chose the least conspicuous spots to take it down a notch during the walk.

As we sit there debriefing and surveying the vista, the ocean breezes waft over us. It's cold, but the sun is smiling down as if it were summer. I can see the vague forms of people sitting nearby us, tossing morsels of food to the birds. At the moment, these little creatures look like black specks moving around, but I've been here often enough that the visual snapshots are firmly imprinted in my memory.

"We'll need to make a time for next week," says Susannah. I squint across to see her tapping at her phone. "Is Wednesday good for you?"

Oh, God. That's nearly a week away. "Um… I know you're busy, but can you bring him back again sooner?"

Susannah lowers her phone and turns her head my way. "Oh, no. He's staying with you, of course."

Well, spank my arse and call me Charlene. I'm so relieved I could hug her if I knew her better. *My boy. I'm getting my boy back.* I throw my arms around Brendan and he lunges at my face again, rolling with me on the blanket and covering me with sloppy kisses. Jesus, I'm glad I packed the wipes.

Bruno arrives then, calling out to us as he's striding through the park with my picnic basket. "I brought food. You're more than welcome to stay and eat with us, Susannah."

"Yeah, you should. Bruno makes a mean sandwich."

Susannah smiles and shakes her head. "I'd love to, but I'm already going to be late for my other client."

"No worries. Next time, eh?" Bruno plops the basket beside me. "You stay here and I'll be back after I drop them off."

"Just Susannah." I'm grinning like a twit. "Brendan's staying."

As the two of them leave, Brendan sits there watching after them. I feel a pang of sorrow as I realise he's spent weeks and weeks with Susannah. Of course he's going to miss her. To my surprise, Brendan soon flops down, resting his head on my leg. As I pat him, I see all too clearly how worn out he is. Suddenly it dawns on me why he's so exhausted, and I want to cry.

"He's been trying his best in front of her. He knew this was his test, and he didn't want to be away from you for another second."

Mum is leaning back on her elbows next to me, her sandal-clad feet casually crossed. She's wearing one of her flowery hippie dresses, and a huge sun hat obscures the upper half of her face.

"I can't tell you how relieved I am, Mum. I was so scared I'd never get him back."

She looks over at me, tilting up the brim of her sunhat. A kind smile lights up her features. "Things we hold dear to our hearts often have a knack of finding their way home to us."

Her simple wisdom never fails to shed a light exactly where I need it. "Well, *you* did, Mum. I don't know how I would have made it through all this without you watching over me."

"Bradford, you've always been my ray of sunshine. This chance to be around you again has been a blessing and I've cherished every moment."

My chest tightens as I notice her use of tense. I don't want her to say anything else. It's something I can't face hearing right now. Maybe I will never be ready.

A dark figure hops up to me. I squint sideways to see a magpie. It's up so close I can make out its head cocking quizzically from left to right. Very carefully, I sit up and reach into the picnic basket. My hand lands on a soft square lump, and I pull it out to find half the loaf of seed bread I bought this morning. Slowly, I take out the crusty end sliver, pick off a small piece and place it on the ground next to the blanket. The bird doesn't dash and grab, he swaggers over and picks it up. Gulping it straight down, he stares at me for more. Now he's right here, I can see his colouring. He's very young. So trusting. Untainted by the cruelty of the world.

One by one, I feed him tiny morsels. About halfway through, I place a piece on my hand and he calmly takes it. When the sliver of bread is all gone, he seems to understand there's no more. I'd keep feeding him, but I don't want to overdo it and make him sick. He does this kind of little thank-you dance, then off he hops towards some other people nearby.

"You always had a magical connection with animals, darling. I could see your compassion from the time you were a baby. You'd reach out from your stroller and pat the dogs you saw with such gentle reverence. It was a wonderful thing to watch."

Mum's shared similar observations with me before, of course, but never with this kind of detailed recollection. It's touching to know that forty-eight years down the track she remembers these things so vividly.

Shrieks, swearing and aggressive human squawks ring though the air to my right. My head whips around and I see people throwing things at a small dark object. It's the little magpie friend who just visited me. He's not flying away. He doesn't know any better. One of the human figures jumps up and runs towards him, stomping all over the place.

"NO! STOP!" I'm on my feet straight away, running and tripping over myself. As I approach, I see some feral young guy standing there with a girl sitting next to him. "Please leave the bird alone. He's only a baby."

"Mind your own fuckin' business, dickwad," snaps the girl, in a common fishwife tone.

The guy is straight up in my face. "Yeah, you heard her, *faggot.*" He shoves me hard, but he's underestimated my sturdiness and I don't budge.

My heart is thundering. Steam is erupting from my ears. I may be panicking, but I'm seeing red.

I will not be helpless. I will not be helpless.

Drawing in the biggest mother of a breath I can, I steel myself. "Keep your hands off me and LEAVE THE BIRD ALONE!"

He takes a step forward, butting into my chest with his wiry frame. He's taller than I am, but I can still smell his rancid breath. "Whatcha gonna do about it, *faggot*?" He draws the last word out, wringing it for everything it's worth.

"You have *no idea*..." I growl.

"HEY! What do you think you're doing?" Bruno's voice booms from behind me on rapid approach. "Get the hell out of here!" The guy doesn't budge. "You think I'm joking? FUCK OFF!"

With a scowl, the guy turns his head and spits on the ground. Taking his sweet time, he slinks off after the girl. When he glances back, Bruno charges forward several steps, making him scuttle faster. After he's reached a safe distance, he swivels round to face Bruno again. "Fat cunt," he snarls.

Behind him, I spot Mum, who kicks something that's lying on the ground. The guy turns and scarpers like a scared rabbit, stacking it over whatever Mum's laid in his path and landing on his hands and knees. With an impish grin, Mum holds both thumbs up to me. "I *knew* you could do it, darling," she whispers, her sound reverberating in my mind as her image vanishes.

CHAPTER 24

"Looks like I won't be needing these anymore." I'm standing here in just my Y-fronts, flicking through the rack of jackets and jumpers Brie brought over back in winter. "Getting too bloody hot now."

"I dare say you'll need one tonight for the concert. Things'll still get a bit chilly outside after sundown."

I glance over and smile at Bradford, who's sprawled naked in the bed with the quilt kicked down to his ankles. It's six-thirty and the first rays of sun for the day are streaming in the window. I study the way they dance over the side of his arse as he lies there facing me. His cock is lolling against his thigh, still half-hard for lack of attention. This residual arousal is due to my standard daily alarm for him. The first thing I do whenever I wake up is bury my face in his beautiful arse and balls. Sometimes, though, Bradford beats me to it. On those days, I feel like a king. The way he continues to love my body never fails to lift my spirits.

"Come back to bed and finish what you started," he croons.

Normally that would work, but I ignored my actual alarm for too long today. As a compromise, I pull on the uniform I've just located, then slip in beside Bradford fully-clothed and cup my hand on his bum. My fingers stroke over the furry surface, relishing the way his body hair becomes denser as I delve further into his crack. "If I do what I really want to do to you, I'm gonna be late." I nuzzle against his ear, kissing his neck the way he likes, getting the precise kind of moan I want to hear.

"You know, I reckon Brie was making a statement back when he brought all your winter stuff here. I was hoping you'd stay for good."

Bradford is shyly avoiding my gaze, and I lift his chin till his stormy grey eyes are looking right at me.

"We have a real home together now, *Blinky.*" I lean forward and brush my nose against his. Things did indeed work out perfectly. When Brie and I sold our apartment, he took the living room furniture, and I moved all the bedroom stuff into the empty room here at Bradford's place. It all happened so organically. Once I'd had a taste of domestic bliss with this wonderful little bear, there was no way I wanted to leave.

With one final grope of his arse and a long kiss to his lips, I peel myself off the comfortable new mattress and stand up. "You are an evil temptation."

"I'm trying to con you into calling in sick." Bradford grins at me, sliding his hand up and down his rigid dick.

"Ha! I wish. I had to swap this shift if I was gonna have tomorrow off for Summer and Nathan's housewarming."

"Well, I want you at their party, so you're excused." Bradford shoots me a wink before scooting across and hauling himself out of bed. "I need to take Brendan for his morning stroll, anyway." Sauntering around towards me, I watch his dick swing at a ninety-degree angle, its metal ring glinting in the sunlight. As he wraps his arms around me, my fingers make a beeline for the offending piercing, jiggling it and marvelling at the way his cock jumps in response. "You'd better go," he chuckles. "Make sure you're not late tonight. I'm gonna get there early so we can score a reasonable spot in the park."

Bradford's all excited about this gala concert. It's not at the Opera House, it's one of those public open-air events, kind of an amphitheatre setup in the Domain. Apparently, a few famous opera names are performing, people Bradford knows well. I've never heard of them, but I want to learn more about this part of his life. He's been taking regular lessons and practising away in his study these past few months. I'm thrilled that he might be considering a return to singing.

***

It's a good thing Bradford insisted I meet him at the venue straight from work. The park is already becoming crowded, even though the concert doesn't start for quite a while. It's not hard to spot him down near the front on his picnic blanket with Brendan. As always, he's prepared well, making sure we have reasonable proximity to the bathrooms—no stumbling all over other people when you're dying for a piss after too many champagnes.

As I stroll over towards him, picking my way through the many picnic blankets and folding chairs, the crisp September air soothes me. It's probably the last bit of cool weather we'll have before the heat well and truly sets in, and it seems just the right atmosphere for tonight.

"You got changed," says Bradford, smiling up at me.

"I took advantage of the shower at work. Good thing I did—look at you!" He's swapped his usual winter bear attire of jeans, t-shirts and flannies for a beautiful button-up and chinos. His hair is swept back and his beard looks glossy and immaculate. Fuck, I adore this gorgeous man.

His hug is warm and tight as I settle next to him on the picnic blanket. Brendan is on duty tonight, so his usual enthusiasm is muted, though he responds with wags and licks as I reach across and give him his hug in turn.

"As promised, I bought champagne." I hold up the cooler bag stuffed with four chilled bottles I grabbed on the way here.

"You're too good to me," coos Bradford. "I brought the ice bricks and a cheese platter." He busies himself pulling out a board, knife, plastic cups and a box. "Sorry, it's just one of those pre-packed assortments from Woolies."

"Babe, I couldn't imagine anything better." I constantly marvel at the way Bradford prepares for every outing. He's always lugging around a backpack and he's never failed to forget a single thing we might need. Bringing the booze was the least I could do tonight.

By the time the concert starts, we've worked our way through the first bottle of plonk and made a huge dent in the cheese and crackers. I'm eternally grateful he thought to bring along something to line our stomachs with, otherwise I'd be pretty pissed already.

I don't really know what these people onstage are singing. Sometimes it's a whole chorus, sometimes it's a solo singer and sometimes it's both. Vaguely familiar tunes sail out through the speakers. Dad would very occasionally play some opera when I was a kid, though he was always much more into popular Italian songs.

A man with a booming voice is singing now, and the chorus is standing behind him. "Oh… I know this one!" I say, a little too loudly. "What is it?"

"It's the Toreador's song from *Carmen*," replies Bradford, keeping his voice at a more respectable level. "That's Peter Coleman-Wright. I've done masterclasses with him and he's amazing."

The man onstage he's talking about is all classy and debonair. You can definitely tell he's a total professional the way he's commanding our attention. The other singers' voices weave in and out during what sounds like the chorus of the song. It's the perfect complement to the powerful leading man.

I can hardly keep my eyes off Bradford as he sits forward, his attention fully focused on what's happening onstage. Every now and then, he turns and smiles hopefully at me, checking whether I'm enjoying it too. If only he realised how much I would enjoy anything so long as he was by my side.

At one point well into the show, a woman pretty much floats onto the stage in a stunning gown and launches into one of the dreamiest, most sensual songs I've ever heard. Her voice lingers on every note as her intensity builds. It's not big and dramatic, it's soaring and delicate. Bradford is sitting there transfixed, and I really shouldn't disturb him, but I need to know more. "Who's this?"

"Cheryl Barker," he says *sotto voce*, leaning closer but keeping his eyes on the stage. "It's *Depuis le Jour* from the opera *Louise*."

Bradford turns and smiles at me, his eyes crinkling at the sides. Seeing as he's not annoyed by my question, I decide to ask more. "What's it about?"

"It's an example of *verismo.* You know, a regular girl falls in love with a regular man. And despite everything and everyone trying to keep them apart, they make it through stronger than ever."

There's a tightness in my chest. It sounds exactly like Bradford and me. This woman Cheryl is growing more and more rapturous by the minute. It's bloody exquisite and I'm mesmerised. "Do you know what she's singing right now?"

Bradford leans back a bit and shoots me another grin. It doesn't seem like he's indulging me; he looks genuinely chuffed that I'm reacting this strongly. "I don't really know a lot of French, but I've taught this aria in my Form and Analysis class." He faces the front again, turning his head slightly as he recites the lyrics line by line. "What a beautiful life… Oh! I'm so happy… too happy… And I'm trembling with delight… from the charming memory… of the first day of our love."

When the music draws to a close, I watch Bradford there wide-eyed as a small tear makes its way down his cheek. He's never looked so perfect. I've never loved him so much. "Marry me." The words blurt out of my body by instinct. Bradford turns around, shock written all over him. "Oh, Jesus, I'm fucking this all up." I can't help sounding flustered as I fumble around in my jeans. "Don't say anything now. Please. It's just… this has been burning a hole in my pocket for months." I open the small box I've dug out. "Mum gave this to me when we got back from Italy. It was her dad's." Bradford reaches out slowly and runs his finger over the ring. *That's a good sign, isn't it?* I'm babbling, but I can't stop. "I know it's only been eight months. But Bradford—" I grab his hand and squeeze it tight. "I spent twenty years with a man I knew I was never gonna marry. Time is precious and with you it's… this is forever for me."

"Yes." His response is resolute. He looks up at me. His eyes are shining. "I've wanted this since the first night we spent together."

Yanking him into my arms, I muscle him down onto the grass and roll back and forth, slamming my lips into his and delving my tongue inside his sweet mouth. Bradford giggles into me, holding my face in his hands and moving back to stare fondly into my eyes. "We'd better stop before I give everyone else here more of a show than they can handle."

I glance around, brushing off my shirt as we right ourselves into a respectable position again. In the background, the chorus is humming some kind of lullaby. I'm already high on all the champagne and excitement, so I'm not surprised when tears spring to my eyes as I recognise it. "*Madam Butterfly*. Dad used to play this record on his old stereo when I was little."

Bradford turns his head towards me again, giving me a lingering look. "I really love how close the two of you were."

"He'd be so happy for us right now, *Blinky*."

Bradford gazes at me a moment longer and I see a kaleidoscope of emotions flash across him. The joy and exhilaration that lights up his features is tempered by a faint sadness. He never really mentions his own dad, but I know it's still painful for him. I doubt people ever get over that kind of abandonment. I'm desperate to appease him, but he averts his eyes and looks to the front again. He's focusing on something high; far above the stage. Maybe he's wishing on a star, the way his lips are faintly moving. Ever so slowly, he reaches up. It's almost as if he's trying to touch the sky.

CHAPTER 25

Nathan and Summer's apartment is in one of those old sixties blocks along Rainbow Street on the way to Coogee Beach. There are a few flights of stairs for us to climb, being on the third floor above the ground-level garages. However, I noticed it was high on the hill, so I'm betting there are some nice district views.

Ryan answers the door, giving us both a hug. "Sorry, Nath's busy in the kitchen and Summer's getting the girls dressed." I love Ryan's quiet, reserved manner. I also love the way he's helped Bradford. Attending their support group has become a fortnightly ritual for the two of them, and I know I have Ryan to thank for it all.

"Wow! Look, it's Goldilocks and the Three Bears!" A slim Hispanic-looking guy has appeared in the hallway. This could only be Ryan's fiancé Dominic, someone I haven't met as yet. Glancing at our little group huddled by the door, I laugh as I take stock of me, Ryan, and Bradford in descending order, with the yellow lab panting away in front of us.

We're whisked inside and Bradford is swamped by little girls who predictably adore him. I stand back and smile as I observe the family dynamics. It's been a real pleasure seeing the way Bradford interacts with these guys. Given the way he looked after my folks, I'm hardly surprised how loved he is. My heart swells as I think about all the opportunities we're going to have to unite our two clans.

Summer and Nathan have put on a really nice vegetarian spread. Their balcony is long and narrow on one side of the apartment, and the food is set up on a table near the open sliding doors. Fresh spring breezes wind their way through the lounge to the balcony on the other side, where Ryan and Dominic are hard at work on a kettle barbecue. “Oi, Bruno!” Dominic pokes his head in the door, holding out a stubby of beer for me. “Come join the real men while we cook dead animals.”

I glance at Bradford, who grins up at me with a raised eyebrow. “Go on, you enjoy yourself. I’m gonna join the knitting circle.”

I must admit, I’ve curbed the amount of meat I usually eat since I’ve been living with Bradford. His cooking is amazing and I never feel like I’m missing out, but whatever carcass those two men are chargrilling out in that Weber has me intrigued.

Once we’ve all eaten our fill, Nathan and Summer get the girls settled in front of the TV with Brendan, then reappear on the main balcony with flutes of champagne for everyone. “OK, folks,” says Nathan, holding his glass aloft. “There’s a reason we only invited family to this housewarming. Um, as you know, Summer and I have been together for ten years, but my hippie other half has never agreed to officially tie the knot.”

We all laugh as Summer gives him a coy slap on the shoulder. “Excuse me! We had a *spiritual* ceremony, didn’t we?”

Nathan makes a puppy face, putting his arms around her shoulder and squeezing her close. “You know I wouldn’t swap that day for anything, babe.” He looks back out to the rest of us with an impish grin. “But now I’ve finally worn her down and we get a *proper* one.”

Summer beams as she holds her hand up, complete with glinting engagement ring. Amongst the back slapping, hugs and congratulations, she shrieks at the top of her voice. “YOU!” She’s pointing right at Bradford. Bustling forward, she wrenches his hand up, studying the antique ring he’s wearing. “When did *this* happen?”

Bradford’s gone all shy. His face is visibly red. “Um, last night.”

Summer squeals like a little girl as she throws her arms around her blushing brother and jumps up and down.

“You reckon the church’ll give you a two for one discount?” pipes up Dominic.

“Not on your life,” chortles Summer. “I want a barefoot beach wedding. In the summer. At dusk. No awful speeches or anything, just lots of food and friends and family for one huge party.”

“Sounds like my kind of wedding.” This comes from Ryan. He’s been hanging back most of the evening, looking on from the sidelines.

I’m expecting some boisterous, cocky reply from Dominic—after all, he’s been one playful joke after another since we got here. To my surprise, he snaps to attention at the sound of his man’s voice. Taking Ryan’s hand, he looks straight into his eyes. “You know, big bear, if this is what you want, I’ll make it happen.”

"Well, I've been waiting over a year for you to make an honest man out of me, *lontra.*" Ryan pulls Dominic towards him, engulfing the slender man in a crushing bear hug. "We can't stay engaged like this forever, you know."

Summer's eyes meet mine. She looks to Bradford, then to Ryan and Dominic, and finally to Nathan. "This may sound like a lame Hallmark movie, but I have an idea…"

CHAPTER 26

The hot summer sun beats down on us as the Kingswood careens south along the highway. We're fairly close to the ocean now; I can smell it in the air. Every kilometre we cover brings my anticipation up a notch.

It was Dominic who really came through with the goods in the end. Summer had all the ideas, of course, but I think the rest of us were pretty pleased with them. Dominic had jumped to it, organising a secluded beach venue on the south coast. He also booked out a whole motel in the nearby town, and teed up a shuttle bus for family and friends too drunk on champagne to drive back after the reception.

Summer and I had taken care of the alcohol and food, including all the barbecued stuff for the meat eaters. She'd also organised the celebrant, the decorations and outfits for all six of us.

I've been craning my head, staring out the window trying to see if there's a glimpse of ocean yet. It took six months, but I eventually regained the sight I lost last winter. Thankfully, I made it through the rejection episode without needing a new corneal graft. With close to ten percent vision now, the tunnel in my better eye is able to see some detail again. I'm able to walk faster with Brendan, focus properly on my massive computer screen, and make out some of the faces when I watch movies on my big TV. I'm relying less on feeling around for things, but you know what? I've regained a skill that I didn't know I'd lost. Being forced to depend on tactile recognition for the first time in six years has come in so handy.

I'm also excited about the coming year. Earlier in January, my opera coach talked me into replacing the tenor soloist for a huge production of Beethoven's *Missa Solemnis* at Easter. I still have a good couple of months up my sleeve to rehearse, but every day my voice gets closer and closer to how it used to be a few years ago.

As for Jarrod—well, his court case hasn't come up yet. Who knows when that will happen, but the police LGBT liaison officer has been diligent with keeping me up to date. I have zero interest in spouting tired clichés about forgiveness and understanding. Jarrod tried to destroy me and he very nearly succeeded. If that was all he'd done, then I'm sure I could find it in my heart to show him some compassion. But he lost me entirely when he hurt Brendan. No, I do not wish him all the best. I hope he's miserable, I hope they throw the book at him, and I hope I never, ever have to speak to him again.

These days, I focus on my family. On the beautiful fiancé who's driving right now, smiling over at me from time to time. On my best friend in the back, the furry fellow who made a full recovery and has been taking me on long power walks again for months. On the wonderful blended bunch of relatives who have come together more than once to date—for birthdays, for Christmas and now for this wedding. *Our wedding.*

***

I can't believe how nervous I feel as we pull up into the car park at the beach. I'm glad we've been really informal about this. The six of us—plus Brendan—pick our way down the path to where everyone is waiting on the sand. All of us five men are dressed in Hawaiian-inspired shirts that match the flowing fabric of Summer's dress. Summer's long dark hair is cascading down in her usual hippie style, though she has a stunning array of tropical flowers worked into it. And all of us guys' arses are snuggled into—you guessed it—slutty little shorts. Of course, that part was my idea.

As the beach comes into view, I gasp audibly. I've been running around the last four months helping prepare all of this, but I haven't actually put everything together in my mind. This is all *real.* This is *actually happening.* Who would have thought that just a year ago—and on this very day—a man would walk into my life and turn it upside down so profoundly that we'd be getting *married*?

People are scattered everywhere, drinks in hand. From the guest ratio, a small slice of the pie seems to belong to Summer, me, Nathan, Ryan and Dominic. But Bruno? I swear, the entire crowd from his and Gabriela's fiftieth must be here. As they see us approach, the party music that's been playing in the background dies down and Abba's *I Do, I Do, I Do, I Do, I Do* starts up. I'm trying desperately to stifle a snigger as Summer turns and smirks at me. God, the amount of times we must have watched *Muriel's Wedding* together all those years ago.

My heart is thundering as Summer, Nathan, Ryan, Dominic, Bruno, Brendan and me walk barefoot through the gathered crowd towards the celebrant. The late summer sun is behind us to the side, its rays still high enough in the sky to bathe our gathering in a bright warm glow. I'm barely able to concentrate as, one by one, we recite the brief vows we've all rehearsed. All I can do is gaze at the man I love and try not to cry. When it's our turn to kiss, we cling to each other, our heads buried tightly together. The connection between our hearts is electric; the utter devotion that unites us flows from chest to chest. Slowly, Bruno moves back and gazes at me. Tears begin to spill down his cheeks. "Blue," he whispers. "Your eyes are *blue*. The storm has passed."

As the crowd begins to disperse towards the long tables laden with food, Summer takes Brendan over to the relatives she's organised to entertain him. After all, Brendan deserves the night off to party too. From my vantage point at the front, I scan from right to left, taking in the sea of guests. In the background, I spot a man standing there by himself. I'm drawn to him for some reason. As I'm trying to work out why, he turns and starts to make his way off from the party. I barge through the crowd, giving automatic apologies, stumbling over the sand till I reach the long pathway that leads to the car park. It's dark here. Trees are everywhere, blocking the residual light which is fast dipping below the horizon. This man has had a big head start, but I can see him not too far in front of me, slowly walking up the hill. "Dad!" I blurt. I don't know why, but it *has* to be. The man turns around as I stumble closer. He's old. Time may have ravaged him physically, but it's unmistakable. "Jesus, Dad. How…"

"Summer tracked me down and invited me." The sound of his voice sends my mind hurtling back decades.

Now that I've found him, I'm standing here dumbstruck. How do you talk to someone who checked out of your childhood—who disappeared during all those years when you desperately needed them? "What did I do wrong, Dad?" The words slip out automatically, a natural progression of the thoughts that are crashing around in my skull. "I loved you so much." The searing hurt I feel right now has me all but falling to my knees. It's a shock. Wasn't I over this decades ago?

"I have no excuse, Bradford. I made a lot of mistakes."

I hate that word. "No, Dad. 'Mistake' makes it sound like an accident. You *chose* to abandon me. I was a scared kid and all I wanted was my dad back. I would have done *anything* to hear from you. Every day I'd hold onto whatever shred of hope I had left, but eventually it died." I'm breathing hard now. "Twenty-one, Dad. I was *twenty-one* before you ever made any effort to contact me. Is it any wonder I'd given up by then?"

Dad isn't looking away. He's gazing right into my eyes, nodding in recognition during every stage of my tirade. "It's my biggest regret and I've carried it with me every day these last forty years. I may have divorced your mother, but I'll never forgive myself for turning my back on you."

I'm doing my best to calm down. Deep breaths, in and out. I've thrown my toys out of the pram for now and it's time for me to keep my voice even. "I'm gonna ask you one question, Dad. And I want an honest answer. You think you can do that?"

He nods slowly, his lips drawing into a line. Deep in his eyes I can see a faint flicker of hope.

"Why did you come here today?"

He doesn't even pause to think. "Bradford, I'm seventy-nine. I won't be around much longer. I know the odds here are impossible, but I have to at least try."

My brain is in so much turmoil, I don't even know how to respond. We need to put a pin in this discussion. The pent-up emotion inside me works its way out into a long, turbulent sigh. "Don't go, Dad. Come back to the wedding. Please."

Dad smiles. He looks tired. "Thanks, but I've intruded enough for one day. Although—" he stops short, swallowing visibly. "I'm not going back home straight away. I'll be in Sydney for a couple of weeks, if you feel like… I don't know. Talking more. Summer has my number."

I gaze at his features for a few seconds. Gone is the powerful father I remember—or at least, who I built him up to be. In his place is a weak, elderly man. His vulnerability is palpable, and I could crush his spirit in my bare hand. But the truth is, I don't want to. Cruelty is not in my nature. Right now, I realise he's given me the offer I've always craved. I'm not fooling myself. I don't know if we can ever repair the damage that was done. But maybe a little patch-up here and there won't hurt. I do my best to generate a smile. "Sure. OK, Dad. I'll be in touch."

There's visible relief in his eyes as he turns and begins to walk off. After a few steps, he looks back for a moment. "Congratulations, Bradford. It was a beautiful ceremony." Capping off with a slight nod, he continues on his way. I stand there and stare at his careful gait, watching as his body becomes darker and darker and he disappears into the night.

"You gave him the chance that he never gave you." The warm tones of Mum's voice waft towards me as she moves into view from my right. She comes to stand directly in front of me, making sure she's completely within my field of vision. "I've always been so proud of you, Bradford, but never more than I am today." Her gentle smile betrays the sense of melancholy reflected in her glistening eyes. She pauses for a moment, and I watch as she studies every part of my face. "That was the last piece of the puzzle, sweetheart. You don't need me anymore."

The pain of reality is swift and severe. It reaches deep inside my chest and grabs so hard I feel like I might faint. "You can't do this, Mum. Please." My voice wavers and cracks. I'm scrambling to stop myself sobbing, but I've already lost the battle. "I know it's selfish. I know this wasn't supposed to last. But I can't lose you again."

"Sweetheart, leaving you is the hardest thing I'll ever have to do." Mum's trying her utmost to sound strong, but through the veil of my tears I see it's not working. As she begins to weep openly, her hand reaches out towards my chest. Energy hums louder and louder all around us. At long last, I feel her make contact as her palm presses over my heart. A colossal wave of warmth rushes straight through my body, filling every inch of it with urgent intensity. "I'll be in here forever, Bradford. You have to believe that."

My sobs are tearing into me now. "Please, not yet. Just a bit longer. *Please*!" I wipe like mad at my useless eyes, desperately hoping to get one last look at her, but when I open them again, she's nowhere to be seen. That smile, that voice, that loving presence is gone for good.

I'm shaking so violently that I'm starting to keel over, but a warm hand suddenly grips my shoulder. "Baby, what's wrong?" Bruno pulls me around, gathering me against him. "Who was that man you ran after?"

"It was my dad."

Bruno doesn't ask any more questions. He just stays here, holding me tight, shouldering my full body weight till he's sure I'm OK.

***

The party moves in full swing when I return. The food is amazing, the dancing is shambolic and wild, and the entire place hums with an exuberance that sends my spirits soaring once again. After the cake has been cut by all six of us, Bruno approaches me carrying two plates loaded with huge slices and whipped cream. "You wanna take a bit of a stroll along the beach?"

We wander down towards the shore, then head south along the edge of the water. The gentle waves lap at our feet as the glow of the wedding behind us gives way to the moonlight ahead. The blazing hot day has nicely segued into a balmy night, which wraps its fingers around us in a comforting warmth.

Bruno stops, taking our plates and putting them down out of harm's way. Coming back to me, he slowly unbuttons my shirt. "This is what's gonna make tonight perfect for me," he says.

"You reckon they'll catch us?" I crane my head around, trying to see how far from the party we are.

"Nah," he says, pulling down my shorts and underwear before removing his own. Taking my hand, he leads me out into the water. "One year, Bradford. One year, and look where we are."

Once we're in deep enough, he draws me against him. I wrap my legs around his waist, my arms around his shoulders. As we hold each other, bobbing in the water, down below his cock flexes against my arse crack. My own cock is raging as my knob and PA rub against his belly, but it seems like this is enough for us right now. Off in the distance, the wedding party is going as strong as ever. I can hear the strains of Italian music now. "Your family must have taken the DJ reins," I chuckle.

"Well, it was gonna happen sooner or later." Bruno shunts his dick firmly back and forth over my arsehole, causing my cock to grind against him repeatedly. He smiles at my instant moan. "I really need to fuck you now," he growls.

"Um, you might have trained my arse to take your dick super fast, but I still don't think it's gonna happen without lube."

He considers this for a moment. "We need to get back to shore." His tone is urgent, and I follow him closely, wading as fast as I can. I watch his burly arse in the moonlight as he steps out, rubbing my penis slowly at the sight of him bending over to get the wedding cake. He lingers there a moment for my benefit, his arse cheeks spread, his balls hanging low. It may be dark, but I know and love every part of this man so comprehensively that the picture I'm making out couldn't be more vivid. Returning to me, he takes me in his arms and I feel his hand slide straight into the cleft of my arse. Fingers probe at my hole, working their way directly through my tight ring. "Oh God," I groan. "Is that the whipped cream?"

"Got it in one." Bruno gives a lascivious laugh as his hand vacates my arse, then comes round to the front to coat my cock with a few firm strokes. Guiding me down to the sand, he turns me on my side and cuddles in behind me. Heaven hits hard as his penis slides straight into my arse. The stretch is so divine that my hand is on my dick straight away, rubbing in a fast frenzy. His arm reaches around my chest and his fingers start to caress my nipple. I can barely fathom how overwhelmed I am right now.

"Am I allowed to pound this beautiful cunt as hard as I want?" Bruno pants in my ear.

"Not if you'd like me to last." I'm masturbating with full force. I know I should be trying to resist it. I can't come yet. Bruno needs to get there first. *I* need him to.

"Red rag to a bull," he growls, and immediately begins slamming into me. "Fuck lasting for ages. We have a lifetime ahead of us, baby. I need to breed you so fucking badly right now."

The pure lust in his voice sends the tension in my erectile muscles sky-high. I hook my right leg behind his thigh, grinding my arse into his crotch to give him the best angle possible. As his warm breath strafes my neck, his lips kiss behind my ears, and his finger teases the hardened nubs on my pecs, I feel myself beginning to float. My pleasure is so extreme it's almost unearthly. I'm a balloon about to burst, a geyser about to shoot skyward. The glorious ache in my taint is so deliciously intense I think I might even be wailing. This man—this man who loves me more than anyone else in the world—he can make me feel like *this*. And I get him for the rest of my life. A huge, ecstatic sob chokes me as I finally detonate. The firm strokes I've been giving my cock speed up frantically, blasting every missile right across the sand in front of me. With each ejection, my arse tightens hard around Bruno's dick, causing his moans to double in pace.

"I love you so fucking much," he gasps, clutching me even harder to his chest while his body seizes up. His hips convulse against my arse, and I feel the strong peristaltic throb of his dick delivering its promise deep inside me. I am his, he is mine, we are each other's. Wholly, entirely, eternally.

I never knew I was going somewhere. But in the warmth and safety of my husband's arms, I marvel at the unbridled joy emanating from the crowd over yonder, and I know I've arrived. I've reached the end of the race, broken through the tape and there's nothing but green grass as far as the eye can see.

Bruno relaxes into my body while familiar musical strains sail out from the wedding party. "Listen, *Blinky*," he whispers. Once the chorus begins, I hear the chant of the crowd all singing along. In perfect time, Bruno's gentle words resonate in my ear. "*Sarà perché ti amo*."

THE END

DEAR READER

Hello there, beautiful people! I'm so glad you've come along on Bradford, Bru and Brendan's journey with me. If you enjoyed their story, I'd be thrilled if you would drop a little note somewhere—Goodreads, Bookbub—wherever takes your fancy. These reviews make all the difference for us little ol' authors and I'll be forever grateful.
Big bear hugs!

If you'd like to connect with me or tag me on Instagram, you can find me @colindereham

These reviews make all the difference and I'll be forever grateful.

Big bear hugs!

Colin

ABOUT COLIN

Having started with a clear mission to create a hybrid of kitchen sink drama and gay erotic romance, Colin's books are gritty and realistic depictions of same-gender-loving life in the Australian urban landscape. His other books include the novels Nervous Kid, Hound and The Lookout, and a collection of short novellas called One Night Stand. He lives in Sydney with two great blokes, two rowdy Italian Greyhounds, and his trusty seeing-eye dog, Hedy. You can connect with him at: https://linktr.ee/colindereham

Colin puts out a weekly newsletter with book news, new releases and a bunch of pics of NSFW hairy men. Subscribe here for weekly bawdy banter!
https://colindereham.wordpress.com/newsletter/

Colin Dereham's Den is a relaxed reader group dedicated to gay fiction, erotic gay romance and furry bears of the gay variety. Come join the fun at:
https://www.facebook.com/groups/derehamsden

BOOKS BY COLIN

Bondi Bears

Hound

One Night Stand

The Lookout

Nervous Kid

Bradford, Bru And Brendan Too

www.ingramcontent.com/pod-product-compliance
Lightning Source LLC
Chambersburg PA
CBHW030135010826
48973CB00002B/568

* 9 7 8 1 9 5 9 5 5 3 2 1 2 *